continued ...

D1051206

"There's nothing better than a rip-roaring adventure, a mystery, an interesting mix of legend, myth, betrayal, prejudice, and justice as opposed to what's legal. . . . If you haven't read Richardson before, treat yourself to a Greywalker novel."

—SFRevu

Labyrinth

"Richardson's once-playful Harper is clearly evolving into a supernatural force to be reckoned with." —*Publishers Weekly*

"This is one urban fantasy series that is not to be missed."

—SciFiChick.com

"Harper continues her metamorphosis into a grave paranormal entity in this delightfully evolving urban fantasy. The story line is action-packed. . . . This is a complicated superb entry in an evolving series growing stronger and deeper."

—Genre Go Round Reviews

"A wonderful unique heroine . . . [and] a compelling place . . . [a] wonderfully intense ending." —Night Owl Reviews

Vanished

"Full of thrills, chills, and mystery . . . easily my favorite in the series so far. Greywalker is a unique urban fantasy series that won't disappoint." —SciFiChick.com

"Richardson has such a natural knack for storytelling . . . completely captivating. I think Harper is one hell of a protagonist and I can't get enough." —*CrimeSpree Magazine*

"Richardson hooks readers from the start with her storytelling talents, and offers up a multifaceted mystery that's sure to keep fans riveted." —Darque Reviews

"A terrific tale. . . . The story line is fast-paced and filled with plenty of action." —Genre Go Round Reviews

"This fast-moving tale boasts lots of action, a complex plot, and meaty characters." —*Booklist*

"Richardson continues to develop strong, intriguing plots."

—*Publishers Weekly*

Underground

"In many ways this is a book that brings together all that Harper has learned and felt over the previous books. She's stronger and more centered. . . . She's a very human and humane character." —SFRevu

"Following in the tradition of Tanya Huff and Jim Butcher, this is a strong addition to the growing body of urban fantasy mysteries." —*Library Journal*

"If you are looking for a new addition to your urban fantasy collection, then look no further than Kat Richardson."
—Night Owl Reviews

"This powerful urban fantasy whodunit will appeal to fans of Charlaine Harris." —The Mystery Gazette

"Part Indian folklore, part detailed urban history, part PI procedural, part monster-from-the-depths horror story."
—*Booklist*

Poltergeist

"Richardson's view of the paranormal has a nice technological twist and features intriguing historical notes that lift this whodunit a cut above the average supernatural thriller."
—*Publishers Weekly*

"The story line is fast-paced, hooking the audience from the onset . . . and [it] never lets go until the final altercation."
—Alternative Worlds

"Gripping, stark realism . . . a truly excellent blend of detective drama and paranormal thriller." —*Library Journal*

"Richardson is really striking out in new territory with this series. . . . This is urban fantasy at its best with new ideas, crisp dialogue, great characters, and exciting stories." —SFRevu

Greywalker

"Nonstop action with an intriguing premise, a great heroine, and enough paranormal complications to keep you on the edge of your seat." —Charlaine Harris

"A genuinely likable and independent heroine with a unique view of reality." —*Library Journal*

"Contemporary fantasy meets urban noir in Richardson's intriguing debut . . . well produced, pleasingly peopled, with a strong narrative and plenty of provocative plotlines."
—*Kirkus Reviews* (starred review)

"This book kicks ass. . . . Like Charlie Huston's *Already Dead* and Simon R. Green's Nightside series, *Greywalker* is a perfect blend of hard-boiled PI and supernatural thriller. It'll grab you from the first page and won't let you go until the last."
—*CrimeSpree Magazine*

Also by Kat Richardson

Greywalker
Poltergeist
Underground
Vanished
Labyrinth
Downpour

Anthologies

Mean Streets
(with Jim Butcher, Simon R. Green, and
Thomas E. Sniegoski)

SEAWITCH

KAT RICHARDSON

A GREYWALKER NOVEL

A ROC BOOK

ROC
Published by the Penguin Group
Penguin Group (USA) Inc., 375 Hudson Street,
New York, New York 10014, USA

USA | Canada | UK | Ireland | Australia | New Zealand | India | South Africa | China

Penguin Books Ltd., Registered Offices: 80 Strand, London WC2R 0RL, England
For more information about the Penguin Group visit penguin.com.

Published by Roc, an imprint of New American Library, a division of Penguin
Group (USA) Inc. Previously published in a Roc hardcover market edition.

First Roc Mass Market Printing, July 2013

 REGISTERED TRADEMARK — MARCA REGISTRADA

ISBN 978-0-451-41545-5

Printed in the United States of America
10 9 8 7 6 5 4 3 2 1

ALWAYS LEARNING   PEARSON

For my sister: Thanks for being here, yet again.

ACKNOWLEDGMENTS

The year 2011 was a very difficult one for me and my family, and getting this book written, revised, and through the whole process was a bigger team effort than ever before. It's impossible to quantify my appreciation for even the seemingly small things people did to help me bring this off, but the following is, I hope, at least some measure of recognition.

Thanks to:

Armando Marini for help with the rivers and estuaries of Rhode Island and for letting me steal his wife for a month—including her birthday.

Michael Kinsella for help with small craft routing across the Strait of Juan de Fuca.

Cherie Priest for lunches and being there.

Elizabeth Rose-Marini, for being the best and most patient sister in the world.

Jacque Knight for agreeing to be bad.

Rosanne Romanello for sympathy and help beyond the call of any publicist.

Richard Foss for the guest room and wonderful conversations and for being gracious about my forgetting to mention him in the previous book for suggesting the Ley Weaver.

Robin MacPherson for beta reading, good suggestions, and common sense as well as, y'know, friendship.

Julie, Judy, Peggy, Jacqueline, Aliza, Kirsten, Mita, and the rest of the folks at the Swedish Hospital MTC in Ballard for everything.

Shawn Speakman for carrying on.

Kelli and Lance Zeilinski for the BBQ.

John and Susan Husisian—you rock.

The fabulous staff of Murder by the Book in Houston, Texas, and Duane Wilkins, Fran Fuller, JB, M'E, Christelle, Synde, and the rest of the booksellers who keep on pimping my books—I love you guys.

Jon Jordan for letting me graciously off a hook.

Jen Jordan for being ... well, Jen.

Mary Robinette Kowal for being utterly wonderful and so much more, and Rob Kowal for much help and even more help after that.

Laura Anne Gilman for professional advice and personal charm, plus the occasional kick in the head.

Janna Silverstein for help and letting me hide in her home.

Sally Harding for picking up my professional pieces and being a wonderful friend as well as a fabulous agent.

Anne the Amazing Editor and the rest of the crew at Roc—you make me look smarter than I am.

Janet, Carolina, Linda, Mario, and my unknown copy editor who corrected my Spanish.

Chris McGrath for Oh My God gorgeous cover art. Again.

The Minions for picking up the promo slack when I couldn't and for being the best minions in the world. No evil overlord could ask for more.

Paul Goat Allen for saying wonderful things in very public places.

Mario, Caitlin, Mark, Richelle, Jeanne, Jaye, Nicole, Chuck, the Rainforest folks, Nova, Sandra, Jilli, Bruce, Arinn, Erin, Blake, Charlaine, Toni, Dana, Patrick S., Shanna, Cat R., and the rest of my mad writer friends.

Diana Rowland for mutual venting and being amazing.

My husband, Jim, for pirates, cutlasses, dogs, passion, compassion, and heaters as well as all the other things that are too numerous to list.

PROLOGUE

I am trying to break my habit of dying. I've had my turns on the dance floor with death at least three times that I know of. So far, it has never lasted more than a few minutes and I hope I won't be staying longer anytime soon. Although I fear my next pas de deux with the Reaper will be the last and lasting one, I prefer to put that bow off as long as possible.

Each time I've died, I've awakened changed in ways normal people can't see. These unexpected and unwanted adjustments have stuck me with a strange job: to protect the Grey, the fringe between the normal world and the world of the purely paranormal, from which rise the ghosts and monsters of our collective nightmares, where magic sings across the blackness of this world between worlds as clouds and lines of gleaming energy. Sometimes I must also protect the rest of the world from the Grey and things that are birthed there. I am not a magical creature myself—at least not in the way a ghost or a vampire, a witch or a sorcerer, is. I'm just the legman and general dogsbody for the thing that guards the place; I'm a Greywalker—Hands of the Guardian, Paladin of the Dead.

None of these titles is on my business cards or my office door. As far as the normal world of Seattle is concerned, I'm Harper Blaine, private investigator. It's the job I was doing long before an angry man killed me and helped introduce me to the Grey. I continue to do it partly because I'm good at it and largely because ghosts tend to stiff me on the bill. Some days I long for the boredom of background checks, personal-injury fraud, and missing persons handed off from an overworked police department. But something always seems to lead me back to the Grey, whether I want it to or not. My friends and family—such as they are—get the short, hard end of the stick too much of the time. I am sorry for that and I know I owe them something better. When the living nightmares are bleakest and thick around me, these ties are all that keep me anchored to what is good and right and human, and I will hold those things close, because this is not a job you quit—it's one you die from.

ONE

The news called it a ghost ship. I didn't detect any ghosts from the outside, but the boat was enshrouded in thick, colored skeins of Grey fog and ghostlight in gleaming, watery shades: aqua and cerulean with thin whispers of violet twining through them all. I didn't see any ghosts per se, but there was definitely something paranormal going on—more than any reporter was likely to credit.

I stood in the fog near the end of B dock, waiting, looking at the *Seawitch*. The insurance paperwork called the old wooden boat a fantail motor yacht, designed by someone named Ted Geary—which I guessed was a big deal. I've dealt with boats before, but I'm certainly not an expert and a lot of the technical information about this boat meant nothing to me. It had a long, low profile—relatively speaking—with a round stern and rakish angles that exuded a Jazz Age sense of power. I knew the family had money—the boat wasn't the only expensive object the insurance company that had hired me had covered for them—but the vessel wasn't flashy; in its current derelict and stained condition, freighted with mystery, it was grim.

By all reports—official and speculative—the *Seawitch* had cruised away from its berth in this same marina twenty-seven years earlier and vanished from the knowledge of men, taking four passengers and one crewman with it. They had never returned but the boat had; suddenly and without any sign of hands aboard, it had simply been found one recent morning, standing at the end of its old dock. The derelict boat had been moved to B to rest with the abandoned, broken, seized, and foreclosed vessels until the truth of its reappearance could be ascertained.

The story in the newspaper claimed that the boat had sailed into port under its own power, but, really, the *Seawitch* seemed to have arrived under cover of the strange, low-hanging morning fog that had swelled around the edges of the Sound and skulked below the bluffs every June morning in Seattle that year, making the hills and spires of the city appear as islands afloat in a haunted sea. Here it was, a lost ship piloted by no one living, returning to its berth after being presumed lost with all hands. Of course, that wasn't quite the truth of the matter but it was close enough. And it raised the hit rate at the news Web sites by a thousand percent, which was far more important than veracity; advertisers pay for eyeballs, not for unvarnished truth.

The insurance company had paid the claim long ago, and when the *Seawitch* reappeared, they were far more interested in where the boat had been all this time and why it wasn't a hotel for fish at the bottom of Puget Sound than in unraveling any ghostly sea stories. They felt it far more likely that someone had defrauded them than that the boat and its crew had somehow vanished and remained hidden for all this time. They wanted prosecutable answers.

The case would have landed back with the original investigator but he'd retired, and since freaky circumstances are my specialty, it didn't take long for the file to end up on my desk. This case had the smell of something that would taint your life and haunt your dreams for years afterward, so I wouldn't have blamed anyone who passed on it, especially since insurance investigations of this kind don't come with high-end recovery fees—just lowball hourly wages and the occasional dinky bonus. Insurance investigators are sometimes known to play fast and loose, so once the cops got involved, my colleagues were even less interested in contesting my assignment.

Lucky me. I not only got the case; I knew the cop.

And so I stood in the shreds of morning mist, waiting for Detective Rey Solis to arrive, show me aboard, and explain why the Seattle Police Department was involved in what should have been a matter for the maritime lawyers and insurance actuaries to scrap over in court. Something large and dark—maybe an otter hunting in the salmon run—splashed in the water beside the dock and made me jump.

In the swirling fog, the sound of footsteps on the floating cement dock bounced off the water in a disorienting fashion. I turned my back to the boat and the unseen otter and stood still, waiting for someone to emerge. Solis, looking like a specter in his dark raincoat with his wet dark hair plastered against his head, seemed to resolve from the murk as he drew close enough to see me, and I him. He nodded to me and stopped at the foot of the steps someone had provided for boarding the *Seawitch*.

"Good morning."

I wasn't so sure of it, but I nodded back. "Morning, Solis. How did you get stuck with this one?" I knew he'd been promoted to detective sergeant not long ago and he probably had the seniority to avoid an assignment like this one. Homicide had been separated from other major crimes a few years back and this sort of thing wasn't their usual beat. They were still top dog where any suspicious or violent death was concerned, but the vagueness of the jurisdiction might have put it in some other agency's bailiwick or given a senior officer an excuse to push it onto someone else.

He cocked his head in what I thought of as his half shrug, but didn't explain himself. His aura didn't give him away, either, but it rarely does.

I can't say I was unhappy to be working with Solis—he's a good detective and I respect him—but I'd never thought Solis was comfortable with me or the creepy cases I seemed to attract, so this was going to be interesting, most likely in that Chinese-curse sort of way.

"Well," I started, not sure what I should say, "*I'm* glad it's you. Better than working with someone new."

He gave another small nod and turned to look at the *Seawitch*. "It does not look like a ghost ship, does it?"

"Looks solid enough," I replied. The structure was intact as far as I could tell. I was more than ready to go aboard and not worried about the physical side of the boat: I couldn't recall ever being seasick except when experiencing the sensation of the world heaving underfoot when I'd first been introduced to the Grey. I'd gotten over that eventually.

Solis led the way on board, up a set of plastic stairs that were a little too short—the last step to the deck was about eighteen inches above the last riser and a couple of feet away across empty air. With my long legs it was only annoying, but Solis, being five inches shorter than I, had to stretch a bit. He then used a key on the padlock affixed to a makeshift hasp on the main hatch. Someone had taken a drill to the original lock inset in the narrow wooden door and the remains sat loosely in their case, making a metallic rattle as Solis pushed inward.

"Did your guys drill the lock or was it that way when you got here?" I asked.

"It was one of the Port Authority employees," he replied, stepping inside, since there was no room to move any other direction with me standing on the side deck behind him.

"They can just do that?"

"Yes, if safety is in question."

The boat didn't seem like a hazard—just a bit old and abused—but in this day of terrorism, I suppose the thinking was, Who could be sure that it wasn't a bomb or a floating biological attack waiting to happen?

I nodded as Solis watched me slip through the doorway. I nearly recoiled at the smell inside.

The room reeked of mildew and wood rot. We'd walked into a huge upper salon with scattered sofas and tables around the room and sturdy wooden cabinets and shelves built into the walls below the window line. The cream and blue upholstery on the seats was striped with green and black stains, and the filthy blue carpet felt moist and spongy underfoot. The matching blue curtains had rotted to shreds, and the tables and cabinet doors were warped and discolored. From inside I could see out in almost any direction between the ruined hangings. I would bet the sun shining on all that glass had done its part to advance the rot, and at the same time, the spotted windows made the room seem both open and trapped in its own personal fog bank.

I sneezed and coughed a little as the smell aggravated my nose and throat. "Ugh," I muttered. The movement of the boat was barely noticeable, but the stink was compensating for the lack of *mal de mer*.

"It is unpleasant," Solis responded. "It's worse below."

"Oh . . . goody," I replied, turning my attention back to the room around us.

A squared-off arrangement of the furniture defined a lounge area that faced the rear of the living room–like space—I knew real hard-core boat people would have called it the saloon, as it was labeled on the plans, but damned if I would. I wondered why the seats were oriented to the back until I figured out that the entire rear wall was made of wood-and-glass panels that folded aside to open the back of the space to the round, covered aft deck. Passengers could sit inside reading, chatting, or eating while enjoying the outdoors without having to be in it—back when the interior was still clean and dry—and if the weather went sour could still use the area just by pulling the doors across. Judging by the moisture level, the weather had invaded at some point, doors or no doors.

"Could we open those up and air this place out a bit?" I asked.

Solis considered it, then nodded and went to open up the doors himself, scowling at me when I moved to help. I ignored him. The sooner we had the boat open and full of fresher air, the better, as far as I was concerned. It wasn't as if we were trampling up a clean crime scene here. Whatever had happened aboard the *Seawitch*, it hadn't taken place recently.

I touched the nearest of the folding doors and felt a cold frisson race up my arm and across my scalp. I must have gasped or twitched, because Solis cocked his head and glanced at me from the corner of his eye.

I shook him off. "Just one of those creepy feelings."

He grunted, nodded, and went back to opening doors. Once we had the back of the boat open, fresher, cold air rushed in, swirling around and, to my eyes, raising filaments of violet, blue, and green energy off the floor and furnishings as if the magical residue of whatever had happened in the boat had dried out like sea grass left on the shore. The fine threads were the same colors I'd observed outside. I helped Solis shove the last of the resisting, warped doors aside and took a moment to peer harder at the Grey—that thin space of magic and possibility lying between the normal and the paranormal worlds.

The misty material of the Grey was acting stranger than usual here; instead of the foggy, airy movement I normally saw, the boat seemed to be filled with two separate Grey fluids that refused to mix. The brew flowed and crested in the space as if held in an agitated fishbowl, the walls warped and rough around it. At the far end and to the right was a staircase where one of the substances flowed down, taking all the amethyst color with it as well as the cerulean and emerald, while the other remained above, showing only thin watery shades of blue and green. The air felt colder in that area, piercing right through my jacket like winter ice.

I stared a moment longer at the strange tide of the

Grey. It looked . . . as if something powerful had passed through the boat from back to front, sinking down where it found access and leaving this lingering stream as a reminder. How long ago had it been at full flood?

I turned my attention back to the normal world, to Solis, who was frowning at me nearby.

"This . . . evidence of something foul that brought you here—is it downstairs?" I asked, thinking about the direction and flow of the energetic traces.

He raised his eyebrows. "Yes. Come with me."

He continued to frown as he turned to lead me to the scene of whatever crime the SPD suspected had happened aboard. Judging by the way his usually quiet aura spiked and jumped, I'd rattled him—which was no mean trick.

We bypassed the rest of the upper deck and I followed him down the narrow staircase—a "companionway," to sailors—submerging into the oily, swirling Grey. For an instant I thought I was drowning, the rising spectral liquid bringing a cold recollection of a certain teenage summer when I'd gone swimming with my cousin Jill and not entirely escaped my first brush with death. Jill had not escaped at all. I was glad I was behind Solis and he couldn't see me jerk my head back in suddenly remembered terror as the uncanny fluid seemed to rise over my face and push into my mouth and nose. In a moment the sensation passed as I continued to breathe normally, but my heart was still racing for a while afterward and the scent of the sea stayed in the air around me as long as we remained aboard the *Seawitch*.

From the foot of the stairs, Solis led me forward along a narrow corridor that ran about a third the length of the boat. As we walked I felt colder and colder and the sense of damp became oppressive. I realized I was slowing, as if I were fighting a current and feeling tired from it. Nearly to the end of the hall, Solis, who was several steps ahead of me, stopped and turned toward a narrow door on his left.

I moved to catch up with him—he hadn't even opened the door yet—but a sudden blast of wet cold smacked me down. I stumbled to one knee, bowing my head against what felt like a deluge of icy water. Solis whipped back to stare at me and took a step away as I planted my hands on the walls and shoved my way back to my feet. Keeping my hands braced, I stood firm and shook back my hair with a sharp flip of my head. Water from my drenched locks spattered against Solis's coat and face—seawater that reeked of dying things struggling in poisoned currents.

He caught his breath short and stared at me, his head pulled back, murmuring under his breath, "*Madre*—"

I took a couple of steadying breaths and fought off the sense of being battered by a riptide only I was caught in. "Welcome to the freak show," I muttered.

TWO

The hall ceiling above me was dry—or at least no wetter than any other part of the ceiling—yet I stood in a puddle of seawater. My head, face, and the front of my jacket had taken the brunt of the unseen wave—for that's what it had felt like—while my back and lower body were mostly dry. Solis, usually dead-calm unflappable, was fully flapped and had taken a step away from me. I must have looked like something from a horror film, judging by his wide-eyed expression. I'd never imagined the quiet Colombian could be so shaken, but I suppose it's one thing to imagine someone you know is a little on the weird side and a different thing entirely to have it thrust upon you in a hallway the size of a Volkswagen's backseat.

I was just thinking the wave was a onetime thing when I felt it rushing upon me again as the liquid Grey pulled back, just like the ocean before a tsunami, making a tugging sensation in my chest. I wasn't worried about Solis—it seemed to affect him not at all—but I wasn't in the mood to be soaked to the skin by invisible waterspouts. I didn't pause to worry about what he'd think as I threw myself into the Grey, deep into the churning tide of this strangest manifestation yet.

A current of green energy "water" tore at my legs and I crouched to make a smaller, denser target as I looked for the cause of the surge. The Grey looked strangely white here, like a day of unbroken, high, thin clouds reflecting the sun in directionless glare. The harsh whiteness felt wet and cold and rippling curves of colored light rose in waves ahead of me. At their core I saw flickers of amethyst light that stretched and receded as the waves grew and rushed toward me. I plunged forward, diving into the approaching wave, and gripped the violet light.

It slipped from my hand like a fish and rushed away with one final flick that sent me head over heels through the suddenly becalmed Grey. I fell toward the normal and tumbled backward over Solis.

He jumped aside with a yelp of alarm, one arm coming up as the other reached for one of my flailing hands and twisted it behind my back. I didn't fight—even if it hadn't been Solis, I was too dizzy from the spinning transition to catch my balance.

Solis pushed me toward the wall by force of habit as if he were going to snap the cuffs on me, then realized what he was doing and let go. I sagged forward, catching myself against the wall beside the door. I gasped for breath and turned, leaning back against the nearest firm, upright surface.

Solis faced me, braced, his hands slightly raised as if he expected me to lunge at him, but wasn't sure I was actually dangerous as much as confused, like a holiday drunk. His eyes weren't quite so wide, but his stance and expression were wary—no, alert, like a fighter waiting on the next move of an unpredictable opponent. That was interesting. . . . He wasn't freaking out, though his aura was jumping wildly and the tension in his body spoke loudly of a willingness to meet his fears rather than run from them.

I caught my heaving breath and kept my hands where he could see them. "I'm sorry. I didn't mean to fall over you like that," I said.

"Fall?" he repeated. "Say more like flying, as if someone threw you. What . . . was that?"

I chewed on my words before I let them out. "I . . .

sometimes have little disagreements with . . . um, with reality. And physics." I offered a very thin, uncertain smile. As far as I could recall, Solis had never seen me interact with the Grey before—I usually kept that aspect of my job hidden and most especially from him, though I knew he thought I was strange and that strange things happened in my proximity. Once or twice he'd even come close to accusing me of criminality—or at least lying through my teeth to cover up an unpalatable truth.

"So I see." He seemed to be mulling over a few difficult thoughts of his own, but he didn't speak them. He straightened up, letting his hands drop to his sides but still keeping a jaundiced eye on me. Maybe he thought I was going to lunge at him again. Then he asked, "Are you all right now?" Which I interpreted as "Are you going to do anything else disturbing?"

I never *plan* to be disturbing. . . . "I'm fine," I replied, trying to look innocuous and predictable. "Thanks."

He turned his head a bit so he was looking at me from the corner of his eye—a posture I was familiar with from the many times I'd used it to peer deeper into the Grey without falling in. "How did you get past me?"

I shrugged. "I'm slippery."

"Yes, and you are, as always, not telling me something."

I pulled a rueful face. "Can I explain later? Right now I just want to get a look at the problem and get out of here so I can change into dry clothes."

He nodded and opened the door, keeping one eye on me the whole time.

Nothing new came out, but the tide of Grey surged a bit, as if he'd opened a gate at the locks and let a gush of water through. I waited for it to calm before I stepped into the doorway, mentally bracing myself, and looked into the cabin.

The room was cramped and not very square—or at least it looked that way with the wall opposite me sloping and curving outward on one axis and inward on the other. This was obviously the boat's hull near the bow, where things got narrow and pointy. The narrow bunk made me think this was a crew cabin, not guest accommodations. Judging by the slopes and angles, part of this room—as with all the rooms and corridors down here—was below the waterline. The smell was strong here but not identical to the stink above; this had the additional odor of burned driftwood and the harsh sting of iodine. The room itself seemed just a bit out of focus, as if the swirling liquid Grey clouded my eyes, and everything was filthy with decayed ocean flora as well as the same sort of black and green mold stains we'd seen upstairs. That was ugly enough, but the floor and the built-in bed must have been the things that caught the SPD's attention.

A low moan seemed to issue nearby and I jumped a little. Solis didn't look quite as startled, but even he was unsettled by the sound. It took a moment for me to realize it wasn't a ghost—it was a foghorn—before I could return my attention to the strange sight on the cabin floor.

A pattern of rust-colored arcs and markings started on the floor and carried on over the surface of the bed and back to the floor, incompletely enclosing a twelve-pointed star in a circle of intertwined curves that looked like cresting waves. Smeared letters or numbers had been sketched at each point of the star with barely enough room between the point and the circling, painted waves. In the middle of the star something had bled a lot and matching spatters crusted in mold marked the walls. Incongruous dots of luminous color and rainbow shimmer were scattered throughout the weird markings. One edge of the ring and some of the figures had been wiped out, creating a gap in the circle. I'd never seen this before yet it felt familiar in a way I couldn't pin down. . . .

I crouched, keeping one hand on the doorframe to steady myself as I studied the circle of symbols. Something gritty rubbed against my palm. Resting my weight against the doorpost, I looked at my still-damp left hand. The dry substance from the wall made a bright red stain on my hand. I held it out to Solis.

"Is this blood?"

He nodded. "It's human."

"Crap," I muttered, and I knew what had tripped my sense of the familiar: This was some kind of blood magic—not like what I'd seen before, but I recognized the general sensation and stink of it. Magic really wasn't my strong suit; I'd have to wing this one on my own, since my friends the Danzigers were out of the country and I usually brought this sort of problem to them. "Any idea *whose* blood this is?"

Solis shook his head. "It's hard to tell with samples so old and broken down, but it appears to be mixed with something else as well as the blood of more than one person. Who is not yet known."

"And may not be if the bleeders have no match in the DNA database. Any suspects?"

"Everyone who was on board when the boat was reported missing."

I stood up again and turned to face Solis directly. "You have a working theory?"

He gave a small shake of his head. "Empty speculation has no point. This is the only cabin with such markings, although there may be traces of blood in many others. Traces only."

"May be? You're not sure?"

"This is a low priority case for the SPD and the risk of false positives is too high in this environment for extensive use of the Luminol test. I've had to take test scrapings from the obvious stains and submit them to the lab." He pointed to the small, numbered evidence-location tags stuck here and there in the cabin. "The results are not yet available and stains have not been easy to find or identify."

"Do you think they were cleaned up or just . . . decayed beyond identification?" I asked.

"It's the discovery that has been difficult, but if this stain survived, why not others? The whole boat has the dirt and mold, so if this marking is a sign of crime, why only here? If the passengers and crew were killed, why isn't there more blood elsewhere? What does this symbol mean? This is where my questions begin."

I nodded. "Dirt. Blood . . . Where did the seaweed come from?"

Solis raised his eyebrows. "From the sea."

I was still wet and the room was unnaturally cold, so I was distracted, scowling, and shivering a little, but not enough to miss that rare spark of sarcasm. Or was it rare? I'd never spent much time with Solis beyond a cumulative hour or two of mutual info swap and occasional interrogation. I'd assumed the taciturn detective didn't have much of a sense of humor, but that wasn't likely. Homicide investigation is one of those fields that demands an outlet for the purging of the disillusion and disgust that come with the territory. A lot of cops and forensic investigators tend toward a sense of humor as black and dry as gunpowder; others become callous and irreverent or just plain crass. Only those about to crack lose their ability to laugh, however gruesome and unfeeling that may sound. Rey Solis was apparently—though quietly—just as odd as any other cop and possibly more stable than most.

I felt I should ask him some insightful, buddy-bonding sort of question at this point, but I couldn't think of one. Or have some clever comeback for his snarky quip—if he'd have been Quinton, I'd have called him a smart-ass at the very least—but that also seemed to come up blank for me. Instead I just gave the eye roll I awarded to most bad jokes and puns.

"You guys find anything like this in the rest of the boat?"

"Not guys. Only me. But there is nothing else quite like this. Other stains, other similar materials, but not arranged as so." He made an indicative circle with his finger at the blood-painted symbols and their collection of muck.

I stood back as far as I could and still see the whole space. I gave the encircled star and its mess a sideways glance through the Grey; it writhed and wavered in liquid colors that circled the bloody star like the edges of a whirlpool. I couldn't detect any sign of who had made the circle or what it was for, but I did see some holes in the pattern—just two or three. . . .

"Is this exactly as you found it?" I asked Solis.

"No. I removed one of the pebbles and some of those shiny flecks for testing. I believe the flecks are fish scales."

"And the pebbles?"

He shrugged. "Very old glass that's been sand-scoured."

Beach glass, though they didn't look much like any kind of glass from where I was standing. Dull surfaced, pitted, dirty, and partially smirched with filth and blood, they looked more like small, colorful river rocks or broken marbles of almost a dozen colors: cobalt, apple green, gold, cherry red, kelly, aqua, brown, violet, white, jade, and black with a rainbow sheen barely seen beneath the crud. They were irregular shapes that ranged in size from shards no bigger than my pinky fingernail to clods as long as my thumb; when you consider how large my hands are, that's a good-sized chunk of junk. But even knowing what the material was, I still didn't have any idea what had happened aboard the *Seawitch*.

I shook my head, disquieted and cold. "Let's see the rest and get out of here."

Solis raised an eyebrow at me—this was the second time I'd made a point of my desire to leave quickly when he knew me for a tenacious pain in the ass more likely to throw herself right in front of trouble than run from it. But I'd made a resolution not to get in Death's face anymore; I was pretty sure I was no longer bulletproof, and I had someone else's pain to consider now that I seemed to have an official significant other.

"C'mon. Do you really want to stay here any longer than you have to?" I asked.

He gave it only a moment's thought. "No."

I took a few reference photos using a small digital camera Quinton had lent me. Then Solis and I backed out of the cabin and I followed him through the rest of the boat. We looked into the other crew cabin, washroom, and storage area in the front part of the boat, finding more dirt and stains and a single, empty duffel bag abandoned at a random angle under a bunk and now glued to the floor by creeping black mold. Collectively, the boat had room for up to five crew members—providing they were very slim and not picky about privacy or claustrophobia. We also found a large compartment under the pointed bow where the stems of two large anchors poked into the hull through steel-lined sleeves, and a heap of chain and rotting rope sat to either side of a large electric winch so rusted that the chains would have to be cut free before the anchors were ever dropped again. I hoped we wouldn't need to dig around in there for clues, though the twining, colored mist of the Grey that tangled in the chains gave me a sour feeling.

When we finished with the crew cabins, we went through the engine room, which connected to the crew area by a narrow door hidden in the wooden paneling at the aft end of the corridor. The twin engines were massive to my mind, the size of Smart Cars crouching in the middle of the boat, isolated from the rest by walls lined in foamed-lead sound insulation, according to the report. It looked like dirty cappuccino foam under a layer of aluminum foil. They, too, had a drapery of dried seaweed, but the engine room was not nearly as filthy as the room with the strange, bloody circle on the floor, in spite of having a patina of old oil and engine dirt on the floor and ceiling. I spotted a dense black coil of ghost energy roiling in one of the back corners, but with Solis present and my clothes still damp and itchy, I didn't have time to investigate it thoroughly. Nothing as obvious as a face or figure presented itself in the time I was staring at it. I made a mental note to come back and take a closer look....

We passed out of the engine room through another narrow door and into the aft, where the guest accommodations awaited us. Here the signs of something gone wrong were more present, if strangely inconsistent. In one cabin we found a collection of more of the pitted bits of glass and a few round white objects I thought might be either bones or pearls, but they were so crusted with dirt it was hard to tell and we were both unwilling to move them without gloves and evidence bags. Everywhere we found mildew, muck, and stains that ranged from green to rust-red to grainy black. Every room held the sense of disarray and hasty, unexpected departure— and the smell—and yet nothing seemed to be missing besides the people themselves. Personal possessions had been abandoned in situ—even duffel bags with clothes and supplies packed inside and a woman's purse with its 1980s contents intact, as far as I could tell. The bed in the master suite at the back had been torn to shreds by something with claws and teeth. We finished with the cabins and moved to the stairs. Near the aft companionway, I saw a clump of shiny dark brown fur caught in a crack in the handrail.

I pointed at it. "Any idea what that came from?" I asked Solis.

He frowned. "No confirmation from the lab, but I thought, perhaps, a dog."

"Doesn't feel like dog fur," I said, fingering a few strands. They were thick and soft like something torn from an expensive fur coat. "And there was no dog aboard. So . . . you're thinking someone boarded the vessel and brought an attack dog of some kind to drive the passengers up on deck?"

"It is a possibility. Though I don't like the theory."

I humphed under my breath. Solis didn't usually advance a theory he didn't favor. Both of us were a little out of our depth here. I returned his frown and studied him in silence a moment, waiting to see if the creeping disquiet I felt was unsettling his nerves, too.

Finally he added, "There are no Somali pirates raiding shipping in Puget Sound."

"Not right now," I agreed. Besides, pirates used guns, not dogs, and they didn't worry about bloodstains—of which we'd found so few. We'd also found no bullet holes, and the boat was still intact and appeared to have been unused since the day the passengers and crew had vanished. Pirates don't just let their prizes float off to be found later like bottles cast up on the shore.

From the foot of the companionway I looked back into the aft corridor and its strangely empty rooms. "It looks like they left in a hurry—possibly under threat, considering the mess—but they didn't take anything and the boat doesn't appear to have been sinking. . . ."

I frowned, wondering why they'd left and where they'd gone. The final report of the original loss investigator was that *Seawitch* must have had hit some bad weather near the Strait of Juan de Fuca and been wrecked, sinking with all hands on board and so swiftly no one had even seen her go down. It's not unheard of for pleasure boats to be ill prepared for the kind of severe weather and adverse currents the strait can dish out. Even large commercial vessels with all the right equipment have come to grief in the upper Puget Sound and straits, and this was neither of those, just a hundred-year-old yacht with the sort of equipment current more than twenty-five years ago—which hadn't included vessel tracking beacons, GPS chart plotters, or weather radar.

From southern Vancouver Island in British Columbia down to Coos Bay in Oregon, the coast has rightfully earned its nickname the Graveyard of the Pacific. From what I've read, more than two thousand ships have been lost here since white men started plying the waters of the West Coast, and the ghosts of the seven hundred shipwrecked and drowned are thought to haunt the storm-wracked shore. Is it any wonder I don't spend more time at the beach?

"We shall have to return with proper collection equipment," Solis said, interrupting my thoughts.

I shook myself. "Huh?"

"If we wish to know what happened to this boat and the people on board, we will need to examine what they left behind. Assuming your employer continues to be cooperative."

The insurance company technically owned the boat since they'd paid off the original loss claim, but the cops could kick up a fuss if they wanted over the possible crime scene and so could the Coast Guard—and the FBI, as their investigative representative—if they liked. The insurance company preferred to keep this simple and cordial and move it through to closure with all possible speed and silence. They weren't pleased with the public notoriety of the ghost-ship story, so they weren't yelping about anything yet, even though Solis's involvement was in the gray zone between legal necessity and professional courtesy. He was maintaining a politic front and I thought I understood why he'd been assigned to this messy mystery in spite of his disgust for cases that read more like Agatha Christie novels than police files: He was thorough and quiet and didn't ruffle feathers. And it didn't hurt that he was now a sergeant.

"The company already knows I plan to remove things for investigation," I said. "They want this over with as quickly and quietly as possible. They won't kick as long as everything is logged and returned when we're done."

He nodded. "Have you seen all you care to down here?"

I gave the clammy corridor one last look for now and replied, "Yeah. Let's finish this up."

Going upstairs, we left the worst of the stink and

damp behind and came back up into the main salon by a
different staircase. Then we went toward the bow and up
a couple of steps to investigate the galley and a kind of
formal dining room/library sort of area that lay forward
of the galley and main salon. These were not quite as
filthy as the rest of the boat, but they, too, had been
touched by mold and rot. In the galley we found mold-
crusted dishes and cookware standing in a now-dry sink,
waiting to be washed with water that had seeped away,
leaving a crusty soap ring behind. A medical kit lay open
on one of the galley counters, but the only things that
seemed to be missing were some gauze pads and waterproof bandage tape. The big table in the shelf-lined dining salon supported a centerpiece of driftwood and
shells and was set for a meal for four, but the dishes were
slimy with mildew and the books were too swollen to
move on their shelves. Twin doors led out of the dining
room to the triangular foredeck and from there a quick
turn and another narrow, open stairway led us up to the
pilothouse and its accompanying deck stretching aft to
shade the rounded stern.

This topmost level was mostly an open area bounded
by a railing that edged the roof of the deck below. A pair
of dinghies sat on matching blocks to either side of a tall
winch sort of thing. Obviously no one had escaped in the
lifeboats. The canvas covers on the boats and around the
railings had become tattered where they remained intact
at all. A single wooden lounge chair lay collapsed on the
grimy white paint of the deck, one of its broken legs
wedged between two heavy metal stanchions that supported the safety rail. The control deck — or bridge
house — lay forward of the boat winch, so the bridge
crouched over the galley with part of the dining room
roof sticking out in front of it and forming a little eyebrow over the empty foredeck, to protect the dining
room windows from heavy seas or wind.

The bridge was one of the least-damaged parts of

Seawitch—merely musty and a bit mildewed with some muck tracked on the floor. It really did seem like a sort of bridge from one side of the boat to the other, since you could walk in the door on one side and out an identical door on the other, coming down another companionway to the opposite side of the dining room. I supposed it made sense to have easy access to the bridge from either side of the boat. Two cushy-looking chairs on fixed pedestals faced the front—one behind the wheel and the other off to the left in front of a chart table spread with a mildew-spotted map, a large book, and a heavy ruler. Against the rear wall there was a bench for the convenience of the nautical version of backseat drivers, I supposed. A row of pegs near the right—starboard—door held a collection of rotting foul-weather gear, but none appeared to be missing. A latched flare box and fire extinguisher were clipped into holders on the wall near the other door, both untouched. A pair of binoculars lay on the floor, apparently fallen from a rack on the right side of the steering station. Aside from the tumbled binoculars, there was no sign of violence here. Even the ceiling-mounted radio's microphone still hung neatly from its clip, its spiral of rubber-covered cord sagging downward in an uneven, frozen squirm as the material had deteriorated.

I moved to the chart table—navigation station, really, since it had its own array of tools and electronic instrument displays placed so either working position could see them without moving much. Screens marked loran, depth sounder, and radar were inset across an upright panel, as well as simpler displays for the boat's speed, the wind speed and direction, and the more mundane issues of temperature, humidity, and barometric pressure. The instruments were no longer state-of-the-art and looked as if they'd been roughly treated, though they had been only a few years old when *Seawitch* went missing. The chart, with a clear plastic overlay marked up in grease pencil, had become bonded to both the table and cover by mildew and moisture. It was going to be a bitch to get it off that surface, so I took a picture of it as it was in case removal destroyed it.

I picked up the large, flat book and looked it over. The leather cover was rotting and the pages inside had warped into a rippled mass from exposure to the damp. I held it up for Solis to see.

"What do you think—ship's log?"

He considered the venerable book. "Most likely. Useful, perhaps."

"We'll take it with us," I said.

He nodded and I laid the moldering volume on the bench to be carried off when we left.

Under the chart table there was a series of shallow drawers meant for flat charts, and a grid of cubbyholes farther down for rolled charts. It was three-quarters full but the rolled charts had become too delicate to open without risking their dissolution into dust and useless fragments.

There didn't seem to be any other clues to pick up and even to my Grey-adapted sight there wasn't much else to see. We stepped back out on the opposite side than we'd entered by and started down the other stairs. A brassy gleam caught my eye and I stopped, turning back, looking for whatever I hadn't quite seen. Solis watched me from a step or two below.

I turned back toward the bridge door, squinting in an errant shaft of sunlight that had cut momentarily through the fog. A bronze bracket was mounted to the back of the bridge roof, but nothing hung from it. A hole lined with a plastic grommet pierced the wall just below it for something narrow to pass into the pilothouse—a thick bit of string, maybe. I frowned at the bracket and hole.

"Solis," I said, waving at the empty mount, "what do you suppose went here?"

He returned up the steps and peered at my find. He cocked his head slightly, then looked up at the roof of the pilothouse and around the back wall. "Perhaps a bell? We haven't seen one anywhere on board. Don't ships usually have a bell?"

I supposed some didn't, but a boat like this, kept in its original vintage style except in the bridge and engine rooms, where no one but the captain would see it, should have had a bell—a big, clanging brass bell with the ship's name on it and a string into the pilothouse so it could be rung without having to step outside. This was the place I'd expect it to be. But for the *Seawitch*'s bell, there was only an empty space.

THREE

The ship's log would require some drying out before we could get a look at it without doing damage to the pages. I had a list of names for the missing passengers and crew, but since they were presumed dead, it didn't seem worth our while to look them up. But the owner's widow—presumed widow, at least—was still around. As the sole beneficiary of the insurance, she was the party my employers most suspected of fraud, so it made sense to me to go talk to her next and find out what she knew about the vanishing and reappearing *Seawitch*. Not that *I* suspected her of fraud now that I'd seen the boat and its cargo of weirdness for myself, but disgruntled spouses are known to speak impulsively and I am known to take advantage of that.

We closed up and left the boat, stepping into fog that seemed to have thickened instead of burning off. *Seawitch* looked even less inviting than when we'd gone aboard, the ropes of colored energy writhing now like tentacles trying to crush the vessel in their grip. The low moan of the foghorn seemed more like the voice of ghosts than ever before.

Something splashed in the water and Solis and I both stiffened, looking for the cause. An otter poked its whiskered face out of the water nearby and stared at us a moment before snorting and diving away in a burst of bubbles. We exchanged a glance of relief and conferred quickly about what to do next. Solis took the log book back to his car—to be transported to the lab later— while I changed out of my wet shirt and jacket in a dock-side restroom. Then we drove separately to the home of the late Castor and still-living Linda Starrett.

You don't meet many people with a name like Castor—especially if they aren't a twin—so background stories about him had been easy to find in the newspaper archives when I did my preliminary checks on the case. At the time he and his ship had vanished, most people in Seattle knew who Castor Starrett was and no one had to brief them, but in twenty-seven years he'd become obscure. He was the great-grandson of a lumberman who had made a lot of money chopping down Western Washington's cedar and fir forests at the turn of the previous century. His grandfather had turned that pile into a recognizable fortune, and his mother had carried on the tradition by marrying well, investing better, and driving her husband into an early grave in time to rake in another, larger fortune in the postwar housing boom. Even before Castor had inherited the lot—including his grandfather's custom-built fantail yacht—he seemed to like nothing better than being seen running with the most glamorous people passing through town. He didn't work; he was just . . . rich. Filthy rich. There were lots of photos of Castor and his pretty blond debutante wife at social functions and even more of Castor with his high-profile friends, and yet there seemed to be so little substance beyond the pictures—just beautiful clothes, beautiful people, and beautiful smiles fronting lives as substantial as cotton candy.

Linda Russell Starrett lived beyond the end of a cliff-side cul-de-sac street that, ironically, overlooked Shilshole Bay Marina and the moorage of the Seawitch. We had to park most of a block away and walk to the end of the street to find the narrow brick-and-stone driveway that wound between another house and the cliff edge to the Starretts' house—a sort of mock-Tudor thing an English novel might have called a cottage that was more than twice as tall as it was wide and pointy with attics. It was cute and well maintained, as far as I could tell from the front in a waist-high bank of fog that spilled over the cliff to the marina below. A florist-shop odor hung in the air and made me frown at the incongruity.

Solis watched me a moment, then took a slow breath through his nose. "Flowers."

"Yeah . . ." I agreed, but there was something more to the smell . . . something too sterile, as if the scent came out of a can. The view through the Grey looked much like the one seen through normal eyes—mist, mist, and more damned mist. I shrugged it off and we went up to the small brick porch with its arch-topped door.

It was still early and we hadn't called ahead but that didn't seem to matter. Mrs. Starrett was at home, though she wasn't very welcoming and I was sure *that* had little to do with the time or the murky fog lurking around her cliffside yard like an incoming tide of trouble. Solis made the official knock, since most people will give way to a badge, but the widow Starrett wasn't impressed. She gave us a sour look with narrowed eyes and pursed lips that made unattractive creases in her pale lipstick. She hadn't looked her age until she frowned; now she looked every minute of fifty-six and then some, but at least her face hadn't been Botoxed into immobility.

Linda Starrett, dressed in elegant white lounging pajamas swamped by an incongruous fluffy sweater that reached to her knees, was petite to the point of tiny—her twenty- to thirty-year-old photos hadn't given an accurate idea of her stature. Cultivated blond, bobbed, and bitter, she heaved a sigh through her nose and stepped back to invite us in. "I suppose you think I know something about this boat business," she said. "Which I categorically do not. But you might as well come in and relieve yourselves of the notion sooner rather than later."

She waved us in and then led us, tiny heeled slippers

clicking, to a glassed-in porch at the back of the house. It was a little chilly with the fog outside and the watery sunshine still blocked by the bulk of the house. "Have a seat," she ordered, remaining on her feet beside the cluster of furniture. "I'll be right back."

She didn't wait to see if we sat, but turned and went through another door that plainly led to the kitchen. I moved to watch her through the window in the door while Solis took a wicker chair that gave him a view of the backyard and its crop of mist if he turned a bit sideways. If she ducked out the front we might have a problem, but I figured we'd hear her if she made a break across the hardwood floor of the hallway. But she didn't bolt. In a minute she returned to the glass porch with two clean coffee cups on saucers and placed them on the wicker table at the middle of the seating group, where a small coffee service was already set. She handled the new cups with care, turning them in the saucers so that their handles were neatly parallel to each other and pointed to her left.

Then she perched on the padded seat of the wicker sofa, her spine poker straight—and gave me another glare. "I said you could sit." As if permission were the same as an order.

I ignored her tone and took the remaining seat on the sofa, which put me between her and Solis. I could have penned her in by taking the other chair, but that would have made the conversation awkward and she clearly wasn't going to run away. I received a thin smile for my pains as Mrs. Starrett reached for the first clean coffee cup and turned her eyes on Solis.

She forced her smile a little wider, as if trying to apply herself to a job she had no heart for. "I never met a policeman who didn't like coffee," she said, pouring the black liquid from a large French press. She managed it very smoothly in spite of its obvious heft. This was a woman with old-school hostess training, and I wondered that she'd made such a lot of coffee for just one person. Maybe it was just a habit she'd never broken. . . .

Solis gave her a small nod. "It's very kind of you," he said like a guest at a fancy tea party. "I am quite fond of coffee. When I was a child there was always a pot of coffee on in the house."

"Really? Your parents let a little boy drink coffee?" Mrs. Starrett asked, offering him the cup.

He took it gently. "It's very common in Colombia. Everyone drinks coffee."

"How do you ever sleep?"

Solis smiled. "We take more milk."

I was having a hard time keeping a straight face. Was Solis—dour, quiet Solis—making a joke? Mrs. Starrett seemed confused, as if she didn't know whether she should be charmed or insulted. Finally she settled on flustered and offered him the creamer and sugar bowl. I noticed he used quite a bit of each.

Mrs. Starrett glanced at me and her face got a little harder again. She poured my coffee—which I took black.

As she was topping up her own cup, Solis started to speak.

"Mrs. Starrett, I know this cannot be a pleasant topic—the reappearance of your husband's boat—but I hope you'll help us understand what happened."

"It was his grandfather's boat," Linda Starrett replied in a sharp voice. "To Castor it wasn't so much a boat as a . . . a floating Playboy Mansion with hot and cold running bimbos."

Solis raised his eyebrows slightly. Mrs. Starrett blushed and bundled her sweater closer around herself before huddling over her coffee as if she were icy cold.

"Joshua—Castor's grandfather—just doted on him when he was little," she said. "I doubt he ever really acknowledged what a pr—what a pig he was, even when it was obvious Castor didn't give a damn about anything but his own pleasures." Her voice grew sharper and the color eased out of her face as she went on. "Joshua died about a year after we were married and I often thought Cas married me to allay any qualms his grandfather had that he might not settle down. Of course he never did. I wasn't so much a trophy wife as a token of respectability. Cas always made sure we were seen together in public, being ever so perfect, whenever he'd come too close to crossing the line with Joshua or his mother. He kept on using me as his . . . his totem of rectitude when he'd been made a fool of in the press or gotten in trouble with the law."

She paused and sipped noisily from her cup, her hands shaking with suppressed anger. "He was a pig!" she repeated. "A spendthrift fool who nearly bankrupted us. He was only saved from total disaster by selling the big house and moving down here."

"You said 'us,'" I observed. "Did Castor control your money, also?"

Her voice was bitter. "Most of it. Not all. It's mostly my own money that keeps me in this so-luxurious style now," she sneered.

I found the house rather nice, but I suppose if you're used to cashmere and caviar, anything else seems like a fall from grace. "Why did you marry him?" I asked.

"Because I was stupid," she spat. She rolled her eyes in self-deprecation and took a long, disgusted breath, settling herself back down. She sat back and took a steadier sip of her coffee before she went on. "Cas was six years my senior and I thought he was just kicking up his heels a bit—a sort of last hurrah—and would settle down a little once we were married. I thought we'd have fun. I didn't understand that I wasn't a person to Cas and certainly not a partner. I was a thing: a shield of respectability he could throw up when he needed it. I should have divorced him—it's not like people didn't do it all the time then—but I just couldn't stand the idea of the failure it represented. I'd never failed at anything in my life and there I was, the only girl in my class whose marriage was as much of a wreck on the outside as it was on the inside. At least my friends had husbands who *pretended* to be respectable and hardworking. Cas didn't

even try. He was . . . a wastrel. That's the word: 'wastrel,' "
she repeated with an angry hiss and bared teeth.

She raised her eyes suddenly and skewered me with
her glare. "And you know the most insulting part of it?
It made me look ripe for the taking. Cas treated me so
badly that other men thought I'd just fall into their beds
and be grateful. I wanted to kill him for that. I wanted to
just kill him! I was never so happy as the day that
damned boat didn't come back." Her eyes flicked toward
the windows as if she could see the *Seawitch* right
through the cliff and the fog. Then she looked back to me
and to Solis—appealing to his chivalrous instincts, I
imagined. "I was happy he was gone. But I never realized
how awful it is to be a sea widow. To think someone's
dead and out of your life but to never really *know*. It was
terrible. It was as bad as when he was here."

Her face knotted into a hideous expression of pain
and horror. "And then it came back."

Solis and I were both taken aback by her outburst for
a moment. "Do you know how it came back?" Solis
asked.

Mrs. Starrett snorted. "How? Why would I? As far as
I'm concerned it might as well have precipitated out of
the fog."

I found that an interesting choice of words since I've
seen ghosts materialize in that very way—particles of
mist gathering and assembling into a recognizable form.

Solis had no outward reaction to her phrase but I did
see a spark of blue jolt from his aura. "Do you believe
your husband had anything to do with the boat's return?"

Mrs. Starrett scowled at him. "I do not. Castor's dead
and I don't think he brought the boat back to harbor
from beyond the grave—no matter what the sensation-
mongers are saying about it being a ghost ship."

"And yet its presence disturbs you. Why?"

At first she didn't reply, and we let the fog-wrapped
silence lean on her, exerting pressure to fill the void with

words before something worse could enter. "I think . . . I'm afraid that there might be something to that curse folderol," she whispered.

"Curse?" Solis asked. He didn't shoot me a glance, but the rising tension in his body and the growing brightness of his aura stretching toward me was almost as good. "Tell me."

Mrs. Starrett dropped her eyes and stared at the floor, unblinking. "At first the press didn't have much to say except that it was a tragedy, but when the ship didn't come back and Odile was already dead they made a big deal about the boat being cursed—which was a total fabrication. They claimed the boat was built with parts from another boat that went aground—not parts taken from the boat but parts meant for the boat that weren't used—and they made up this wild tale about a curse that would take everyone who had anything to do with the boat. First the crew and passengers and then the family. They said I'd be next, but of course I wasn't because there isn't any curse, but . . . I wondered if there was something else, even at the time and . . . What if there is?"

"Who is Odile?" Solis asked.

"Odile? My—she was my best friend. Odile Carson. She was married to Leslie Carson." She blinked at us, waiting for us to fill in the blank. I knew it but I wasn't going to say where I'd seen the name before; it was more valuable to see how she filled in the blank herself. Solis also gave her a slightly owlish look and waited.

She took a long, deep breath and pressed her lips tight for a moment before answering. "Les was on the boat when it disappeared. Les and Odile were our social satellites. We did everything together, once upon a time. Odile and I were very close. The 'boys,' of course, did that man thing of pairing up by gender and going off to do manly things without the 'girls.' So, Odile and I . . . we spent a lot of time together."

Solis sat back and nodded a little. "You were very close."

Linda nodded again, not quite meeting either of our gazes. "Very," she repeated. "More than sisters. But not—not below the line."

That was the kind of phrase my mother would have used to mean lovers without actual sex—the line being the waist, below which one did not venture. Above it was OK, however, since it was acceptable for women to kiss and hug their female friends, even if those caresses were a bit more intimate and frequent than most people were comfortable with or would admit to.

I had new insight into the insurance company's ideas about why Linda Starrett might have had something to do with the original disappearance of the *Seawitch*; they thought she and her female lover might have plotted the whole thing to get rid of inconvenient husbands. It still didn't wash with me, but it would be worth a bit more looking to see if Odile Carson's death had any bearing on the boat's disappearance.

"What happened to Odile?" I asked. I could look it up, and I would later, but I found Mrs. Starrett's replies more illuminating than a recitation of mere facts on a computer screen.

Linda's mouth puckered, holding back a sob with a frown until she had mastered the urge to cry and could speak calmly again. "An 'accident.' She was electrocuted or drowned . . . I'm not sure which they said. In the hot tub. Those converted wine-vat kind of tubs that were the rage then. Odile had trouble with her back—she had mild scoliosis of the spine and sometimes it hurt her quite a lot. She would go sit in the hot water and listen to the radio. I think she used to do it more than she needed just to get away from Les. Les hated the classical music she listened to." Linda smiled a little. "Sometimes we'd go together, Odile and I, and drink some wine and listen to the music, and just float in the water in the tub, out on the little terrace that overlooked the cliff and the beach. . . . Nothing but birds and trees and the wind dancing in the branches over our heads . . ."

She let out a sudden gasp and began crying, tears streaking down her pale cheeks and leaving tracks in her face powder. "I miss her so much! Why couldn't *she* come back instead of that horrible old boat? I hate it! I hate that boat. I hate it!"

"Do you believe the boat's disappearance and your friend's death were connected?" Solis asked.

"Don't be stupid!" Mrs. Starrett snapped, but it seemed like she was protesting too much. "I used to think Les managed to kill her somehow—he was so jealous while he was being so selfish—but that's not"—she gulped and continued—"that's not how things work. Is it? Even if it ought to be. So, no, I don't think the boat came back for some kind of magical revenge. But now that it's here I can't stop thinking about Odile and what happened to her. I miss Odile! I don't want that horrible boat—I want Odile back!"

Now Solis did turn his head and look at me, the slight lift of his eyebrows asking me to step in.

"Linda," I started in a low voice, "we can't bring Odile back, but we'll find out if what happened to her was connected to what happened to *Seawitch*. I know you don't want the boat. You don't have to worry about that—the insurance company will take responsibility for it now. We'll find out what happened. Now, can you tell me who was on board besides Cas and Les Carson?"

She snuffled and gulped her way back to something like normal. "I don't know. I—let me think. Who went with Cas . . . ?" She closed her eyes. "There were five all together. Cas, Les, some bimbo friend of Les's . . . Ruth . . . Ireland, I think. One more woman—I remember it added up to two couples and the captain, but not Reeve that time. . . ."

"The captain?" I asked.

Linda opened her eyes and blinked at me, not sniffling in spite of her reddened nose and eyes. "Yes. Cas hired a professional captain—John Reeve—to manage the boat most of the time. Cas wasn't really very good at handling her and he was too lazy to sit behind the wheel when he could be on deck, getting a tan or fishing or just drooling on his female guests. This was kind of a rushed trip, so the group was smaller than usual and Reeve didn't go—it was usually seven to ten guests, plus Cas, Captain Reeve, and another hand or a cook." She paused to dab at her eyes. "But not this time, which I suppose is why I . . . thought it was something it wasn't."

I looked at her expectantly.

She shook her head. "No cook or extra hand this time. The boat had been modernized and didn't need as many crew as it did originally, so it could go out with just two as long as the passengers weren't picky. The usual hand was booked, so Cas was doubling for the crew. Reeve wasn't available, either, so they took his assistant, a guy named . . . Gary Fielding. Really young. I wasn't sure he was competent, but I didn't really care until the boat didn't come back and then everyone was asking me about the crew. I didn't know anything. I thought it was John Reeve who'd been with them until he turned up talking to the press. Reeve said this Gary kid had his license and had crossed the bar a dozen times as a pilot—whatever that means. It seemed to make a lot of people shut up, so I suppose it's important, but I don't know."

She stopped, an odd look on her face. Then she said, "Janice. Janice Prince. That was the other woman they took. She was a boater. One of those floating trash that tramp from marina to marina, looking for a trip anywhere in exchange for crew work." "And other things," she implied with a lifted eyebrow and a cynical quirk to her mouth.

Starrett, Carson, Fielding, Ireland, and Prince . . . that matched the list the insurance company had given me. The messes in the cabins had left me with the impression of more, but maybe it was just the remains of whoever—or whatever—had invaded the boat and taken or driven the passengers and crew away. . . .

FOUR

There wasn't a lot more we could get out of Linda Starrett. In spite of her own protests about its implausibility, she seemed to cling to the idea that the death of her friend was connected to *Seawitch*. Even a crazy idea can be comforting when you're confused and upset, which she clearly was. She didn't hold up much longer and soon asked us, her voice shaking, to go. Solis and I walked down the curving brick drive to the sound of her heavy wooden door thumping closed behind us like the seal of doom.

At least the fog had begun to thin a bit and returning to our cars was less of a passage through mystery than arriving had been.

"What do you make of it?" Solis asked as we neared the cars.

I shook my head. "The whole curse thing is ridiculous. I've got the paperwork and there's nothing about questionable parts from another boat being used on *Seawitch*. Part of the boat's value was that it was all vintage and intact—a lot of wooden boats that age aren't. And Mrs. Starrett's idea that her friend's death was somehow connected to the boat seems more like the sort of hysterical fancy some people glom onto when they're upset and can't ever shed. I suppose we could ask for Odile Carson's autopsy report, just to be sure. . . ."

"I also think it's unlikely to be a homicide, but I'll make the request. What of the rest?"

"I think we need to get that log book dried out and find out who was really on board. Those cabins didn't look like accommodations for two couples and a single crewman. All four of the cabins had been occupied and more than one of the crew cabins looked used."

Solis cocked his head. "Only one had the symbols in it."

"But it wasn't the only crew cabin that had been used, so it sounds like Mrs. Starrett was wrong about who was on board."

"Gary Fielding would have used one. But, yes, that does leave the other. . . ."

"It seems to me," I added, "that the insurance company has come to the late and erroneous conclusion that Mrs. Starrett and Mrs. Carson may have colluded to get rid of the boat with their husbands on board so they could enjoy their . . . friendship in peace. How they would even manage that, I don't know."

"It is also at odds with Mrs. Starrett's statements about her friend and the timing of her death. I'm as disinclined to credit that as you are."

"Agreed. Even without the complication of Odile's death, a conspiracy to sink the boat would have required help from someone on board, which wouldn't include either husband or the ladies they brought with them."

"Leaving Fielding."

I nodded. "But he's apparently as dead as the rest, and what's the profit in scuttling a ship if you drown in it?"

"Very small," Solis agreed. "Perhaps we should talk to the original captain, Reeve, about his late protégé. . . ."

It shouldn't have taken very long to find Reeve—I did have his address in the file—but it proved to be out-of-date and we had to look for him. Or, rather, I volunteered to do some computer work to find him while Solis took the log book to a documents expert the cops contracted with for this kind of problem.

We finally discovered John Reeve in a retirement village in Des Moines—a cliffside town on the Sound south of the airport but far enough north of Tacoma's Poverty Bay to be free of the paper-mill stink of the mud flats at low tide. The locals pronounced the town's name with the S at the end and sometimes in the middle, too. Des Moines sprawled along the shore in a wedge that was honed to a point by the westward swing of Interstate 5 near Saltwater State Park on the south end of the bluffs. On Zenith—the tallest ridge overlooking the sea and right in the middle of Des Moines—stood a shining edifice called Landmark; it looked like a grand country estate from an English period film, but in fact it was a fancy Masonic retirement home. John Reeve had lived there for a while, but he had moved when the market crashed and now lived in a humble one-story duplex in a seniors' complex of identical duplexes on looping private streets on the north side of town, within walking distance from the beach and the Des Moines marina.

The seaside town wasn't pretentiously quaint yet, but it was working on it, keeping the buildings short and widening the sidewalks near the boardwalk and municipal marina to encourage foot traffic to the little commercial district along Marine View Drive. The east side, near the freeway, was nowhere near as picturesque as the west side. Reeve's home was kind of the same: cute on the outside and much less charming inside.

It was just after three o'clock as we pulled up in front of the building. I thought it looked like the suburban equivalent of a hobbit's house: low and rambling with arched window frames and doorframes and green stucco that blended into the landscaping. The plants in the yard were just a little wild and seemed to have been miniaturized in some fashion, not to bonsai tiny, but to Kincaid-cottage cute. Straight cement walkways to each door slightly ruined the effect, but I thought it was probably a concession to canes, walkers, and wheelchairs. There was no front stoop in front of Reeve's door; the porch was just a slightly sloped cement rectangle. A cast-concrete figure of a semireclining mermaid sat on one corner of the pad, patchy remnants of sparkly blue paint making her supporting tail look leprous, while the red color that had adorned her hair had flaked and gone gray-brown. A scatter of shells and a wisp of sea grass circled the base. Just beyond the porch I saw tiny white and blue sparks in the Grey that darted through the foliage near the house and danced fleetingly across the mermaid with a sudden blush of emerald light that faded as quickly as it had come. Other than that the building was magically dull.

Because Reeve was now approaching eighty, according to the Department of Licensing, we did not attempt the tactic of simply showing up to ask questions. We called first, which netted us a civil greeting at the door, though it took some time for Reeve to open it to us. He didn't move very fast; he wasn't using a cane or a walker but it was obvious to me from the way his whole right side seemed slightly collapsed that he could have used some kind of assistance.

"Ah, the cops!" Reeve exclaimed in a mushy voice that issued only from the left side of his mouth. He had been a big man in his younger days but now he was stooped and withered. His shaggy white mustache—now gone a little yellow—and large ears seemed to be compensating for his hair, which was white and had thinned to expose a spotted scalp between the fluffy strands. "Come on in. Don't mind the place—I hate it. We'll go out back."

Inside the house was faded and too full of once-fine furniture that didn't really fit the small rooms. The whole thing had an air of benign neglect to it—it was clean enough but nothing was really kept up. We followed Reeve through a grim little kitchen that even yellow paint and matching wallpaper hadn't perked up and out into a small yard made private by a vine-covered fence. A large tree cast pleasant shade over the green-painted iron table and matching chairs he directed us to with a jerky wave of his left hand.

"The sundeck—if you will," he said with what might have been a chuckle or an incipient cough. A plate of misshapen homemade cookies and a sweating pitcher of iced tea large enough in which to sink a small flotilla of bathtub toys awaited us.

As we sat, something rustled in the bushes behind a tiny dried-up fountain with a flurry of Grey sparks that glittered green and gold for a moment, then vanished as the sound died away. Reeve grunted as he lowered himself clumsily into one of the chairs. "Neighbor's cat's always slinking around in the shrubs. Looking for rats, I say. She always squeals like a lubber when I say that. Don't know why; killing rats is what cats are best for." He seemed to fall the last inch or so into his chair and sighed heavily. Then he looked up at Solis and me. One of his eyes wandered a little, but the other was a piercing blue that seemed to cut right into us. "Now. What was it you want with me? Something about the 'Witch, I suppose."

We both gave him our best bland expressions. I spoke first. "Why do you suppose that, Captain Reeve?"

"I'm a little slow these days, but I ain't stupid and I watch TV. Saw her on the news the other night. Though why the police are interested after so long, I can't guess. So tell me and I'll think on how I might help you."

"I have to be honest with you: I'm not actually with the police," I explained. "I was hired by the insurance company."

Reeve snorted. "Money grubbers. Probably think the boat's a scam, don't they?"

I made a noncommittal noise.

Reeve turned his sharp gaze on Solis. "And you?"

Solis returned a small nod. "I *am* with the police. We wish to know more about your apprentice who captained the *Seawitch* on her last voyage."

"Gary? That scamp. Never could decide if I was glad or sad over him."

Solis lifted an interrogative eyebrow but said nothing.

Reeve made another of his scoffing snorts. "He was an able seaman and captain—had the paperwork to prove it and the skill—but like a lot of young fellas then, he had a bit of an eye for skirts. Thought being a sea captain was sexier than being a bar pilot—it was all about getting the girls."

"Excuse me," I said. "What's a bar pilot? Mrs. Starrett mentioned something about crossing the bar . . . is that related?"

"Columbia Bar," Reeve replied. "River comes down to the sea mighty strong and dirty—you can see the silt spill from space—and deposits the mud and debris for a couple miles at the mouth of the Columbia River, making a shoal. That's a sort of moving underwater sandbar, missy. What with the current going out and the tides moving, it's a damned dangerous place to cross. But you want to navigate the coast here, you've got no other choice 'cept to sail out a hundred miles or so to avoid the current push. Takes a skilled and experienced pilot to cross the bar more than once—'cause once could be luck, but more than that is skill. Gary had that skill—had a feel for the bar you don't see in every ship's pilot. Could take damn near any craft across and never so much as scrape the barnacles off a hull." He gave me a wink and added, "Gary once told me he'd been kissed by a Columbia River mermaid when he was a kid and I half believed him."

"He sounds remarkable."

Reeve nodded. "He was. I worked with him first time on a yacht delivery coming up from Alameda. He fair impressed me. And he hadn't his captain's papers yet, so I offered to take him aboard so he could get his hours. Didn't hurt me any to have another able man around and I thought I might start me a service, but I dropped that plan when Starrett come along with his offer. Hard to refuse."

"What was the offer?"

"Prep, maintenance, and permanent on-call at thirty thousand a year. Doesn't sound like much, but I could do whatever else I liked so long as I always had the *Seawitch* ready to go and took her out for him whenever he said. I also brought on a cook and extra hands if wanted and I could take the *'Witch* out on my own for shakedown cruises and the like whenever he wasn't using her. I made some right good money taking youngsters like Gary out for their training hours and doing the odd private party when Starrett was out of town."

"Did he know about your sideline?"

"He did. Only kink in the line we ever had was Starrett blowing up rough at me over fuel costs. After that I paid the fuel myself, but I was charging the trainees and party folk for it already, so that was fair, yeah?"

"Captain Reeve," Solis cut in, "why were you not on board the *Seawitch* for her last voyage?"

Reeve peered at Solis, his energy corona pulling in and fading to a watery apple green color. Then he looked away. "Truth to tell, I wasn't fit for duty. First time since I'd taken the job."

Solis didn't say anything for a moment or two and the silence in the yard stretched, broken only by a new rustling from the cat in the bushes. Finally he asked, "In what way were you unfit?"

Reeve flushed a mottled red that continued into his aura, but he didn't yell or demonstrate his anger. He just said quietly, "I was drunk. Three sheets to the wind and didn't give a whore's damn. Thought I could hold my liquor better than that. Guess I was wrong. Starrett wasn't pleased at first, but then he didn't seem to mind so much when I said I'd send Gary along. He liked Gary—they had that skirt-chasing hobby in common. And I won't say I was entirely disappointed to miss the cruise. Kept thinking I saw the dobhar-chú hanging around the boat."

I frowned at the foreign phrase that sounded like "dovr koo" and saw Solis do the same. Reeve noticed our confusion.

"Dobhar-chú—the water hounds. Bad-luck beasts. You see one by a river, you run away fast or they'll catch you and drown you. You seen one hanging round your boat, you can be sure something bad's going to happen on board. That's what I saw the last day I piloted *Sea-witch*: a dobhar-chú. It came out of the water and right up the boarding ladder. Then it just stood on the fore-deck and stared at me like it was memorizing my face, planning some kind of mischief. I went straight to the bar with the old hands and their gals once I got ashore and had a few drinks—maybe more. And I told myself it wasn't anything but an otter, but you know what happened later, and I say it was the fault of the dobhar-chú."

"This . . . water hound is some kind of sailor's omen, then?" I asked.

Reeve shook his head. "Not an omen; the real thing."

"A mythical beast . . ." Solis muttered.

Reeve's aura flashed red again, but this time he didn't hold his temper back. "You think I'm crazy? You think I'm lying?" he shouted, leaning farther forward with each angry sentence. His half-slack face twisted into something from a nightmare and his words came out in a wet slur. "You think because sailors are superstitious it must *all* be hokum and smoke rings? You'll take it more seriously when *you're* the one looking a devil dog in the face and you see those teeth shining, hear its voice. . . . You won't think it's a myth: You'll think it's going to rip your throat out and dance in your entrails. You will *believe* you are staring Death in the face!"

"Captain Reeve," I started, leaning and reaching toward him, hoping I could touch that angry energy around him and maybe—if I still had the ability—calm him down. But he wrenched sideways in his chair as if my impending touch were poisonous, and he fixed me with a glare of utter malevolence.

"Don't you try to gentle me, missy!" Reeve snapped. "I'll put you over the side with the rest of those fish-tailed bitches." And he made a jabbing gesture at my face with three arthritic fingers from his left hand. He seemed to look right through me or even past me as he continued. "You—you—you—" He started choking, the word catching in his throat like a bone and his face going crimson.

Still glaring through me and gagging on whatever curse he was trying to pronounce, Reeve began to topple from his seat. Solis swore and jumped up to help as I dove to catch the old man. But even falling and now turning blue in the face, Reeve jerked himself away from me, landing hard on the little cement patch of his patio. I could hear his head knock on the paving and he started convulsing and twitching, keeping his eyes pinned over my shoulder as Solis pushed me aside and tried to help him. I backed away from Reeve's accusing stare and grabbed my cell phone to call 911, looking around to see what it was that was upsetting him so much—if it wasn't actually me—but all I saw was the shuddering of leaves in the shrubs and a glitter of Grey sparks.

I turned my attention back to the men. The energy around Reeve's head and body was blackening, as if ink were flooding into the psychic space around him, and I could feel a twisting, breathless pain in my own chest as I watched him in horror. He was dying right in front of me and there was nothing I could do for him and no way for me to avoid the wrenching shock of death that would strike me when he stopped fighting.

I started to kneel down and help even as I tried to tell the emergency operator what was happening, but Solis, cursing quietly in Spanish, pushed me away. "You frighten him," Solis whispered. "Back away."

I moved back a little, out of Reeve's sight and where I could no longer see his accusing eyes. In a few minutes the EMTs arrived and hustled past me to the still-thrashing man. I could see Reeve arch and writhe, his eyes rolling up in his head, and I expected to feel the ripping pain of death slam through me. . . .

But it didn't come.

I backed up against the plant-draped wall of the

building and slid down into the Grey. I wanted to see what was happening to Reeve in the magical realm, since I wasn't experiencing what I expected.

Reeve's little garden was hot in the Grey. The plants were all a-rustle with green and blue energy and a spiked line of black and orange defined the wire fence along one edge that had become overgrown by plants. But there wasn't much around Reeve himself except an exceptionally thick cloud of energy of mingled dirty-green, violet, and red threads that seemed to pour from the dry fountain and twist from the foliage, wrapping and swirling around him in coils like a boa constrictor slowly squeezing. . . . As I watched, the green-smoke snake of Grey loosened a little, unwinding a bit, and the pain in my own chest eased.

I looked for the source of the torturing mist. . . . Something was moving along the fence line, heading for a ragged hole where the flow of energy had been disrupted and towing the stream of ugly smoke. I dropped as deep into the mist world as I dared, knowing I was probably as incorporeal as a ghost to normal eyes, and started after whatever was slinking toward the magical exit.

In the deep Grey, where the mist is thinner and energetic strands and shapes of magic dominate the senses, everything living or magical looks like a child's scribble executed in burning, colored light. The thing creeping away from Reeve, dragging the Christmas-colored rope of agony, was about the size of a large dog and wound of blue energy threads so dark they gleamed like sapphires dipped in running, liquid tar. Barbs of red erupted from the thing here and there, as if it had spikes and extra claws jabbing outward through its skin. I fixed my eyes on it and moved closer. . . .

It stopped and turned its ill-defined head to pierce me with a glare of furious light from eyes like a volcano's seething heart. More eyes glared from the writhing green cable. I twitched backward, rising a bit out of the Grey without intending to. In the more normal zone, the beast that glared at me from the thicket had a heavy black head, a humped back, and luminous eyes, but was so dark it was difficult to see. Until it bared its teeth—a double line of sharp white serrations meant for crushing and tearing.

We stared at each other for a charged moment, then the hard-to-see creature sucked in the ugly skein of torment and turned away with a grunt as if brushing me off. It dove through the hidden hole in the fence, trailing sparkles of gold and green and a flicker of red and disappeared as if it had dissolved into the very fabric of the Grey.

I drew a long, slow breath and backed away, stepping out of the Grey and smack into Solis.

He blinked in surprise and took a step aside. "I thought you—" he started, then cut himself off. He looked back toward the EMTs, who had just finished loading Reeve onto a collapsible gurney. I turned my head that way, too.

The EMTs raised the gurney quickly, locking it into position to be pulled out to the aid car, and rushed their burden through the yard and house. We trailed behind. After loading Reeve into the back, one of the EMTs paused long enough to say, "He's holding on but he's not stable. We'll take him to Highline—it's the closest trauma center."

FIVE

The emergency medical crew left us in the front yard in a swirl of retreating sirens and a cluster of concerned neighbors. Solis and I had to find someone to look after Reeve's home until he came back—if he did—before we could leave, too.

I walked back to Reeve's garden to grab my bag and paused to look at the dry fountain that had seemed to pour out so much of the Grey energy that had attacked Reeve. The bottom was painted with a brown scalloped pattern, like waves, obscured by a handful of sand, colored stones, and dried grasses.

Solis called to me to join him in the more pressing business of securing Reeve's house. As we answered questions discreetly and asked after someone to take charge, I kept catching him scowling in my direction. I wasn't surprised when he buttonholed me beside my truck as I tried to slip away from the diminishing crowd.

"I did not see you when the EMTs arrived. Where did you go?"

"I didn't go anywhere."

He frowned at me. "You did. As you did on board the *Seawitch*. You were not where you were."

I crossed my arms over my less-than-impressive chest—I'm not built to win any wet T-shirt contests—but I felt suddenly defensive in the beam of Solis's intensity. "I didn't actually go anywhere. I saw something and I had to take a closer look. And my way of taking a closer look . . . it's complicated."

I knew he wanted to say something else but he settled for, "What did you see?"

"Come and take a look for yourself." I led him to the backyard again and pointed into the bowl of the dry fountain. "Does that look to you like what we saw on the boat down in that crew cabin?"

Solis knelt and studied the red-brown figure under the blown sand and dried grass. "Similar . . . the same encircling waves . . . But what lies at the center?" he added. He took a pen out of his pocket and poked the dried grass aside. A tiny spark of oily green energy flared and died out as he moved the detritus.

Small fragments of beach glass and shell rolled around the bottom of the cement bowl, playing hide-and-seek with the tiny twelve-pointed star drawn at the center of the figure. It wasn't as complex as what we'd seen on *Seawitch*, but it was similar enough to claim kinship. "It doesn't look like the same person made it, but it's got to be related," I said. "I think some of the grass and stones are part of the figure, but they're out of place now, so we'll never know exactly what it looked like."

Solis grunted. "I shouldn't have touched it."

"You couldn't have known." But I took a photo of the revealed sigil with my little digital camera, anyhow.

"You did."

"No, I didn't. I saw something that looked familiar, but I'd have done the same thing. It just looks like trash. At least you didn't touch it with your hands. That's probably blood."

"What else did you see?"

"Excuse me?"

Solis stood up. "You weren't near the fountain when I tripped over you. What were you pursuing then?"

"Oh. Um . . . this will sound pretty loony."

"I'm prepared for that."

"All right. What I saw . . . might have been a dog."

He raised his eyebrows. "Really. How did you see it? I saw no dog and I am hardly blind to something of that size."

"Well, it was not exactly . . . here. I mean it was here, but only partially."

Solis continued to stare at me without saying another word. His tight-clinging aura flicked out whips of aggravated orange and red, but he didn't let it show on his face.

I sighed. I couldn't have dodged this particular push coming to shove once I'd dived for the Grey aboard *Seawitch*, so I had no one to blame but myself for this corner I was in. I didn't like it, however, and I wasn't pleased to be risking this tenuous partnership so soon with the big reveal of just how freakish I was. "Do we have to do this here? It's kind of public."

"Where do you prefer? I tell you, I will not let this drop."

I resisted an urge to roll my eyes. "So it's better for me to get it over with. Yeah, yeah. I know. But you aren't going to like my answers—that is what *I'm* telling *you*."

"I understand."

"My office?" I offered reluctantly.

He glanced at his watch. I did the same. It was five fifteen. He looked skeptical. "Closer will be better."

I waved in the direction of the waterfront. "Something here? Not likely to be very private, though."

"Agreed. But there is privacy to be found in the open. Let's take a walk along the shore, then."

I raised my eyebrows in amusement. "How romantic of you, Solis."

He snorted and turned away. "At the boardwalk by the marina in five minutes."

We drove separately to the parking lot next to the marina and shops and met up again on the shorefront walkway. Without a word we turned together and started strolling north along the shoreline and away from the buildings. The fog had burned off here long ago and we would have been a curious sight on the strand if there had been anyone looking: tall, skinny me dressed for urban hiking more than beachcombing, and older, shorter Solis in his suit and overcoat in spite of the pleasant warmth of the early-summer afternoon.

When we were inconveniently distant from the last building, Solis spoke. "So. Tell me what you saw or how."

"It's a little more complicated than that," I replied, not looking at him but still walking and keeping a moving eye on the area around us.

"Then explain. We're stranded here until the rush hour is over. I see no reason not to put the time to use."

"Well," I started with a sigh, brushing my sea-breeze-tangled hair out of my eyes, "you're aware of how I seem to attract strange things. . . ."

From the corner of my eye I saw him nod. He, too, was keeping his gaze on the scenery more than looking at me. That was the way this was going to go: talking without looking at each other, as if we didn't have to acknowledge anything unpleasant if we didn't see the truth in the other's face. It felt strange; I'd never been totally honest with Solis but I'd always tried to keep my evasions small and cleave to omission more than outright lies. It's a bad idea to get in the habit of lying to cops.

"I see things most people don't. These things see me, too. That can be . . . troublesome."

"What sort of things?"

I shot him a desperate glance, then turned my head away again, letting the wind off the surf blow my hair into my face and hide my expression. I don't manage fear very well—I get angry, aggressive, or snarky instead—and here I had no choice but to be afraid. "Do I really have to say this?"

He nodded. "*Sí.*"

I took a deep breath, not because there was much to say but because it was stupid and annoying to heave the words out, and turned so my face was less obscured by my hair. "I see ghosts. There. OK?"

"Ghosts."

If the chips were down, I might as well go all in. "And other things," I said. "Monsters, magic, things that go bump in the night . . . all that stuff." I didn't feel much better having said it.

"So . . . you say that such things are real?"

"I wish they weren't and I wish I wasn't saying that, but I am. Most of the . . . paranormal is the best word for it . . . paranormal things aren't strong or active or any kind of threat to regular people. Every once in a while, though, they are. Do you remember the Mark Lupoldi murder?"

"I will never forget it."

"Did you ever really buy the explanation I gave you for how he was killed?"

"No, but the case didn't go to trial, so . . . the rigor of proof was never needed."

"But it bugs you still, doesn't it? Like all the little odd things about me and my cases bug you."

He nodded.

"That was one of the cases where the paranormal became dangerous. One of those moments when what should be impossible happened anyhow. And that's pretty much where I fit in the world: working with the stuff that logic rejects but that exists nonetheless."

"Are many of your cases like that?"

"No. Most are the routine investigative stuff, but there's plenty of the other to keep me busy while a lot of my colleagues are looking for new lines of work—what with the Internet making it easier to invade anyone's privacy. . . ." I slammed the lid on my gripes with that particular aspect of modern living.

Solis ignored that last bit and nodded, his expression thoughtful. I wondered if he actually believed me or if he was just doing a great job of humoring the madwoman. "You are implying you saw something at Reeve's home that was . . . paranormal. That you see such things frequently."

"Constantly, in fact."

He turned his head suddenly and frowned at me.

"It's always here. Most of it's like air," I explained, waving my off hand through the salt-scented breeze. "Most people can't see it until it's so thick they choke on it. But I see it all the time. And I can look harder at it to see more if I want, but then I tend to get a little . . . ghostly myself."

He almost covered it up, but I still saw the rapid flicker at the corners of his eyes as he repressed the impulse to widen his stare in surprise. "You saw that at the boat and again at Reeve's," I said. "You almost said something, but then you caught yourself. Didn't you?"

He hesitated—I'd never known Solis to do that. Then he tightened his mouth into a stubborn line, looking angry, and took in a long breath through his nose.

"Oh, damn it. Just look. Look at me. Look as hard as you can. This isn't some kind of illusion," I shouted, and I dropped into the Grey, letting it slam up over me like a steel trap snapping closed.

I hadn't fallen that fast and hard into the Grey in years and I wasn't entirely prepared for the sensation of dropping through cold water and mist, falling into the grip of something uncanny and ungentle. I lurched and stumbled onto uneven ground that seemed to shift and roll beneath me, and the sea of mist swirled into hints of faces and forms that snatched and snarled before they resolved into nothing more than raw ghost-stuff. I elbowed something icy aside, mentally counted to ten, and shoved my way back out to the normal world.

This time Solis actually did take a step away from me and his eyes were larger than they should have been. His right hand twitched upward and he stopped it and his movement away from me. Then he put his hand out and touched the edge of my coat.

"I told you it's not a trick. I'm really here."

"And a moment ago, you really weren't."

"Not quite. I was here but not in a state you could observe. At least that's the best explanation I can make."

He frowned, muttering as if to himself, "I didn't see you, but then you were where you could not have been." He pinned me with his gaze, as if having made up his mind: He wasn't going to let me out of his sight now. "It startled me every time. I thought I must have missed your movement, but I'm not that easily fooled. This makes me no happier, but for now . . ." He shrugged, dismissing the rest of his thought. "But tell me what you think you saw at Reeve's."

I sighed and shook my head, letting the sound of the lapping breakers fill the pause while I pretended not to hear the insult of his doubt. "Something was watching us from the bushes and it wasn't a cat. It was some kind of paranormal creature about the size of a large dog."

Solis snorted. "A dobhar-chú?"

"Oh, now you're scoffing . . . ? After I do the Harper Blaine, Disappearing Girl act?" I shook my head in exasperation, but I did notice his expression wasn't as doubtful as it had been. I put off my annoyance for the sake of getting on. "Really, I have no idea. It wasn't something I've ever seen before. It wasn't a ghost. It was something smart enough and mean enough to frighten Reeve into a heart attack, though. It wasn't me he was staring at but whatever was in the bushes. And then there was some kind of . . . magical smoke from the fountain and that's when the shit hit the fan."

"Huh," Solis grunted, and turned his gaze away again. "If he were afraid of something watching him—be it a monster or not—that implies someone who feels threatened by what he said."

"Or what he would have said if they hadn't stopped him," I suggested.

Solis nodded. "Possibly. But he had already departed from a logical discussion. . . ."

I scoffed this time. "According to you, everything you've heard and seen since Reeve sat down is a departure from logic. That doesn't mean it's not true and that he wouldn't have—or hadn't—given us useful information that would lead to someone who has an interest in keeping the truth of whatever happened aboard *Seawitch* quiet, whether the explanation is paranormal or not. That is, if you believe all I've told you and shown you and that I saw someone or something that frightened Reeve nearly to death."

"I do believe that Reeve was frightened and I apologize for blaming you. I am . . . struggling with the rest."

"There *was* something in the bushes and there is or has been something uncanny on that boat."

"Perhaps. Can we stick to that which is provable in the world *I* inhabit for a while longer?"

"I live here, too, Solis. I understand the problem of legal and material proof. Believe me, there aren't many people who have the fine grasp of this problem that I do."

"Yes, I concede! But someone brought the boat to port and abandoned it," he thought aloud. "Someone of flesh and blood, not a ghost."

"Don't be too sure," I muttered, but realistically I knew that ghosts didn't have the physical power to move something like the *Seawitch*.

He glared at me but ignored my jibe to say, "Someone wants this investigation to happen. . . ."

"And someone else doesn't. Someone skilled brought that boat back to port—it didn't drift in and it wasn't brought in by a novice. Someone good at keeping secrets hid it for twenty-seven years. It's possible they're the same person, but I'm not sure of that."

"Do you suggest that one of the crew or passengers is still alive?"

"I am not suggesting anything except that there are still living people to question. And when we run out of the living, I may have to start on the dead, whether you like it or not."

Solis grunted again. "Let us start first with the log book—with the *normal* evidence. If Starrett was the hedonist his wife described, he may have written revealing and personal notes as well as maintenance records and the names of the marinas they stopped in."

It was my turn to snort in derision. "Reeve would have been the one to write the actual records. If Starrett were writing it, I imagine that book reads like excerpts from letters to *Playboy*."

"At least it is unlikely to read like a Stephen King novel," he snapped, and that surprised me more than anything else I had seen or heard that day. He was deeply unsettled and it made neither of us happy.

And I had no choice but to make it worse. "You're going to have to get used to the creepy factor, Solis," I said. "Because we're hip-deep in it."

SIX

I got back to my condo about six thirty. The trip had been short once traffic cleared and there hadn't been any point in lingering or stopping elsewhere. I'd type up my notes for the insurance company later; I'd been on the job for only twenty-four hours officially and they didn't require a report so soon.

I didn't see any sign of Quinton when I came in so I assumed he was busy elsewhere. We're a couple but we don't spend every free moment together, not least because we both have strange jobs, dangerous associates, and eccentric habits. Two born loners living—mostly—together requires a degree of laissez-faire most people haven't got. I took off my boots and hid them in the hall closet to save them from possible predation by the ferret. Then I flipped on the TV to the first channel I found running a nature documentary and let Chaos out of her cage for a romp around the living room. Chaos loves nature shows, except for any part of Shark Week, which I think demonstrates a lot more common sense than I'd normally credit to a furry mammal the size of a sneaker who looks like an animated kneesock with teeth.

I was staring into the fridge and wondering why I never seem to have any food in the place when I got a whiff of an unpleasant odor that wasn't coming from the icebox. A cold feeling ran down the back of my neck and I turned around slowly.

My kitchen and living room had vanished behind a wall of Grey mist and a gleaming doorway shape awaited my attention. I hadn't seen this phenomenon in years—not since I'd first been introduced to the Grey. I'd seen it only once since then and none of these occasions had been pleasant. Apparently the Guardian Beast wanted to see me and was sending a formal invitation, for once. Usually it just showed up and beat me into doing what it wanted—not the most articulate of monsters, it tended toward violent demonstration more than discussion. Since it is, effectively, my boss in the Grey, when it shows up, I pay attention, especially since I'm pretty sure it could take me out permanently if it wanted to. I sighed and gave up on dinner.

"All right, I'm coming," I muttered, and stepped toward the glowing portal of ghost-stuff, sinking out of the normal world and fully into the realm of shadows and magic.

The Guardian resolved from the boiling fog of the Grey, a long, sinuous, and coiling shape of silver reflection and ghostlight. The unpleasantly dragonlike head swooped down to my own eye level and looked me over, breathing cold and the odor of forgotten crypts on my face. Cold wisps of Grey mist suggested the imminent shapes of sharp horns and fangs.

I pushed the head back with the flat of my hand. "What do you want?" I asked. I would have demanded, but where's the point in that?

"*Seawitch*," the Grey sighed around me, silver-mist faces momentarily evolving from the cold steam of the world between worlds to give voice to the Guardian's thoughts.

"I'm already on it, but I don't have much to go on yet. You have to be patient."

"Valencia," the voices whispered.

"What?" I had no idea what the Guardian was alluding to. A city in Spain? An orange?

"Find . . . the lost."

Not helpful, that. "That was on my to-do list already. If you have a more articulate or specific clue, I'd really appreciate it. I think I liked you better when you couldn't speak at all."

It laughed at me, the Grey rippling and rolling with its amusement. Then it coiled around me, wrapping its snakelike length up my body in cold loops that sent a metallic shock over my skin like touching the live contacts of a small battery. This time it didn't pull me up and drop me down again, as it had once, but spun me round and round, the Beast uncoiling into a dark panorama before my dizzy gaze.

I reeled out of its clutches and stared at the scene it had composed of the Grey. A dark place with two large humped shapes and a black stain that thickened the air in one corner. . . . I'd been there, but it hadn't looked quite like this. . . . Where was it?

As I looked, the dark clot of something widened and became more solid, spreading out to form an impossible crowd of black human shapes that couldn't really fit in the confined space, yet they did—all contained as if warped into the area by some freak of black-hole physics. I thought there must have been a hundred or more, trapped behind the large, cold iron shapes of engines. . . . Yes, that's what they were: engines. The space was *Seawitch*'s engine room. Not as I'd seen it last, but as it might look from within the Grey.

I pulled back from the Guardian and its vision with an effort. "OK, I see it. The engine room. I'll go there tomorrow and take another look. Is that what you want?"

The Grey made a hissing noise that slowly faded to a chuckle as the mist drained away, leaving me flat-footed in the arch between my kitchen and the living room. "Wait," I cried. "What sort of creature—" But it was too late and I couldn't call the Guardian Beast back. I felt cold and my skin was damp and stiff. "Thanks," I muttered. "Next time I'll bring a towel."

"Don't you always know where your towel is?" Quinton asked. "What sort of Hitchhiker are you?"

I whipped around to glare in the direction of the front door from which his voice was coming.

Quinton was smiling at me from just inside the closed door. "Hi. Sorry if I startled you. I didn't realize you were . . . here/not here."

"Just having a little conference call with the Beast and its Greek chorus."

"And this leads to towels . . . how?"

I shook my hands out, flinging salty water at him. "I'm wet. This case revolves around a boat that was lost at sea and has now returned like a bad penny—a very wet bad penny. So I got drenched. The new Guardian has what passes for a sense of humor. Mostly on the verge of nasty."

He looked at the puddle developing around my feet, which had now attracted the ferret, who darted in to take a taste and then backed off, making a face that clearly said the water was vile and she disapproved of it intensely. "You need a towel. Luckily, like a good Hitchhiker, I know where they are."

"What is with the hitchhiker reference?" I asked, grabbing a dish towel off the drain board to wipe the worst of the moisture off my face and hair.

Quinton ducked into the linen closet in the hall and brought back a large bath towel. "You might want to change out of your clothes here, where the floor's easier to mop up. And haven't you read *The Hitchhiker's Guide to the Galaxy*?"

I took the towel and rubbed some more water out of my hair before I started to disrobe. "Nope," I replied. "If it isn't shelved in the mystery section, I haven't read it."

He heaved an exaggerated sigh and scooped up the ferret as she rampaged past. "One of the guiding principles of intergalactic hitchhiking is 'Always know where your towel is.'"

I gave him a blank stare.

"I guess you had to be there," he replied.

"I guess," I echoed, taking off the last of my damp clothes. "This is the second time I've been soaked today by water that wasn't there. Maybe I *should* be taking a towel with me."

"The point isn't that you have the towel with you—although that is implied—but that you know where it is."

"Huh," I grunted from under the terry cloth. "That almost makes sense."

"How did you end up soaked with invisible water the first time?"

"Something on the boat we're investigating doused me."

"Who's 'we'?" he asked.

"Rey Solis—of all people to get stuck with a cold case that's straight out of the *Twilight Zone*."

"How's he taking it?" Quinton asked as I popped back out from under the towel.

"Better than he could have but not as well as I'd like. I think he's actually taking in the idea that I'm not normal in a way that goes beyond his usual experience. We had the Chat."

"The I-talk-to-ghosts chat?"

"Yup. And then I had to show him."

Quinton snorted. "I'll bet he loved that."

"About as much as you'd expect." I peeled off the last of my wet clothes and wrapped the towel around myself.

"Hey, you don't have to cover up for my sake," Quinton objected, smiling.

"I'm cold."

His smile widened into a wicked grin. "I can tell." He walked over and wrapped his arms around me, putting the ferret on my shoulder as he started to kiss and nibble at my opposite ear. "I can warm you up. . . ."

I laughed and tried to wiggle loose. "Silly man. Dinner first."

Suddenly Quinton twitched backward. "Ugh! Ferret tastes disgusting!"

Chaos made a leap for the kitchen counter as I started laughing. "You're the one who put her there!"

"I hadn't considered that she'd stick her tail in my mouth," he added, making a face and turning toward the sink in search of water to rinse from his mouth the taste of ferret fur.

I chuckled and caught the fuzzy miscreant so I could return her to the floor where she belonged. Not that I hadn't enjoyed the kissing, but I was still wound up from the long day and once we got to the sexual gymnastics I wanted to do more with Quinton than rush through a quickie on the kitchen counter. I took his distraction as an opportunity to slip away to a quick shower and some dry sweats.

When I returned, Quinton was pulling things out of the fridge. Neither of us was much of a cook, but Quinton at least had the skill of recognizing what bits and pieces might go well together. I'm strictly a prepackaged dinner girl and if I tried to put a dish together from leftovers, we'd end up dining on something like cream of beet on toast. I like food well enough; I'm just lousy at making it. On the other hand, I have never put things in the microwave that don't really belong there.

Later, when we were sitting on the couch with dinner in front of us and Chaos was occupied with reorganizing her stash of toys, I recapped my day to Quinton at his request. I told him about the *Seawitch* and her missing passengers, my first soaking of the day, Linda Starrett, and then our conversation with Captain John Reeve.

"What worries me," I said, "is that I don't know if whatever was watching was there to begin with or if it was summoned in some way."

"You mean because of the spell thing in the fountain or because he called it in some way?"

I gave a half shrug. "I'm not quite sure. That is, I'm not sure about the connection or if there is one or if he somehow conjured the thing into existence."

"I'm not quite following you. . . ."

"First, I'm not sure what it was that I saw. It could have been what he was describing—a large doglike thing—or it may just have been something that size and I filled in the idea of a dog thing myself."

"Does it actually matter?" Quinton asked.

"It may. If I could figure out what the creature was, I might be able to get a line on what powers are involved here and if it's one of those creatures that is attracted by its name or if it's something that can be tethered or . . . what. Most of what I've seen so far is pretty foreign to me except for basic principles. It all seems to be about water, which I haven't had much experience with up till now."

"Except for up at the lake last year."

"Yes, but that was freshwater and it didn't feel like this. The water was just a carrier of magic in that case, but here . . . it's like the seawater or the sea itself is a power of its own. And I'm not ignoring the fact that there's blood magic involved and that blood is also salty. I'm not quite getting a handle on this."

"Well, you are dealing with sailors and boats and there's a lot of tradition and superstition there. If, as you've said, this stuff is influenced by the things people close to it think and feel and fear . . . then that's a lot of influence and shaping over a very long period of time. And not all of it will be homogenous. You could have more than one tradition in the mix on this coast. I mean, we have everything from English legends to the local Indian lore and the Viking myths that came over with Leif Eriksson."

I gave that a moment's thought and nodded. "True. Could very well be any or all of them. Or maybe I'm just a little thrown off by working with Solis. He's kind of hard to read. Even when he's freaked-out."

"That's what makes him a good cop. You're not easy to read, either, you know. Most people find you a little . . . aloof."

I raised an eyebrow and looked askance at him, feeling a bit prickly. "Aloof? Doesn't that imply dislike?"

"Not from me, but you can understand how your tendency to keep your distance may look like distaste or disdain to some people. I know it's part of the job—you need to keep your thoughts to yourself and not become a factor of your cases—but it does put you in the position of disinterested observer and that unsettles some people. *They* don't separate their observations from their emotions and they don't really understand someone who does."

"Do you speak from experience, O Wise Sage?"

"Yup. My dad's one of those guys." His aura gave a brief, panicked flash of red before he shut his emotion back down, but I still felt it. "He makes you look like a passionately impetuous mayfly. I don't think I ever saw him smile spontaneously in my life. Now, *that* is aloof."

"I can honestly say Solis is not that chilly. I might be able to *like* him if he'd just crack the ice a little. . . ."

Quinton snorted. I cut him a narrow look as he said, "Oh yes, Ms. Pot. Meet Detective Kettle."

"All right," I said on an aggravated sigh. "I admit I'm a hard shell. But I did try to let him in."

"Yeah, but what you let him in on is not an easy thing to get your brain around. Give him some time. You guys have to work together on this and he'll either get it or he won't. You can't force him."

"Yeah, yeah, yeah," I groused, dismissing the problem for the moment, though I knew it was going to come back on me later.

Quinton just gave me a doe-eyed look and raised his eyebrows. I frowned back at him. I could feel something wasn't right. The strange and tenuous magical connection between us vibrated like a drawn string and I didn't know what he was concealing from me, but there was something. . . . I'm curious by nature and I wanted to pick and poke at this hidden thing until he told me what it was, but my better instinct said I shouldn't.

I took a long breath and decided to redirect the subject back to the problem of whatever I'd seen in the Grey at Reeve's house. "Maybe I should drop an e-mail to the Danzigers and see if they know what Reeve was talking about and if what I saw is the same thing."

Quinton shook his head. "Mara and Ben are in Europe, working on his book," he reminded me with a small frown of annoyance. "They're not exactly glued to the Internet, waiting for you to cry for help."

"I'm not crying for help," I objected.

"Yes, you are, and you need to stop that."

"Excuse me?"

He sighed. "Harper, I know you don't want to hear this, but you've gotten lazy about doing your own research—which is ironic, considering that's essentially what you get paid to do. They've been gone most of a year already and you still send queries to Ben and Mara as if they have nothing better to do than answer your questions about magic. And, yes, yes, I do know they're a great resource," he added, putting his hands up to stop my objections. "And there's no one out here half as useful, but that's just the problem: You can't use your friends that way."

I gaped at him. "I don't."

"Yes, you do. And most of the time it's all right—we don't mind. But you said it yourself: You have to stop taking your friends for granted. I know you can manage to get through this stuff without treating people like resources."

I felt stung and didn't know what to say to that; at the same time I had the feeling there was more behind Quinton's concern than he was saying. It was true that I tended to rely on my small circle of friends too much and, frankly, to put them in situations that weren't always safe or comfortable because I needed something and I hadn't weighed the possibility that they wouldn't want to or might get hurt by helping me. And because I have an unnatural gift for persuasion, they didn't tell me no when they probably should have. I looked down, suddenly uncomfortable. "I guess I'm a hard friend to have," I muttered. "Or maybe . . . I just don't know how to be a friend."

Quinton wrapped one arm around my shoulders and pulled me tight against his side. "That is not true and I'm not trying to make you feel bad. I'm just reminding you—as you've said you wanted—that you need to think about these things before you presume on friendships. Ben and Mara and I would all walk across burning coals for you, but you shouldn't assume that we don't mind."

I bit my lip hard. I didn't like being reminded of all the ways I'd abused my friends, but while Quinton was only doing as I'd asked—kicking me in the conscience where I tended to have a blind spot—it was pissing me off. I can be a jerk—I'm not saying I can't—but I wasn't thrilled by being reminded of it. Especially when I had the increasingly strong feeling there was something he didn't want to tell me and this conversation was at least partially a dodge to avoid it.

I took a few more long slow breaths and unlocked my jaw. "I'm not saying you shouldn't remind me how to be a better friend, but maybe we should put further discussion of this off for now," I suggested.

He looked hard at me, as if he were searching for a sign in my face that I apparently wasn't giving. "All right," he said at last. "But I don't want to leave it like this."

I shook my head in confusion. "Leave what?"

"No. I mean 'leave' as in actually go away: I have to go back out. I just wanted to . . . see you before I did."

I frowned at him. "What's wrong? Where do you have to go?"

"It's just more work stuff. I have to do it."

"Work stuff? Like with the three-letter acronyms?"

He made an uncomfortable shrug.

"I thought you were done with that."

"Me, too," he said, his voice rueful as he glanced away from me.

I wanted to ask a half-a-hundred questions, but I stifled them and we spent the next quarter hour trying to pretend we both weren't uncomfortable and lying about it.

Finally I gave up. "Does this have an end?" I asked.

He squeezed his eyes shut and gave a tiny shake of his head. "I don't know." He stood up and took the plates out to the kitchen to keep the ferret from helping herself and, I guessed, to avoid making more of a reply.

I caught him before he could slip out the door. "Are you coming back?"

"Yeah. Just trust me."

"I do." I wanted to ask why he didn't trust me, but I knew that would be a big, fat mistake. So I shut my mouth, which made our parting kiss a cold, narrow, and unsatisfying thing.

As soon as the door was closed behind him I wanted to scream in frustration. I was trying to be a better friend, even to my lover, to give as well as take, and here was something I could do nothing about. I couldn't complain, I couldn't remonstrate, I couldn't even be sure what the problem was, though I'd have put money on the chance it was something to do with his mysterious family, since he'd been more forthcoming about having worked for the government than he was about them.

I growled and threw the nearest object: a coffee mug that shattered against the doorframe.

Broken ceramic showered down onto the floor and the ferret scampered to it, hopping in fury.

I watched her a moment, fuming, until her antics worked past my annoyance and left me shaking my head in self-disgust.

"That was a stupid thing to do," I chided myself, fetching the dustpan and broom from the kitchen.

I went to clean up the mess, having to field the ferret away from the sharp bits of former mug. And afterward I sent an e-mail to Mara and Ben, anyhow.

There are few things more emotionally terrible than interviewing family members of missing persons presumed dead for twenty-seven years. When someone's been missing for a short time, the family usually has strong

ideas about whether they are dead or alive and what
may have happened to them. They will even argue with
one another and with the interviewer about it. But when
someone's been gone without word or trace for so long,
the sadness and confusion settles in and some of these
people who can otherwise manage their daily lives become painfully disconnected when they talk about the
missing. Time seems to flutter around them, shifting the
phase of their reference from now to then to . . . some
strange, unspecified time that is neither future nor past.

Gary Fielding's family was in Portland, so Solis and I
had chosen to leave them aside unless necessary and
started with the family of Janice Prince—one of the two
women who'd been listed with the passengers. But we
hadn't made a lot of headway with the Princes. Janice's
mother, now in her early seventies, kept breaking into
tears. Her father was stony, glowering at us and offering
nothing but negative comments such as, "I always knew
it. I knew she was a bad one," which threw Mrs. Prince
into fits of crying and arguing against him. Mrs. Prince
countered with, "No, Janice wasn't bad! She was confused, poor thing. She just—she just didn't fit in!" and
similar statements, when she could make one at all between bouts of upset and tears.

The conversation went in circles of blame and recrim-
ination that broke down into Mrs. Prince sobbing about
what a good girl her daughter had tried to be while her
husband just shook his head in judgment.

"She couldn't help falling in with that fast crowd
down at the marina," Mrs. Prince cried to me. "They
were so—they seemed so charmed."

"Boat trash," her husband muttered.

Mrs. Prince gave him a pleading look. "They were so
glamorous. Even the ones without any money always
seemed to be going wonderful places and doing exciting
things! How could a little girl like our Janice not fall for
that? There weren't bad people. They weren't! They were
just—"

"Trash!" Mr. Prince spat.

"No, they weren't. Besides, Janice worked there. How could she avoid them?"

"Excuse me, Mrs. Prince," I interrupted. "Your daughter worked at the marina?"

She turned her reddened eyes to me. "Yes . . ."

"What did she do there?"

"She . . . she worked in the convenience store at the end of the fuel dock."

"So she knew a lot of the regulars?"

"Oh yes! Janice would have such interesting stories when she came home! Who was going to Mexico or Alaska or out to the islands or taking their boat out for repairs. It was like all of them were her personal friends!"

"Was she particular friends with anyone?"

"Oh . . . I don't know. I suppose. I don't remember names now. . . ."

"Did she have other friends around the marina—other workers or anything like that?"

"Well, she and Ruthie Ireland spent a lot of time together. . . ."

"How did she know Ruthie?"

"Just from the marina."

"More trash," Mr. Prince declared. "Loose!"

"Now, dear, that's not fair."

"Sluts, the both of them," Mr. Prince declared. "Better off dead and gone."

Mrs. Prince broke into wailing sobs for the third or fourth time. I eyed Solis and wondered if we could just call this one done and go on to the next sad family on the list. He glanced back and shook his head in resignation. Then he got to his feet.

"Mrs. Prince, Mr. Prince," he started. "We apologize for bringing up such painful memories. You've been very helpful."

Mrs. Prince grabbed for his hand and turned her face up to his. She hiccupped and gulped as she asked, "Will you be able to tell us what happened to our little girl?"

"We hope so, Mrs. Prince."

She let go of his hand reluctantly and covered her face with the tear-soaked handkerchief she clutched in her hands.

Mr. Prince saw us out, still hard, still disapproving. He opened the door and held it for us, scowling. He didn't say anything as we left.

I walked behind Solis to his car—a blue Honda sedan so bland it would disappear in a bowl of oatmeal. Beside the car, Solis reached into his jacket and brought out his cell phone. It was one of those big-screened smartphones blinking with little messages and clever applications. He poked it a few times and smiled. "Our manuscript technician has had some luck. He should have some legible pages photographed for us within an hour," he announced, looking back at me. A momentary frown flitted across his face, as if he was unsure of me, but it vanished almost too fast to see.

I supposed he hadn't really forgotten our strained conversation from the day before, even though he'd put on a good show of it. I played along. "I hope they're useful," I said. The chances of the pages holding anything but chart headings and maintenance information were slim, but I still hoped for a break from the "normal" side of this damned investigation.

"I asked him to concentrate on the pages near the end, where the most recent entries were. We'll see. . . ."

And in the meantime Solis and I would pretend strange things hadn't happened yesterday and carry on to the home of Walter Ireland to find out what he had to say about his missing daughter.

Ireland, like the Princes, was elderly, and a widower besides. We got lucky in that he was one of those guys whose family was helping out rather than dumping him into a retirement home. His two remaining children were at the house when we arrived, and it appeared we'd interrupted a lively game of poker—the dining room table was spread with cards, chips, and snacks, and the elder

Ireland was comfortably parked at one end in a wheel-chair that was slightly ratty but lovingly padded with a crazy collection of brocade pillows and clashing blankets.

We'd been met at the door by a woman in her late thirties with black-walnut hair that was unashamedly straight out of a bottle. She introduced herself as Jen and her older brother as Jon and waved at her father as we drew near, saying, "Hey, Dad, what you been up to? The cops are here! Have you been drag racing again?"

Walter Ireland's laugh was a weak, wheezing thing that shook his chest like an earthquake nonetheless. Judging by his thin, olive green aura, the oxygen bottle strapped to the back of his chair, and the way the riot of pillows propped him up, we'd get more of our answers from his kids, not because he was going to hold out on us, but because he simply didn't have the breath to speak for long.

We introduced ourselves to Walter and he gestured to us to sit down with the family. The table had enough mismatched chairs to seat eight, so we picked one on each side near the poker party. I sat on the side next to Jon — a tall man in his early fifties with receding hair the color of dust and a mustache stolen straight off a cowboy in a cigarette commercial. Solis took the seat next to what must have been Jen's currently empty chair, judging by the cards facedown on the table.

"You want anything?" Jen asked, still standing between the table and the doorway and glancing around at everyone. "Dad is going to have his go juice."

Walter shook his head and made a face.

"Oh yeah, you are," Jen replied. "It's after noon and the doctor says you have to drink it twice a day. I know it's gross, but, hey, it could be worse — it could be blend-ered liver powder and wheatgrass like Dotty drinks. Num num!"

Walter's mouth turned down and he coughed out, "All right. Nasty gunk."

"I want some of that red stuff," Jon said. "We've still got red stuff, right?"

"You mean red-red or pinky-red?" Jen asked.

"Red-red. Pinky-red is that dragon-fruit goop. Pfah!"

She looked at us. "We have Vitamin Water in whatever color you like and soda and plain, old-fashioned tap water. Or I can make some tea if you want."

"Water is fine," I said.

Solis nodded to indicate the same.

Jen raised her eyebrows at us. "Ooo . . . living on the edge—drinking tap water."

"I hear fish fart in it," Jon said with a wink at me.

Jen hustled around the open-plan kitchen that adjoined the dining area and fetched the drinks. She brought her father a small plastic bottle of some thick orange liquid and plopped down a bottle of purple Vitamin Water next to it before she sat down beside him and pried the lid off the orange goop. She pushed it into Walter's hand, saying, "There y'go, Dad. Slug that crap down and then you can have the good stuff to wash away the taste." She shot a look over her shoulder at me and Solis. "Acai and blueberry. I think it's horrible, but Dad likes the stuff."

"Better'n this," Walter mumbled, lifting the small bottle in a shaking hand.

"My theory is that the combined tastes must be much better than the individual ones," Jon added, "because that acai berry stuff is kind of weird."

Walter started to offer him his orange glop. "Wanna find out?" It came out as a near whisper.

Jon waved him off. "Nope. You drink it, Dad. You're a better man than I am."

Walter wheezed another laugh, then guzzled his drink with a downturned mouth and a scowl.

"OK, so . . . what's the question of the day?" Jen asked, turning to us as her father reached for the bottle of purple liquid.

"We have some questions about your sister, Ruth," Solis replied.

Jen blinked and Jon scowled. Walter looked stunned.

"Ruthie?" Jen asked. "She's been gone a long time. What kind of questions could you have? Have you found her?"

"No. But the boat on which she disappeared has been found and we wish to know more about the passengers."

Jen blinked a little, her mouth working like a fish's, and couldn't quite form a reply.

Jon leaned forward, helping his father with the lid on the bottle of Vitamin Water, but keeping his focus on us. "What sort of thing do you want to know?"

"Did she talk about the trip?"

"Not a lot that I remember," Jon replied. "But I wasn't around much then. I suppose she would have been excited, though."

Jen snorted and Walter shook his head.

"So she wasn't looking forward to the trip?" Solis asked.

"She wanted it like fire," Walter mumbled, wheezing.

Jon reached over the wheelchair and adjusted the valve on his father's oxygen bottle. "Ruthie was boat crazy, so if she was going to go out with those high-roller types, of course she was excited. She loved that stuff."

"Well, she liked her friends, too. I don't think she'd have been as excited about it if they weren't going along," Jen added.

"Which friends, specifically? Do you remember?"

"Oh, Janice, of course—they were BFFs." She looked at her brother. "What was that other girl's name? The crazy one."

"Which one? Half of Ruthie's friends were crazy."

"The one with the funny hair." She turned her gaze back to me and Solis. "One of those blondes whose hair goes all green in the swimming pool. You know. Kooky. She was like a deckhand or something." She looked back to Jon. "What was her name?"

"Sally?"

"Nooo . . ." Jen said, shaking her head. "That's not right."

Walter coughed around a word. Jen and Jon both leaned close to hear.

"What, Dad?" Jen asked.

I could barely hear the whispering of his breath as he repeated the word.

Jen looked up again. "Shelly. Dad says her name was Shelly." She looked at her brother. "Does that sound right to you?"

Jon nodded. "Oh yeah. Now I do remember her. Shelly Knight. Which I remember because Janice didn't like her as much as Ruthie did and she called her One-Night Shelly. They used to argue whether Shelly was a friend or a floozy."

"Like I would remember that. I was, what, twelve?"

"Well, you might if you'd paid attention."

"What came to my attention was the way you mooned around after Janice Prince."

"Mooned around? I never moon—unless I drop my pants first."

Solis cut into their developing argument. "Do you believe Shelly Knight was on the boat when it left?"

"I'd be really surprised if she wasn't," Jon said.

Jen nodded. Walter seemed to nod, too, but it could just have been that he was tired, since the energy around his head and body was very low. "Shelly," he whispered, a slight scowl on his face. He motioned to his children and Jon leaned in to listen before Jen could turn around from looking at us.

Jon nodded for a few seconds at what his father was saying, then raised his head, frowning. "I think Dad's really tired and he's not making sense. He says he saw Shelly the last time we were down at the marina. But that couldn't be right."

"Why not?" I asked. "When was he last at the marina?"

"About a year ago. Before he went into the hospital

this last time. We went down with the broker to finalize the sale of Dad's fishing boat—nothing fancy, but he wasn't going to use it and we kind of needed the money for the medical bills. But, anyway. He's sure he saw Shelly sitting on the dock when we were there. I don't remember that but he says he did. I think he's imagining things, myself."

Jen smacked him on the arm. "Don't say that. Dad's not senile."

"I didn't say he was. I just don't think he's remembering quite right. It was a year ago. A lot's happened since then."

"How could you misremember a girl with green hair?"

"These days there's a lot of them I'd like to misremember. Ecch. Green hair."

Jen made a face at him. "Bigot."

"I don't make fun of *you* for dyeing your hair."

"That's because I look good."

"That's because you dye it a nice color, not green. You look like a femme fatale from an old movie."

Jen beamed at him. "Thank you!"

Solis's cell phone vibrated and made a rattling sound against the chair where his pocket touched the seat. He reached down and silenced it without looking. "So," he started, "your sister didn't have any fear about this trip?"

"Oh, heck, no!" Jen said. "It sounded like a great adventure. I wish it—I wish it hadn't been. I wish she'd stayed home." Her face went suddenly and deeply sad.

Jon put his hand over hers on the tabletop. "It's all right, honey. We all miss Ruthie."

"I just wish I'd been nicer to her. I wish I hadn't been such a brat to her."

"You *were* a brat; you were twelve."

"I said some mean things to her before she left. I guess I was jealous, but I wish I could take them back. And I can't."

Jen teetered on the verge of tears until her father interrupted with a soft snore. Both adult children jumped a bit and looked at their father. Walter had fallen asleep in his chair.

Jen wiped her eyes, smearing a bit of eyeliner on the back of her hand and sniffling around a wobbling smile. "Oh, Dad. Silly old Dad. Maybe we'd better put him to bed...."

Jon stood up, unfolding to a comfortable six feet and stretching his arms a bit. "All right. Let's do it. You get the door; I'll drive."

They paused and glanced at us. "Umm . . ." Jen said.

I stood up and Solis followed suit. "We'd better be going," I said. "You've been very helpful. Thanks. If you think of anything else about Ruthie's friends or the trip, you'll let us know, right?" I added, holding out my card.

"Oh. Sure." Jen took my card and another from Solis and tucked them into the back pocket of her jeans. "I hope you find out what happened to her. We—we all really miss her."

"We will let you know," Solis offered.

Jen nodded and we let ourselves out as the Ireland kids put their father to bed.

Outside, Solis glanced at his cell phone and poked it a few times. Then he held it out to me.

I took it, not sure what I was going to see. On the big screen there was a photograph of a sheet of paper that was stained with green and black marks and yellowed unevenly all over. I couldn't see more than that and started to hand back the phone, scowling in confusion. Solis reached over my arm and made the picture suddenly zoom larger.

"Oh," I said in surprise, looking down at the photo of a page from the log book floating in a shallow tank of water. "Oh . . . my." It was the passenger and crew manifest for the last voyage of the *Seawitch*. For the crew, two positions were listed: a captain/navigator and a cook.

Solis looked over my arm at the photo, then up at me.

"Do you suppose the cook listed there could be Shelly Knight?"

"I'm not sure it could be anyone else. But if it was Shelly ... who did Walter Ireland see on the dock last year?"

"Perhaps Shelly Knight."

"Then why hasn't she come forward before this?" I asked, mostly to get the question into the air, since I was sure we were both thinking it.

"We should see if we can find this woman."

"Marina?" I asked.

Solis nodded.

SEVEN

As we returned to the marina, I remembered what the Guardian Beast had told me: "Find the lost." Was Shelly Knight one of the lost or was she something else? Had she really been on board *Seawitch* at all? And if she had been, was the woman Walter Ireland had seen really her or someone who merely looked like her in the memory of an old, sick man? How many women with pale green hair were there in the area? There were plenty of places to go swimming around Seattle, so any number of blond women with swimming-pool hair might have been mistaken for her, and we had no picture to go by. We'd have to find someone at the marina who could remember her. If we were very lucky they might have an old photo or we might get an ID photo or a hit on the Internet, though the chances weren't good for a woman of no notoriety who may have vanished for twenty-seven years. And I hoped Solis's magical technician was able to salvage more useful information from the log book to confirm or deny the presence of Shelly Knight on the fateful final voyage of *Seawitch*; if she were still alive it would be our first real break.

The marina had just thrown off its morning coat of fog and the pavement and docks still gleamed with moisture when we arrived. Sailors are a ridiculously early lot, I noticed. But I suppose when you plan your voyage by tide tables, you don't waste time sleeping in when the tide is in your favor. There wasn't a throng of people, but the place was far from deserted. It would be a busy place in a few weeks, when school was out, but for now the residents, workers, and boat folk were up and about in scattered groups and singles, going about their business. The boat-repair yard at the south end was already busy and we could hear the hooting of the travel lift backing away from the edge of the dock as it trundled into the yard with a midsized sailboat hanging from slings between its chunky metal trusses. The boat must have been thirty feet long or more and it looked like a toy in the blue-painted arms of the massive lift.

Seaview Boatyard was a busy little place with nearly every available space in the yard filled with boats getting fixed or cleaned up for summer—every kind of boat you could imagine, from old classics built of wood to high-tech racing sailboats, from fiberglass motor yachts to charter fishing boats built of steel. But in spite of the number of boats in the yard, the activity was laconic.

I took point on this one, being a female and therefore not in danger of losing my street cred by showing some ignorance of boats. We followed various directions from the staff until we found the boatyard manager, a curly-haired, rough-skinned man in his mid-fifties named O'Keefe—called Keefer, naturally. I asked why the packed yard was so sparsely busy.

He rocked back and forth from toe to heel as he spoke, as if the ground were too still for his taste. "Well, it's midweek and a lot of these boats are in for yard work—that is, we're doing the work, not the owners—so they have to wait their turn, since we only have so many crew here. A few have their own contract crew in—shipwrights and specialists who come in on contract to the owner—and we're fine with that. So only a couple are being worked on by the owners themselves, and a few by my guys, a couple more by contractors. It'll be about twice as busy on the weekend when people come in to do their finish-up work and splash the boat."

"Splash?" I asked.

"Put it back in the water. Not a tricky thing with steel or fiberglass, but you have to be a little delicate with wood since they can dry out if they're standing on the hard—up on dry land, that is—for a protracted time. Three or four days is no big deal for a large boat, and with the fog we've been having, that's like putting a nice, wet blanket on 'em every night. But when it's hotter, old woodies can dry out pretty thoroughly in a week or two and the wood shrinks up. Then you have to lower 'em back in slowly and sometimes leave 'em in the slings overnight to swell up and seal all their seams again. That takes a little patience."

"I imagine so. How long have you been working here?"

"Here? Only a couple of years." My heart sank. "I've been in the business near thirty, but I was at the old yard on the canal until last year when they closed up and moved out here."

"Would you have met a woman named Shelly Knight? She was some kind of cook or deckhand for hire out here between twenty-five and thirty years ago. Blond. We heard she was back in the area."

"Well . . . maybe. Boat people get around, y'know. You always run across people you knew from some marina you moored up in five years ago or some regatta you went to or something like that. Can't say the name rings a bell, though." Keefer shrugged. "But it's not like itinerant crew are running around with name tags on their chests, either. Sometimes you only know these guys by first name—or, worse, just a nickname—and pay 'em in cash or kind and never see 'em again."

"What do you know about *Seawitch*? The boat that came in a few days ago, abandoned."

"Oh, our ghost ship?" He let out a short laugh. "She's a legend, that one. Custom built out at the old Lake Union Shipyard back in the twenties. Port Orford cedar on white oak frames to a Ted Geary design. Steel keel shoe and bow protectors. Twin engines—upgraded to diesel in the fifties. All hand-fitted mahogany and such inside. Nice boat. Well kept up until she went missing. Nicely fitted out, too, I hear. Pity what's become of her."

"What's the rumor mill say about it?"

"About *Seawitch*? That she's haunted. You know how sailors are. One old dog says she was doomed from the start—that she was built with parts from a wrecked ship, which is patently not true. Another fella on the dock claimed he heard sounds from her the other night, like someone was tearing the boat apart, but he says there was no sign of anything amiss when he went to take a look."

"What was he doing out there?" I asked. "I thought B was the legal-status dock."

"Nah. It's all mixed up. He lives out there—Stu Francis his name is. Out at B Thirty. The marina wouldn't admit it, but they kind of like to have someone living on every dock if they can. Kind of like getting free security, though the Port of Seattle may not feel the same way—they have a bit of a love/hate relationship with live-aboards because of the legal and environmental bullshit—pardon my French. One thing you can count on, though: Live-aboards will always check up on strange noises and come to a call for help. Save many a boat from damage by being first on the scene. Funny bunch; know what everyone's doing—how could you miss it with such thin walls and neighbors five feet outside your window?—but they look away when it's not their business. They all act like they don't know a thing until someone's in trouble. Then they're on it like it's their own boat shipping water or beating itself to death in the wind. Even if they can't stand you, they'll jump in and save your ass and your boat, too." He shook his head and repeated, "Funny bunch."

We didn't get a lot more out of Keefer and we couldn't go wandering around the docks without a key, so we headed for the marina office, past the large and oddly proportioned statue of Leif Eriksson mounted on a stone plinth and surrounded by smaller standing stones in a boat-shaped oblong. I'd long ago discovered that the people of Ballard prize their Nordic heritage, but I still found the tribute to Seattle's Scandinavian immigrants a bit bizarre. Foreshortened as it was from below, Leif's head seemed a bit too large, and I always half expected him to raise the ax he was leaning on and demand I answer a question about the air-speed velocity of an unladen swallow. I admit I gave the big bronze statue a wary look as we passed by, but it remained inert.

Inside the office, we met a pleasant Asian-American woman who offered us an electronic key and answered a few questions. She was far too young to have been around the marina for twenty-seven years, unless she'd toddled into the office during a preschool outing.

"Do you know of anyone working here now who might have been here when the *Seawitch* was last moored at this marina?" Solis asked.

She thought about it and shook her head. "No, I think there's no one on staff who's been here that long, but I do know some of the live-aboards have been here for a long time. You could try a couple of the boats on F dock, I think. . . . It didn't change size during the renovations a few years ago so a lot of the same people are there who were there before. It's late enough now that some of the residents might be barbecuing—they have a little party on Thursdays out there. Ask around. I'm sure someone will have an idea."

Solis nodded. "Thank you. We'll do that. Have you heard of a woman named Shelly Knight around the marina? Possibly working for one of the boat owners?"

Again the clerk shook her head. "No, I don't think I've heard of her. We do keep track of all the keys—they each have a discrete code that is recorded when they're used on any of the electronic pads at the marina. That way we know who's been on a dock or in a building where there's been a problem. But we don't have any control over owners who lend out their keys to employees or friends without telling us. Let me check something. . . ." She looked down at her computer and typed for a moment. "I don't see the name," she said, looking up again. "The vendor keys we loan out for short-term use don't tell us anything about who's using them, just that it was that key at that lock. If she's here, working for someone, she hasn't been introduced to me and she isn't on the vendor or staff roster. You could ask in the offices next door to see if any of the businesses have a temporary employee. I could send out a request to our vendors who've used keys recently to let you know if they have her on their lists, but that's about all I can do and it would take a few days for them to reply—most of them are busy or out of the office on weekends, so if they don't reply tomorrow, I couldn't tell you anything until Monday or Tuesday at the earliest."

"We would be grateful for any help you can lend with the vendors," Solis replied. "And we will continue to search, also. Thank you for the use of the key."

The woman gave a faint smile. "It's no problem. Just bring it back when you're done. And if we're closed, you can put it in the drop box for transient moorage payments. That's in the hall."

It was amazing how laid-back the system was while it still had an overlay of security. But not great security, as we discovered when we approached F dock and were willingly waved through the big glass-and-steel security gate by a man coming out to walk his dog. "Heading for the barbecue?" he asked.

"Yes," I answered with no hesitation. It's just smarter to agree with people when you want to get past them.

"They're almost at the end of the dock—can't miss 'em. See you later!"

Solis stopped on the way down the dock to poke at his phone again and offered me another look at several photographs the manuscript guy had taken. I'd figured out how to zoom in by the third page and took a closer look at one of the pages. And there it was: Shelly Knight—deckhand/cook. I looked at Solis.

"She was there. How long do you think it'll take your guy to get the whole thing photographed or dried out enough to read the original?"

Solis shrugged. "Perhaps another day or two to photograph the pages, but the whole book may never be dried out in a readable condition. He says in the e-mail that he's made good progress with the separation process, but not all the pages were salvageable and many will have to be photographed wet, which is harder to read. There will be missing information even with the best recovery."

"Still," I said, "it's more than we had yesterday."

"There might be more than that. An electronic scan of Odile Carson's autopsy and the accident reports are being sent to me."

"We'll have to go through those, too, I suppose, if only to rule out any connection between the two events."

"It is an upsetting coincidence that the boat disappeared within days of Mrs. Carson's death. . . ."

"And it may be nothing more than that—a coincidence."

"Yes. But we'll look over the reports, anyway. For now, we need to find Shelly Knight—if she's alive and near this marina."

"You can't find a picture of her online using your magic phone, can you?" I asked.

Solis gave me a long look. "I already tried and got nothing. I'm waiting for the DoL to reply to a query I sent earlier, but they may also have nothing. Transients often don't use their real names, as you know."

I agreed unhappily, and we carried on up the dock in search of a barbecue.

EIGHT

A massive shoal of salmon had come into the marina and the water was restless with their endless circling and sudden leaps as they rested before heading to the fish ladder at the locks a mile or so up the passage to the east. Their splashing made occasional punctuation to conversations drifting from the decks and portholes of the boats along the floating sections of F dock.

About two-thirds of the way to the end of the quarter-mile-long dock, we found a group of five people sitting in camp chairs or standing on either side of the floating walkway upwind of a large propane barbecue on a cart. There were chairs set out for more people and a few bowls of chips and salsa sitting on top of the nearest dock box. A few cans of cheap beer and plastic glasses of wine were in evidence, but the party was obviously only getting started.

A tall, dark-haired man in his early sixties, sporting a luxuriant mustache, was tending some beef ribs on the barbecue. He looked up as we drew near. "Hi, there! Hope we're not in your way," he added, trying to step aside to let us pass without falling in the water or sending his ribs to feed migrating salmon.

Solis glanced at me and raised his eyebrows. Apparently he wanted me to take this one. "Not in the way at all," I said. "You're actually the people we were searching for."

They all looked at us in surprise, and we were no longer the strangers passing by but a focus of piqued attention. I introduced myself and Solis, who flashed his badge, just to make it official. "We were told there might be some residents on this dock who were here twenty-seven years ago when the *Seawitch* was regularly moored here," I said.

"*Seawitch*?" asked a seated man wearing a floppy sea grass hat to shield his bearded face from the sun. "Which one is that?"

A short woman with cropped dyed-brown hair pointed south across the docks with her free hand; the other held a sweating plastic stem glass half-full of white wine. "The ghost ship. You know." She turned her attention back to me and Solis, smiling a little as if she didn't want to seem unfriendly but wasn't going to just give up the information without knowing more. "Why are you looking?"

"We hope to find anyone who might have information about who was on board the day the boat left here on its last trip," Solis replied to her. "We also hope to discover if a woman named Shelly Knight has been seen in the marina recently."

"Is she associated with the ghost ship?" the man in the hat asked. A salmon leapt nearby, sending a patter of water drops onto the dock.

"She may be," Solis replied with care.

"Huh," the hat wearer grunted. "Imagine that." He looked at the short-haired woman. "Isn't that young lady on *Pleiades* named Knight? The one who sings all the time. . . . Something Knight—can't remember her first name."

"The woman we're looking for would have to be approaching or past fifty," I said.

"Then this couldn't be her. Our Miss Knight is much younger than that," Hat Man replied.

I glanced at Solis before saying, "She may be a relative, though. Where is *Pleiades*?"

The man in the hat looked over his shoulder and pointed south. "Over on D dock. The big blue ketch on the far side. Oh, and it's a beauty, too! They just refinished the masts and all the brightwork on the sheer and up the sprit—"

The short-haired woman shook her head a little in amusement. "Silly, she doesn't know what a ketch is." She looked at me and Solis. "It's a two-master. Shorter mast in the back. The hull's dark blue with varnished woodwork, gold trim and lettering, and it's got matching blue covers on the sails. She's a really pretty boat."

Solis looked at the man in the hat and the woman who'd spoken before saying, "The office did not have a record of anyone named Knight keeping a boat here."

"Oh, she's just boat-sitting and prepping her," the woman replied. "The owners are back East and they haven't gotten out here for the season yet."

"When did *she* arrive? Miss Knight, that is."

The woman looked around at her companions, seeking consensus. "Oh . . . back in March, I guess. . . . Does that sound right to you guys?"

The rest muttered among themselves and nodded in general agreement.

"All right, then. March. Which would have been when the boat came out of the maintenance yard. They did the hull and bottom paint and reset the masts after winter storage so she'd be ready for opening day, and then the owners couldn't get back in time. Isn't that sad? Anyhow, Miss Knight must have come with the money or Keefer wouldn't have let the boat out of the yard. A lot of people don't keep boats in the water year round like they used to, but once you've got a nice boat like that in, you have to keep her up every minute, so hiring a reliable caretaker is a good idea."

"How would you know they were reliable?" I asked.

"Oh, mostly references from other boaters, or if they have a bond posted or come from a company that does moving and service stuff."

Solis didn't look at me, but I saw his aura flare up for a moment in bright gold sparks. He was very interested in Miss Knight, but he only nodded and thanked them all while making a quick note on his cell phone. A few more salmon plashed around, making a slapping sound on the surface of the water.

"I see," I said, redirecting the conversation before the momentum dropped off. "What can you tell us about residents who might have been here in the mid-eighties?"

The crowd looked at one another and muttered names to one another. Then they turned back to us and the guy in the hat said, "It's a pity the old restaurant is gone, because you could have found a lot of the old hands just hanging out there, but try Paul Zantree. I think he moved here in the seventies. He's out at the end of the dock here on *Mambo Moon*—it's a big old motorboat—but he might not be home yet. I haven't seen him, at least. Any of you seen Paul today?"

"Not since this morning," said the man at the grill, turning the ribs again and brushing sauce on the meaty side. "He volunteers at the library a couple days a week now, but he should be back soon to finish up that trim work while the sun's still out." He looked up from his cooking and caught my eye. "He's a feisty old coot. Trying to get his boat all fixed up to take the grandkids out fishing this summer. The little one's about eight and loves to hang a line in the water with Grandpa."

The short-haired woman walked up beside him and elbowed him lightly in the side. "You're a feisty old coot yourself."

The cook laughed and gave her a one-armed hug. "Well, I don't know about the 'coot' part—what is a coot, anyway?" he called to the rest of the group.

A slim woman in shorts, who'd been silent up till now, raised her head and said, "I think it's some kind of badger."

The man in the hat objected, "It's a bird. Isn't it?"

The last man in the group fished a couple of beers out

of a cooler and brought one over to the cook. "It's an old guy who won't admit he's old. That's what a coot is. I, personally, am a young coot and I intend to stay that way by drinking this beer. You better join me, Rick."

"Well, I think that I shall," Rick, the cook, replied, letting go of the woman and accepting the beer. Then he turned back to us. "Oh, I'm Rick Hines and this is my wife, Rhonda, by the way," he added, slipping his arm around the short-haired woman's waist again. "This is Phil Rhineman"—he indicated the beer bringer—"and his wife, Laura. Peter Black is the fella with the hat over there. Would you like to sit down and wait for Paul here? We're always glad to have more people. . . ."

It was a generous offer, but I was pretty sure our continued presence would put a damper on the party—and on the gossip, which would be a mixed blessing. More talk might generate more memories, but it might also warn off the mysterious Miss Knight, if she was related to the woman we were seeking. Still, I really had no interest in sitting with strangers when I could be getting more of this business nailed down. Solis seemed to feel the same way.

"Very kind of you to ask, but we need to continue with our work," he replied. "Thank you for your help. If you think of anyone else who might have been here in the mid-eighties, please let us know." He offered his card to Rick Hines and I followed suit. Then Laura Rhineman and Peter Black asked for cards as well and we handed them out quickly with a few more thank-yous before we made our way past the barbecue and farther out the dock toward *Mambo Moon*.

"Friendly," I commented once we were well past.

"Chatty. I hope word will not travel too quickly to Miss Knight. I would like to talk to that young woman without her being warned of our interest. . . ."

I was glad to hear Solis was as wary of the gossip grapevine as I was. "Do you want to split up? I can take Miss Knight if you like—she might prefer to talk to a woman unofficially rather than on the record to a policeman."

"I prefer we stay together as much as possible. This case is too complex for me to wish to divide our attention." A few odd sparks glittered in his aura as he said it, but I wasn't sure what they meant. Solis may have been coming to trust me . . . but that trust only went so far, as long as he was undecided on the point of my paranormality. "And if we do discover a prosecutable crime," he continued, "I will not want to have undermined any witness statements."

Ah, thinking like a cop. I sometimes forget that my priorities aren't like those of most investigators. I nodded. "All right. I can work with that."

"Can you?" he asked, giving me a sharp look.

I frowned at him. "Of course. Do you think I'm not aware of the necessities of police procedure?"

"I think you are not a cop and that you . . . take all advantage of the flexibility that offers you."

I was perversely amused and my smile quirked a little as I raised an eyebrow to him. "I see. I'll bear that in mind."

He nodded and turned his head to watch his step along the dock until we reached Paul Zantree's boat. *Mambo Moon* was one slip from the end of the dock, bobbing comfortably as a larger boat swept by in the channel beyond. Small waves reflected off the breakwater to move the floating dock with gentle swells that sparkled sunlight into our eyes, punctuated by the shadow of salmon. The boat was completely unlike *Seawitch*: half the length and made of white fiberglass that had been recently cleaned and waxed to a shine. With its flying bridge on top and almost a dozen canlike fishing-rod holders attached to the stainless-steel railings at the rear of the two open decks, *Mambo Moon* looked like a boat meant for long, lazy fishing trips in ridiculous comfort.

We walked down the finger dock beside the boat,

looking it over and trying to figure out where the thing that passed for a door was. Most of the living space must have been contained within the hull, and the cabin that rose out of the main deck looked like an iceberg waiting for *Titanic*. The rear of the main deck had a sort of built-in ice chest the size of a double-wide coffin with two big lift-off covers. I guessed it was meant for storing the catch of the day on one side and in the other any bait or drinks that might be needed for a long day of fishing from the built-in chairs on posts that faced the aft rails. An extension from the floor of the flying bridge deck made a small roof over the lower deck that was further shaded by a canvas cover stretched from the edge of the roof's lip to a pair of upright poles that folded out of the railings. Despite our having been told that the owner probably wasn't in, noises were coming from inside the boat.

We stopped beside a set of molded plastic steps that led up to an opening in the rails that stood at about Solis's head height. This was the front door, for lack of a better description. I felt odd about stepping aboard a boat onto which I had not been invited, so I glanced at Solis for ideas. He shrugged and reached out to knock on the hull. The noises stopped. Solis knocked again and called out, "Mr. Zantree?"

"Are we supposed to say 'ahoy' or something?" I asked.

Solis started to reply but was cut off by a pirate coming around the edge of the cabin from the rear. The buccaneer was a dark, grizzled man with a broad chest showing a few gray hairs through the opening of his billowing cotton shirt. His hair was covered in a red bandana that sported a skull and crossbones on the front, but a few bits that stuck out were as gray as the rest and matched the scruffy whiskers on his jaw that weren't quite long enough to be called a beard and were too pronounced to be a five o'clock shadow. Black trousers bloused into knee-length brown boots and a bright red sash tied around his waist completed the bizarre outfit. The man himself was just as odd, his brown skin and mixed-up features defying racial typing.

"Avast! What be the cause o' this bangin' and hallooin'?" the pirate demanded, squinting at us with a snarl.

"We're looking for Paul Zantree," Solis replied, flipping open his ID.

The pirate straightened up and blinked, his entire demeanor going from aggressive to passive in a heartbeat. "Oh," he said in a perfectly normal voice and let out a small nervous laugh. "Well, that's me. I—I was trying on my pirate outfit for Seafair. I hope I didn't startle you—thought you were my neighbors. Am I in trouble for something? And, gosh, I hope so—it's been such a long time since I was in trouble."

"No, sir," Solis answered. "We merely have some questions about the past we hoped you could answer for us. Your neighbors were kind enough to refer us to you."

"Which neighbors?"

"The Hineses and Peter Black."

"Oh. Well, then, you'd better come aboard." He unclipped a chain that barred the way through the railing at the top of the steps and waved us up. We followed him on deck and back to the fishing area at the rear.

He flipped a couple of the chairs around so they faced in rather than out and settled himself on the edge of the built-in ice chest, shoving to the deck a decorative belt and scabbard from which protruded the worn steel hilt of an old navy cutlass. It fell with a clatter and he winced, but didn't stoop to touch it again. "Have a seat," Zantree said. "Can I get you a drink?"

We both shook off the offer politely and sat in the fishing chairs. Zantree pulled off his bandana and scratched his shaggy gray hair before shoving the piece of cloth into his back pocket. He still looked like a pirate from the neck down but his uncovered head definitely made him grandfatherly, in an exotic, eccentric fashion.

"Mr. Zantree," Solis began, "we are seeking information about *Seawitch* and those aboard it before its disappearance. Your neighbors suggested that since you had been a resident here for many years, you might be able to help us."

He smiled and looked relieved. "Oh, the '*Witch* was a fine old boat then. She used to be moored just down at the end of E dock in those days," Zantree offered. The energy around him bloomed into a soft gold corona laced with thin blue threads. "Right across from here, in fact."

"How long have you lived here, sir?"

Zantree grinned, his teeth showing a bit yellow. "Thirty-four years. I was just thirty and my wife and I couldn't afford a house, but we both liked the water so we bought an old wooden boat—bit of a wreck, it was—and moved aboard. We fixed her up real nice—taught ourselves how—and lived on that old boat for about . . ." He glanced aside and nibbled his lip as he thought about it. "Six years. Had two of our three kids on that boat. When June got pregnant again, we bought this boat so we'd have room for the baby. We could have moved back up on the hard—we could afford it by then—but we just didn't want to." He paused in memory, his face clouding. "Or, really, *I* just didn't want to . . ." he added. Then he shook off his mood as swiftly as it had come. "So we had moved up here with the big boats about a year and a half before *Seawitch* went missing. Back then there weren't very many live-aboards but a lot more people just hung out around Charlie's—that was the bar and restaurant in the lobby of the old harbormaster's building. Had a big tower on it like an air-traffic-control tower so the harbormaster could look out and see the whole place. They tore all that down and redid the docks a couple years ago."

"You've always been in this slip since you moved onto this boat?" Solis asked.

"Yep," Zantree replied, nodding.

"And you could see *Seawitch* from here?"

"Oh yes! Such a pretty boat she was then. Old man Starrett had kept her up real well. The boy—Castor—he was a bit of a layabout but he had the smarts to hire himself a good captain and give him both the money and the time to keep the boat up for him."

"So you knew John Reeve."

"I surely did. Haven't seen him around much in a while. He worked for a few other folks after that, but I always thought that losing the '*Witch* took the heart out of him. He made a bunch of money in the stock market and retired. I hear he lost most of it again recently, but I always thought old John was a rubber-sole sort of guy: bounces right back."

Solis adopted a thoughtful expression but said nothing more about Reeve. Instead he asked, "Did you also know his apprentice?"

"Gary? Oh yeah. Kind of an odd fellow, Gary. He always had a sort of mischievous air to him, but in that kind of desperate way, like he knew he was getting too old for that sort of shenanigans—not that he was old, but . . . you know."

Solis nodded. "Mrs. Starrett indicated that the *Seawitch* occasionally used temporary crew. Did you know any of them?"

"Well, no, not really. Reeve had a couple of hands who'd usually show up to handle lines and so on when they'd cast off or come in. Didn't really know the sort of people they hired on for parties and the like—caterer's folks, mostly. Well, except for Shelly—everybody knew Shelly. She was sweet . . ." Zantree added, blushing.

"Shelly Knight?"

"Oh, she was a beauty. So mysterious and charming—like a Gypsy fortune-teller—and she could cook . . . mm-*hm*. Best crab boil you ever tasted."

"Do you know where we could contact her now?"

"Well, no. She's dead. She went off on *Seawitch* when

it put out to sea for the last time. Gary took her along as the cook."

"Another boat owner said he thought he had seen her here within the past year. Is it possible she's still alive?"

"Shelly? Well, no. I don't mind telling you I had a terrible crush on that girl. Terrible. I was brokenhearted when they declared the '*Witch* lost at sea with all hands. I doubt I was the only one, either."

"What of this other young woman in the marina now, staying aboard *Pleiades*? Her name is also Knight, isn't it?"

The colors around Zantree's head darkened for a moment to shades of grim green and brown, then brightened again in a sudden flash. "Here at the marina? The singing girl? Of course it couldn't be her. Shelly'd have to be in her late forties or fifty by now and, besides, the hair's completely different. And this girl sings. Shelly never sang, not even to herself."

Solis and I asked disparate questions at the same time: "Are you certain you remember what Shelly Knight looked like?" he asked. And I asked, "What do you mean her hair was different?"

Zantree looked back and forth between us. Then he stood up. "I'll tell you what. I have an old photo of some of the wharf rats from back in the day—I mean, I have pictures of the folks who used to hang out here all the time. Let me go get the photo. I'll show you they can't be the same...."

He went into the boat, leaving the large sliding doors of the cabin open and moving as if dazed. I cocked my head and tried peering sideways through the Grey at him, but the difference in light and shadow inside made me unsure if I were truly seeing a thin pall of sickly color around him or if the dim electric bulbs just cast an unpleasant glow off the dark wooden wall. I could see him shuffling through a shelf of old-style photo albums until he found what he wanted. He hesitated, almost putting the big book back into the shelf before he tucked it under his arm and returned to us, flopping the volume open on top of the ice chest. He paged through it in a strained, mechanical way and finally pointed with a shaking finger to the second in a series of photos showing a group of people working on what looked like a parade float that had somehow run aground on the beach. The round-cornered photos had taken on that faded yellow-and-blue tinge that was typical of the one-hour-processed snapshots I remembered from my own youth.

"This was taken in 1980," he started a little stiffly, almost defensively, "which was my first year as a Seafair pirate. My wife took a lot of pictures of me and the crew—she and the kids were so tickled. And this is all of us working on the pirate landing craft. That's me," he said, his voice and demeanor suddenly animated and his aura aglow in bright gold pleasure as he pointed at his younger self in plaid Bermuda shorts, white sport shirt, and a floppy straw hat much like Peter Black's. He was in the middle of a pack of people dressed in similar clothes, who were pretending to push back the tide of pirates surging out of the painted-plywood sailing ship. The were all cheating over their shoulders and grinning, while the people dressed as pirates bared their teeth in mock fury and held aloft their plastic—and some not plastic—cutlasses and pistols.

Off to the side a laden picnic table poked into the frame, a handful of women and kids gathered around a huge boiling pot set on a portable burner about eighteen inches across. Zantree moved his finger to the woman who was stirring the pot and neither smiling nor looking up at the photographer. "That's Shelly Knight—and about thirty Dungeness crabs."

The focus was a little blurry on the group near the pot and Shelly's face wasn't as distinct as we might have liked, but the general idea was there: a slim young woman in a pink bikini top and a colorful sarong wrapped around her hips as a skirt, her long blond hair drawn back into a braid that flopped over her shoulder and down to her waist. Her hair was a pale apple green, but I thought that could have been caused by the shifting of the old photo's color.

I looked up at Zantree and asked, "This other woman on the dock recently—how did she look different from Shelly?"

Zantree nodded a little mechanically. "Well . . . her hair's red."

"But otherwise . . . ?"

He struggled with the words. "Not much . . ."

"Not much different? Or not much the same?"

He quivered and shook his head, his mouth drawing tight in discomfort. I took a deep breath and shook my head, too. "Never mind. Don't let it bother you."

Zantree's stiff shoulders softened and he looked at the photo again as if for the first time. Then he smiled at it. "She was so pretty. So charming. She'd tell our fortunes with cards and weave the most wonderful ghost stories over the bonfires on the beach at night. . . . Everybody loved Shelly."

"And yet no one seems to know anything about her," Solis muttered.

I gave him a sharp glare. He blinked back at me.

I pointed at the photo again. "Did Shelly really have green hair? It looks green in the photo, but in real life . . . ?"

"It was green, all right. A touch more yellow and paler than that photo shows, but definitely green. In the right light, it looked just a pale blond color, but up close in the sun, or under a fluorescent bulb like we had in the old marina building, it was actually green."

"How do you remember that?"

"Who forgets a girl with green hair?"

Solis rejoined the conversation. "What about this red-headed woman from *Pleiades*? Have you spoken with her?" he asked.

Zantree shrugged. "Sure I have. Why?"

"What did you say? What were the circumstances?"

"Well . . . it was on the fuel dock . . . I was pumping out the holding tank. Smelly business. She was . . . she was just sitting on the dock. She was sort of singing to herself and dangling her feet in the water."

"At the fuel dock? Kind of an odd place to do that, isn't it?" I threw in.

Blue-green sparks circled around Zantree's head in my Grey-adapted sight. "Oh. Well . . . I guess it is. Didn't think of it at the time."

"What's her name?"

"Name? Well, I didn't ask."

Solis scowled. "You didn't ask this woman her name when you introduced yourself? This woman who did not look different from your old crush?"

"Well . . ." Zantree started, and then he went quiet and looked very confused. Peering at him through the Grey, I could see a wisp of the same dirty green color I'd seen suffocating John Reeve stroking around Zantree's head and then sliding away. "I guess I just don't remember anymore," he said in a flat voice. Then he shook himself and added, "Hah! Guess I really am getting old."

Solis rolled his eyes as if giving up the fight. "Do you have any other photos of Shelly?" he asked.

Zantree blinked, hesitated, and then pointed to another picture lower on the next page. "Just this one. It's not very good."

"Not very good" was an understatement. The color was less faded on this photo, but the photographer hadn't been trying to shoot Shelly, so her part of the picture was even more out of focus than the last—and she had been caught in the act of turning so her braid was twisting and flinging around like a whip, her face obscured and her upper body looking misshapen. But I could tell her hair was a silvery green, not the apple green it had looked in the earlier photo. It wouldn't have been too outlandish a color now—in fact it would have been too subtle for a lot of people to bother taking note of—but in 1985, when the only people wearing Kool-Aid–colored hair were rock stars, it must have been much stranger. The idea popped into my head that Linda Starrett must never have met Shelly because, as people kept telling us, you didn't forget a girl with hair like that.

"May we take these?" Solis asked Zantree.

"Let me copy them for you," Zantree offered, picking up the album and walking it back inside. "I have a scanner on my computer in here—my son helped me with it a couple of Christmases ago. C'mon in and I'll fix you right up."

We trailed after Zantree into the dimly lit main cabin and then down a short set of steps to a galley. A laptop computer and multiuse printer sat on a pull-down shelf hanging over the hull side of the built-in dinette. Zantree hauled the machines down to tabletop level and carefully removed the photos from the album to press them onto the glass plate of the printer.

As it scanned and spat out the photos, Zantree said, "Terribly clever thing my son made, yeah? He's an engineer. Works for Boeing now. The other two kids moved out of state during the bank failures a few years ago, so Hale and his wife and kids are the only family I have left up here now. I really miss my family, but . . . I have the boat and all my friends here, which is more than a lot of people have."

I was hesitant but went ahead and asked, "What became of your wife?"

Zantree's face fell. "Ah. She left me. Back when the kids were all off to college, June up and said she was tired of living on a boat and it was time for us to move into a house like 'real people.' I disagreed. I love the boat life. I don't want to move back up on the hard like a bug crawling on a tabletop. I never even knew she was unhappy. I guess she told me, but I must not have listened. . . ." He looked more shaken and sad than I would have expected, even for such a revelation.

"Where is she now?" I asked in a soft voice.

"She died last year. Complications after surgery. She had cancer, but she didn't tell me about it and she asked the kids not to, either, so I never knew till it was over. That's why I like to spend as much time with the kids and grandkids now as possible; I don't want to miss anything else."

We took the copied photos and left behind a much sadder pirate than we had met.

NINE

Pleiades was impressive. It shone like its namesake; every inch of paint and trim gleamed. Even in the Grey the big blue sailboat had a sheen to it that exuded a low hum of self-satisfaction. We stood on the finger dock and admired it for a few moments before Solis tried knocking on the hull as he had with *Mambo Moon*. This time there was no answer except the tiniest of shivers in the Grey. The moment of waiting silence passed and he glanced at me.

I shrugged. "If she's in there, she's not going to come out."

"And we may not board without permission. Do you believe Miss Knight is inside?"

"I don't think so. But I think she's probably got some kind of alarm system, so even with permission from the owners, we still wouldn't catch up to her."

"If we entered under a warrant, the alarm would be directed to the police. We would already know the situation and ignore the call."

I shook my head. "That's not the sort of alarm system I meant."

He eyed me askance. "You imagine something . . . extra?"

"I'm not imagining anything. I can see it, remember? When you knocked, it sent out waves and I don't mean in the water. There's something not normal about that boat."

Solis stood still and studied me a moment in silence. Then he turned away, saying, "What do you suggest now?"

"I suggest you leave," answered a voice from the main dock, a strange harmonic vibrating under the tone.

We both looked up. A pretty young woman stood at the beginning of the finger dock with her arms crossed over her chest and glared at us belligerently. She was a dead ringer for Shelly Knight except that her hair was red. I've known blondes who dye their hair red to combat brassiness or a tendency to go green from chemicals in water, but this didn't look like a bottle job: It looked like her hair was alive in some strange way I couldn't put a finger on that turned it the vibrant red of oxygenated blood. I didn't dare sink deeper into the Grey right in front of her and everyone who might be looking this way, but even restricting myself to a mere glance, I saw her energy corona as a huge, writhing, barbed tangle of green, blue, and red that stretched out to each side and down toward the dock and the water like a thirsty vine run amok, rustling with the sound of talons on glass.

She narrowed her eyes as Solis produced his badge and ID card and walked toward her. I kept a step behind, letting him partially hide me from her view; I didn't like the cold, squirming sensation that her scrutiny brought and I'm not always sure how much a paranormal creature can tell about me from a glance, so I preferred she get as short a glance as possible. The fish didn't seem to like her, either, raising a drumroll of splashes just out of sight. The corner of her mouth twitched in irritation at the sound but she didn't turn her gaze from us.

"I beg your pardon for the intrusion," Solis began, drawing closer. "We're seeking Shelly Knight or any relatives or friends here who may have known her twenty-five to thirty years ago."

"I don't know her."

"Is not your name Knight?"

He didn't say anything else, just looked at her with

that bland, inquiring glance that tricked people into talking just to fill the silence.

"*Jacque* Knight. Not Shelly."

"Related?"

"She's not my mother or whatever it is you imagine." Her voice swooped like poetry.

"I do not imagine. I only ask, since you bear a striking resemblance."

Knight tossed her head and the coiling strands of her aura flexed and tightened like snakes constricting on prey, throwing off a cloud of gray-green mist. "How lucky for her. Now shove off."

Solis shrugged and cocked his head slightly. I couldn't see his expression, but I thought he'd probably raised his eyebrows in an expression that needed only a muttered "meh" to imply her anger was a meaningless inconvenience. He'd pulled it on me often enough. "I apologize for taking your time." He stepped around her and I followed him, cutting only the swiftest peek at her as we passed. I caught a disconcerting glimpse of something only half-human with hair that reached and coiled the same way as her aura. . . . I shivered, my skin instantly clammy.

A chilly whisper song and an urge to move on and forget I'd ever met Jacque Knight blew over the raised hairs on my arms and neck but I refused to give in to it. And I could tell by his stern posture that Solis wouldn't, either—which made me frown in thought, pushing the unnatural suggestion out of my mind.

"You feeling . . . disinclined to loiter?" I asked under my breath.

"Yes, but I won't run."

We walked along the dock toward the gate in silence and spoke only once we'd stepped out onto the public promenade. We both shivered a little and exchanged uncomfortable glances as the pushy sensation faded.

"You felt that," I said. "That insistent 'Get the hell out of here' sensation."

"Only the desire to put distance between myself and that young woman—who's too young to be Shelly Knight," Solis observed, continuing to stroll along the pavement at an easy stride no longer edged in restraint. So he'd felt it but he didn't want to discuss it, at least not yet.

I took the hint. "But definitely related, in spite of what she said," I added, staying on the case. Two women with such similar names couldn't look so much alike and have no family in common—no matter how distant. But there was the small matter of her aura, which boiled with energy. I'd met plenty of magic users and strange creatures whose power let them live long beyond a single human lifetime—hell, I'd been told I probably would, too, and I would bet my abilities weren't even a flickering match light compared to Jacque Knight's, whatever she was. And that, of course, made me wonder more about Shelly. . . .

Solis paused on the walkway and turned to lean against the railing, his back to the docks. "I agree. I shall have to look into her records—and Shelly's—once I'm back in the office. We'll have to wait for the log pages, so there is no point in pursuing that at this moment. I could put some time in on other cases. . . ."

"If you like. I'm actually slow right now, so this is the only big thing on my agenda; I'd still like to close it as soon as I can, though. So right now I want to take one more look at *Seawitch*. You don't have to come along if you prefer to avoid my weirdness. Or, you know, you want to get back to those other cases."

He turned his head and regarded me with that odd silent glance of his. Then he shrugged. "I *prefer* not to leave you alone in my crime scene. My other cases can wait a little longer."

I caught myself starting to laugh at the absurdity of it but I didn't let it slip out. "All right. Time for act two of the Harper Blaine Creep Show. I should have brought my tap shoes," I muttered to myself.

Solis accompanied me to *Seawitch* without any further comment. He was back to inscrutable and I wasn't sure how I felt about that. On the one hand, it was normal for him; on the other, it was *so* normal, I wasn't sure whether it was a sign of acceptance or rejection.

As we neared the boat I saw a man standing on the bow of the boat in the slip across from it. He had his hands on his hips as he faced *Seawitch*. With the sun lowering toward the water ahead of us, it was difficult to see anything but his shape: average height with ropy-looking limbs and a hard hemisphere of belly that defied gravity. The shape of his head in shadow was curiously elongated at the bottom and, as we got closer I saw he had a long ponytail tied low at his neck. It reminded me of Quinton's now-cropped queue, which hadn't yet regrown long enough to gather into a proper tail, so it just stuck out awkwardly, revealing cowlicks neither of us had known he had. A touch of chill seemed to reach from *Seawitch* and I momentarily wished I was at home with Quinton, teasing him about those cowlicks, instead of here, walking toward a haunted ship.

The man on the near boat turned to watch us as we walked toward *Seawitch*'s boarding steps. I stopped and looked up at him and he returned my stare with a slightly out-of-focus gaze from eyes red rimmed and gummy due to lack of sleep. I remembered what the yard manager had said and called out, "Are you Stu Francis?"

He gave an affirmative grunt and nodded. "Who're you?" His voice sounded rough, as if he'd been smoking unfiltered cigarettes since grade school.

"My name's Harper Blaine. This is Detective Sergeant Solis. We're investigating *Seawitch*."

Another affirmative grunt and nod from Francis. "Wouldn't want to be you guys. Damn thing's spooked."

"Spooked?"

"Got ghosts like a freighter's got rats." Several heavy splashes spattered water onto the end of the dock. "Damn fish! Crazy-ass salmon!" Francis shouted at the water. "Get the hell out of here!" Then he fixed his watery stare on me. "It's this damned boat, I'll betcha. Got the fish acting crazy. Saw two otters and a harbor seal in here, too."

"Is that unusual?" I asked.

"You betcha. Salmon follow the water scent up the river; they don't pause to rest until they clear the locks. They never come in here on the way up, only on the way down. But this year they're in here like a swarm of cockroaches. Kept me up all night, banging on the hull, chattering."

I must have looked skeptical because he added, "And don't tell me fish don't talk. They make all kinds of noise up against the hull. Sounds just like a bunch of teenagers whispering in class. 'Blah, blah, blah, yak, yak, yak.' Man can't get any sleep! Talking about a shipwreck in Spain. What are salmon doing in Spain, anyway?"

Spain? I thought, something tickling at my brain. I reconsidered the origin of his rheumy eyes—they might have resulted from consuming a considerable amount of alcohol regularly as well as from a handful of sleepless nights.

"Mr. Francis," Solis interrupted. "Why do you believe the *Seawitch* is haunted?"

"Screams. Couple of nights ago she started screaming."

"You heard screams from inside the boat?" Solis clarified.

Francis glared at him and shook his head adamantly. "No, sir. I said *she* screamed and I meant it. The noise inside came later. Boats make noises all the time—when the wind comes down off the point in winter and plays on the masts and rigging, it can sound like a chorus of wolves and lost souls. But this wasn't the north wind. There wasn't any wind! I never heard nothing like this before." He jabbed a finger at *Seawitch*. "That thing screamed."

Francis made a noise in his throat that could only be

called a harrumph and swung on his heel to stomp away
into his own boat. Somehow he managed to slam the
hatch as he did.

Solis and I exchanged puzzled frowns, then turned
around to face *Seawitch*.

The boat looked less inviting than ever, especially
when contrasted with the boats we had just come from;
it was neither shiny nor homey and I could not imagine
anyone wanting to hang out with friends on the dock
near it, either. In just a single day the boat had gone from
sad and spooky to outright nasty, the coils of Grey that
hung on it now churning and billowing like a nest of angry snakes. For a moment I thought of Jacque Knight's
grasping aura and shivered.

Solis watched me. "You have changed your mind?"

"No," I answered. "But I think this is not going to be
as much fun as the last time."

"You have an odd idea of fun, Ms. Blaine."

I don't know why that torqued me, but it did. Maybe
it was the malevolent energy bleeding off *Seawitch*,
Francis's weirdness affecting my thoughts, or just my
own discomfort left over from the day before and Solis's
reserved silence on matters freaky, but I turned and
glared at him. "I think you can drop the 'Ms.' now, since
we're stuck together on this. I don't expect you to like or
respect me—or even believe me—enough to be friends,
but I'd appreciate it if you didn't mock me."

Solis raised his eyebrows and looked genuinely surprised. "I find you strange but I do not mock you. What
would you have me call you?"

I bit my tongue; I was being unreasonable. I was good
at my job and I'd helped him out plenty of times—
sometimes more than he knew—but I was worried that
my revelations about just how "strange" I was were
straining the relationship when I wanted it to be smoother,
not harder. So if I overreacted now, any breakage would
be my own fault. I took a long, slow breath and replied

more evenly, "I'm sorry. Just Blaine, or even Harper, will do. What do you call the cops you work with?"

"I call them by their last names—it's written on their badges."

I laughed. It just came over as amusing that he implied he couldn't remember people's names without a label on them. Solis flushed a little and looked aside. He cleared his throat and waited for me to wind down. When I stopped chuckling he glanced at me and then at the boat again.

"Shall we proceed, M—" he caught himself and re-started. "If you're ready, shall we proceed, Blaine?"

I grinned at him. "Yes, we can, Mr. Solis."

"I like 'Sergeant Solis,'" he replied with the hint of a smile. "It makes me feel taller. Which, beside you, is a feat. And my wife likes it."

"I didn't know you were married," I said. Apparently we had broken some serious ice.

Solis nodded. *"Sí."*

I raised my eyebrows, but he didn't volunteer any more. He only gestured toward the boat and waited for me to precede him.

We started up the stairs to *Seawitch*'s aft deck. On the third step I felt cold and the pressure in my lungs increased as if we were diving into deep waters. I made the last steps and paused, catching my breath with an effort. Solis watched me and started to raise his hand as if to take my arm, but I waved him off and headed for the interior. He followed wordlessly, a frown of curiosity on his face.

Just inside the salon I turned back to him. "This is where things get . . . weird," I said. "You ready?"

He gave it a moment's serious consideration—he wasn't taking this lightly and I felt a wash of relief, pretty sure that before replying he was recalling what I'd shown and told him yesterday. I didn't push him to find in my favor; he had to do it himself. He seemed to brace himself, then gave a tiny nod. "Yes."

"If . . . you can't see me, call out. I don't want to get separated." Then I let myself slide a little closer to the Grey without getting too thin in the normal world. I would be glad of Solis's presence if things got too rough but he'd be no help if he couldn't see me. And I did expect it to get rough: The slice of the energetic world within *Seawitch* was aboil with colored mists, not just the thin threads I'd noticed the day before. A volume of foggy shapes seemed to battle in knots and whorls of green and red and blue that tangled and roiled against one another. It was like walking through the fringe of a war zone where the fighting had broken down to small but desperate skirmishes.

I stepped forward with care, resisting the urge to sink to a more elemental level and dodge some of the mist world's turmoil. Streamers of animate fog buffeted me like ropes cut loose in a wind. The slender, bright thread of purple energy that had led down the stairs the first time I'd been aboard was missing this time. Shredded or removed, I wasn't sure, but I had the strong impression that the energetic conflict up here was only a diversion from whatever was waiting in the engine room. I glanced around to spot Solis, seeing him as a ghostly version of himself with his carefully contained energy much brighter and more colorful than I normally saw it: a vibrant yellow with swirling sparks of blue and gold. Interesting . . .

I eased out a little and motioned to Solis to follow me down the stairs to the lower deck. Then I slid a bit back into the Grey and pursued the sense of something waiting. Through the crew quarters and down the passageway to the engine-room doors, the writhing smoke let me know I was taking the right path. I considered slipping through the doors in the Grey, but I didn't want to lose Solis, so I stepped back to the normal plane one more time and waited for him to catch up to me. He was a lot closer than I'd realized and we both started a bit, coming nearly nose to nose. He hadn't seemed that near, but the Grey does strange things to time and distance.

"Sorry," I muttered.

Solis gave a tight smile. "*De nada*. So, it's the engine room?"

"Something is. What, I'm not yet sure, but there's a lot of paranormal disturbance here."

He nodded.

I frowned. "Do you feel or see anything, or is that just the conversational acknowledgment nod?"

He cocked his head slightly. "I have . . . an unsettled feeling. Like an intuition."

That intrigued me and I hmphed a bit in agreement. I knew the feeling, that something trivial is actually important or that a subject is about to do something revealing. I also knew most successful cops are hunch players and instinct followers and I wondered if that wasn't some unacknowledged touch of the Grey.

"See anything? Anything at all?"

"No . . ."

"Are you having an urge to look over your shoulder for something that you don't *quite* see in the corner of your eye?" I knew that urge, that sensation of flickering motion that makes you turn to find . . . nothing. Of course, something *is* there in the ghost world but most people have no clue and they truly wouldn't want one.

Solis squinted, his eyes shifting back and forth. Then he tightened his mouth and forced his eyes back to me. I guess that was as good an answer as his nod. I remembered I'd started out much the same way, learning to look around the filters we raise between ourselves and what we don't want to see. Most adults can't make themselves drop those filters—the habit is too strong and self-preserving—but a few find a way to peep in, however limited the view. And then there are those rare cases, like me, who get the unlimited pass and wish they never had.

Such an encouraging thought to hold in mind as I opened the engine-room door . . .

Even barely touching the Grey, the room was black with a darkness no electric light could dispel—gleaming, energetic darkness that moved and writhed and muttered with voices at the threshold of hearing. It wasn't like the voice of the Grey that I'd once, in near madness, listened to; this was the babble of something contained in it, not the voice of the Grey itself. I could hear Solis catch his breath behind me as I stepped through the opening and was plunged deep into the source of the icy cold that had risen through the boat. My lungs froze and I stretched upward for a surface that was not there, striving for light and air and warmth as the blackness clutched me within its ever-collapsing folds. I stumbled forward and down . . . through a sheet of mist that shattered and hung in the space around me, so frigid that the air itself seemed filled with crystalline ice. I felt my legs buckle and the hard floor of the engine room struck hard against my knees. I was in the normal world yet I wasn't, drowning in the darkness that struck and shook me like storm waves. I heard screams, prayers, and the fury-roar of a hurricane as it battered us, overturning the lifeboats and drowning the women and children before our eyes. . . . and the crew lashed in the rigging, crying out, mouths filling with salt water—

I wrenched myself away from the invading sense of the storm-battered dying. These were not my own thoughts but those of others—hundreds of others.

Stop. I could not even gasp the word, only let it shout in my mind across the blackness as I begged and hoped. . . .

The storm around me eased and I gulped in sea-wet air. Coughing, I choked out, "I want to help." A flood of thoughts burst against me from all directions and seemed to cut through my flesh in cold iron needles of fury, panic, horror, and a thin, keening hope as dim and ephemeral as a will-o'-the-wisp. I stretched toward that spindly thread even as my body seemed to be buffeted by blows from unseen objects careening through the air on the eldritch hurricane's rage. That thread of possibility flickered near me and I clutched it, reeling it in and pressing the growing, glowing skein to my chest.

The tiny warmth of it seemed to ease my breathing and loosen the gasping terror of drowning that clawed at my brain and clutched my lungs. "I want to help you," I repeated, a little stronger now. "Show me . . ."

The storm ebbed down slowly, the troubled blackness diluting to a more ordinary darkness. The ghost-filtered illumination showed me a room lit by insufficient light through an open doorway partially blocked by a human shape.

I looked around. Still the engine compartment and closer to normalcy, but somehow . . . it was filled with hundreds of ghosts. They pressed close and yet fell back into the hull of the ship, continuing on into the Grey to an impossible distance and density somehow contained within the *Seawitch*'s engine room. They were black tangles of energy, barely human shaped with flickering storm light for eyes. I stared around at them all, infected with a sliver of their own panic.

Solis stepped through the doorway and strode to me, reaching down as if he were going to raise me to my feet. Then he glanced around, his eyes as weirdly illuminated as those of the ghosts, and stopped moving, his hands clutching my shoulders. He shivered and pulled me up, his eyes still moving, still taking in . . . whatever he was seeing.

A voice rose from the collective in the hissing of sea spume against rocks. "We did our part. Now uphold the bargain. Save us."

Solis glanced at me. "Do you hear . . . ?"

I nodded. Then I put one finger to my lips, afraid his presence might disrupt the conversation I needed to have.

"It wasn't my bargain," I started. "I don't know what happened or what to do. Tell me. Show me."

The darkness of spirits shuffled and opened a narrow

path between them. Solis and I both turned our heads to see where it led, but the only view was a hard green-gold gleam lying low in a sea of grime.

"You see — ?" I started in a whisper.

"There is a light that cannot exist, gleaming where I cannot go." His voice was low and unsteady.

"Yes, you can. Hold on to my arm and we can't be separated. This is like walking a tightrope: Don't look down and don't look back until your feet are back on solid ground."

I sucked in a preparatory breath, squared my shoulders, and felt his grip on my elbow. I started toward the glow. Solis came along a step behind me. I could feel the warm impression of his presence at my back, even though I didn't dare turn to see him. I did not want them — whoever *they* were — to take any notice of Solis, nor did I want to lose sight of whatever it was they were showing me, leading me toward.

The ghosts remained nebulous and thready as we passed between them. I heard Solis breathing a little harder and faster than usual and I wished I knew what he was seeing, but it seemed a bad time to ask.

It felt like an hour but it must have been only a minute or two until we reached the gleam, walking slowly out of the Grey and back into the normal — or nearly normal — world. It lay near our feet, a reflection of light obscured by mucky water in the crook of the floor where it met the hull and gapped a bit here and there between the boat's ribs. The reflection was duller here and the ghosts had become less present, though they were far from gone. I stooped and reached out for whatever the green-gold flash was coming from, shivering as my hands pushed into gelid water thickened with algae and gunk.

There was something cold and metallic below the water's surface — just the merest inch or less of a curved edge sticking out. I pushed my long fingers between the hull and the thing to get a grip on it. It was hollow, and once I had hooked my fingers under the edge I pulled upward with care. The thing was chilly and heavy and felt too large to come back up through the narrow gap between the boat's ribs.

Something clanked against the floorboards. Solid, *normal* floorboards. I risked a glance back over my shoulder at Solis, hoping he was really there, or really *here* depending on how I thought of it. He was and he stared down at me with a frown that was too tight around the mouth and too white around the eyes, but he was solid and willing.

"There is something?"

"Yes, something real, but it's too big to pull through the hole. We need to lift this section of floor if we can."

Solis reached into his jacket and brought forth a penlight. He sighed relief as the unexpectedly bright light came on at his flick of the switch, nearly blinding me. The flashlight cast a bright, shivering circle on the floor and hull just around the gap where my hand vanished into the hole. The illumination bounced off the metal edge I held on to and rekindled the strange spark of color we'd seen earlier. Solis played the light shakily across the floor until he spotted a seam nearby and, turning slowly, followed it to more seams.

"You will have to move to your right," he said, his voice deadened by the insulation on the walls but no longer quivering. "Can you hold on to the object if you move?" Our return to the normal world must have reassured him everything was all right. I was a little less sure, but I've had more experience with ghosts.

I kept my own counsel on that score and replied, "I think so. It feels loose in here. . . ." I shifted the heavy thing into my left hand and shuffled awkwardly to my right like an injured crab with one claw dragging. It pulled on my fingers and made my knuckles feel swollen and overworked as it clunked along beneath the floor, jamming on ribs and thudding to a halt. I had to stoop like an ape and pass it from one hand to the other around each rib, then back into my left to drag it on until I'd moved my weight clear of the floor seam Solis was illuminating. My back, shoulders, arms, and hands ached from the strain and the chill, but I held on.

Solis bent and stuck his fingers into a depression in the floor to get a grip and lift the segment of floorboards. The thick planks came up with the screech of swollen wooden structures reluctantly scraping open. The smell of cold swamp water and brine wafted on the updraft.

Solis leaned the hatch against something bulky and denser than the ghosts. I guessed it was one of the engines, but I wasn't sure and I wouldn't risk my grip on the thing to look around. I wiggled the metal object loose from where it had lodged next to a rib and pulled it upward. It felt huge and ridiculously heavy for something hollow. . . .

Solis shone his light on it and it gave back another sickly green-gold shimmer.

"A bell . . ." I whispered as it came up into the light.

"Our soul . . ." the ghosts sighed, melting away and taking the remnant Grey with them. I didn't think they were gone for good, just exhausted and satisfied that we had what they wanted us to have.

I turned the bell in my hands, letting the filth-crusted bronze catch the beam from Solis's pocket flashlight as I wiped the worst of the gunk away. The bell was huge and weighed more than ten pounds, easily. I wasn't sure, but it seemed too large for the bracket we'd seen the day before up near the boat's bridge. The light caught on the cast edges of a deep engraving along the bell's mouth. I read it aloud as Solis picked out the words with the penlight's illumination: "S.S. Valencia."

TEN

The penetrating chill of *Seawitch*'s engine room was too uncomfortable to encourage any further investigation once we had the bell in hand, so Solis and I agreed to head topside and catch the light and warmth before discussing what had just happened. The sun was still up, even though it was definitely heading for the western horizon, but at this latitude and so close to the solstice the light would linger until nearly eleven at night. We carried the slippery bell down to the dock and rinsed the worst of the slime off it. Solis kept a wary eye on me throughout the move and cleanup.

"I did warn you things were going to get weird," I said, not looking up from the bell.

"You did. I had not expected quite what happened."

"What did happen?" I asked, glancing at him as I brushed off the worst of the muck from the bell.

He gave me a puzzled frown in return. "You were there...."

"Yeah, but I'm pretty sure that what I experience isn't the same as what you do. So what was it like?"

Solis sat on his heels and thought about it. "Cold. Like a nightmare I used to have in my youth: darkness like sharp black lines that crowd in from the edges of vision, thicker as they draw together until I can only see straight ahead. Yet things continue to be there in the corners of my vision, stabbing at my eyes. I could see you—shining silver but dim, as if light barely touched you. Your arm was cold and hard to hold on to—insubstantial. There was sound, whispering that sometimes rose to sharp words and then quieted again, like people arguing when they don't want to be heard but can't stop themselves. And then the reflection of light off this bell was like . . . a distant star, so small and yellow. It shone where it could not have. It was under the floor but I saw the light. And then . . . just cold. But I felt as if someone watched us from concealment."

"Huh," I grunted, taking it in. It wasn't so far away from parts of what I'd experienced, just less intense. It was his admission of nightmares that was most interesting, since the Grey tends to reflect and produce what the people in an area impress on it. This was the first time I'd had any proof that the experience of the Grey was individually tailored. It also made me wonder what other odd things had happened in Solis's life to let him get that close—because even pulled into it by me, a pragmatic hard case like him shouldn't have experienced that depth.

Solis shook off the mood he'd created and turned his gaze back to the bell. "*Valencia*. Not *Seawitch* . . ."

"It's obviously been there for quite a while."

"Perhaps it was taken from another boat for service on board *Seawitch*."

"Are you giving credence to the idea of a curse brought on by mounting parts from a doomed ship?"

"No . . ."

His voice wavered a little and I guessed he didn't actually believe it was true but he was unsettled enough at the moment to let the idea slink into the back of his mind. I stuck a pin in that trial balloon. "It's too big for the bracket we saw on board *Seawitch*. This bell never hung on that boat. Someone hid it in the engine room. I admit, I'd like to know why, and how it got there in the first place."

"Do you wish to continue tomorrow? It's after five now. . . ."

I hesitated. I wanted more answers and I wasn't ready to stop for the night just yet, but I didn't want to presume he had nothing better to do—he was married, after all, and I assumed from the way he'd mentioned his wife that his was not one of those barely functioning misery marriages that are too common among cops.

He echoed my own thoughts. "I would like some answers rather than endless questions. If you're willing to bring the bell to my house, perhaps we can find some." He raised his eyebrows, issuing a silent invitation.

"All right. I think there's still a lot to talk about, too."

He nodded and got to his feet, letting me take possession of the bell. "Agreed."

Technically the bell was part of the boat's inventory and therefore mine to oversee, so I appreciated the courtesy, but the damned thing was still pretty heavy and awkward to carry. Still, we could look at the bell in better light and more comfort at Solis's house than *Seawitch* offered, and the other reports and photos would be available through his computer. So I wrestled the bell into the back of my Rover and followed Solis to his place.

Solis's house sat on a moderate lot near the middle of the block on a street that wasn't quite in trendy, yuppified Madrona and hadn't quite bootstrapped itself out of gritty, poor, crime-ridden Central District. With its old foursquare houses straight out of a Sears catalog from the first quarter of the twentieth century, the neighborhood was mostly in the process of gentrifying. A couple of the neighbors hadn't gotten that memo and their homes were still paint-peeling, weed-yarded hovels from which the sounds of TV and gangsta rap blared forth while packs of angry-looking young black or Hispanic men sat on the stoops and wandered in and out of the open doors, drinking beer, smoking, and conversing loudly. One of them hoisted a sarcastic salute at Solis as we drove past.

As he parked and got out of his car, Solis gave the boy

and his seedy residence a narrow glare but he didn't say or do anything more. Carrying the bell in a small canvas duffel I'd had in the back of my truck, I followed him up a short flight of concrete steps to his own neat, fenced yard and onto the raised wooden porch of the big, square two-story house. We opened the door on an old-fashioned foyer and an uproar.

A boy about ten years old raced from one doorway to another, hollering like a pig outracing a butcher. Solis reached out and caught the boy by the shoulder, turning him around with a firm curl of his arm. An irritated frizzle of orange sparks erupted around him in the Grey. The boy came to an abrupt halt, his eyes flashing wide and his own glimmering golden aura falling to a narrow band around his form as he stared at Solis and caught his breath with hastily compressed lips, smothering his shouts instantly.

Solis looked down and lifted one eyebrow, then shook his head, flinging a few sparks into the ghostlight while wearing an expression of severe disappointment. The little boy seemed to shrink, his shoulders slumping as he glanced at the floor. Solis relented, scooping the boy into a hug, followed by a whisper in his ear and a swift kiss on the cheek. Then he put the boy down again and asked him a question in Spanish. The boy pointed back toward the doorway he'd come from, his energy rising to a more normal range as he whispered something too low to make out and patted at what looked like a scorch mark on his sleeve. Solis nodded as if satisfied, examined and then kissed the reddened skin exposed by the burned sleeve, and shooed the boy away. The kid scampered off with a relieved smile up the staircase to our right.

A more distant ruckus continued farther back in the building. Solis glowered a second, his energy corona sparking orange and red. Then he reined in his temper with a visible effort and waved me on. We went under an arch and down a narrow passageway toward the noise, passing a large closet and a small bathroom tucked in under the staircase. Then we walked through a dining room with built-in cabinets that were partially refinished, making a low half wall between the dining room and a large, disarrayed living room on the left. We continued ahead through a scarred swinging door that was painted yellow on one side and white on the other.

We emerged in the yellow kitchen, where a petite woman in her thirties—his wife, I assumed—was trying to tear herself away from a flaming pan to go to the rescue of three very young children being herded into the rear utility room by a tiny, elderly woman in a white house dress and an aura so chaotic it looked like a furiously animated scribble of olive and red drawn by a deranged child. The children seemed to be objecting to the older woman's harrying while Mrs. Solis—her own energy a harried orange shade flashing with tiny lightning bolts—snatched up a lid and slammed it over her pan, smothering the flames. Then she turned to intervene in the child herding, to which she seemed to object, judging by the way she flung her hands in the air and tried to separate the kids from their shepherd, muttering in Spanish as she did.

Solis cleared his throat and started, "¿Ximena? ¿Qué está—?"

Ximena Solis whipped around with a gasp, bringing her hands to her mouth, and I assumed some of the words she'd used weren't appropriate around children or police detectives. A cloud of dismay seemed to envelop her. "Rey!" she squeaked, then launched a stream of flustered Spanish accompanied by a flurry of hand waving and gesticulating at the older woman. She broke off suddenly to bound over and wrench one of the children from the older woman's grasp and push him toward Solis before she turned back to try to rescue another, scolding and pleading by turns, if I guessed the tone correctly.

The older woman picked up the smaller of the two remaining children—a little girl in a slightly grubby striped dress—and plopped her, shoes and all, into the wash sink. A splash of soapy water erupted along with a shriek and a spike of acid-yellow outrage from the girl.

Ximena, tiny red lightning bolts leaping from her, shoved the last free-range kid toward her husband and turned back around, planting her hands on her hips for a moment before throwing them into the air again in exasperation and letting out her own cry of indignation. "*¡Mamá! ¡No hagas eso!*" She tried to reach past the older woman, who, though short, angular, and possibly addled, was apparently no weakling, and shouldered the younger woman away with insouciant ease. The other looked ready to explode.

Solis eased between them and pushed the two women apart. He kept his gaze on the older one, but he was clearly speaking to his wife when he said in carefully clipped syllables, "*Ximena. Vuelve a la cocina.*"

The moment she had flounced away to remove the other children from the kitchen, Solis reached past the old woman and her belligerent shoulders to pluck the now-wailing little girl out of the sink. For a moment, the sparking energy in both the adults' auras seemed to hiss and coruscate as if on the teetering edge of flaring into furious white heat that would consume everything near it in a flash fire of destruction.

Solis set the girl on the floor and snatched a bath towel off a stack on the clothes dryer nearby to wrap her in, and the moment's potential faltered, sending a shiver into the Grey.

The woman let out a screech of her own and turned around to berate Solis, bony little claw fists propped on her hips and her beaky face thrust forward like a furious crow, her energy blowing outward into a harsh, violent tangle of red spikes. Her posture was so much the full-bore version of Ximena's aborted stance that I knew the woman had to be her mother. She cawed at her son-in-law in a glass-shattering voice, dropping Spanish words I knew nice old ladies didn't use in polite Colombian company.

Solis whipped a fisted hand up between them, pointing his index finger at her in a warning gesture as his aura flushed a deep, vibrating red. Unlike his mother-in-law's, his energy seemed to pull inward, intensifying and burning in a tightly controlled band around him. His expression was stern enough to give a charging rhino pause. "*Mi casa, mis reglas,*" he snapped.

The old lady shut her mouth with a snap, her tangled strands and spikes sucking inward but not really dissipating, and glowered at him before she also spun around and marched out of the room.

"*Bruja vieja y vil,*" Solis muttered, rolled his eyes, and stooped to pick up the sodden child. The hard red energy around him drained away, leaving a slightly too-bright residue that gave off occasional low sparks and glimmers of white and orange. He turned and saw me and I could tell he'd momentarily forgotten my presence in his house. His sparks died away.

He cleared his throat. "Have a seat in the kitchen. I will take Claudia Elena upstairs but I won't be gone long."

I wasn't sure if that was an apology in advance, a warning, or what. I shrugged. "All right."

Solis offered a small smile and walked past me. I followed him into the kitchen, where I could just glimpse two children's faces peering into the room from the hallway beyond until they saw their father coming and disappeared from sight. I took a seat at the oversized work island in the middle, putting the bag full of bell down on the floor beside me. Ximena Solis stood at the stove, her back to me. She was mumbling and working with jerky, angry motions, occasionally tossing her head in dismissive fury. She turned suddenly with the scorched pan in her hand and let out a fearful yelp as she saw me, jumping in shock and barely keeping hold of the pan and its burned, goopy contents. She started to question me in Spanish, then stopped, made an exasperated face while shaking her head, and restarted in English.

"Who the hell are you?" she demanded, tossing the burned pan into the sink with a clatter and a look of disgust. Her English was more heavily accented than Solis's, but she spoke more casually—as if she were more comfortable with the language than her husband and didn't give a damn how she sounded.

"I'm Harper Blaine," I replied. "I'm working with Sergeant Solis for a few days."

Her eyebrows pinched together as she looked a bit askance at me. "Harper Blaine? Really? You don't look spooky to *me*."

I let out a short laugh. "Is that how your husband describes me—spooky?"

"Espantoso," she replied, nodding while keeping her eyes locked on mine, as if I might do something untoward at any moment. Then she shrugged. "But no one's really that scary compared to my mother."

I pointed in the direction the old woman had disappeared. "Was that her?"

Ximena rolled her eyes. "Oh yes. She is having one of her 'bad days.' She decided the children all needed to be scrubbed of their sins and she was going to do it with Tide and a wire brush." She glanced around the kitchen in sudden anxiety and added, "I don't know where Oscar Luis went. . . ."

"Is he about ten, has a burned shirtsleeve?"

She nodded. "Yes. Did you see him?"

"He met us in the foyer. Your husband calmed him down and sent him upstairs. He didn't seem badly burned—just a little red on his arm."

Ximena looked stricken, her aura going an unattractive green for a moment, and she seemed to buckle at the knees before she caught herself and stiffened her spine with the help of a loud, long inhale. "He stumbled against the stove trying to get away from Mama and he caught his sleeve on fire."

She must have noticed my raised eyebrows; her face tightened and she shook her head. "It's not what you think. We don't abuse our kids. Once in a while Mama just goes crazy in the head and then things always get bad. She's locked herself in her room now and she won't come out until morning, probably."

"Really."

"Yes!"

"Do you think it's safe for her to be upstairs with the kids at all?"

Ximena growled under her breath. "She isn't upstairs. She has the bedroom down here." She pointed to one of the doors leading off the kitchen. "I'm not stupid enough to let my lunatic mother sleep near my kids. I'm not sure I should let her sleep near the stove or the food, either, but she's my mama and I can't put her in a home. Rey is kind enough to let her stay." She stopped suddenly and looked at the floor.

I glanced over my shoulder, thinking Solis must have returned, but he hadn't. It was just us girls.

"Don't you both worry?"

Mrs. Solis sniffed and said, "She's not like this very often. When she's all right she's a lot of help and she loves the kids. But when she's bad . . ." She glanced back up at me as if my understanding was a prize she coveted.

"She's horrid?"

Ximena didn't get the quote and just nodded. "She is . . . delicate. My parents were both artists. Papa died when I was very young and then Mama fled Colombia for the United States with me and my brother—"

"Fled?" I asked.

"Yes. Papa was killed in an accident and that was when Mama started to go a little crazy. She said he'd been murdered by the police in Cali—we lived in an artists' colony in the foothills and she thought of Cali as a wicked and filthy city, so of course Papa couldn't just die in a bus accident there; he had to have been assassinated over his art," she explained with a touch of eye rolling and hand waving. "She was sure someone would come to our door one day and kill us all. She had family who had come here and they said they could get her a job and so we ran away in the night like criminals."

"Did you believe it was true?"

She shut herself down with a shrug and glanced away. "Sometimes. I stopped when I was in high school, but"—her eyes swung back to mine from under her lowered brow and falling hair—"the first time I met Rey and he said his father was a policeman in Cali . . . for just a moment . . . I thought that maybe it wasn't just one of my crazy mother's crazy stories."

"She thought I had come to kill her," Solis added from the doorway behind me.

I turned my head toward him. "Ximena or her mother?"

"Ximena," he replied. He walked across the room and snuggled one arm around his wife. "Didn't you?"

Ximena nodded, biting her lip. "It's so stupid of me, but . . . you know. . . ."

He kissed the top of her head, which forced him up on his toes since Ximena was only an inch or so shorter than Solis. "I know." He whispered in her ear and kissed her cheek.

She made a shy smile at the floor.

"So," Solis started, giving his wife a little squeeze. "Pizza?"

Ximena giggled and finally looked up at him. "I don't want to feed a guest pizza!"

Solis shrugged. "As you like, *mi reina*. But Blaine is not a guest." He raised his eyes to mine and a momentary desperation flashed in his glance and sent a shower of anxious olive sparks into the Grey. "Are you?"

"Nope," I agreed. "Just here to make the sergeant's life harder."

"Then you should go upstairs and get started," Ximena suggested, stepping out of her husband's arms. She made comic shooing motions at us both. "*Marchaos*. I can clean this up myself."

Solis caught her nearer hand, his expression serious. "You are certain?"

"Of course," she replied, but her voice was a touch brittle. "I'll be fine. I'll call you when dinner is ready."

"And Mama?"

"I can manage Mama. I'll pull the curtain over the door."

Solis seemed reluctant, but he squeezed her hand a little before letting go and shrugged. "All right."

He motioned for me to come along and headed out of the kitchen. I picked up the bag full of bell and followed, glancing back at Ximena for only a moment as I went. She stood at the sink with her back mostly turned to us and her hands covering her face. She wasn't crying, but she seemed very close to it. I had the urge to turn back, but I didn't because Solis didn't and I know that the comfort of strangers is rarely appropriate when teetering between tears and rage.

ELEVEN

Solis led me back to the foyer with its polished wooden floor and up the stairs. He stopped at the top and glanced toward the back of the house. "The children are in the boys' room. They should be all right until dinner. My office is in the attic; we'll hear them if they misbehave." I wasn't sure he was talking to me as much as reassuring himself.

In a moment he opened the door to what I'd thought was a closet and started up a steep, narrow staircase to the attic.

The space under the roof was roughly divided by a partially finished wall that cut across near the back of the house. The much larger area in the front was plainly an artist's studio with easels and drawing tables arranged to take maximum advantage of the light through the large dormer windows on three sides. Work in various stages of completion hung or leaned everywhere there was room. There was even a covered lump on a half pillar that I guessed was a small sculpture in progress — progress that had stopped long ago, judging by the accumulation of dust on everything. The floor was dusty, too, except for a trail leading to a door in the rough wall.

Solis unlocked the door with the ease of habit and waved me through as he stepped aside to fetch a chair from the studio.

His office was wide but shallow, taking up the whole

width of the house at the back, but only eight feet or so of the depth. Unlike the studio, his office had only one dormer window and that was partially shaded by a huge old tree in the backyard. His desk—a pair of cheap folding banquet tables set at a right angle—took up the area under the large dormer. Piles of cardboard and plastic file boxes and a few battered two-drawer steel filing cabinets took up some of the remaining space on the floor at each side, but most of the area was empty. The walls, on the other hand, were covered with papers and photos so numerous it was difficult to see the surface on which they were pinned. I even saw scraps of fabric and small objects in plastic bags pinned, clamped, or tied among the pages. Various lamps stood here and there or were fixed to the table edges and exposed joists. I stared at it all, turning slowly, with the bell in its canvas sack swinging gently against my knees.

Where my office was carefully buttoned up—all files and notes put away and hidden from clients' eyes—Solis's private space was like a murder board for a serial-killer investigation. It looked as if every case he'd ever worked haunted the walls with paper ghosts.

He watched me until I stopped to blink at him, amazed and stunned. He gave a half shrug and quirked one corner of his mouth. "My wife's family has their madness. I have mine." He removed his coat and suit jacket and hung them on a hook at the back of the door before holding his hand out for my own coat. I gave it to him and he placed it on top of his. Then he turned back into the room and his close-hugging energy corona flushed a bright gold color as he seemed to brace himself or change mental gears. "Now let us take another look at the bell," he added, dragging the spare chair up to the desk.

I followed him and he removed a small pile of file folders to a box on the floor to make room for our prize. I put the bag on the table and pulled out the bell, keeping it over the bag to contain any glop we'd missed earlier. Solis pulled one of the lights down closer and drew up the desk chair beside the other one. He pulled a handkerchief from his pocket—I didn't think anyone actually carried them anymore—and wiped the bell with care, clearing water and the last of the embedded goop off the engraving.

The bell was made of bronze all through as far as we could see, but nothing new was revealed by the wiping, except a small loop on the top for a lanyard to be threaded through. The lettering still read s.s. VALENCIA and nothing more.

Solis frowned in thought, murmuring, "*Valencia*. So, whatever the neighbor, Mr. Francis, thought he heard, it most likely was not about shipwrecks in Spain," he added, shooting me a sly look from the corner of his eyes.

"Maybe the wreck of *Valencia*," I suggested.

Solis nodded his head a bit, but I wasn't sure he was conscious of it. "Ghosts . . ." he muttered, keeping his eyes on the bell. His aura pulled down to a thin line of cold blue for a moment. Then he abruptly swung the chair around and scooted it to face his computer, a boxy old desktop machine that squatted like an electronic gargoyle on the corner where the two tables met. He clacked away with his ancient keyboard and mouse and the printer made some grunting noises. "I'll start printing the other case files while we search for *Valencia*," he said, barely glancing up.

He didn't touch-type comfortably, looking down several times even though his fingers were hitting the right keys most of the time. In a minute or so the browser coughed up a Google search; all the visible listings related to a steamship named *Valencia* that had been wrecked in 1906. We read through the top six articles, including a Wikipedia entry and one from HistoryLink. org that revealed a grim story:

On January 20, 1906, the passenger steamer *Valencia* had left San Francisco heading for Seattle. It was stand-

ing in for another ship that had been dry-docked for repairs, but though the *Valencia* was a little older and of a
less-hardy design, it was thought to be up to the task. On
the night of January 22, *Valencia* attempted to enter the
Strait of Juan de Fuca in the teeth of a storm that quickly
proved to be more than the ship could weather and the
steamer's hull was gashed open on unseen rocks. Water
gushed into the interior compartments—most of which
were not watertight—and the boat was in danger of
sinking. The captain tried to turn and beach the ship
safely, but the stern ran up, not on soft sand but on a
rocky reef along the southwest coast of Vancouver Island. *Valencia* was trapped on the rocks below a cliff
twenty miles north of the strait and unable to move in
any direction or safely put out the lifeboats—of which
there weren't enough to save everyone, anyhow.

The fierce storm beat at the ship without mercy and
began to tear into the structure. Abandoning everything
in the cabins and holds below, everyone on board—most
still clad in their nightclothes—huddled on deck or in
the stern cabins that were still dry and whole. At the first
break in the storm the captain attempted to put the
women and children ashore in six of the seven lifeboats,
with two men per boat to row, but as the men left on
board watched in horror, the tiny wooden boats were
capsized by waves or crushed on the rocks, killing all
aboard them, save nine of the men, who made landfall
alive. The nine climbed to the cliff tops, but in the slash-
ing rain they turned the wrong way and wandered away
from the lighthouse that could have saved them. On the
ship the remaining men climbed into what still stood of
the rigging, trying to keep out of the raging surf that battered the crumbling vessel to pieces.

The last lifeboat was finally put down with just three
men aboard, under instructions to reach the cliff top
and drop a line to the boat so the remaining passengers
and crew might climb to safety. This time the boat
reached land and the men found a sign directing them

to the lighthouse. Abandoning their instructions, they walked for two and a half hours to the lighthouse, where they were finally able to call for aid to save *Valencia*'s surviving men. But even when help arrived, many of the boats were unable to safely draw close enough to the sinking steamer to remove anyone and had to turn away. Some of the remaining men of the *Valencia* were rescued by the responding boats, but not all, and when another party arrived on the cliff with ropes to haul the last ones up, the ship broke apart and sank before their eyes, taking several dozen men, who clung to the rigging, to their deaths. They had weathered two days in the storm, watching their fellow passengers and crew die and their ship tear away and sink in pieces beneath them, seen others rescued, but not them. . . . Of the men, women, and children who had been aboard when *Valencia* left San Francisco, only thirty-seven men survived.

The stories differed as to how many people perished in the tragedy—maybe 117, possibly 136 or 181, since records didn't include children or late-arriving passengers who paid when they boarded—but of the unknown total who boarded, not a single child or woman had survived. Twenty-seven years later the *Valencia*'s lifeboat number 5 was found adrift in a cove nearby. The nameplate was preserved in a museum, but the rest of the ill-fated steamer was left to her grave on the rocks below Pachena Point.

The wrecking of the *Valencia* was later dubbed America's *Titanic* and was accounted to be the worst peacetime shipping disaster in North American history. And we had found its bell hidden in the engine room of another ill-fated boat.

Solis leaned back in his chair and tapped his lower lip with his right index finger. "What connects them?" he murmured, capturing my own thoughts as well. "How did the bell from one come to be in the engine room of the other?"

"I can't imagine. *Seawitch* wasn't a salvage vessel and

there's no record of any diving equipment on board, so they didn't go out to explore the wreck. Almost eighty years apart, totally different types of vessels coming from opposite directions . . ."

"Both were in or near the Strait of Juan de Fuca when they were last seen."

"That's not much to start with," I said. "*Seawitch* was heading up to the San Juan Islands, but it's a big area inside the strait and we don't know for certain that the boat ever made it out of the south sound."

"Perhaps the pages from the log will say," Solis suggested.

I didn't turn to watch him, taken by a stray thought. "Did you notice that the last lifeboat was found twenty-seven years after *Valencia* sank?"

"I had not, but it is an odd coincidence that the *Seawitch* also returned after twenty-seven years lost. Do you have any suggestions about what that means?"

I had to shake my head. "No."

Solis looked unhappy and turned to pick up the sheets that had been spilling out of the old printer while we'd been reading about the wreck of the *Valencia*.

The first document he picked up was nothing but text and he started to put it aside. I took it from his hand and looked it over.

"Odile Carson's death reports. I'd almost forgotten about her."

"I thought it best to be certain of what happened. It seems unlikely, but if hers was not an accident, it would link the *Seawitch* definitively to a homicide—which is my area of investigation."

"That would keep you on the case."

He nodded. "For a while."

"But if not, then would you be able to close the case at your end?"

"No. There would still be the matter of the blood and the condition of the boat's interior. If there is a link in that to a major crime, the case will remain with me."

"Unless there's something in the log pages to give us a clue, the only lead we have on the condition of the *Seawitch* may be this bell," I said. "The connection to the *Valencia*—if we can figure it out—is unlikely to be admissible evidence of a major crime. I mean, there *is* something going on, but it might not be ... solid enough to force you to remain on this case."

Solis cocked his head. "Force?"

"Yes. I think you can wiggle off this hook pretty easily as long as Odile Carson's death wasn't a homicide." I reached again for the report.

Solis put his hand over mine, holding it down on top of the pages. "One moment, Blaine. You believe I've been forced onto this case and want to 'wiggle' out of it?"

"Well, I assumed so."

"Why?"

I drew away to sit back in my chair and shrugged at him. "You hate mysteries and you especially hate this sort of case full of coincidence, unexplainable circumstances, and, frankly, the weird crap that lands on my desk."

"I requested the case."

That stopped me cold and I blinked at him, puzzled and frowning.

Solis graced me with a tiny smile. "My captain made the same expression."

"I imagine so," I replied. And though it sounded incredibly stupid, I added, "But why?"

"I have heard," Solis said, looking down at his hands, "that a definition of insanity is continuing to do as you have always done while expecting a different result. Here I saw a case that could not help but fall into your hands and I thought I might learn something if I observed it from within—if I approached the mystery from a new angle: yours. I don't find myself liking the sensation—I don't believe I ever shall—but *am* finding it ... illuminating." He glanced up and I could've sworn his eyes sparkled. "And why should I inflict your ... affinity for the bizarre on some innocent policeman?"

I snorted and started to reply, but found myself lurching forward and gasping as a spurt of fight-or-flight adrenaline shot through me. My chest felt hollow and battered as my heart rate accelerated like a sprinter from a standing start. This wasn't my emotion. . . .

Solis reached for me in concern and I shook him off, forcing myself up to my feet, trembling as I fought off the sensation with long breaths. "I'm fine," I gasped at him. "I'm fine." I fumbled in my pocket and clutched my cell phone.

I brought out the suddenly slippery thing, turning it on as I did, and started poking in a message as fast as my shaking fingers could manage. Damn Quinton's security paranoia that favored dumb pagers over smartphones. I tapped one last key and sent the "Call me *now*" code and wished we had established one for "What the hell was that?"

"Are you certain?" Solis asked, and for a moment I wasn't sure what he meant, but I nodded, confirming that I was all right.

"Yeah." I offered no explanation and he continued to watch me, niggling threads of curious yellow and anxious green leaking into the Grey around him. "Let's just . . . get back to the case in hand," I suggested, putting my phone on the desk as I sat back down. My heart rate was sliding back to normal already, but I'd be happier once I heard from Quinton.

Solis scowled at me for a moment and I almost laughed. It was like old times. He shook it off and took the autopsy report from under my hand. "I will read this, since it is a past case and department property. You review the log pages." He moved his chair aside so I could park mine in front of the monitor and flip through the digital images from the log book. I appreciated the distraction.

The log entries were mostly dull and out of order. Some of the pages hadn't been salvageable and others were still unavailable, but I read through a few, including a couple with some diary-style notes courtesy of Gary Fielding, including one that referred to a "strange feeling" he had whenever he was near Shelly Knight. I wondered if that was an actual sensation or an emotion. I clicked onto the next page and found an entry that read in part, "Carson totally flipping out about his wife—"

"Odd," I muttered.

"What?" Solis asked, looking up from his reading of the Odile Carson death report.

"There's an entry here that mentions Odile . . ." I replied.

"Is the date June nineteenth?"

I peered hard at the image and increased the size on the screen, but it didn't help. "It's hard to be sure, but, no, it looks like the eighteenth."

"That is the day *before* Mrs. Carson's body was discovered." He scowled.

"When did she die?"

"The night of the eighteenth. What more does the passage say?"

"It's very smeared, but what I think it says is that Les got into an argument with . . . someone . . . after dinner and then . . . he wanted a record that he had been on board continuously since they left port. Fielding's note says, 'This is to affirm . . .' There's a further note about fishing—making a change of plan to go fishing at . . . Port Townsend. Then it appears that Les Carson received a call via the radio about Odile's death . . . but when isn't recorded here that I can see, and the next page seems not to have been salvaged."

Solis paged through the report and found a call log. "June nineteenth at eleven forty-four a.m. A call was made to *Seawitch* via the radio telephone service for the purpose of notifying next of kin."

I closed my eyes, slightly nauseated by the idea. "The log says they were going to stop at Roche Harbor that day . . .

but there's no record in the insurance report that they did. It looks like Les Carson knew his wife was dead before she died. . . . And *Seawitch* went missing later that day without making port or being reported in trouble by any other boat or either coast guard. What the hell happened? Did Les Carson kill his wife and use the trip as an alibi?"

Solis shook his head. "The timing is impossible, and Mrs. Carson killed herself."

"Really?"

"The medical examiner is very clear. Mrs. Carson left a note and the disposition of the body was consistent with suicide by electrocution in water." I thought I saw him shudder before he added, "She was thorough in guaranteeing her death."

"Could it have been murder for hire?" I suggested.

Solis shook his head, rolling his eyes. "It is my experience that the clever professional assassin exists principally in the minds of thriller authors and Hollywood scriptwriters. Those who kill strangers for money rather than the satisfaction of their own psychotic impulses are most frequently violent thugs with criminal records and the minds of twisted children."

I almost smiled at his vehemence. "So . . . not a fan of Barry Eisler's novels, I'm guessing."

He gave an amused snort that didn't quite bloom into a laugh. Then he shook off the moment and looked back down at the report. "It appears that the coroner certified the death as 'misadventure,' in spite of the autopsy and scene investigation."

"Maybe the family brought pressure to keep the suicide ruling out of the public record," I suggested.

He nodded. "Possible. No city is perfectly without corruption."

"Seattle's built on it." I would have said more, but my phone rang, jiggling across the surface of the folding table where I'd left it to fall onto the floor near my original position. I dove for it as the office door opened and a small brown face peeped through the gap.

"Blaine," I barked as I answered the phone, falling onto my shoulder on the floor and trying to keep an eye on the newcomer at the same time.

"Papa?" the face asked.

"*Sí*, Mario?"

The little boy started in Spanish, then switched to English after Solis frowned at him. "Mama says dinner's ready and Grandmama came out of her room again. But she's OK now."

Solis nodded. "We will be downstairs in a moment. Tell your mama we'll wash up first. Just like you."

"*Sí*, Papa."

Mario withdrew his head and closed the door gently. I couldn't hear him leave over the sound in my ear from the phone.

"Harper!" Quinton yelled over the sound of traffic, "I'm sorry. I'm at a pay phone in downtown. It's really loud here."

"I can tell. What happened earlier?"

"When earlier?"

I checked my watch. "About forty minutes ago. I *felt* something."

Quinton didn't reply for a moment and only the sound of cars on the street filled my ear. Finally he spoke. "I saw someone from the past. He shouldn't be here and he wants me to do something I can't agree to."

"I understand. Are you OK?"

"I am now. I . . . I'll tell you the rest later. Here and now is not good."

"I'm with Solis at his place—we're going over files. Do you need me to meet you somewhere soon?"

"No. Whenever you're done, page me. I'll come home then. I want to stay out here until the last minute. Just in case."

"If it's *that* past, then they already know who I am and where I live, if they want to find you."

"Yeah, but . . . humor me." Then he cut the connection.

Goody. More fun and games dodging Quinton's scary ex-boss.

Solis lifted an inquisitive eyebrow as I put my phone back into my pocket.

"Boyfriend trouble," I said.

He grunted and made a lifted half nod with his chin. "Do you need to leave?"

"Not yet. I'd like to get through this paperwork while we can. Qu—He'll be all right."

"I'm sure he will." He stood up and put the death report back into a neat, squared-off pile on the table before motioning for me to follow him. I went along and I noticed that he paused to lock the office door behind us as we left.

TWELVE

Dinner at the Solis house was served in the dining room under tension that seemed to have less to do with my presence than that of Ximena's mother—whose name was the long and rolling Maria del Carmen Gomez Baranca de Moreno, but was shortened by everyone to Mama Gomez. Chatter was carefully regulated and dish passing was accomplished with a degree of solemnity I had rarely seen in a house full of subteen children. The table seemed a bit unbalanced with both me—in the uncomfortable middle—and Ximena's mother on the same side and three of the four kids on the other. Ximena was at the foot of the table with the two youngest—Martha Carolina and Claudia Elena—seated on either side. Solis sat at the head with the older boy, Oscar Luis, on his left. Mama Gomez was on his right and I thought it wasn't so much for any honor the place conferred as the ease with which Solis could keep an eye—and if necessary a hand—on her. Directly across from me sat the youngest boy, Mario Diego, who at seven years old was still a bit too small to manage his own plate and the serving bowls at the same time, which made the progress of dishes go backward: Food started not with the head of the table, but with the youngest children and Ximena, then passed on to me and Mama Gomez, and finally to Solis, Oscar Luis, and Mario. This seemed to annoy Mama Gomez and she muttered continually while casting me black looks from the corner of her eye and eating mechanically.

The food was more a collection of meats and a few side dishes than a specific meal, but it was delicious. The amounts were ample and no one complained, though the feeling of something about to shatter hovered over us. Eventually Mama Gomez said something under her breath that brought a low-voiced reprimand from Solis and a giggle from Martha.

"She called you a witch," Martha said, looking at me with big, sparkling eyes.

Solis pressed his lips together and seemed about to say something but I forestalled him with a wave.

"It's all right," I said, addressing the little girl. "I've been called a lot worse and I recognized the word, anyway."

"Do you speak Spanish?" Martha asked. "Papa says it's rude to say things the guests don't understand in front of them, but if you speak Spanish, we can talk normal now."

"No, I don't really speak Spanish. I'm sorry. I know only a few words and they are mostly very impolite ones."

Martha was crestfallen. "Oh."

Mama Gomez grinned and repeated herself a little louder, staring at me as if issuing a challenge. I returned her stare with a bland face and didn't use any of my precious store of profanity, waiting to see what she'd do now. I'd caught exactly three words of what she'd said: "silver," "gold," and "witch." The rest meant nothing to me with my terrible Spanish.

Ximena gasped and looked taken aback.

Solis narrowed his eyes but it was the only outward sign of his irritation. "Apologize, Mama."

Mama Gomez whipped her head around to face him. "Why should I?"

I'd already figured out that she understood English perfectly, so I wasn't surprised she spoke as well as her daughter did. I kept my face and body still: This show-down wasn't really about me.

"Because you have insulted our guest," Solis replied.

"I spoke only the truth," she objected.

"Truth or not, you meant harm. When you do harm to my guest, you will apologize or you will leave. My house, my rules."

From the corner of my eye I saw Ximena bite her lip. Both her daughters looked to her in confusion and she glanced back, shaking her head and laying her finger over her mouth.

Mama Gomez also turned to look at Ximena, but she didn't like what she saw. "Ximena!" she demanded.

Ximena's eyes were huge and her lip trembled but she replied quietly, "Apologize, Mama."

Mama Gomez made a strangled noise and flew to her feet. She glared back and forth between her daughter and her son-in-law, eyes bulging and mouth pressed tight to suppress her rage that sent violent red shocks into the Grey. Finally she looked at me. Since I was sitting and she was tiny, her face was just about level with mine.

"I'm sorry you're a witch!" she shouted, and wrenched herself around to rush from the room, knocking over her chair and lurching into the built-in sideboard as she went. The room seemed to shiver as she left it, some glimmering residue of anger dying out of the air.

The whole room seemed to draw a breath of relief. The children dove back into their food and it appeared normalcy would return.

"So," I asked, "what did she say?" I glanced at Martha Carolina and added, "Aside from the witch part."

"She said you have gold and silver in your . . . umm . . . Mama, what was that word?" Martha asked.

Ximena didn't look up from helping Claudia Elena with her food. "Aura. It's like a light some people have around them."

"Like a halo? Like a saint?" Martha asked.

"Sort of . . ."

Martha looked at me again, grinning. "You have a halo! You must be very good!"

Solis made a quiet snort.

Now, here was a pickle: I'm not much of a kid person, so I didn't know what I was supposed to do, but it felt incumbent upon me to do or say *something*....

"Umm ... no, I don't think it's a halo," I started.

"Ms. Blaine hasn't got that kind of goodness," Solis said.

"Is she bad, then?" Martha asked, frowning.

"No. But not everyone who is good is a saint. That takes a holy kind of goodness all the time."

"And I'm only good some of the time," I added, hearing the obvious cue in his voice.

"Oh," said Martha. Then she brightened and declared, "I'm good all the time!"

Ximena laughed and turned to her older daughter to smile and tap her lightly on the nose. "You only wish that were true, Martita. Now stop pestering our guest and eat your dinner."

The boys giggled and elbowed each other until Solis frowned at them. They stopped immediately and the rest of the meal was civilly quiet.

As we rose afterward, Ximena sidled up to me, chivvying the three older children into the kitchen to bus their dishes, and whispered, "I'm sorry about my mother. Sometimes she ... sees things...."

"That's all right. Sometimes I do, too," I replied. Then I noticed Solis motioning for me to go with him.

Ximena gave me a trembling smile. "You do?"

I nodded and she nodded back, her smile strengthening. Then she said, "Go on. You and Rey have work to do. The kids will help me clean up."

Feeling a little guilty, I went with Solis, heading back up the stairs to the office in the attic. On the final steps I asked, "What was that about with your mother-in-law?"

"I apologize. She's very rude when she gets like this."

"Like what?"

"She is taken with strange ideas, with visions. And as an artist she refuses to constrain her mind, and, to our frustration, her mouth as well."

He paused to unlock the office door.

"That's not quite what I meant. She may be a little nuts, but that wasn't the crazy talking at dinner. She was trying to get a reaction out of you."

"Her feelings about me are . . . unstable." He opened the door and waved me inside, then shut the door behind us before he continued in a low, intense voice. "She knows how I love Ximena and our children, that I will do anything to keep them safe. Sometimes that means keeping them safe from her, which she doesn't like. And sometimes she hates me for being blind to the world as she sees it—the world, perhaps, as you see it."

I frowned at him. "As I see it?"

"Yes. I . . . have begun wondering if there *is* something I don't see. For years I've thought Maria del Carmen was mad. And she is, but not all of her madness is lies. And Ximena . . . I fear she is becoming like her mother."

"You're afraid she's going crazy?" I asked.

He nodded. "When we met I knew she was . . . fragile. I had no idea . . . what she might become. Now I see it in her mother and I know she will get worse. But"—he turned his face to me suddenly—"if there is something else—something that is true, even though it is hidden from the world—then perhaps she isn't doomed to madness."

"And that's why you wanted to work with me. Because you think I'm like them and that gives you some kind of hope."

"Yes. And you are *not* insane. I may not agree with all you say, I may find it hard to believe everything you've been telling me and even some of the things I experienced today—even in the face of proof, it can be difficult to change the"—his eyes darted around and he made a frustrated gesture, rolling his hands in the air as if trying to grasp something incorporeal—"the habit of mind. But

if there are more things to see than I *can* see, then perhaps a way can be found to manage the difference between us and I . . . won't lose her."

I blinked at him and found I'd been holding my
breath. I drew in a shaking lungful, but it didn't help
much. I still didn't know what to say even when I had the
breath to say it. "I—I'm not— That is, what we experience is not the same."

"You and Maria del Carmen?"

"Me and . . . anyone. It's different for each of us. What
you experienced in the engine room on board *Seawitch*
wasn't the same as what I experienced—similar, related,
but not the same. Even what Ximena and her mother
both . . . see won't be identical."

"It is a matter of depth, then?"

"No. It's not. Or not just that. It's not all vision and it's
not all just a matter of what you see. There's the intensity
and kind of experience, what you can do with it or what
you can't do, and whether you can turn it off or not. . . ."
I could tell he wasn't quite getting it. "Look, I can see
things and touch them, experience them pretty intensely,
but I can't *do* anything with them. Nothing significant. I
can't work magic—" I cut myself off as Solis made a sour
face.

I sighed. "Now, don't tell me you're starting to believe
in ghosts but you can't make yourself believe in magic.
What we saw in the lower cabin on *Seawitch* and what
we saw in the fountain at Reeve's house were spell circles. I don't know what they did—"

"Why not? If you know they were magical, why don't
you know what magic they did? And why can't you do it,
too?"

"I just can't. It's a talent I don't have. Like I can't draw,
or sing, or play an instrument, or . . . do high-level math
functions in my head, but I can dance. It's all different,
even where they're related. Like . . . circuit boards. I
know one when I see one, but I can't tell you what it
does. The board for a microwave is not the same as the

board for a blender, but I couldn't tell you which one was which, just that they aren't the same. Magic comes in a lot of specializations, and I can tell some from others but I can't cast a spell or tell you what a spell circle was meant to do after it's burned out."

Solis scowled and walked to the desk to sit down. I could see the telltale glimmer of gold around him that I'd seen before; he was shifting mental gears, putting away the intimacy of his situation with his family to concentrate on the case, distancing himself from the personal discomfort of the discussion. "So . . . how are the two circles related?"

I crossed slowly to the desk myself. I wasn't as ready to put aside the other subject as he was, but I knew it wouldn't help my cause to pester him. "They're the same . . . school of magic, I guess you'd say. But not drawn by the same person. The wave figures were the same symbol but the handwriting—for lack of a better word—was different. The big circle on the boat was complex, which implies a complicated or complex spell. The one at Reeve's was small and pretty simple, so I'd say it was a specific and simple spell—which doesn't mean it wasn't dangerous."

"Could the spell on board *Seawitch* have had anything to do with Odile Carson's death? And I don't say I believe it, but if the possibility exists . . ."

"You mean could she have been killed by magic? At that distance it's not likely, especially since she killed herself."

"Could she have been influenced to it?"

"Possible, but, again, not very likely. It's hard to magically convince someone to do something they are mentally opposed to. If she'd already been suicidal, though . . . the possibility would be better. But it could explain how Les Carson knew his wife was dead before the cops called him."

"What about the spell circle at Reeve's?"

"I'd guess a rudimentary trap of some kind. If it were

keyed to him personally it wouldn't go off except when he was near it. And since he's an old man with health problems it wouldn't have to be a spell that could kill someone, just one that would cause a lot of distress."

"Is it likely the person who drew the symbols at Reeve's house would be completely unrelated to whoever drew the symbols on *Seawitch*?"

"No. That particular strain of magic is relatively rare—thank your lucky stars—and it tends to run in families, like a genetic disease. The only other person I've met who does that particular kind of magic doesn't tolerate others of her kind nearby and she's nasty enough to enforce the distance. So whoever drew those spell circles was either far enough away to be ignored or more dangerous than she is."

"But who were these people, how are they related, and what is the connection to *Seawitch*?"

"Your guess is as good as mine."

Solis grunted to himself and turned his attention to the papers on the desk. "Perhaps there is more in the log. . . ."

We resumed our places, reading through all the available log pages. Solis started with the ones I'd already perused and printed while I looked at the newer ones on the screen, waiting for the printer to finish spitting them out on paper. The last page stopped me. It was blotched with red and brown stains and numerous small slashes and tears and a single rambling paragraph of poor penmanship:

. . . she cursed me and now this! I didn't stop him from forcing himself on her, so I guess I'm just as guilty as he is. Now it's too late to be sorry. She won't stop. The storm is going to wreck us unless I can make the cove and even then I may have doomed us all. I think Starrett is dying—that's my fault, too. When people say "hostile waters" they don't know what that can mean. I do. Now I do. I don't know

*how I'll live if I survive. My skin feels like it's on fire
and this hair is everywhere. And the blood. My
hands ache—*

The words ended in a red-blotted scrawl, and a long
location number and heading were written below, large
and messy, as if drawn by a child with a leaky pen. I
swung away from the monitor and waved Solis's attention to it.

"Hey," I said. "Read this. It's the last entry in the log."

Solis turned and took my place at the monitor as I
stood up to pace.

"A strange thing to say," he commented.

I stopped pacing and turned back. "What is?"

"The writer says 'I don't know how I'll live if I survive.' Not *if* he will survive or *if* he will live, but *how* he
will live. As if there's something beyond survival that is
just as frightening as death."

"Interesting. You focus on that. What jumps out at me
is he says someone is guilty of forcing himself on a
woman—and that Castor Starrett's death is also his fault.
Sounds like a rape and a homicide, though the writer
almost seems confused by it all. He also mentions a cove.
But where? Are the numbers and heading at the bottom
an indication of where he was going or where he was at
the time?"

Solis gave me a wry look. "I did not ignore the rest of
the statement; I merely found the one sentence very odd.
It should be telling, but what does it tell? I agree that the
writer seems upset and confused. He almost seems to
imply that the storm was caused by the lady in
question. . . ."

"Which one of the three?" I asked, not wanting to
think about the question Solis was really raising.

Solis made his half shrug. "Who knows?"

"What's the statute of limitation on rape in Washington?" I asked.

"Ten years, but if a death results, none."

"What if the rape victim survived the wreck?"

"Why would you imagine she did or that she would not reveal herself?"

"I'm just thinking . . . someone had to bring the boat back to port, someone who knew where it had been and what had happened on board, or they would have come forward. If the victim did it, maybe it's because she knows her rapist also survived. But it's been too long for her to file a legal complaint so . . . she plays dead and waits to see if the reappearance of *Seawitch* will bring her rapist—now apparently her murderer—to light."

Solis shook his head. "It seems woefully complicated."

I frowned. "Possibly, but regardless, the writer— probably Gary Fielding, since the handwriting looks about the same as the entry we know he wrote, even though it's deteriorating here—says he's taking the boat somewhere. If he made it, the odds are good the boat stayed there all this time."

"The whole twenty-seven years?"

"You saw its condition. That boat didn't move from the time it docked after whatever happened on board until the day it turned up at Shilshole. Nothing had been disturbed enough for the boat to have moved under its own power. No one's started those engines in years.

"Maybe, if we can find the place where it's been sitting all this time, we may be able to find a witness to say who brought it and kept it there, at least. They might even have information about what happened aboard, who survived, and who died. Because I'm still betting that whoever brought the boat back to Seattle was aboard it when it was lost."

Solis looked thoughtful and started to say something but was interrupted by the bleating of his cell phone. He answered it and listened for a moment, then killed the connection with a bitter expression on his face. "John Reeve is dead and it may be a homicide."

THIRTEEN

Reeve had died at Highline Hospital, which made his death a Seattle PD matter, but not Solis's case. He wasn't "on deck" when the call came in and the connection to the *Seawitch* investigation was tenuous, so it had been assigned to someone else. Still, the circumstances were strange enough that the detective on the case wanted to talk to Solis and me once he'd heard we'd been on the scene when Reeve had the heart attack that brought him to the hospital in the first place. We drove down separately and I found myself annoyed at the lost opportunity to pursue the discussions we'd begun at Solis's house.

My disgruntlement took a backseat when we arrived at the hospital. Crime scenes at hospitals aren't managed in quite the same way as they are anywhere else, since the place is always busy and space is generally at a premium and you don't usually get to leave the body in situ for long. Reeve had already been removed from his cubicle in cardiac ICU and the area was screened off for privacy while a pair of technicians finished picking up what they could in the way of forensic evidence. Other patients had been rearranged to optimize the isolation of the scene, and we met with Detective Julian Plant in the cafeteria downstairs—it was empty since the regular meal service had already closed and no one seemed to be raiding the vending machines at the moment, though we could hear the patient nutritional services crew clattering away in the kitchen behind the metal curtain barrier.

I'd met Plant before. He was one of those tall, pale, lanky guys who always looks like he's in desperate need of some sun, sandwiches, and sleep. Competent enough, but I'd never been overly impressed. He didn't seem to go any further than he had to with anything and I had the impression he was marking time until he could retire. He wasn't sloppy or a bad cop, but he was one of those aging, old-school detectives who'd gone the route of no longer caring rather than care too much. He gave us both a basset-eyed stare as we came and sat at his table.

"You two want some coffee?" he asked. "They've still got some in the patient services hatch round the corner if you don't like the vending machine kind."

We both shook our heads and sat, facing Plant at the awkward round table.

"Well," Plant started, curving his hands around his dented paper coffee cup on the table. "So. Here's the thing: seawater."

I made the "Huh?" face at him, and Solis said, "Clarify, please. Seawater?"

Plant nodded. "Yeah. Mr. Reeve was either smothered with a wet something or he died of drowning. In seawater. In his bed. Now, they would have said pneumonia—which I guess they considered—except the bed was wet. Not that they aren't wet a lot of the time when folks die, 'cause you know what happens. And there was the dog. So we're waiting for confirmation from the coroner, but the attending medical team is saying Mr. Reeve was attacked by a dog that smothered him with a wet pillow. What do you think? Any connection to your case?"

Solis and I exchanged incredulous glances. "A . . . dog?" I asked.

"Yeah. Big dog, they said. Brown with a white stripe on its back. Mr. Reeve was resting and they'd pulled his curtains closed for privacy when the monitors started going crazy, and the first nurse through the curtain sees this big, wet, brown dog wrestling with a pillow on Reeve's chest. The nurse said there was a stink in the room like"—he flipped open his notebook and paged around a bit—"like rotten vegetables. And the dog was sitting on Reeve's chest, shaking the crap outta this wet pillow that was covering Reeve's face. So the medical team can't get near the guy and they call security to come shoot the dog, but Reeve's already dead and the dog takes off. They couldn't revive him and the attending physician called it at"—he looked at his book again—"six forty-one. Well, technically they're saying cardiac arrest due to animal assault, but the amount of water in his mouth and on the bed is making the ME want a deeper look. So, what do you two think?"

"Are they sure it was a dog?" I asked again.

"Yeah, though they can't decide on what breed. One guy said it was a German shepherd. Another said it was an otter hound. Another said it was . . . umm . . . a Portuguese water spaniel—you know, like the president's dog. And one said it was a pit bull. A fat pit bull."

"Fat chance."

Solis smirked—there was nothing else to call it.

Plant made a sour face at me.

"Oh, come on," I said. "No one can seriously believe a dog was trained to run in here, find Reeve, jump on his bed, and smother him with a wet pillow. When we saw Reeve he was afraid of something, and we saw something or someone moving at the back of the property. But if anyone did kill him—"

"Someone did," Plant said, cutting me off. "He sure didn't die of smothering himself or inducing his own heart attack." He looked at both of us, then focused on Solis. "What do you think, Rey?"

Solis lowered his gaze to the tabletop, his brow creasing, then drew a slow breath before he looked back at Plant. "I think Mr. Reeve may have been frightened by a stray dog that got into the hospital. Or he may have been smothered by an attacker who was frightened off by a service dog, but that's all I can imagine, if Reeve didn't die of a simple heart attack, which seems far more likely. Doesn't it, Plant?"

Plant sat back, closing his basset-hound eyes. "Yeah. And I hope that's how the coroner will rule when he's done. But if not . . . I guess I'm going to be looking for people who had it in for the old man and made a habit of carrying pillows soaked in seawater and training dogs to smother people with them." He shook his head in disgust. "You two can go. I'm sorry I bothered you."

We stood and Solis bent down to ask Plant to keep him in the loop; then we walked toward the exit together.

"Who murdered Reeve?" Solis whispered to me as we neared the door.

"Why ask me?"

"I hoped you had seen something."

"Nothing you didn't. We got only a glimpse at the scene before we had to go down to see Plant."

"But what did you see that I did not? You have that look on your face, so no evasions. We are partners on this case, remember."

"All right. I saw the same gray-green color around Reeve's bed that I saw around him when he had the original heart attack, and I'd bet the description of the dog people claim to have seen here would match the thing I saw at Reeve's place. Whoever killed Reeve is involved with *Seawitch*."

"That is my thought, too."

We walked on through the hospital without another word. Solis walked like something heavy and morbid had settled on him. I stopped him just outside the lobby doors in the dim greenish light of the emergency room driveway.

"Are you really ready for this? I don't think we can pretend this whole business, from the boat to Reeve's death, isn't paranormal. And it's going to get worse now that someone with the stink of magic on them is willing to risk exposure by coming into a hospital to kill an old man who was probably dying, anyhow."

"This was not something accomplished from a distance?"

"No. There wasn't enough magical residue or a spell circle around his bed for Reeve to have been killed by magic at a distance. Someone or something came here in person to do it."

"If this person has magic at their disposal—"

"It costs. Magic is not free, especially not this kind. The farther you want to reach, the harder you want to hit, the more you have to pay one way or another. Both the spell circles we've seen were drawn in blood. That has to come from a live person or animal, not a plastic container stolen from the hospital blood supply, which means our spell flinger is powerful but has a major crutch and can't do much without literally spilling blood. Smothering wouldn't pay the piper. No blood here, but the residue was otherwise the same, so no major spell was cast but something or someone magical was in the room and they killed Reeve—or made sure he couldn't be saved, at the very least."

Solis looked troubled.

I sighed and felt like I was kicking a puppy. "Up to you to believe it or not," I said, "but I am telling you the truth where magic is concerned, and I don't see any other explanation or any other way of solving this without heading into the weirdness."

"I am sorry I'm ... difficult. Forcing my mind to go in these directions is ... is like changing religions."

"Have you tried that?" I asked.

"No. I think it wiser to challenge only one ingrained practice at a time."

"You might find that some changes just come along with the package."

He nodded. "That may be true. Your ... partner. Mr. Lassiter? Mr. Purlis? Which does he prefer?"

Ah, so Solis *did* know the whole long, strange tale of Quinton. "I've never asked him," I replied, which was true. I'd just assumed he was content with the nickname and didn't really like either his alias or his real name much. One he'd adopted on the fly and the other he'd tried to walk away from. "I just call him Quinton and we go on from there."

"Ah. How does he cope with this . . . blindness? I assume he is not like you. . . ."

"You assume correctly. He trusts me—most of the time," I added, thinking of his unexplained discomforts and alarms lately. "And he has enough personal experience with things that don't fit the standard paradigm that he's developed his own Theory of the Invisible by observation and deduction. Most of the time he's right. Sometimes he's not. Some things you can't see still leave observable traces—like, say, gravity. Some leave nothing concrete behind to prove your experience was anything other than imagination. Well, *I* have some unexplainable scars, but I'm strange that way."

He seemed intrigued but he didn't ask. He grunted to himself and nodded. "I see."

I had the urge to put my hand on his shoulder, but I stifled it. I wasn't sure this tiny, forced bud of acceptance could withstand any ham-handed gestures on my part yet.

"Just don't go slamming any mental doors. If you can do that for a while I think you'll figure the rest out. And I . . ." I hesitated, then finished, "I'm here."

"So you are," he said. "And I should return home. To see how things are."

I smiled. "Understood. I'll call you tomorrow if you don't call me first. Then you can tell me if you're still on board this crazy investigation or not."

He nodded and turned away to find his car. I went to mine and started back toward home.

It was only ten minutes from Highline to my place in West Seattle, but when I reached the turn that would put me irrevocably on track for the condo, I went the other way, heading up to Ballard and back to *Seawitch*.

When I got to the marina, I didn't go straight back to the boat, though I had thought I would. Instead I found myself walking up and down B dock as the last rays of our late-setting sun faded into purple and umber smears on the horizon. I wanted to confirm something I hadn't been able to get a good look at before, and with the evening closing in, my ghostly act would be less noticeable than it would have been earlier. C dock and *Pleiades* were just across the water. . . .

I sank into the Grey, the chilly mist and ghostlight washing up over me until the world was a dim shape beneath shadows of memory and bright lines of energy. I walked out to the end of the finger dock closest to the big blue sailboat and sat down in the slow-pressing cold at the edge of the blackness that was water. From here the power grid of the Grey was easy to see in all its burning color and searing light. *Pleiades* looked like the cold shadow of a boat surrounded like Sleeping Beauty's castle by a magical hedge of waving emerald and aqua vines spiked with fury red thorns that rose from the water in a tangled pillar. And over it all lay a coiling cloud of gray-green smoke. The same color and misty snakelike form I'd seen around John Reeve when he collapsed at his home and again lingering around his empty bed at the hospital. Was it attacking Jacque Knight or was it protecting her? I was pretty sure I didn't want to attract the attention of our murderous magic user, even if he or she was depleted after killing Reeve. I eased back from the Grey, feeling as if I were swimming upward through thickened silver steam as cold as Siberian graves. I broke free, back to normal, and found myself gasping for air, not realizing I'd been holding my breath.

Something splashed and nudged my foot where my toe overhung the edge of the dock. I glanced down, looking for the surface ripples left by a leaping fish, and caught the limpid brown stare of a furry, whiskered face. I froze, hoping not to frighten it off before I could see what the creature was, but there was no danger of that when the beast heaved itself up, throwing the bulk of its upper body onto the dock beside me.

It bared its fangs, like the gigantic version of Chaos panting in excitement. I started at the creature, all wet, dark fur and compact, muscular body. Much too big to be a harbor seal and too hairy to be a sea lion. An otter of tremendous size but with a head bizarrely large and misshapen. It pawed at me and rubbed its weird head on my calf, soaking my jeans leg instantly. I thought about reaching out to pet it, but another glimpse of those teeth changed my mind. Whatever this thing wanted, I wasn't going to tempt it to lose its temper by patting it on the head. Especially since that head was nearly the size of mine, to accommodate the finger-length incisors it flashed. It wriggled and the dying light flashed on its wet back.

"What do *you* want?" I tried.

"Har-per!" it barked. "Booooad!"

"Boat?" I asked. "Which boat?"

The noises it made didn't make any sense to me this time; they were hisses and grunts cut off by a harsh barking scream as it thrashed back into the water, apparently dragged or shocked by a sudden eruption of energy from *Pleiades* that started with a whistle and a rising cry of sound, then flashed out in shades of red and searing white like lightning bolts directed by an angry god. The otter creature dove and dodged through the water, breaching the surface and cutting back down and around, faster and more nimble than the slickest fish. A trail of phosphorescent bubbles twisted through the water in its wake, the strange sound of it making ripples on the surface until the creature disappeared from view, tangled up in a gleaming creeper of jade and sapphire energy that faded into the depths as the gigantic mustelid swam away. Then the twining energy flashed bright and lashed through the surface in a shout of strange harmonies, recoiling toward me. I threw myself down on the dock and with a shriek, a crackle, and a whir of angry wasps, the bright line of energy whipped through the space my head had occupied. Then it reeled, fading as if exhausted, back to *Pleiades*, sighing like a broken wire pulling through a hole in a steel wall—a wire drawn too taut and snapped by a sudden flick of a giant's wrist.

I converse with ghosts and work for vampires; one freakish, talking otter was barely a blip on my personal radar of the weird. That said, the short, swift violence of the moment startled me far more than having even a truncated and garbled conversation with a giant seagoing ferret. Not much fazes me anymore, but the sudden blink of magical conflict did leave me a little unsettled and mildly abraded on my palms and knees.

I sat up with care and peered sideways into the Grey, looking for a sign of what had happened to the otter creature, but the cold depths of the bay were obscured by a scree of visual noise—like the Grey version of a dust devil kicked up in the otter's wake. I turned my Grey-tuned sight toward the sailboat, but that, too, seemed hidden in a flurry of dimming energetic particles writhing in the water like clouds of agitated, dying krill. I muttered some curse words under my breath and backed away from both the Grey and the precarious, wet end of the dock. I considered walking over to *Pleiades* to investigate the apparent source of the magical flash, or down to *Seawitch* to see if I could get more out of the ghosts, but the fallen night, ringed around with sudden, creeping fog, made me think I'd rather return with Solis in the daylight than face the ghosts of *Seawitch* or, possibly worse, the resident of *Pleiades* alone.

Rattled, I walked back to my car, paged Quinton, and went home.

Quinton had arrived first. Even before I got inside I could sense his frustrated annoyance. He was muttering to himself and swiping at the dishes in the sink as if they had done him wrong. Every angry swish of the scrubber felt like a slap. We've had this strange emotional tie for about a year, but while the intensity had faded, the worst sensations apparently still bled through. Quinton was royally pissed and a touch scared and I felt every second-hand stab of it.

"Hey there," I said, putting down the bell and my bag with care so as not to squish the ferret, and coming over to kiss him on the cheek.

He flinched.

"What's wrong?" I asked.

"Nothing," he snapped, throwing down the scrubber.

I raised my eyebrows. "I don't think so."

He glared at me. Then he turned away with a jerk. "This hasn't been as easy as I'd thought it would be—the things I feel, the things I try to shut off in my own head. I didn't even realize I was this . . . angry about so many things until I started trying to turn it off."

I watched him and I hurt—my very own ache of sadness and pain for him, not just his upset turning inward and stabbing us both. "It hasn't been a problem at my end. I don't want you to shield me from your bad parts; I want you whole—bad things and all. You know I'm not any good at keeping my own horrors at bay. Is that the problem?" I was all too aware of Solis's worries about his family to discount such a risk to what counted as mine. "Is being privy to my feelings driving you crazy? I'm sorry if that's the case," I said. It was so much easier to apologize now than it had been a few years ago. I knew it wasn't a weakness to own up to causing distress or having made a mistake, or even to take a share of the blame whether you did something blameworthy or not.

"No. No, that's not it at all." He still sounded angry, but the fluctuating colors around him told me it was frustration as much as anything. His shoulders were stiff and the set of his head and a ghost pain in my jaw made me think he was clenching his teeth. He kept that posture for a moment, still turned away from me; then he took a deep breath, held it . . . and deflated, the orange sparks around him dying out to only sparking glimmers as his aura settled down. "I'm sorry. I'm overreacting and I'm making this worse. I'm not sure how it could get worse, but I'm pretty sure it will."

"No. You're still getting used to a strange situation. It took me a while to accept what I am and what that does to me. Although it's still hard for me to take what it does to you.

"And what could get worse?" I thought of his hints the night before. "Is it connected to Fern Laguire?" Laguire, his former boss at a government agency people don't like to talk about, had finally retired and given up her search for the computer geek that got away when she had been persuaded that Quinton—or, as she knew him, J. J. Purlis—was dead. Her obsessive focus and fury went well beyond the normal profile for government spooks as long as her retirement had been at stake, but it appeared she'd let it go once her financial security had been assured by the removal of the threat she had seen in Quinton's unresolved disappearance from her fold.

He stiffened and swore. "Oh yes. Much worse than Fern. I forgot I mentioned it."

"You thought I wouldn't remember what you said earlier? That your past is leaking back?"

"Not just the business past. It's not Fern this time. It's my dad."

"I thought you'd dealt with your dad. . . ."

"I thought I had. But I continue to be wrong every time I think I've got the upper hand at last. I saw him today. Or, rather, I heard from him. . . . That's not quite right. It was a meeting, but it wasn't a meeting. Telepresence, but I know he was actually nearby. I've seen him around Seattle recently."

I went to him and put my arms around him. "You're sure? Why would he be in Seattle?"

"Because he's figured out some of the same things I did—that there are people like . . . well, not like you, but like some of your clients. People like the late Edward Kammerling. And didn't he make hay out of that. . . ."

"Excuse me? I'm not following you."

He rubbed his hands over his face, then turned and put his arms around me. The embrace felt a little desperate and more in need of comfort than I had expected. I tightened my hug. "Try again," I whispered. "What did he want?"

"He's in charge of a new project. He calls it the Ghost Division and he thinks that's funny because it's the sort of project no one wants to admit exists. And it's looking for . . . paranormals."

"I see." Actually I wasn't sure I did. Various governments have looked into psychic phenomena and other paranormal topics in the past and in the end they all give up or the projects get canceled. It was hard to believe anyone was green-lighting a project like that again. But maybe enough time had elapsed for the collective memory of the government to fade. "How did your father manage to persuade anyone to go down that road again?"

"I have no idea. He's the proverbial silver-tongued devil to have talked his way not only out of his last debacle but back into a position of autonomous control. Hell, he's just a step from Satan, anyway. Why I'm surprised, I don't know. And I wouldn't care except that he *knows* I know . . . the right people. I don't think he knows about you—if he does, he's playing dumb or hasn't had time to threaten you yet—but he may make the connection once he starts finding the people he's looking for and notices how many have connections back to you."

"Is it just the bloodsucking fraternity he's after or . . . everyone?"

"Everyone, everything. I don't even know what he's planning to do once he finds them, except I know what the standard operating procedure is and . . . well, he's pretty much by the book on that front: Catch it, contain it, examine it. If it dies, get another one."

"This isn't good."

"No. Very not good. And he's putting a lot of pressure on me to do the street work. I don't want this. I never wanted to be on anyone's hook again and especially not his, but this is a nightmare."

I always think of Quinton as strong and balanced, so calm and logical, that it was odd finding this anger and confusion in him. I didn't know how we'd get past this, but we had to find a way. And we'd have to do it without becoming lunch for the sort of paranormal creatures that enjoy chaos, anger, and fear. I didn't need any of them hanging around. But I did need Quinton. "We'll find a way," I whispered.

"I wasn't intending to drag you into this. . . ."

"I know that. But I'm glad you're not keeping it from me. We can't stay ahead of him or anything else if we hide things from each other. I have your back. I'll always have your back."

He gazed into my face, making an effort to turn his emotional state. His eyes sparkled with a distant twinkle as the corners of his mouth fought upward. He rubbed his hands over my spine and shoulder blades. "I have yours, too. And it's very nice."

I chuckled at him—I refuse to think I giggle—and gave him a tiny peck of a kiss on the mouth. "You're wonderfully odd."

"Am I?"

"I think so. Let me try that again." I gave him a bigger kiss. "Hmm . . . yes, I definitely taste some odd there."

"How can you call me odd when I'm concerned for the welfare of the entire paranormal world?"

"Wouldn't you have to be odd to be concerned about that in the first place?"

"I would think that was your field of expertise."

"Are you calling me odd?"

"Strange, even."

"Wonderfully strange? Or just the garden variety of strange?"

He broke down and laughed, a flush of pink and gold sparks zipping around us like champagne bubbles. "Exquisitely, marvelously strange." He chuckled and kissed me again, spinning us both around like a top until we lurched to a stop against the drain board.

I glanced over his shoulder. I wished I hadn't.

"Umm . . . what's that?"

"What?"

"In the sink."

He blushed. "I burned a pot pie."

On a stove or a hot plate, Quinton can make a decent meal out of anything—or almost nothing. But where a microwave is concerned, he's jinxed. I suspect that nature compensates for genius in one field by making people stupid in a related one. Quinton, who plays with electrical and quantum theory and can build an alarm system from a greeting card, two rolls of wire, and a tube of toothpaste, can't use a microwave without setting his dinner—or the oven—on fire. I've been told Albert Einstein had difficulty tying his shoes.

"Oh, my," I muttered, trying not to break the fragile mood.

He sighed first, the brightness of the moment fading but not collapsing completely, I was glad to note. "I'll clean it up," he said, turning back toward the sink.

I held him back long enough to kiss him again and then left him to it while I went to write up some notes on my home computer.

Chaos the ferret was sitting on my chair, attempting to heave herself up onto the desk to wreak some havoc on my paperwork. I picked her up, giving her a quick scritch behind the ears, and deposited her on the floor, much to her ire. As I watched her dance in mustelid fury I remembered the way Solis had kissed his kids and his wife with casual ease, and for a moment I felt a pang of loss that I had never had that comfortable acceptance of place with a family. My family was Quinton, the ferret, and my annoying mother. I didn't dare bring a child into the world; I didn't know what might happen to it developing half in the Grey all the time. And if it emerged into the world healthy and human, what might happen to it then, surrounded by ghosts and monsters? It wouldn't be like Brian Danziger, who seemed to be a perfectly normal little boy except for the educational effects of growing up with a witch and a paranormal researcher for parents.

I sat down, feeling a little melancholy, and turned on the computer. I logged in to check my e-mail while the word processor started up.

There was still no message from Ben or Mara Danziger. I typed up my paltry notes for the insurance company, then sat and poked at a few Web sites, trying to find some information about dobhar-chú, but it's not easy to search for something you can't spell and don't have any keywords for. I swore under my breath and muttered, "Damn it, Mara, why don't you write back?"

I hadn't noticed Quinton walking up behind me and I jumped a bit when he said, "You wrote to Ben and Mara."

I replied a little defensively, "Yes, I did. I know you thought I shouldn't, but they are the experts . . . and I miss them. But what does it matter, since they didn't write back?" The thin glow of our good humor of minutes ago collapsed and I felt cold and dreadful.

"You're still treating them like resources, not friends."

"That's not fair. Or true. Even if you think it's selfish and unfair of me, this at least gives me an excuse to communicate with them. I have to say *something*. . . ."

Quinton humphed.

I was a little ashamed of myself, but that wasn't going to stop me asking them questions. "I suppose the issue is whether picking people's brains and asking favors is the *only* interaction I have with people. . . ."

"Not entirely, but it's a big one."

"Would it help if I wrote back about something *other* than the only thing we have in common?"

He sighed and rolled his eyes. "*That's* the problem: You assume that you have *nothing* else in common, nothing else *to* talk about. So you don't bother."

"I do! I just don't know what to say! What the hell else *should* I say? I don't have kids. I'm not married— well, not the same way they are. And we don't have any other activities or hobbies in common. Where does the conversation start?"

"Do you like Mara?"

"Of course I do! I like Ben, too."

"And Brian?"

I thought about it. "I don't know. He's a kid. I guess he's all right. For an alien."

Quinton laughed. "I will grant you that most children are like aliens to many of us who don't have any of our own. But he's a good kid."

"You know I *am* trying. I can fake friendly long enough to interview someone, but I don't know how to just . . . *be* friendly. It doesn't come easily to me, and if I'm faking it, I'm plainly not being a real friend."

"Sometimes you just have to fake it until it's true."

"I can try, but I'm a cold, prickly bitch. So I hear."

He sighed and I could feel him trying to exorcise the last of his own pique. "Not from me. I'm sorry. I shouldn't ride you about it. I was out of line the other night. I know that social butterfly is not in your repertoire."

I made an effort to turn the conversation to a lighter note and swiveled my chair around to face him. "Oh, come on. I don't have to learn the whole butterfly thing, do I?" I teased. "You have to wear toe shoes for that. I hate those."

"Your call, but you'll look silly in the wings and hiking boots."

"I think I'll just stop when I reach the chrysalis stage."

"What, all encapsulated away from the world and mutating?"

"Hey!" I said, directing a mock glare at him. "I could be a very dynamic chrysalis."

"You *are* a very dynamic chrysalis."

"Ooh, low blow, J.J."

He blinked at me. "Why do I find it disturbing when you call me that?"

I winced, mentally cursing myself in light of the conversation we'd just had. "I am sorry. I promise I won't do it again. It's just that your name—umm, names—came up with Solis. He doesn't know what to call you and I guess that got me wondering, too. I mean, I call you by a nickname, but we're . . . almost like an old married couple. It suddenly seemed strange."

"I prefer it. I don't really like being named after my dad. My grandfather was OK—he was the Jason. But being 'James,' or—worse—'Jimmy,' kind of curdles my blood. I'd rather be Mom's son than Dad Junior."

I nodded. "Yeah. I can see that."

And we both seemed to have decided to drop the subject. I went back to my computer and he went back to removing the burned pot pie from my dish. The ferret ignored us both and stole the keys from my bag, which I'd foolishly left on the floor, and we later spent twenty minutes looking for them. We found them behind a stack of ancient videotapes I'd forgotten I owned. Which led to laughing about old movies, then finding some online and watching them together. Which always leads to snuggling and snogging and then, of course, to various bed gymnastics and horizontal dancing. I had a feeling I'd be sleeping late. . . .

FOURTEEN

Morning comes too soon when it starts with excited phone calls from cops. Especially when I've been in bed only a few hours, and not asleep for most.

"What?" I mumbled at my phone.

"The lab has forwarded their report on the samples from *Seawitch*," Solis repeated. "Also, I can find no records for Jacque Knight nor for Shelly Knight."

"Mysteries on enigmas," I said, which made more sense when it started out of my mouth than by the time I'd finished. "What do the labs say?"

"I would like you to see the reports for yourself."

I grunted and dragged myself upright. "Where? When?"

"I am in my office. Where are you?"

"In bed. I went back to *Seawitch* last night and stayed up too late. Don't yell at me; I didn't go aboard. I just wanted to look at *Pleiades* from a different angle," I explained, staggering toward my closet with half-closed eyes. I hate morning on my best days and this wasn't starting out to be one of those. I had that persistently groggy and startled feeling that comes from being rudely forced awake in the midst of a dream.

Solis paused before he asked, "And what did you see?"

"Something creepy and very interesting—but you'll have to take my word for it, unless I can track down the otter."

"Otter?"

"I'll explain when I see you. Which won't be for an hour or you'll be embarrassed to be seen with me."

"I will meet you at your office in an hour." He hung up without further ado.

I turned my head and glanced at Quinton, who was still mummified in the bedding—the rat. "Why can't breakthroughs happen after coffee?" I asked his shape.

"Because they wouldn't seem as interesting if you were fully awake," the lump replied.

"You don't think this is interesting?"

"What? The only interesting thing I heard was the part about being in bed."

I threw a pillow at him. "Sex fiend."

"Ah! There's my girl, casting aspersions."

"Next time I'll cast a shoe."

He let out a muffled chuckle but didn't emerge from under the pillow. I was tempted to let the ferret sneak in and nibble on his toes, just for spite, but I restrained myself.

I managed to shower and get dressed with my eyelids still at half-mast, and get out of the condo looking more like a human than I felt. I stopped for coffee and still managed to get into my office before Solis knocked on the door. I hadn't checked my watch, so I don't know if he arrived late or if I was just moving faster than I thought. I suspected the former.

I let him in and returned to my chair behind the desk, picking up the coffee cup as I sat down. "So . . . what was in these reports?" I asked.

Solis handed me an envelope with a few pages in it and removed his coat while I read them. He sat down and waited for me to finish, which didn't take long since the report was pretty short.

"So . . . there was human blood, but also something from a nonhuman mammal—specific genetic tests on that haven't been completed yet so we don't know what animal we're looking for. But since we didn't find animal remains at the scene, whatever it was probably didn't die there. Still, it looked like a lot of blood. . . ."

"Less than life-threatening amounts if there was more than one donor."

I nodded, my eyes feeling loose and gritty in my skull even under the influence of coffee. "With an animal in the mix it's even less blood per . . . donor. And the rest of this . . . fish scales, mammal fur," I read, "and nematocysts from some variety of jellyfish, all of these species unknown." I looked up. "Does that mean they haven't yet determined the species or they can't identify it at all?"

"I believe they have been unable to identify them *yet,*" Solis replied.

"OK. And what's a nematocyst?"

"I also asked that. It is the part of a jellyfish that stings."

"So jellyfish stingers. But no jellyfish or remains of them. What sort of Frankenstein's otter are we dealing with here?" I wondered aloud.

"Again you mention otters. Why?"

I drank more coffee and hoped I wasn't just about to shoot the infant trust between us in the head. "I had a few interesting words with one last night at the marina."

Solis scowled. "Words? With a large aquatic mammal."

"It sounds crazy, but that's kind of what you get with me."

"I know."

"Let me start at the beginning rather than giving it to you in pieces. Remember I said I saw something at Reeve's house and again at the hospital?"

"This green mist you mentioned and the dog."

"No, we didn't see the dog for ourselves at the hospital. It was only hearsay. But the mist, yes. It's some kind of energetic residue that was present at the hospital, but it was a more active thing at Reeve's and I saw it wrapped around his chest like a snake that was constricting his ribs."

Solis frowned, but his expression was less skeptical than in the past. "I still don't understand what this is that you see."

"I can't be sure, as I said, but it's related to what I suspect your mother-in-law sees—and that's why she said what she did about me. She probably believes this is mystical in nature, that she's crazy or 'touched by God' because she can see it, and she's got preconceived notions about what sort of people have certain types of energy signatures. But I'm getting off the point. This paranormal energy is visible as light, or a reflection of light, under the right circumstances. In my case—and Maria del Carmen's and probably Ximena's, too—some energy that *you* can't see is still visible to me and I perceive it as having color and radiance, even substance in some cases. Sometimes it just looks like light—like neon or a laser show. Sometimes it looks more like colored smoke, steam, or light reflecting through clouds and mist. In this case what I saw was a sort of dirty green smoke with brighter pinpoints of red light—like sparks—inside it. That's what I saw wrapped around Reeve and squeezing his chest when he had his heart attack. The dog—or whatever it was—was at the other end of the smoke, but I don't know if it was generating the stuff or trying to tear it away, now that I think of it. Because it was on the receiving end last night. . . ."

I shook my head. "I'm getting ahead of myself again. Anyhow. I saw remnants of the same gray-green stuff around the bed where Reeve died. So my guess was the stuff came from the dog or—"

"Or whatever it was," Solis finished for me. He wasn't comfortable with the discussion and his energy corona was flickering through several colors and fluctuating in size and shape, surrounding him with spikes of color one moment, then pulling in and blazing in fast-flickering hues the next. I guessed it was an indication of a more intellectual distress than I'd seen in most people, but he was trying to take it in or the energy wouldn't have been

so manic. Positive progress, but it must have been ex-
hausting.

"Right. Or whatever it was. And I'll get to that in a
moment. At any rate, I thought I'd like to get another
look at *Pleiades* and see if any of the indications I saw
before were similar when observed longer and from a
better position, since I had no time to examine the boat
earlier. So I went back to the marina and I walked
around on B dock until I found a good position from
which to observe *Pleiades* and I took a look there—I
didn't go on board or even near *Seawitch*. And the same
sort of smoky energy I saw with Reeve was all around
the sailboat. It was thick and very active."

I watched him for a moment, gauging his reaction, before I went on. "While I was there I heard some more
splashing like we'd heard before. I thought it was just
fish, but then something touched my foot and I looked
down. A very large otter—and I mean a huge, mutant
sort of thing—was in the water, looking up at me. Then
it heaved itself partially onto the dock and it barked my
name."

"Are you quite sure?" he asked. "Many people imagine their pets talk to them, but they do not; it's only
sounds that the human mind interprets as words."

"In this case, I'm pretty sure. But the interesting thing
I want you to consider is this: The mammalian blood and
fur found on *Seawitch* may well have come from an
otter—the fur certainly looked like otter fur—and now
that we know it's possible, the lab should be able to confirm it or rule it out easily. Also a large—make that
huge—otter and a medium-sized dog aren't that far
apart in size or appearance if you're not really paying
attention and see it only in a moment of confusion. So
the creature that was reported at the hospital might have
been an unusually large otter. Or, more to the point, an
otterlike thing."

"A dobhar-chú, perhaps?"

"I hate to say yes, but yes. I tried to get some information on the name Reeve gave us, but since I wasn't sure how it was spelled, I had to try a description. Wasn't very helpful and all I got was a small number of Web pages about an Irish lake monster that killed a woman in the eighteenth century. None of them said anything about talking, and the only thing any of them agreed on was a certain phrase, 'The Father of All Otters,' and that the creatures are vicious and look like giant otters."

"But they are mythical."

Now I was a little annoyed with him. He said he wanted to understand this and he'd been opening up to it slowly during the past two days of the investigation, but now he was digging in his mental heels. He reminded me a bit too much of myself in the early days. How had Ben and Mara stood me? "Biologists used to think the fossa of Madagascar was mythical until they found one," I snapped. "And what about this investigation rules out the possibility of monsters? You saw ghosts! You *saw* them. You *heard* them. You saw me fade from the normal world and come back—twice. You even went with me into whatever occupies that engine room now and found *Valencia*'s bell, under the direction of ghosts! On the one hand you say you want to believe—for your wife's sake if not any other—and I'm endeavoring to help you. On the other you have a head as hard as a brick wall and start kicking up rough when *believing* is actually required. You can see there's something strange here—you admit it—so why are you balking at the idea of one more bizarre thing in this case?" I demanded.

I shut up quickly; I may have gone too far but I hoped not....

As he blinked at me, trying to form his reply, I kept my mouth shut over the one thing I wasn't going to reveal to him, at least not yet: The Guardian Beast had bullied me about finding "the lost" and had also given the name Valencia. If the ghosts in the engine room of *Seawitch* were actually the remnants of the people who died on board the steamer *Valencia*, then I had, indeed, found "the lost" when we found the bell in *Seawitch*'s bilge. Lost souls . . . What had the ghosts said? "Our soul"? The Beast hadn't pestered me since we'd found it, but it also hadn't let me off the hook, so there was something more to it than just finding the bell. . . .

I scrambled around on my desk and realized I didn't have the information I was looking for. "Solis, what's Paul Zantree's phone number? Did you get it?"

He shook himself. "What?"

"Paul Zantree—the pirate. Did you get his phone number?"

"I did."

"Give it to me. I need to ask him something while you make up your mind about your position on the paranormal."

He brought his notebook from the breast pocket of his suit and flipped it open, handing it to me at the appropriate page. I wrote the number on my desk pad and flipped the notebook closed before I returned it—I didn't want Solis to think I was making an excuse to snoop in his official notes.

I grabbed the phone and dialed Zantree. Apparently old pirates still get up before noon and he answered after only three rings. I went through the usual identification and greeting before I said, "Tell me about ships' bells."

"What do you want to know about them? Usually cast bronze in the old days, mostly spun brass now."

"Is there any superstition attached to them?"

"Oh, a few. Mostly portents of death or disaster when bells ring without human hands or if the bell is lost overboard."

"What's the significance of that—the bell going overboard?"

"Oh, well . . ." I could imagine him scrubbing at his hair as he thought about it. "The ship's bell is considered the ship's voice or soul, so if the ship loses its bell, obviously that's a bad thing and disaster will follow—sailors think disaster will follow on the heels of a lot of stuff, so they have a ton of superstitions about how to avoid bad luck. There's a bunch of odd little rituals you have to go through if you replace a ship's bell. You're not supposed to just swap one out without doing the right kind of magical hokey-pokey—you don't want to piss off that old bastard with the trident down there. If you can make the new one from the old one, that's best, but if that's not possible, you're supposed to smear a little of the captain's blood on the new bell before you mount it to tie the boat's soul back in place. These days we just make do with pouring some cheap cabernet on it and Poseidon doesn't seem to mind. Lemme think . . . the bell is the last thing installed before a new boat is christened. Ideally you want whatever you christen the boat with to splash on the bell, too, but you can get away with just dribbling some on it before you set sail. Motorboats and the like aren't quite as traditional, so there's a bunch of crazy stuff you never have to do with them, but the gist is the same. Poseidon's not that picky, as long as he gets his due *before* you go wandering around his domain. Because if he doesn't, he'll come take it. Or, y'know, so they say. . . ."

"I see. Thank you, Mr. Zantree," I added before hanging up.

I sat for a moment, thinking about what the Guardian Beast really wanted. . . .

Solis spoke up and jolted me out of my thoughts. "What did Mr. Zantree tell you?"

I shook myself and replied, "He said the ship's bell is considered to be its soul. So . . . we found a lost soul aboard *Seawitch*—more than one, it seems to me—but what we're supposed to do about it is still a mystery. Or what *I'm* supposed to do about it, since this sort of thing is not your venue."

"Why would it be yours?"

"It kind of goes along with seeing these things: I—" I stopped myself before I blurted out too much that would probably overwhelm Solis's shaky attempts to wrap his hard head around this stuff. "I just feel I should do something to set things right sometimes. If someone was murdered aboard *Seawitch*, that's your venue. But if someone's ghost is stuck there . . . that's mine. Especially if the ghosts are causing some other problem."

"What problem do you think they're causing? Are you thinking that they're the reason *Seawitch* disappeared?"

"I'm not sure which is the cause and which the effect. *Seawitch* had no history of problems until the last voyage. So . . . if the bell is the soul of *Valencia*, and if that's the cause of the problem or a symptom of it, the precipitating event of this whole case occurred during the last voyage of *Seawitch*. Not before."

"Did you not call the ritual in the lower cabin the precipitating event?"

"I'm not sure now. We don't know what spell was cast, just that it was complex, and I'm guessing it's how Les Carson knew his wife was dead before the cops called him. But I'm not sure if it's a cause or an effect or *where* it lies in the course of whatever paranormal action occurred that made the boat and its people disappear." I shook my head. "I keep coming back to those . . . bizarre log entries."

"If we assume your speculation to date is correct and the information from the log is sufficient to support it," Solis said, "then it would seem that the death of Odile Carson and the ritual in the lower cabin—in whichever order they occurred and however they are connected—set responses in action that sealed the boat's fate."

I started to break in but he waved me down. "As a policeman, whether I believe in the supernatural or not, it cannot be denied that someone aboard *Seawitch* did, and the ritual marks were either made by that person or made to control or frighten that person. And whether it worked or not, the result was the loss of the ship and all aboard. These events must have happened just before Fielding's last log entry, since he alludes to them. And loss of the ship must have occurred very soon afterward at or in the vicinity of the cove he mentioned. We need to find that cove."

"I think I said that last night."

"Yes, and I agreed then. I agree now and I . . . *think*— I do not yet believe—that something extraordinary did take place. And that it is connected to the ghosts aboard *Seawitch*."

I stared at him. I did not ask how he was sure or if his ability to see what he had was anything more than the occasional moments of clarity that hunch-playing cops get or just an effect visited on those who consort with people like me and his mother-in-law. I said only, "We'll need a boat. And a talk with the only available witnesses."

"What witnesses?"

"The ghosts of *Valencia*. If we take the bell, I think we'll find them in *Seawitch*'s engine room."

"Why must we take the bell there?"

"I don't know if they're bound to the bell or the boat at this point—the bell seems more logical, but I don't want to take any chances. Ghosts like this are unpredictable. If we re-create the conditions under which we found them last time, we have a better chance of finding them this time."

FIFTEEN

"**A**re not ghosts more active at night?" Solis asked as we walked down B dock once again toward *Sea- witch*, with the bell in its canvas bag swinging from my arms.

I smiled. "You sound nervous about this." We'd eaten lunch on the way to the marina and I was feeling human enough to have something at least approaching a sense of humor.

"I am not nervous. I'm afraid."

"Of ghosts?"

"For my reputation."

I shook my head, amused and remembering what a dreadful hardhead I'd been about the whole thing once, myself. "Trust me, no one will ever know except me and obviously I won't tell. Well, I might tell Quinton." Solis's aura flushed an odd bilious yellow. What was that? Embarrassment? Fear? I turned to look at him, serious and as calm as I could manage, considering we were on our way to interview ghosts, a process that doesn't always go well. "I'm teasing you. I won't say a word to anyone— including Q."

He looked relieved. "Thank you."

I wondered why he would care. Yet he did so I did, too. Enough to keep it to myself unless I *had* to do otherwise. I turned back and resumed walking and Solis fell in beside me. It was strange to be the lead on this. Yes, the insurance company was the big dog in this case, but I wasn't used to having a superior position to Solis's. Parallel or sneaking around him in one way or another, yes, but equal? No. And certainly not the lead dog. As we walked toward *Seawitch* I noted that the colors and activity near it were brighter and stronger, smoky coils and chains of sparks writhing around the vessel and occasionally reaching out toward the water and other boats, only to be snapped back. I didn't like it any better than I had the night before. *Pleiades* appeared dark and empty in my Grey-seeing eyes and I wondered where the energy, or its owner, had gone. Had *all* the local activity moved to *Seawitch*? I pointed at the boat. "There's a lot of energetic activity around *Seawitch* today. Last night *Pleiades* was the busy one—some kind of sentry feeler took a poke at the ... creature that came to talk to me and drove it off. Then it backlashed and almost hit me, but the charge was fading out and the activity was way down by the time I left."

"I can't detect such activity," he replied, peering at *Seawitch*.

"You'll have to take my word for it. Something's happening but I'm not sure what. And I don't know what happened to the creature that tried to talk to me, though that energy tendril seemed fairly dangerous as long as it was charged up."

"Do they, then, discharge?"

"Well, this one did. Magic has power limits. You have to have sources to draw on and channels to feed it through, and there's only so much energy a magic user or spell can pass before it shuts down or burns out, unless they have something to stabilize or store energy. Magic is not immune to the basic laws of physics." It felt strange to be repeating the things Quinton had explained to me long ago when I'd been the one who was thrashing around blind.

"But ... it's magic."

I cast him a sideways glance, trying to decide if he

were making fun of me or not, but his expression was only puzzled, not sly. "Energy is still just energy, even if it's paranormal," I said.

Maybe it was having thought of dogs or maybe it was coincidence, but as we walked onto the dock beside *Seawitch*, something was there. Something like a large dog.

Solis twitched and stopped moving. "What is . . . that?"

Dripping, it padded toward us with a strange, waddling walk on legs too short for its body. A thick tail touched the ground, leaving a wet, serpentine trail behind it.

"That, I think, is the Father of All Otters," I whispered. "But not the one I met last night . . ." I wondered if the previous one had survived whatever had happened with the magic that had emanated from *Pleiades*, but I didn't want to ask this one. I didn't know if it was as friendly as the other or was more like the woman-eating monster I'd read about the night before. I watched it warily as it approached. No magic seemed to trail from it or reach toward it, though, like many magical things, it had a glow to it that, in this case, appeared as a thin sheen of amethyst and blue, like oil on its pelt.

The creature was dark furred and probably weighed close to a hundred pounds. The guard hairs gathered into wet points along its body, shedding water as it moved toward us. Its thick whiskers bristled forward and I could hear it sniff the air, its lip curled up a little to reveal ivory teeth like the interlocking spikes of a bear trap.

Solis and I stood still and waited to see what the beast would do. It sat down by the steps to *Seawitch*'s deck. As we continued to stare at it, the beast lowered its upper body and lay on the cement dock, making a huffing sound as if it were mildly annoyed with us for making it wait. I glanced at Solis and he at me. We seemed to come to an agreement without actually saying anything and began forward again together, with caution.

The dobhar-chú—if it was one—jumped back to its

feet as we approached and watched us anxiously. Or I took it as anxiety because bright yellow-orange sparks seemed to leap from it and vanish into the air around it with a wet, sizzling sound. But it didn't move toward us. Perhaps it was afraid of scaring us off. . . . I'm not afraid of dogs, but this creature sent a chill up my spine as it stared at us with inscrutable dark eyes. We closed the gap to the steps slowly, watching the beast as we did.

At ten feet or so, the dobhar-chú took a single pace forward, blocking the stairs, and made a noise that sounded like "Who?"

I glanced at Solis, who wasn't quite as calm as he was trying to project. His gaze met mine in a jump that turned away again before it returned more steadily.

The creature barked again, "Who!"

I waved my hand at the policeman. "This is Rey Solis. He's a police detective. He's supposed to find out what happened on board—if there was a crime when the boat was . . . lost."

The dobhar-chú made a derisive laughing noise, then turned and dove into the water, vanishing in a flurry of bubbles.

"I guess that means you're cleared to come aboard."

"And if I was not?"

I shrugged. "I don't know. And we don't have to find out today."

We went aboard and even Solis shuddered at the touch of the boiling, sparking energy that engulfed the boat and reached inside with streamers of smoke like diseased fingers. All the way down to the engine room the air, thickened with magic and must, seemed to resist us and press into our noses with the odor of corruption beyond mere rot. I touched the engine-room door and hoped the ghosts hadn't dissipated.

Inside they rushed toward us, a swarm of darkness and whispers that swirled up from the bell hanging from my hands and seemed to burst from the floor. I saw Solis flinch from the feel of them, like trailing cobwebs. I let myself sink down a bit into the Grey, where they had more substance and appeared as a group of half-formed human shapes rather than an amorphous mass of shadow. They obviously had some freedom here that they didn't have away from *Seawitch*.

They were individuals but still connected in a writhing knot of blackness that muttered of misery and horrors beyond death. I reached out for one of them, certain that engaging one engaged them all. "You are the ghosts of *Valencia*," I started, knowing it's always better to present knowledge before you start asking for favors.

"Harper Blaine," they whispered, nodding collectively.

I was a little taken aback. It's rare for a ghost to know who I am—it's not as if they have the ectoplasmic Internet to look me up on. I dropped deeper into the Grey, to a level where the ghosts began to have more individual substance and the hull of the boat faded to mist. Strange shapes rose with the ghosts: twisted metal, glimmering rods that seemed to fall from the sky, broken steel spars and cables that whipped the air in an unseen gale. I touched one of the rods and felt icy wetness; the rods were streamers of rain and fog catching momentary lights in the storm. They had brought *Valencia*'s last moments with them. I shuddered and pulled back my hand, chilled.

"We came to you," the mass whisper said.

"How did you know of me . . . ?"

"The water hounds."

"The dobhar-chú? Those otterlike creatures?"

They sighed assent. I wanted to turn to Solis and see his reaction, but he was masked by the mist and memory the ghosts had brought with them. I wasn't touching him this time, so he wasn't anchored to my experience of the Grey. I hoped he could see or hear any of what was happening, but I wasn't sure—his ability to see the Grey seemed extremely limited outside my influence, and I felt lucky he was going on trust as much as he was.

"They have hidden us from the water folk and their

witch in the cove. We helped the otter man, who offended the siren, but can do no more. Now is the time we can flee."

"Flee? How did you get here? What are you fleeing?"

"The witch. The otter man brought us here. But we are tired and the gap in the world is narrow. Bring us forth from our enslavement!" The boat shook with their sudden roar. "Bring us forth!"

"How?" I demanded, but they'd spent their allotted energy and they seemed to implode, crushing into a dark point at the center of a ripple of outward-rolling force that shoved me out of the Grey and rammed me back against the nearest hard surface. A sharp pain snapped across my back as one of my ribs cracked against the sudden stop of falling. Breath rushed from my lungs and I doubled over, slumping forward as I rebounded from the hit.

The engine room was shadowed, lit only by the floor-scanning swing of Solis's pocket flashlight as he crossed to me. We hadn't even had time to turn on the lights. . . .

Solis started to stoop and help me up, but I waved him off, sipping at the air, trying to refill my lungs without hurting so badly that I spent all my new breath on crying. If I gave it a moment's thought, I'd notice I'd banged my knees and elbows a bit, too, but they didn't hold a candle to the spiking discomfort of my rib. I hoped it wasn't really broken, but that was probably a forlorn hope. I was ridiculously happy I had left my pistol in my coat pocket instead of putting it in the usual low-back holster, where it could have broken more than one of my ribs.

I managed to get enough breath to tell Solis I was OK, which was true enough since I wasn't dead, dying, or catastrophically broken this time. But, damn, it hurt!

"I saw you fall," Solis said. "I heard something, like someone muttering, but I could not understand all the words. What happened?"

"Ghosts are . . . really angry," I panted. "Blew their budget . . . to yell at me."

"Yell what?"

"Later," I said, waving off his question. I was too uncomfortable to linger and tell the tale that minute.

"How badly are you hurt?" he asked, putting out a hand for me to grab if I wanted the support.

I did and accepted the boost all the way back to my feet. I forced myself to stand straight in spite of the ache in my side and back. "A little dented. I think . . . I cracked a rib."

"Ah," he said. "Left side?"

"Yes," I hissed.

He picked up the bag full of bell and came around to my right to give me something to lean on if I wanted it. I did and we worked our way back to the door. Moving away, I realized I'd fallen against one of the engines. They were built as sturdily as the proverbial brick outhouse. No wonder I'd bent a part of myself.

"You need a hospital," Solis said, as we negotiated the doorway.

I snorted and regretted it. "They won't do anything but tell me to take painkillers and rest," I panted. "I can do that at home."

"First tell me what they said. The ghosts."

"You didn't hear it?" I asked, starting carefully up the steps, trying not to twist my body, move too fast, or bang into the close walls of the stair shaft. Every step jolted a bit and I clenched my teeth, drawing breath in hasty snorts through my nose. I regretted my height that gave me the sensation I was about to bash my skull on the low ceiling and thus compelled me to bend forward even when I knew I shouldn't.

"I heard something. I prefer to know what you heard before I claim I understood any of it."

I cleared the stairs and stepped out into the main salon. I drew a careful breath, straining it through my teeth as the rib protested the expansion of my left lung. Not caring how decayed the upholstery was, I sat down on the edge of the nearest chair and worked on catching a proper breath before I replied.

"Does this mean . . . you believe?" I tried to make it light, but it just came out thin.

Solis worked his lips between his teeth a moment before he nodded. "I do."

"All right, then. They do seem to be the ghosts from *Valencia*—they brought the set dressing with them." My words came out in little rushes between flinching and taking small, nibbling breaths. "Lots of them, but kind of one unit. Tied together, I'd say. They said the water hounds told them I could help them . . . and have protected them from seafolk—not sure what they mean there. The water hounds—or *one* of them—brought them here in the boat. They said 'otter man' for that one. They indicated . . . that time is relevant. They said, 'Now is the time.' And something about a narrow gap closing—I had the impression . . . they meant both time and space. They said they are fleeing from a witch in a cove and the otter man is involved. They also used the word 'siren.' I think they mean . . . like a mermaid? Not sure. They're very angry and scared. No, they said . . . they helped the one . . . who *offended* the siren. And now is the time to flee. From the seafolk's witch. That's right." It was harder to keep things straight in my head when I had to breathe so raggedly. Just sucking in air took more concentration than I had imagined it could and broke up my thoughts almost as much as the stabbing feeling from my rib broke up my breathing. "That sounds . . . like total gibberish, doesn't it?"

Solis was looking at me askance, his head tilted as if he were trying to see me in the Grey. His brows were quirked into uneven Vs and he appeared unnerved. "That is what I thought I heard."

"Good ears. Now, aspirin? Rib is killing me."

"Could this cove be the one the logs mentioned? Where Fielding was taking the boat?"

"That would be my guess."

"I would like to know where that cove is."

"Me, too. Whatever is going on with the ghosts . . . it's there."

"Was *Seawitch* hidden there all this time?"

"I don't know but I think we'll find the answers there, even if it wasn't. Get Zantree . . ."

"Do you suppose Mr. Zantree might be able to tell us where the cove is?"

"Maybe. I can look up the lat and long online . . . but what we really need is a navigator . . . someone who knows the waters and the lore—I don't know much about what creatures we're dealing with. . . . Zantree had a crush on Shelly. He has a stake in finding out what happened to her. He knows the area and he knows the legends. Stories . . ." I squeezed my eyes shut against a sudden welling of nausea tears brought on by talking so much against the prodding pain of my rib.

I could feel sweat break on my face and the world reeled a bit while I tried to swallow down the urge to puke or pass out. "Stories sometimes tell the truth," I muttered.

Solis dug into his coat pocket and offered me a tube that rattled with ibuprofen capsules.

"You have pockets like Quinton," I said, accepting the pills with a quivering hand.

"Thank you. I have great respect for Mr. Purlis's pockets."

"Quinton," I corrected without thinking, shaking capsules into my palm.

"Truly?"

"He prefers it." I swallowed the capsules dry and gagged a little, but held back my lunch.

Solis waited, frustrated at being unable to thump my back with my broken rib, until I stopped choking. "I don't understand the meaning."

I gasped a little and handed him the pill tube. "Nickname from his mother's maiden name."

Solis frowned.

"Quinn's son," I explained. It wasn't as if he couldn't look up J. J. Purlis and get that info for himself. If he hadn't already.

He mulled it for a moment and then he laughed. "I see."

Had I ever heard Solis laugh before? I wasn't sure. It was a sharp sound, short and rough, like something rarely used that had rusted and broken along the edges. I smiled back at him and stood up. A plume of mold and dust swelled into the air around me and I gave a sudden, violent sneeze.

Big mistake. The rib stabbed me and the world wavered and went black around the edges for a moment before the darkness closed in entirely. I could feel myself falling even as my sight blanked and then . . . nothing except the sudden fear of hitting my injured rib again before I lost consciousness.

SIXTEEN

Up and down. . . . Were we still on *Seawitch*? I felt woozy and my chest ached. So did my knees and my back and my butt. . . . "Who hit me?" I mumbled, feeling a stabbing sensation in my back and left side. Broken rib. Right.

"A ghost."

I made a noise like a whale in heat—or I think that's what the sound was like because it was loud and terrible and had a lot of moaning in it. I tried to sit up but someone pushed me back down before the busted rib could force the issue. It smelled like Quinton. I pried my eyes open and checked. Yup, Quinton.

He smiled at me from his position on the edge of my rear passenger seat.

"Where am I and how'd I get here?" I asked.

"Well . . . Solis paged me to your phone so I called you, and he answered and told me you were hurt but didn't want to go to the hospital. Since you were unconscious he figured you didn't have a say but I might, so I said I'd be right there and here I am."

"But . . ."

"Hang on. We're still at the marina, before you ask. We—that is, me and Solis and a guy named Paul Zantree—carried you to the Rover to take you to the hospital. But you woke up. It's only been a few minutes." He could see I wasn't convinced. "I was in the neighborhood," he concluded, throwing his hands up in a theatrical shrug.

"Liar," I muttered. His aura was jumping around and flashing a bit of yellow and orange, which was his lying-for-convenience color. I can't always tell with strangers, but I know Quinton well enough to recognize it with him. I also know cornering him in front of others will not bring answers. I nodded for the sake of onlookers—in this case Solis, who seemed a bit anxious, that rare emotion I'd never caught on him before this adventure began.

Quinton took that as a cue to help me sit up. Even with aid, my breath still caught on the pain in my chest and back as I moved. "I think you now hold the dubious distinction of being the only woman ever to pass out from sneezing," he said.

"Time in the Grey, being smacked by ghosts . . . may be . . . extenuating circumstances," I replied between gasps for breath.

"I blame the cracked rib."

"Yeah?"

"Yeah. A doctor would be a good idea."

"No insurance. . . ." They'd canceled my coverage after my last major hospitalization.

"We'll fake it."

"Don't you dare."

"It's an outpatient urgent-care thing—not even emergency. It'll be a couple of grand, max. We'll find a way to cover it. You can't finish up this case with a broken rib and no help."

"Can too."

"If you think I know the proper field dressing for a broken rib, guess again. Besides, a few painkillers would be a good idea. You can get some sleep and we'll tackle the rest of the problem in the morning."

I shook my head. "I know. Take me home. Do as I say. I'll be fine."

He glanced over his shoulder at Solis outside the truck. "She's being stubborn, like I said she would."

"I could arrest her for impeding an investigation," Solis suggested.

"Bullshit," I gasped. "My investigation."

He shrugged. "True. But we need to find the cove mentioned in the logs—and by the ghosts. I need Blaine with me. We have reason to believe time is short."

"I can find the cove," Quinton said, "if you have a latitude and longitude. And I can pilot a boat but I don't have one."

A new, shaggy head hove into view over Solis's shoulder. "We'll take mine. You guys don't know your way around the Sound—if you'll pardon my saying so—and this isn't a place to go messing around where you don't know the tides and currents. Kills people, and I think there's been plenty of that."

Solis turned and I could see that the owner of the shaggy head was Paul Zantree. "How's Ms. Blaine doing out here?"

"I'm fine," I lied.

He peered at me and snorted. "You'll manage but you're not going to like it. So, are you going to do the smart thing and take an old hand or be a bunch of damned fools? And did you talk to that girl before she took off?"

"Girl?" Solis asked.

"On *Pleiades*. The Knight girl. She took off late last night—no one saw her go, but the hatches were all open when her neighbors went by this morning and her stuff was all gone when they checked on her. The place is kind of wet and mildewed, too. The owners are going to be pissed when they get here. And, damn, she looked like Shelly, but Shelly would never have left a boat in a state like that. I knew you guys were interested in her, and now she's gone. So . . . did you talk to her? Did she know Shelly?"

That might explain the lack of magical energy around the boat this morning—and Zantree's sharper memory of Jacque and Shelly Knight now that no strange tendrils of olive-colored energy were ringing around his head. I wondered what had scared her off: me, the otters, or the ghosts.

"She claimed no relationship and refused to answer other questions," Solis replied.

I caught Solis's eye. "Running."

He nodded. If she was connected to Shelly Knight and the mystery of *Seawitch*—and there was every evidence that she was—we'd have to get to the cove as soon as possible. It seemed highly likely that she was heading back to the place the mystery had lain hidden for so long. She hadn't taken the sailboat, so she had some other way to get there. "We'll need a boat," I reminded him.

"I told you we'll take mine," Zantree repeated.

Solis assumed control of the conversation. "You have a date to go fishing with your grandchildren."

Zantree looked pugnacious. "They canceled. Can't make it out here. I got nothing to do and a lot of questions to answer about my old friends, so why not help you guys? You do need my help."

He wasn't crazy about taking a civilian, but I could see him make up his mind. "We do. But Ms. Blaine is injured."

"Well, get the woman to a sawbones, then! And where are we headed when you get back?"

"Somewhere near Haro Strait?"

"Up in the San Juans? That's a full day or more, depending on tide and weather."

"Can you still take us?"

"Not for six hours."

Solis and I frowned. Quinton made a face. "The tide's the wrong way around, isn't it?"

Zantree nodded. "Coming in. We'd be against it all the way up to Port Townsend. Barely make headway, even on an iron wind off twin Cummins. Better to go out with the next tide and hitch a ride on the outgoing swell. Take about the same time, give or take a couple of hours." He came closer and stuck his head in the truck to look at me.

"You go get a doctor to look at you and if he says you're seaworthy, get your gear and be back here by seven tonight. We'll cast off at eight when the tide turns. OK?" He was grinning like his pirate self again.

Solis frowned in concern. "I must come, too. And there will be some paperwork. Can you accommodate all three of us?" I guessed Quinton had already made it clear he was going to stick to me like gum on a sneaker sole.

Zantree looked at the lot of us and grinned wider. "Hell, we raised three boys on that boat. I got room for all of you. And I'm not afraid of a little paperwork. Bring it on, and bring your woolies, too—it's cold as a witch's tit out there at night. Oops! Pardon me, Ms. Blaine."

I shook it off. "Seven. See you then."

Zantree saluted and trotted off, whistling happily.

I glanced at the men and they returned blinking expressions, as if they'd been swept up in a twister and deposited again without harm in the middle of Oz. "We have a timetable," I reminded them.

"Right," Quinton said, crawling out of the rear and getting into the front seat of my Rover. He turned his head to Solis. "Back here at seven?"

"D dock," the sergeant corrected. "I shall see you *both* there."

We wasted some time at my doctor's office because Quinton insisted. Dr. Skelleher confirmed I had a cracked rib and asked if I wanted an X-ray. I said no, since we knew what it was and taking its picture just wasted time. He said no one tapes up ribs anymore, since it doesn't help and only leads to shallow breathing and pneumonia, which made me stick out a sarcastic tongue at Quinton. I should take it easy, the good doctor continued, have a large and potentially black-market lucrative pill—or smoke some tobacco alternative, as he put it—if the pain was too much to stand, and otherwise come back if I started spitting up blood or had more-than-

ordinary difficulty breathing. "Ordinary difficulty" made
me laugh, which hurt a lot, but I didn't mind too much.
Skelly is weird and probably skirting legality and the
medical board, but he gets the job done—and he'd referred me to Ben and Mara Danziger long ago, which
probably saved my sanity and my life. I gave Quinton the
"I told you so" face as we left and headed back to my
place to pack up some clothes and make sure the ferret
had enough food and water for a couple of days. We also
left a message with my neighbor, to cover any possibility
of the trip lasting longer. Then I took a nap while Quinton searched maps online for the latitude and longitude
I'd cribbed from *Seawitch*'s log book.

I woke to the sound of whispers; for once they didn't
come from ghosts but from living people in my kitchen.
It's a bad idea to discuss secrets in a kitchen or bathroom;
there's not much cushy furniture or swags of curtains to
absorb voices and the walls and floors are usually hard
and slick, reflecting sound like crazy for any sharp-eared
eavesdropper like me to hear without much effort. I lay
on my right side and listened for a minute, making no
effort yet to get up and see who was talking to Quinton
in such an urgent and demanding murmur. It was a voice
washed clean of accent and deliberately modulated so
the consonants were softened and the words mushy.

"... enough time to—" Quinton was objecting in a low
voice.

"You're done."

"Over my dead body."

"Again? Aren't you tired of that fiction yet?"

It didn't sound like my neighbor Rick or any of our
small number of mutual acquaintances. As I listened, I
thought it was a voice and tone deliberately hard to understand at a distance. With that and Quinton's recent
worries in mind, I had a good idea who it had to be, even
though I'd never seen or heard the man before that I
knew of. I eased out of the bed, breathing carefully and
quietly through my nose even when I had to bend and

twist, which sent a kick of pain through my chest and back. Maybe pneumonia wouldn't have been so bad. . . .

On my bare feet I padded carefully down the short hall to the living room, making sure I was between the kitchen and the condo's main door. I didn't want our guest to bolt until I was ready to let him. I needed a good look first.

The man had dark brown hair without a hint of red or blond or even gray in it. I could see only his back—a decidedly well-muscled back above an athlete's narrow hips under the dark rugby jersey and jeans he wore. Something in his stance suggested he was older than Quinton. He was a touch shorter, too, so my boyfriend saw me just fine over the man's head. Quinton tried not to change his expression, but his gaze had flickered to me and that gave us away. The other man spun around, remarkably lithe, and spat out a swearword as he launched himself at me.

Quinton lunged after him. "No!"

James Purlis hit me at a run. It was more of a glancing block as he passed, meant to shove me out of his way, and the blow fell on my right side, not my injured left, but I still buckled and fell from the sharp eruption of pain. He was out the door and gone before I could struggle back to my feet.

Quinton didn't chase after him. He stopped at the open door and gazed out for a moment, then returned to help me up.

"Nice guy, your dad," I said, coughing a bit on my ragged breath.

"I'm sorry," he said. Then he gave me a second take. "How did you know he was my dad?"

"He looks like you."

"He does not," Quinton shot back, indignant.

I tried not to laugh, because it hurt, but I sniggered a bit, anyway. "He does. And who else . . . would it be? Sneaking in. Shoving me. Threatening and belittling you. Had to be him."

Quinton was uncomfortable and he squirmed a bit under my gaze, keeping his eyes on the floor. "I don't look like him," he muttered as he helped me into a chair.

"I said *he* looks like *you*," I replied. "Same beard. Bet he's been letting his hair grow lately. Dyed it recently, too. Not the look I imagined for him."

"Oh? How'd you picture good old James the First?"

"Bigger. Conservative. Dramatically silver-haired. Mean."

"Well, that part's accurate. He's a prick."

"Really? He seemed like such a nice guy."

Quinton gave me a Bronx cheer. "Funny, Blaine."

"What did he want?"

"He wants me back in the business, like I told you, though he tried to play the family card to get me there. He says my mother is upset about my untimely demise."

"Awww, how sweet. Did he really think that was going to work?"

"No. The lies and manipulation were just a fun little side trip before he tries to use you for leverage against me next. Mom knows I'm fine. And I'm not going back."

"Does he know we're leaving town for a few days? Is that why he came?"

"He didn't *know*. He assumed based on operational protocol that I'd run soon. I guess he didn't want to lose me again. He doesn't know how fast I can move."

I gazed at him, breathing in shallow sips, and felt both our mixed-up feelings: fear and anger and desperation and hope all tangling and knotting between us. "Are you planning to keep going? To Canada? It's not far from the strait once we're up there. . . ." I didn't want him to say yes but I'd back him if he did.

He snorted half a laugh and returned an incredulous grin. "No! To hell with him."

The relief was like cool water pouring over me. "Good. Because . . . Chaos would be heartbroken . . . if you left."

He laughed out loud this time. Then he crouched next

to me and put his arms around my shoulders gingerly. "I'd miss her, too. But I'd miss you more."

"You are so predictable."

"Another reason why you love me."

I stifled a giggle and leaned my head onto his shoulder so I could kiss him. Then my phone started making noises and nipped that in the bud.

Quinton grabbed it off the kitchen table. "It's a quarter of seven. We have to get going."

I followed him into the hall to grab the bags and get my boots. "Did you make my phone do that?" I seem to manage the alarm properly only half the time and I didn't remember trying.

"Yeah. I know I should have asked first. . . ."

I rolled my eyes and kept my mouth shut.

SEVENTEEN

Puget Sound is a strange thing—almost an inland sea full of islands and deep saltwater crevasses carved by passing glaciers eons ago. In some places the depth at the bottom has never been mapped, only guessed at, and ships or planes that fall into those underwater canyons never come back—not even as broken bits of flotsam. Seattle lies on salt water so deep that it remains cold year round, yet it's sixty miles or more from the Pacific coast while still touching the same water that eventually passes Alaska and California. Some of its islands are rocky tumbles of cliffs rolled up from the depths, while others are mere piles of sand that sink away at high tide. Orcas cruise by the upper islands in spawning season, following schools of cold-water fish and tipping the occasional tourist into the water when they foolishly get too close. The islands in the south Sound are large and infrequent, while the north end, shared with Canada, is littered with dozens of broken drifts of land wound through with passages and labeled with names like Orcas Island, Deception Pass, and Desolation Sound. It's seductive in its beauty and sudden isolation but not a safe place for a stranger to go alone.

The voyage out from the marina and into the northern Puget Sound was almost too gorgeous to bear as we headed northwest from Seattle up what Zantree identified as Admiralty Inlet. The boat growled along, rocking up and down with a long, mild swell. The water sliding beneath us was a deep, cold blue that reflected the sun as it slowly dipped toward the summer horizon dead ahead of us, reddening and casting the sky in golds and pinks and finally into slumbering purples as we put in at Port Townsend for the night, just as the *Seawitch* had done in a last-minute change of plan, according to the log. We could have driven and taken the ferry across in a bit more than two hours but we'd soon realized we'd never find Fielding's cove without a boat and the experience of Paul Zantree. And the trip at sunset had been an unlooked-for delight in the midst of creeping horrors.

Once *Mambo Moon* was tied up at the dock, Zantree laid out a chart on the navigation table in the pilot-house that sat above the slightly sunken galley and below the rooftop flying bridge. He gave us a quick overview of where we were and where we were going, following the path the Seawitch must have taken as far as the last log entry where Fielding had stated he was heading for an unnamed cove.

"We're here at Port Townsend, so we're in the throat of the Strait of Juan de Fuca. North is Vancouver Island—that's where the city of Victoria is and if anyone has a mind to get off tomorrow, that's where I'll drop you. You can see how the southern point of Vancouver comes down like a tooth. That's Canadian water, but to the east of the big island it's U.S. waters for several more miles north and east to the British Columbia coast and the actual city of Vancouver. The U.S. portion of the northern Sound is small compared to the area as a whole but it's treacherous and the international border runs right about where we'll be heading, so there'll be eyes on us and plenty of traffic.

"We'll go north in the morning, heading for their last recorded destination: Roche Harbor." Zantree put his finger on the second-largest of the San Juan islands, lying to the extreme west of the group and pretty much due north of us. "That's up here on the northwestern tip of San Juan Island itself. The harbor's nicely protected but both approaches can be proper hull scrapers in a storm 'cause they're both narrow and the cliffs can channel the winds and raise their speed to a killing velocity. Not too likely in the summer, but it can be a wild ride in the winter. We'll have a clear run across San Juan de Fuca and up this big open area here, Haro Strait. See how it's running right up between the two big islands, at a right angle to Juan de Fuca? Normally I'd go for the southern passage to Roche from the bottom of Haro, but the position given in the log was on the north end, so for some reason they passed that route and we will, too. It'll take four to six hours to get in and moored up at Roche, depending on how rough the water is, since we'll have to go perpendicular to the current until we're up in Haro Strait, where the current should be in our favor if we time it right. Going to be some hobbyhorsing and crabbing—that is to say, the *Moon* may be rolling up and down the waves coming on the bow or stern and being pushed sideways by the current and wind. So far none of you are turning green around the gills, so I guess you're going to be OK unless it gets rough. We're not in the way of any predicted bad weather, but even so, fighting the motion of the boat in a crosscurrent or wind can tire you out when you're standing or walking around, so get to bed and get rested up. I know this is some serious business but this first part is going to be fun!" he added, his eyes twinkling with glee at the prospect of the cruise.

I slept too easily, fatigued by the constant jostling and bumping the big power boat had served up as it thrust its way through the water, the twin diesels rumbling below our feet until their silence seemed more deafening than their noise had been. Solis and I had both objected to the layover, but Quinton and Zantree had once again pleaded the tides and took us into port just ahead of the incoming turn. I didn't really understand it but I gave up arguing when I found my eyes closing in spite of myself. It was barely midnight and the tide was theoretically going out for another two hours—we had plenty of people to stand watch if we kept on—but I cared less and less as the gentle rocking of the boat at the dock put me to sleep.

We were up again by seven thirty, the smell of bacon and coffee teasing me awake. Quinton was out of bed already but I hadn't felt him leave, since we'd had to share a cabin with separate, narrow bunks, there being only one cabin that had a single large bunk, and that was the owner's. I gimped and staggered into fresh clothes, leaving my gun on the bunk, and made my way to the galley, where Zantree and Solis were making breakfast.

I lifted an interrogative eyebrow at the detective and he shrugged. "I cook on Saturdays. Ximena sleeps in. Except today."

"Who cooks on Sunday?"

"Mama Gomez. If she is of a mind to."

I supposed they ate out if she wasn't.

Quinton had apparently been out on deck and came in with a small portable radio in his hand and a huge smile on his face. He accepted a cup of coffee from Solis and sat down. "I forgot how much I loved boats."

"How's that?" Zantree asked. "How can you miss boats when you live in Puget Sound country?"

"I've . . . just been spending all my time in the city. It's been a long time since I was on a big boat like this, going somewhere." He looked at me. "That little one on the lake wasn't the same."

I was pretty sure part of his enjoyment came from having given his father the slip and I couldn't blame him for that. I smiled without a word and sipped my coffee—it was a bit bitter and very strong. Solis tried not to watch me drink it, but I caught his glance from the corner of his eye. I wanted to laugh at the idea of reserved Detective Sergeant Solis being nervous about his skills in the kitchen but I kept my amusement to myself.

"So, any ideas on where this mystery cove is yet?" I asked.

Quinton looked at Zantree, who took his time replying, swallowing a mouthful of pancakes before he spoke.
"I'm guessing up near Stuart Island, or maybe along the
north shore of San Juan. The position you guys provided
was a bit rough—right at the top of Haro Strait where the
border runs through between San Juan and a group of
smaller islands just north of it. The boat could have been
within a mile or so in any direction of the mark itself,
which is just west of Spieden Channel, at the north end of
San Juan Island. That's a good stretch, wide at each end,
and he could have been aiming to turn hard east of south
and fetch up at Henry or San Juan island, or go to Spieden or Stuart islands or even go on through the channel
toward Orcas. We'll have to give it a bit of thought once
we're up there. Take the weather and current into consideration to adjust the heading provided."

"Umm . . ." I started. "I'm not quite sure I follow you."

"The latitude and longitude info you have is not a
specific location, more of a general position and direction of travel—it wasn't seconds-precise. But the weather's similar at this time of year, so we should have similar
variables once we're in the area and that'll help us figure
where he was going, once we're there. The currents are
strong up here because the channels between the islands
are narrow and a lot of water has to move fast whenever
the tide changes, so even if we get the right location we
may have to play about or lay over to reach it. Can't tell
much from here just yet." He looked up at Quinton. "If
you want to check anything online, you'd better do it
quick—there won't be any Wi-Fi or cell service for most
of the trip. The big islands have antennas but signals
don't always reach ships on the water. The really small
islands have no coverage at all; one of the things I like
about coming up here is the world leaves you alone."

"I can certainly appreciate that," Quinton said.

"How long will it take to reach Roche Harbor?" Solis
asked.

"All morning and a bit more," Zantree replied. "Assuming we have no adverse winds and keep to favorable currents, we should make the dock at Roche by two o'clock or so. Motorboats aren't as susceptible to wind as sail, but we can still be pushed around and if we get caught in a tidal race or current, we could end up going the wrong way. Since it's good weather and a weekend, we'll have to keep an eye out for other vessels—especially tugs hauling barges. If you see the one, start looking for the other, because we don't want to pass between them; the tow cable sinks just below the water and if you cross over it, it'll shear your keel off like a knife through cheese. And where we're headed is right on the border, in the ferry route, so we'll need to be careful of those, too—ferries have the right-of-way and they can push a hell of a wake, even going slow. Boating is fun but it takes some vigilance to be safe. Like wearing those flotation vests every minute you're aboard. Everybody good with all that?"

We all nodded. I noticed that Quinton was the only one of us landlubbers with his vest on and felt a little abashed. Having drowned once, I had no desire to do it again.

"Good," Zantree said. "If you need anything ashore, take care of it now. We're off in twenty minutes if we mean to have the tide with us all the way."

The facilities on *Mambo Moon* were adequate, but I still felt a need to step off and stretch on a surface that moved a bit less before donning my vest and getting under way. I wasn't sick, but the constant small movement of the boat as it floated and bumped the dock made me respond without thinking, my body making continual tiny adjustments to stance and posture to keep my balance, and a lot of those little movements sent twinges of discomfort along my cracked rib. Stretching out wasn't going to be pleasant, but if I didn't try I'd be stiff and out of balance as well as in pain and that would make me an unreliable crew member—something I could not afford to be. I climbed off the boat and walked uncomfortably up the floating dock to the marina's office building, which sat firmly on dry land.

It was still early enough in the morning that there weren't crowds of people in the area and the boaters were mostly going about their own business on board their vessels, just as we had been. They left me alone and cast only a few cursory glances at the tall, skinny woman in jeans and sneakers, using the platform railing as an exercise bar. The leg stretches were all right, but the upper-body stuff was killer and my eyes were a little misty with tears of pain by the time I turned and started back to Zantree's boat. I was swiping the moisture from my eyes as I went, so I suppose I could be forgiven for not paying attention to the shadow that heaved itself out the water and onto the boat's swimming platform at the stern as I turned the last corner to *Mambo Moon*. The splash caught my attention, however, and I finished my turn with a wrench that made me hiss and stop short about twenty feet from the boarding steps.

For a moment I thought the creature on the low platform was a sea lion—it was as long as a man, dark brown, and oddly lumpy. I hurried forward, pressing my hand to my side to suppress the pain in my ribs, as I saw Solis pop out the aft door to see what had caused the boat to lurch to the rear. I came even with the thing just as Solis looked over the rail. Quinton stuck his head out of the door also and called out, "What is it? Are we clear to start the engines or not?"

"There is something on the . . . the rear platform," Solis called back, not quite sure what to call that part of the boat, I guessed.

The creature looked around, moving its large, misshapen head even as its body seemed to writhe and change shape. It spotted me and let out a moaning noise that sounded a lot like "Moooove!"

Quinton ran out and stared down, too. "Holy shit! What is that?"

The creature was still writhing and morphing from a

large furry lump to something vaguely human-shaped and kept its agonized gaze on me as I jumped from the dock to the swim platform, hoping I wouldn't miss or lose my balance and fall in the water. I made it and crouched down, wincing and gasping as I grabbed on to the handrail of a steel ladder attached to the rear of the boat.

I stared at the thing, seeing it tangled in flaring coils of red and gold energy twined with the thinnest threads of bilious green and dimming lavender. The creature shrugged and squirmed as if it were trying to shed its skin. "Harper . . . Blaine," it breathed, exhaling an odor of fish and brine laced with the burning tang of something magical.

"You're the one from the other night," I said. It didn't look quite like it had when it stuck its head out of the water next to *Seawitch* and barked my name, but the voice—such as it was—was the same and the mutant head and body were all too similar.

It nodded its too-big head as its jaw popped and crackled into a harder, more square line. I could see a white scar running over the right side of its face now. Similar white weals like the marks of a rope or whip showed through the brown fur on its body, gleaming with filaments of red and violet energy—perhaps the residue of whatever had reached out from *Pleiades* that night and nearly hit me, too.

"Up, up," the creature yipped, jerking its head toward the deck above us.

"Me or you?" I asked.

"Bofe. *Now!*" it barked. "Moooove!"

I've never been yelled at by a giant sea mammal before but I did as it said and scrambled up the ladder as best I could, wincing and yelping all the way.

Quinton turned back and yelled up to Zantree on the flying bridge, "Zantree! We need a landing winch!"

"What the hell for?" Zantree called back, "and what's riding on my boat?" He started down the steps from the flying bridge and stopped, looking down. "That's not a sea lion, is it? You shouldn't be messing with sea mammals!"

"Not a sea mammal—not like that, anyway. Just trust me! We have to get this up and get out of here."

"Jesus!" Zantree swore, getting an eyeful of the writhing thing on his swim platform. "I'll take your word—and keep it out of my props or there'll be fillet of freakfish all over the place. Flip up the davits and use that winch! Lines are under the transom rail in those lockers!" Then he turned and went back to the control console to flip various switches while the rest of us struggled on.

Quinton apparently knew exactly what Zantree's directions meant and in a few minutes had a pair of lines attached to pulleys on the heavy metal bracket things that were attached to the aft rail. In no time he had jumped down onto the swim platform and passed the lines around the wriggling creature and back up to the deck with him. He handed one free end to Solis and kept the other for himself. "Haul steadily when I say so. The motor will do most of the work, but we have to keep him from tipping or he'll fall off. Harper, get the lid off the fish hold. He'll have to go in there for now."

I turned and worked the top off the big built-in box where Zantree had sat the first time we'd met. It folded in the middle and was a little awkward for me alone with a cracked rib, but I got it flipped back and the fiberglass well exposed as Quinton and Solis pulled the creature up from the platform and wrestled it over the aft rail.

"OK, heave up!" Quinton snapped, and I fell back toward the doors, turning to keep an eye on what they were doing.

Solis and Quinton had the dripping, fur-covered thing in their arms and lifted it like a long sack full of rocks up and into the hold. The creature let out a yelp and the tangles around it flashed red. I winced in sympathy. The men pulled off the ropes and Quinton found a switch that began pumping seawater into the hold to keep the "catch" fresh. Solis stared at the thing with slightly too-wide eyes, crossed himself, and took half a step away before he forced a halt and held his ground. The creature looked back at him, visibly relaxing as the seawater crept up its body.

Quinton finished hauling in the lines and coiling them up. Then he called up to Zantree. "All clear to start engines! I'll go down and prepare to cast off." He turned to Solis and me, shaking his head. "Harper, you watch the monster. Solis, go up to the foredeck and handle the bow line as we cast off. I'll walk us off astern and jump aboard when we're free."

Solis was still a little stunned, but he nodded and went jerkily forward along the side deck. His belief threshold was taking a beating.

Quinton looked at me. "Stay here and find out what gives. He looks as freaked out as Solis."

"He?" I asked, momentarily confused.

Quinton pointed at the fish hold. "This guy here. I think he needs a little help."

I turned my attention back to our "catch" as my boyfriend scrambled off the boat and got busy with the mooring lines.

The creature in the fish hold was roughly man-shaped now, if that man was a bit short-limbed and otter-faced and covered in slick brown fur. There was a distinct manelike growth on its—his—head, and I got one glance that proved he was male and looked away quickly. He squirmed around and tucked his flippery legs under so he was semicrouching in the water of the hold.

"Sorry," he muttered. His voice was still rough and a bit hissy between teeth that seemed too pointy for a face that was stuck halfway between otter and man. His nose and jaw had pushed out to a more human angle, but the upper part was an odd shape, neither one nor the other. His eyes were huge and brown, but they had acquired a rim of white, as if the openings had grown to a more human size and ovalness. He still had bristly whiskers on his upper lip and the side of his . . . "snout" was a better word than "nose," really. I wasn't sure what he was—Quinton and I had discussed the physics problems of shape-shifters before and been wrong at least once, so . . . here again I wasn't sure what I was looking at except that it ought not to exist.

"You're . . . umm . . ." I started.

"Gary Fielding," he replied. "I'm sorry."

I sat down on the nearest chair with a yip of pain and surprise as *Mambo Moon* surged forward and away from the dock.

"I guessed you were still alive," I gasped back. "But this wasn't what I imagined. . . ."

"Me, either," he sighed, curling tighter in the fish hold. "Could you turn the water off? It's getting a little high."

I found the switch and pushed it to Off. "I am having some trouble with this," I said.

"I hoped you would be able to understand. . . ."

"No, no . . . that's not what I mean. I'm a little confused. What are you and how did you come looking for me? And what happened with *Seawitch*? *Is* happening . . . ?"

"That's a long story."

"Start talking. It'll be six hours before we reach Roche Harbor."

EIGHTEEN

As Fielding talked, I peered at him through the Grey. A sort of shadow of his otter self hung around him and I wondered fleetingly how he managed the mass problem. For an otter he'd been enormous; as a man he was a bit on the small side but still heftier than the otter. Well, mostly a man and partially submerged in seawater at that. Quinton and Solis had made their way back to me, but Zantree was still up top, steering the boat out of Port Townsend and striking across the Strait of Juan de Fuca for the lower end of the San Juan Islands.

"Why the water?" I blurted.

He stopped and looked down at himself, half-immersed in seawater. "It's easier to stay in one form when I don't have to concentrate as hard. I can't make the full transition to a man or to an otter—I'm always part the other. This is about the right amount of water to hold this form steady without sweating it too much. More and I have to fight to stay otterlike. Less and I can't stay human enough."

"That sounds backward," I said.

"That's because it's a curse and that's sort of how they work: You turn the nature of something on itself."

"Not always, in my experience."

"Well, maybe not. The dobhar-chú aren't normally magicians so I had to guess based on what the mermaids were doing. They seem to work with elemental magic—according to Father Otter—and then they twist or reverse some aspect of nature. Or that's what makes sense to me after keeping an eye on them from hiding for twenty-seven years."

I waved my hands in the air as if clearing it of hanging, obfuscating words. "Let's get to that later. First, what are you?"

"Umm . . . kind of messed up. See, that's the problem: I'm not really one thing or the other. Part water hound, part human, one hundred percent screwed."

"So . . . the dobhar-chú do exist and they are involved."

He nodded. "I guess you could call them my extended family. They took me in when this happened and they've been trying to help me and the ghosts ever since. But not because they're nice guys or anything like that—you gotta understand that they are so far from human that I'm a freak to them. But I'm family and I'm the enemy of their enemy. So . . . they're on my side."

"Family. So . . . you were born . . . this way?"

"Not *this* way, no. But you could say I was born to have this problem because I'm half dobhar and half . . . normal. But I didn't know about the water hound part until things went cockeyed on *Seawitch*. Well, I *knew* but . . . I didn't really . . . *believe* it."

He glanced around at the men and then back to me. I looked, too, then brought my gaze back to Fielding. He could see we weren't quite following him. "Let me start at the beginning," he said. "When I was a young idiot I used to joke that I was kissed by a Columbia River mermaid. But, see, that's not really a joke. One summer when I was a kid, my mom and me and a bunch of the neighbor kids and their moms went out to Fort Stevens. Our parents really didn't want to take us because the ocean's pretty dangerous and cold in that zone, but it was a big deal for us kids to go to the *ocean* beach. I mean, we all grew up on the river and that was no big deal to us, but to go out in the *salt water*—that was super-cool. My mom couldn't talk me into swimming in the jetty lagoon on the river side—I *had* to swim in the ocean. She couldn't really say no, though I didn't understand why at the time. So we went over to the ocean side of the park. It was a weekday, so not terribly crowded, and of course we all wanted to see the wreck of the *Peter Iredale*, like everyone does, and we walked back up toward Clatsop Spit afterward and staked out a place near the parking lot that was close enough to meet between the swimming area on the lagoon side and the beach on the ocean side. Most of the kids thought the seawater was too cold and they just splashed around in the surf and made a lot of noise but I swam out pretty far. Until I got stuffed by a wave.

"Or I thought I had been, because I'm paddling along fine—I've always been a really good swimmer—and suddenly I'm underwater and I'm scared and then there's this strange woman towing me away. And my mom came out into the water—which she *never* did—and took me away from the woman. I should say, really, they fought for me. Mom won, of course, but the other woman kissed me on the forehead before she let me go and then she swam away very fast. My mother was seriously cranked off about it. She told me to stay away from women like that. Now, see, what I didn't understand, 'cause I was just a kid, was that she wasn't saying I should avoid loose women or ladies who swam topless or something like that, but that I should avoid females of that *species*. The woman was a mermaid, which seemed kind of obvious at the time because she had a tail and gills and even webs between her fingers, but I started erasing that part of the story from my memory because my mom didn't like it and because it sounds babyish to say you saw a mermaid when everyone you know says there's no such thing. And when I got older it was like a joke and I used it to charm people into buying me drinks or hiring me or . . . Well, I used it on a lot of women in bars and at parties. . . ."

At the moment, he didn't look like he could charm anyone, being furry and misshapen and possessing a mouthful of teeth intended for cracking crab legs and ripping open fish the size of a man's leg. But I could see, by concentrating hard on the Grey, two overlapping, massy shadows attached to him: a phantom otter, sleek and dark-furred, with a streak of white down its spine and a crossing streak on its shoulders; and a ghost form of his human self that was dark-skinned, slim, and fit, sporting a thick, curly mane of dark hair that fell over large brown eyes. I suppose some people have a better imagination than I do, since if I hadn't seen it, I wouldn't have conjured such a lady-killer image on my own.

Solis bent forward into my line of sight. I'd almost forgotten the men were there. He scowled at Fielding. "So, you played the lothario." I wondered whether his contempt came from the thought of his own daughters in a few years of if there was some other source of his anger.

Fielding scrunched up his furry brow, puzzled for a moment. "That's from Shakespeare, right? Was he, like . . . Romeo's friend?"

"No," Quinton said. "It's from an eighteenth-century play about a woman who is seduced by a selfish jerk who takes off after he ruins her marriage. Lothario was the jerk."

We all stared at him.

"Hey. I had to read it for a college lit class."

Fielding glanced away. "Oh. Yeah. Well, I wasn't *that* bad. . . ."

Solis continued to glower at him. "In your final log entry, you wrote that you did not stop a rape, that you were equally guilty. . . ." Ah, so maybe it was being a cop as much as a father of daughters stirring up his anger.

Fielding swallowed hard. "Oh . . . yeah. Umm . . . I have had *so* much time to repent that and think about it and try to remember exactly how it went down and why I . . . did what I did."

I turned and glared at Solis. "Can we get back to the original question and catch up to pointing fingers in a few minutes, Rey?"

"'Rey'?" Quinton muttered under his breath.

It seemed better to use his first name and remind the lot of them that once the freaky stuff was in our faces, we were no longer operating on normal protocols and it was now my show. I turned the quelling glance on Quinton next, raising an eyebrow, challenging him to make something of it. He settled down with a sheepish grin. Solis was still fuming but he nodded curtly and sat back.

"So . . . you became a dobhar-chú because you were kissed by a mermaid?" I asked.

"Ah. No. This is the really weird bit."

Quinton smothered a snort.

"Just go on," I prompted.

"See, my mother— No. Let me say this first: The dobhar-chú aren't usually shape-shifters, any more than they're magic users. It takes a special circumstance to be born with two forms. My mom was one of those rare few. Usually the dobhar-chú are not a friendly or social bunch—kind of vicious and unpleasant, actually—but when they moved to North America from Ireland, some things changed and they had to get smarter to avoid being killed for fur. So this aberration started—this is what my mom told me before she took off."

"She left you?"

Fielding nodded. "She left me and my dad a couple of years after the swimming incident and disappeared. Eventually I assumed she went back to her clan, but when I asked the Father Otter here, he had never heard of her."

I stopped him with a waving hand. "Who or what is the Father Otter?"

He hmmed a bit before answering. "Sort of the local clan chief of the dobhar-chú. I'll get to that in a second. Oh, and incidentally, that's how I heard about you; the water hounds are good at gathering information, even though they rarely use it for themselves. They're sort of the information brokers of the local marine paranormal economy, so to speak. 'Cause who can resist a cute otter that's hanging out near their boat or begging for attention at the marina? That's mostly how they stay out of other monsters' sights—by being useful and cute. But they didn't have any information about my mom, so I don't know what happened to her. And I probably never will." He shook his head as if rejecting that thought. "*Anyway*, Mom said the dobhar-chú's origins are that the seventh pup of a seventh pup of a regular otter is a dobhar-chú and then the seventh pup of a seventh pup of a dobhar-chú is a shape-shifter. They're sort of dobhar-chú royalty. And that was Mom. I was her only ... umm ... 'pup,' as far as I know, but I seemed to be just a human. Or I thought so. But, see, the reason Mom wanted me to stay away from mermaids is that merfolk and water hounds are deadly enemies. The mermaid who took me that day at the beach wasn't trying to save me; she was going to drown me or eat me, depending on how mad Mom was at me when she told me the story again."

Seventh pup of a seventh pup rang true—I'd seen that on one of the Web sites I'd found about dobhar-chú, along with references to their viciousness—but I'd never seen any mention of shape-shifting or magic or their presence in North America. Still, I wasn't going to stop the flow of his story now, even if I had doubts about its purity, so I just looked encouraging and leaned on the Grey a touch to give it a little unnatural weight.

Gary went along like a pebble rolling downhill. "But anyhow, I guess that kiss did something—marked me or something. When I met Shelly—um, Shelly Knight—I noticed she always stared at me real intensely and it made me feel strange. I thought it was because she wanted me. That tells you what a conceited ass I was back then, but Shelly was so ... sexy and so ... I don't know. She was special. If we asked her to work on the boat she always said yes, and she'd watch me but she always kept her distance. I thought she was playing hard to get. But that wasn't it."

He was about to continue when Zantree slid down the ladder from the flying bridge and joined us around the fish hold. At first he just glanced around, as if trying to see which one of us had been speaking, but when his eyes passed over Fielding he did a double take and stared. "What in the name of hell are you?"

Fielding seemed to shrink and tried to slide lower in the water, but as soon as he did the water boiled and his skin turned paler and furless. He began to gasp and choke on the water that was suddenly splashing and washing over his face as blood seeped from his mutating nose and mouth.

Solis and I were the first to grab him and haul his upper body above the waterline. He coughed and spat up water for a minute or so, writhing around as his face and body reverted to a half-human, brown-furred state.

Zantree bumped backward into the cabin doors as he twitched back from the sight of Fielding in transition. "Dear God," he muttered. "I never . . . never thought I'd see such a thing." He glanced around with jerky movements. "Do you—you all know about this?"

Quinton caught his gaze calmly. "No. It was a surprise to us as well."

"Well . . . what is that . . . thing?"

"That's . . . Gary Fielding. Did you know him about . . . I guess it's twenty-five or thirty years ago?"

Zantree's eyes were as wide open as Sunday church doors. "Gary . . . ? What happened to him . . . ? And where's he been all this time?"

"That's what we're trying to figure out. He was what was hanging on to the swim step when we cast off at Port Townsend."

"Jesus! I thought it was a sea lion, even when you told me it wasn't. Sure wasn't expecting that," he added, giving Fielding a hard glare.

By this time Fielding had stabilized and was breathing

easier. The blood had stopped flowing from his mouth and nose and now left a red swirl in the water. Salt-crusted tears dribbled from his eyes, leaving a track on the fur of his face. The white scars on his face and body sparkled for a moment with tiny violet stars as the haze around him flashed a bright emerald green that vanished as quickly as it had come. The sight startled me a little and I glanced up from Fielding in a momentary panic. "What was that?"

"What was what?" Fielding responded, glancing around.

"You . . . sparkled."

He coughed up a laugh. "Like an ice skater in sequins?"

I scowled at him. "No, like a spell."

"Maybe because I'm under one?" he replied in a snotty tone.

"Don't start with me, Otter Boy," I snapped back. "You wanted my help and I'm giving it, but I don't have to. We can toss you overboard and go home anytime." Not that I really could with the Guardian Beast lurking around, but that was no one's business but mine.

He cowered a little but not enough to have another fit of uncontrolled shape-shifting.

Solis, looking uncomfortable, broke the tension by asking, "Who is piloting the boat?"

Zantree shook himself and looked away from Fielding. "She's on autopilot. This stretch is clear and empty for a few miles, so I thought I'd grab some gloves. The breeze is chilly up there and it's kicking on my arthritis. Quinton, you want to go up for a minute until I get back?"

Quinton nodded and scrambled up the ladder to the flying bridge as Zantree gave one more scowling shake of his head at Fielding before nipping into the cabin.

Fielding glanced around as if reestablishing in his mind just where he was and that his condition was not some kind of horrible dream. "Was that really Paul

Zantree? He's gotten so old. . . ." Fielding whispered, hissing a bit between his reemerging fangs.

"You'd be only a little younger if you were in your proper form," I said.

"I don't know. . . . Some of us freaks live a long, long time," he replied, looking me in the eye.

I returned a narrow glare and was about to say something cutting when Zantree stepped back out from the cabin, tugging on a pair of lightweight gloves. He took one more hard stare at Fielding and frowned. "We all thought you were dead, Gary. Why'd you let us think that? Did you do it? Did you pirate the 'Witch and hide her all this time? Did you kill the lot of them? Did you kill Shelly?"

"No! I didn't do any of those things! I just— Things went bad. I didn't *do* anything but try to save us . . . but I didn't stop anything, either." He hung his head, but I wasn't sure if it was contrition or an attempt to hide his uncanny lack of expression. "I just ended up stuck in the same place with that damned boat all this time. The way back opens up only every twenty-seven years and it doesn't stay open long. We're almost out of time as it is."

"Time for what?" Zantree demanded. "Are any of the others . . . like you? Did they survive? Are we going to save them or is this just about you—like it always was?"

Fielding cringed, salt tears coming a little faster down his face. "No. They're all dead."

Zantree's face crumpled a little and he looked appalled. "Maybe you should be, too." Then he turned and, without another word, climbed back up the ladder to the flying bridge.

His voice floated back down in a minute, but the wind stole the meaning of the words and they were just sounds snatched from the breeze. Then Quinton returned to our little party on the aft deck.

"He says he wants to hear everything," Quinton said.

"Do you think he'll understand it all?" I asked, thinking of how unbearable some stories from the Grey were.

Quinton looked grim. "Yeah. He's a tough old bird. And he'll keelhaul the lot of us if we don't. So he said." But his glance was directed at Fielding.

"I didn't mean to hurt anyone," Fielding whimpered.

"Yeah, all those dead people were just a mistake. That's what everyone claims," Quinton replied, a storm of little red sparks shooting through his aura. He reached over and flipped a switch on the wall beside the cabin doors on what looked like some kind of intercom system.

An uncomfortable silence fell, scored by the grumbling of the engines below us and the susurrus of waves.

I shook off the feeling first. I didn't like Fielding, but I had other fish—or otters—to fry. "All right. Fielding, you said Shelly was watching you, but not because she wanted to join the bedroom Olympics. . . ."

"Yeah. She watched me and I mistook it for . . . well, something it wasn't. I guess she was really keeping an eye on me, at least in the beginning. I don't know what she was doing at the marina in the first place—it's not like mermaids go and hang out with humans much unless they're trying to kill them."

A snort came from the intercom and I put up my hand to stop his tale. "Wait. Shelly Knight was a mermaid?"

"Oh, Shelly is not just *a* mermaid. She's *the* Mer Maid. And aside from me, she's the only one of us who survived. She's the *daughter* of the sea witch and she's supposed to be a virgin or she won't become the sea witch herself when Mommy kicks the bucket. Which has got to be a load of crap because there is no *way* Shelly hadn't been spreading her . . . tail for someone—"

Solis and Quinton both made low noises in their throats that collectively sounded a lot like a growl.

Fielding was startled and recoiled from them. "Hey! I'm just saying!"

Solis gave him a black glare. "Don't."

Fielding glared back, then looked away with a funny coughing sound. "Well. Yeah. All right."

"So," I summarized, "she's a mermaid, daughter of a sea witch, and you're the child of a royal dobhar-chú. Which makes you . . . what?"

"Ironically, it makes me almost human, but not quite. I guess it's where I got my skill on the water, but the problem was I didn't understand what my mother was telling me that day on the beach or the warnings she was giving then or so many times before she left us. With Shelly and *Seawitch*, I got into a situation I didn't know was dangerous. I didn't know Shelly was some kind of mermaid and therefore my enemy from birth. And . . . all right, I was a jerk. On that last trip with *Seawitch* things started out freaky and got worse and worse.

"There was kind of an uncomfortable feeling among the passengers right from the first, like there was something going on they were all trying not to talk about. And then Les got into a fight with Shelly. He kept saying she was just teasing him and I thought it was a sex thing, but it wasn't that and everyone was kind of out of sorts anyhow because the girls wanted to get up to Vancouver and go shopping, but Cas made us change course to go to Port Townsend for a halibut."

"A halibut?"

"Yeah. Pacific halibut season is really short. That year it ran long—they extended it by two days—and Cas wanted his damned fish. You're only allowed one and he hadn't got his. He took his fishing more seriously than most people realized. I mean he *really* wanted that fish— standing-in-the-water-in-the-dark-with-a-spear kind of want. 'Cause that's what the crazy SOB did. I changed course from the inside of the Sound and brought us out to Port Townsend—and I gotta tell you, it was a hard swim catching up to you guys up here. A lot harder than boating it was."

I stifled a snide comment and just told him to go on with his tale.

"Anyhow, anyhow, so we tie up at Townsend and I take him out in the skiff to the shallows so he can try to swim around with a snorkel and spear one—you're only allowed to use a spear or a longline to get them—"

"A spear?" Solis asked, frowning.

"Halibut are stone stupid, so you have to even the odds in their favor. That's why it's called sportfishing. Anyhow. Nobody else wanted to swim around looking for halibut, so they stayed on board with Shelly and played cards or something. Whatever they did, Les was mad at Shelly when we got back and the girls were kind of . . . freaked out about something and no one was talking to anyone, so dinner was a real cozy disaster. Afterward Les comes up to me, looking all weirded out, and asks me to make that note in the log about his being on board the whole trip—which he was. I had no idea why he wanted me to put that in, but he did and I did. And then Cas and I went out to look for more halibut—night fishing with a spear. Totally wacko.

"We finally got that damned fish about four in the morning. And we should have cleaned it, but I was sick and tired of it, so I just dumped it in the icebox and we went to bed. So in the morning Cas is still obsessing about his fish and he wants us under way on the morning tide so we don't—as he put it—waste the whole day, so I get up and get the boat moving on five hours of sleep, and we're in the middle of the Strait of Juan de Fuca when we get a call at, like, ten, from the Seattle PD via the radio telephone service, saying that Odile Carson is dead. Les flips out. Not because she was dead but because of the way she died and the timing. He says Shelly told him she was dead the night before and he goes nuts. We all did. It was like there was something in the air. Or maybe it was the food . . ." he added, suddenly thoughtful—which looks very strange on a face that's only half-human and covered in wet brown fur. "Shelly was the cook . . . maybe she fed us something that made us even crazier than we were. . . ."

"Don't speculate on what you can't know," Solis warned.

"All right, all right!" Fielding snapped back, his interlocking fangs clashing together in a disturbingly violent bite.

The longer he spoke, the more of the mist of unpleasant green began to draw around him. I didn't like it and I tried to call his attention to it again, but he shook me off and carried on with the story. I tried looking around but I couldn't find a source for the color—it seemed to rest with Fielding himself and I thought its unpleasant shade might have been a manifestation of the dysfunction in his shape-shifting ability. Of course, some people's auras turn sickly colors when they lie, too. . . .

"Les Carson lost his nut and we all went a little crazy with him. It was like Odile died and he had to find someone else to be with immediately or something was going to happen to him. Like he was going to explode or fall apart or something. So the guests were all . . . frisky with each other, but that left Cas out because *he* is still obsessing about his damned fish and I'm up in the bridge, trying to get us across the strait. And that is when Cas finishes up with the halibut and decides it's a good idea to go down below and see if Shelly wants to 'join the action' and to find out if I want to . . . come along."

He made that odd coughing sound and turned his gaze away from us again—his way of showing shame, I supposed, and I felt a bit better about him. But only a bit.

Fielding continued, raising his gaze only as the story swept him up again. "I put the boat on autopilot and followed him down to her cabin in the forepeak. He got a little . . . pushy. . . . She was furious. Her eyes actually sent out sparks! No, really! She grabbed Cas by the hand and she cut his arm open with this little bone knife she had on her bunk, and he started screaming while she shook him so his arm whipped around and the blood made a circle on the floor and the bunk. She was saying crazy things and then she grabbed me, too, and cut my hand and dragged me around the cabin. I couldn't believe she was so strong! She pulled me around, saying things I didn't understand, but they made me feel sick and hot, and she was acting crazy. It felt like . . . like I was burning up inside. Then she screamed something, shoved us both out of her cabin, and came after us with her knife. I pushed Cas up the stairs and I was right behind him. Cas got up to the saloon and out on deck, but then he fell down and he was bleeding and the others weren't there to help us—they were down below, humping like rabbits.

"Shelly must have grabbed the speargun off the table in the saloon and come out after us when I went out after Cas. She followed us and she threw some things into the water. Then she turned on us. She shot Cas! I thought she was going to kill us both but she only spat in my face—it burned like acid—and then she said, and I remember this, 'Half on the land and half in the sea, and never together your halves shall be. Dead by water if on land, burned alive by salt sea's sand. Drown in air and burn by sea, reveal your nature, hound, and cursed be.' More fucking Shakespeare."

Quinton and I both shook our heads. "No," I said, "I think that one was probably an original by Shelly. Did she do anything else?"

"She slapped me with her bloody hand and I fell down as if she'd gaffed me. Then she walked up to the bow and started shouting at the air. That's when the storm came up. Just came. There one minute and not a sign the minute before. Not. A. Sign. I managed to go over, hoist Cas, and get him down to his bunk, but he was in a bad way. I tried to patch him up but he just kept bleeding. When I started back up to retake the helm, we'd just passed Discovery and Chatham islands, I think. We were running late and the sun was going to go down soon so I needed to be back in control of the boat before we left the open water. It should have been an hour or so to Roche from there, but we didn't make it."

"What in hell were you doing in the traffic lane?" Zantree's voice came down through the intercom and, broken, on the wind from the flying bridge.

"We weren't in the traffic lane! I took her around the west side of the banks. We came up from Port Townsend just like you are, remember? I was planning to go up through the inner channels from Anacortes originally, but we came out to Townsend for the damned fish. I wish we hadn't. Maybe if we'd been in the channels around the islands instead of the straits there'd have been some other boat to see us and . . . save us. Or maybe . . . we would have run for Orcas or Lopez as soon as we heard from the cops and we wouldn't have done what we did at all."

"What happened next?" I asked.

The gray-green haze around him had thickened to a palpable smog and seemed to be contracting into tentacles. . . .

"Like I said, we were running late and short of sleep because of the fish, and Cas wouldn't have me take the boat back to Townsend when the call came in for Les from the police. Les lost it and then the business with Shelly . . . I missed Mosquito Pass—" Fielding paused when he saw the confused looks on the faces of us three landlubbers. "It's the southern route into Roche Harbor. We were below it when . . . Shelly happened. I couldn't turn the boat in time because I was down on deck and I was more worried about Cas anyway, since he was bleeding. But I needed to get back into the pilothouse before we got any closer to the northern route, because there's a BC ferry that runs up Spieden Channel. You have to stay out of its way and you have to be careful how you maneuver in Haro Strait before you get to Spieden so you don't get on the wrong side of the traffic lane and get the Canadian Coast Guard on your ass. Right at the channel mouth it's wide, but you can't just charge into it like a bull into the ring—you have to watch the markers and make way for the ferry.

"But by the time we were turning for Spieden Channel we were engulfed in a storm—our very own personal storm. It had taken almost three hours to make the distance up Haro Strait that should have taken just one. So now it's unnaturally dark, we're stormbound, and the boat's starting to make noises I knew weren't good. I couldn't control her enough to shoot the northern passage to Roche Harbor between Henry and San Juan islands, because there's another island between them—Pearl Island—right in the mouth of the pass that makes the channel half the width of the southern route. There was no way to get to Roche safely and the storm and currents would not let me turn her around, so I kept her straight on. Straight down Spieden Channel, thinking I might be able to flip her around at the east end of Davison Head into Neil Bay, or even drag for Lonesome Cove east of that. I was willing to run her aground if I had to. Then the merfolk came on board and that's when people started dying."

"What happened to them?" Solis and I demanded together.

"The merfolk took them overboard. They just flowed on board with the water that was coming over the rails and then they just . . . it's like they swam through the boat and they grabbed Cas and Les and the girls. But they left me. And Shelly went with them. After that . . . it's hard to remember."

"Did you reach the cove?"

"Cove?"

"In your last log entry you said you were trying to reach Lonesome Cove."

"No. Not Lonesome Cove. I passed that, too, and—Oh!" And then his exclamation of surprise turned into a shriek of pain and he threw himself out of the hold and onto the deck, writhing, changing, and making noises increasingly animal and horrifying. He rolled across the deck and flopped upward, barking and moving as if blind and burning, then he toppled over the rail and fell into the water. The splash he raised spattered onto the deck with the same power as if we'd passed too close to a broaching whale.

"It's them! The bell—" he barked just before he sank. The sick-green creepers of energy followed him into the depths.

We all rushed to the rail, but the boat was already too far ahead of the splash and Fielding, writhing in the water, was already changing back to what he had been before. Then he dove and vanished.

"He's gone," Quinton muttered.

"He said, 'It's them.' The merfolk?" Solis asked.

"If so, then I now know a lot more than I did a minute ago," I said.

Both of the men looked at me. I stared for a moment longer at the receding spot where Fielding had sunk out of sight. I didn't feel as bad as I thought I should have. I turned back to the men.

"Everywhere we've seen the paranormal traces of this case I've seen the same energetic residue, the same color. A sort of dirty grayish green. I saw it at Reeve's place when he had his heart attack and I saw it again at the hospital where he died. I saw it yesterday at *Seawitch* and also at *Pleiades*. I saw it just now on Fielding, but I'm sorry to say I wrote it off as an aura shift that usually indicates a lie. But that's what forced him off the boat— that energy. I think he could have stayed, but it might have killed him. It's not from the dobhar-chú, because it attacked him before at the marina and he said the water hounds aren't magicians—though he could very well be lying about that and he's certainly lying about the events of *Seawitch*'s last night. But if that stuff was what was attacking Reeve the first time I saw it, then the creature I saw at Reeve's must have been either Fielding or one of his dobhar-chú cousins trying to protect Reeve. Either way, the party responsible for Reeve's death is one of the merfolk."

"Or a sea witch," Quinton suggested in a soft, unhappy voice.

"Yes. Or a sea witch."

I heard a clatter from above and Zantree came down

the ladder from the flying bridge, landing on the deck with a thump. "What happened? I felt the boat lurch like we lost a marlin off a close-hauled line."

"We lost Fielding."

Zantree looked startled. "How?"

"I'm not sure."

"And what were you going on about freaky spook stuff? Isn't a water hound enough weirdness for one cruise?"

"I think I'd better explain a few things. . . ."

NINETEEN

We moved up to the flying bridge for safety's sake and I tried to bring Zantree up to speed, but it was difficult and there were some things I couldn't discuss or explain that only made the situation feel more outrageous. He watched me with slowly rising anger. I didn't know if it was fury at me or the situation but I felt horrible for it, and I told him we'd be getting off at Roche Harbor to find another boat. I hadn't expected to fall into the path of Reeve's killer on the open water, but now that we were approaching the islands, we were too close and I wanted to shut that connection down before Zantree could become a target for the merfolk or the dobhar-chú. Fielding hadn't painted them as the most reasonable of creatures, and while I wasn't going to take his word for it, no other source made them sound any better. Once again I'd endangered someone without thinking and I'd be damned if I was going to let it go any further. This time I'd end the risk before it got too great. Quinton was frowning at me the whole time, but not an angry frown, just a thoughtful one, and I wondered what he was thinking. I couldn't tell from his aura this time—it was a fuzzy gold-and-green mess of indecipherable lines and moving steam.

"No," Zantree said. "I'm not getting left out of this."

"*This* could get you killed," I replied, "and you

wouldn't even know what was killing you! I won't let you do that."

"That is not your choice, Ms. Blaine. I had a friend on that boat and I want to know what the hell happened to her—and I'm not going to swallow all that mouth gas Furry Face was spitting. I'm not a foolish old man. I have managed myself for more than sixty years and I have a sound idea of what I can and cannot do. And this I will do."

"You don't understand, and I didn't realize how much danger we were putting you in or I would never have taken you up on the invitation to use the *Mambo Moon* for this trip."

Solis tapped me on the shoulder. "This was not entirely your decision, Blaine. I also chose this. And Zantree was not properly informed, it's true, but you do not bear all the responsibility here."

"Are you two trying to make me feel better about endangering you all? Well, you aren't. We will have to put in at Roche Harbor—or any other decent place we can find—and I'll go on by myself."

"You will not," Solis said. "This is also my investigation. According to Fielding, crimes were committed and it's my job to determine if that's true, clear them, and close the file on *Seawitch*. You will not stop me from that duty. That is *my* decision. It is not yours."

"But—" I started.

Quinton nodded at me. "I think you're outnumbered, Harper. Because I'm not letting you go without me—you don't know how to pilot a boat or where you're going. I at least know half of that."

"I can hire someone. I can go on by myself tomorrow. I don't want to endanger all of you over this . . . insanity."

"And it's all right to endanger yourself?"

"No! I'm just saying I have a chance because I can deal on their level and the rest of you can't. This is my job and the rest of you shouldn't be in the line of fire."

"That decision's not up to you."

I growled at him, "You're the one who keeps lecturing me about taking my friends for granted, using them as resources, not treating them like . . . like friends! Now you change your tune? How is this different?"

"We are not your friends," Solis said. "Not this moment. We're your colleagues and partners. You have no *more* say in this venture than any other one of us has. We work together. You haven't coerced me, I know. This is my decision and my case. I'll go with you. Like it or not."

Quinton smiled at Solis and turned his head to nod at me. "What he said goes twice for me. Now, Mr. Zantree, I think, should probably throw us all off at Roche and get the hell out of here before the fecal matter strikes the rotating ventilation device, but . . . I can't speak for him."

Zantree glowered at him and then at me and Solis and then back at me. . . . "Damn and blast you all! I am captain of this vessel and if I choose to go off on a mad reach straight to hell with a crew of lunatics, I'll do it if I so please! And devil take you if you try to stop me!"

I blinked at him. "Umm . . . I guess I'm outvoted. . . ."

"Yes, you are," Quinton replied. "Now be gracious and let's get on with this before the clock runs out."

I shrugged, although I admit the gesture was more uncomfortable than gracious. "In that case, I'm going below for a few minutes. I'm freezing."

"Come back up in an hour and we'll change watch on the wheel," Zantree said.

Solis opted to stay on the flying bridge with Zantree while I went down and tucked myself into the galley. The morning air was still a bit too cold for me without more layers and I felt a little woozy when I looked out at all that water from the height of the flying bridge. I wasn't so much seasick as sea wary—after all, whatever had forced Fielding off the boat had to come from somewhere and I wasn't sure it wouldn't come back, even though Fielding seemed to be its focus.

I sat on one of the built-in settees around the dining

table, blocking myself in the upholstered corner to counter the boat's movement and the strain on my rib a little. I rested my elbows on the table and my chin on my hands and cogitated.

Quinton came in and joined me about fifteen minutes later. "Hey, beautiful. What's eating you?"

"I'm just thinking. If the dobhar-chú were trying to protect Reeve from whatever magic the merfolk sent, they must have been standing guard or watching him in some way. But I didn't see their guard until the magic was already actively trying to kill him the first time. Why did they take so long to act? And why did the merfolk want Reeve dead? He was just an old man who was already retired and far away from his old haunts. They hadn't bothered to try before, so why now?"

"Didn't Fielding say something about time?" Quinton asked, going past me and deeper into the galley to scavenge coffee.

"Did he? Huh . . . yes, he said it, too. Well, that at least gives *some* veracity to his story, since the ghosts said the same thing."

"Which ghosts?" Finding no coffee left, he opened a few cabinets and looked for the raw materials for a new pot.

"The ghosts of the *Valencia*. They said something about time and place. . . . I had the same impression of opportunity dwindling away as I got from Fielding. They both said something to the effect of 'the way back only opens every twenty-seven years.' And that the time it would be open was almost at an end. . . ."

He discovered a can of coffee and a stack of filters for the built-in coffeemaker and started setting up. "That implies a barrier as well as a time frame, like a gate on a timer."

"So . . . when we find this place—if we can find it," I said, "we'll have to get into the right area and work fast." I closed my eyes and swallowed a touch of panic. "We're running on the clock here, without any idea how much time we've got, and I still can't figure how *Valencia* is connected to *Seawitch*."

"Well, there's the bell. . . ."

"That's a clue, not a cause."

"Fielding said everyone on board—everyone human, I assume—died. Just like everyone still aboard *Valencia* died." He filled the coffeemaker with water and snapped the carafe back into its place under the drip hole. He flipped the switch.

"What you're suggesting is that the ghosts themselves—or the deaths—are the connection. Is that right?" I asked.

"Why not? What if Reeve knew about the mermaids? Or at least what they did."

I blinked, considering it. "He must have. . . . He spoke to me as if he thought I was a mermaid. He called me a fish-tailed bitch and threatened to put me over the side—I assume that means throw me overboard—just as if we were at sea and I'd done something dreadful. He also had a mermaid statue on his porch that was a little . . . eerie, and he was the one who introduced the dobhar-chú into the discussion. He knew about the merfolk. He knew about the water hounds. . . ."

"Reeve's an Irish name, isn't it?" Quinton suggested. "Don't you always say that the Grey is shaped by belief? If Reeve was Irish American and had grown up with those stories. . . ."

"He was one old man. I don't think he conjured the dobhar-chú here on his own. The time frame doesn't work either, since Fielding's mother was one and she was the seventh pup of a dobhar-chú—even if he's lying about something, I don't think it's that—which would imply at least two generations of them up here before she was born. But Reeve did say he saw one on his boat and that's why *he* didn't take *Seawitch* out for the final voyage—seeing the dobhar-chú made him sick or so frightened that he made *himself* sick. But I'll bet the dobhar-chú was just looking for Fielding when it came on board. They're the paranormal gossipmongers, so if they heard one of their kind was around, they'd want to check it out. They probably hadn't expected to be recognized for what they were, and when that happened they had to keep Reeve off the boat so they could get to Fielding."

The coffeemaker began to gurgle.

"How would they hear about Fielding?" Quinton asked.

"Maybe Father Otter lied when he told Fielding he didn't know anything about his mother. . . ."

"That's possible," he said, crossing his arms over his chest as he leaned back on the counter, waiting for the coffeepot to fill. "Bending the truth seems to run in the family."

I followed my train of thought rather than pursue the fruitless complaint of Fielding's questionable veracity on some points. "Of course, there's always the merfolk. If the one that kissed Fielding as a kid really had put a mark on him, maybe any of them who spotted him would know he was their enemy, whether he was aware of it or not, and the word might have slipped out through them. Especially if they were planning something unpleasant. They seem to be a bloodthirsty lot."

"Yeah, Zantree was saying so upstairs. The original siren legends are pretty gruesome. It's not all *The Little Mermaid*."

I snorted. "Even *The Little Mermaid* isn't *The Little Mermaid*. Did you know Andersen originally wrote it as a ballet?"

Quinton shook his head.

I continued. "I've danced that, back when I was still ballerina-sized. It's a horrible story: The mermaid gives up her voice to get legs so she can marry the prince she's in love with—and possibly get a soul as well. Every step she takes on land is agonizing, and to get a soul she has to persuade the prince to kiss her so she can take his. To get him to kiss her she has to dance for him. Dancing in terrible pain. And in the end he doesn't marry her—he marries someone else. It's a ballerina's story, really: giving up something you don't know enough to value to gain something that's utterly fleeting, and being in pain all the time until you die of a broken heart. So she dies and becomes some kind of angel and soars off to do good deeds and gain a soul and a place in heaven, but the ending always seemed a bit of an afterthought— Andersen did a lot of those 'but the girl went to heaven and was never cold/sad/alone again' endings. I hated that show."

Quinton made a face and turned to pour us some coffee. Then he came to the settee to join me and brought two mugs of coffee along, saying, "That's a nasty tale. I don't think I'll ever think of it the same way again."

"Now you know how *I* feel," I said, accepting one of the mugs and clasping it in both hands.

"Zantree's stories are equally grotesque, but they don't include kissing princes. Mostly they're about singing sailors to their death on the rocks—"

"Wait . . ." I interrupted him. "I know that story: Scylla and Charybdis from the *Odyssey*. One was a monster in a rocky cave and the other was a whirlpool. . . ."

"Actually they were both monsters—sirens. They used to be sea nymphs; each had been cursed to be a monster but they still had voices that were irresistible. Sailors would hear their voices and either steer their boats into the maelstrom or be wrecked on the rocks on the other side. Then the sirens would eat them. Umm . . . why are you staring at me like that?"

I felt electrified and I must have looked it. The door from the aft deck slid open but I ignored it. Even breathing shallowly with excitement, my chest ached from the clutch of an idea too fascinatingly terrible to ignore— well, that and a sore rib. "The ghosts called them sirens," I said. "I missed the reference. *Valencia* was wrecked on the rocks just the other side of Vancouver Island from here and all but thirty-seven of those aboard died.

Wrecked on the rocks like sailors lured to Scylla, but what if, instead of devouring their flesh, these sirens took their souls?"

"What would they do with them?" Solis asked from the steps. "What use would the merfolk have for souls?"

I shook myself, taking too sharp a breath in my surprise and flinching as I recovered. "Blood magic. I told you how that works, Solis—a spell cast literally in blood. You don't have to kill to do it, but you get more power if you do. Fielding said Shelly was the daughter of a sea witch. Fielding and the ghosts both made a distinction between the witch and the merfolk, and Fielding mentioned elemental magic specifically. Not blood magic. But that's definitely the flavor Shelly cast with that broken circle on board *Seawitch*, so chances are good it's what she learned from her mother. She probably doesn't—or didn't—have the same degree of power or autonomy, so she didn't kill anyone right away. OK, yes, I'm just speculating. But what if she left that aside so *her mother* could collect the important part: the souls? Shelly might not have even had a choice if her mother was using her as a stalking horse. If the sea witch could store these souls, she could have power whenever she needed it without having to take the time and go through the rituals of bloodletting and invoking."

Solis was confused. He narrowed his eyes and blinked at me.

I explained, "Remember what I said about there being several major categories of magic and whatever type you practice, you have to have access to the right power source? In this case, blood and sometimes death. Under the right circumstances any source can be captured in a properly prepared magical storage device. So having this power in storage is like flipping a switch when you're connected to a big bank of batteries, versus having to fire up the generator first. Magically speaking, it's a hell of an advantage."

Solis scowled, rough-edged spikes of color flashing

around his head as he fought with the concept. "You suggest that this sea witch collected the souls of Starrett, Carson, Ireland, and Prince?"

"I suggest a lot more than that: I suggest she first collected the souls of the passengers and crew aboard *Valencia*. That she and her merfolk caused or aided the conditions that wrecked the steamer on the rocks to begin with and they then killed everyone who hit the water."

TWENTY

"Could they do that?" Solis asked. "Lure a ship to its destruction?"

"According to legend, that's their stock-in-trade," I replied. "I've discovered that there's often more than just a kernel of truth to that sort of story. And what happened to the *Valencia* is almost too bizarre to be true—*everything* went wrong, seasoned officers and crewmen made horrendous errors, and when the storm finally died down long enough to launch the lifeboats, they still couldn't get to shore and all the women and children died in the water. Truth really is stranger than fiction, because if that were a book or a movie, people would reject it as over-the-top."

"But why take *Seawitch*?" Solis asked, apparently having decided to throw his wavering disbelief on the junk heap for the sake of puzzling out a killer's motive; it didn't matter what *he* believed as long as he could understand what the *killer* believed. "If she had the souls of *Valencia*, why go to the trouble for a mere four more?"

"Aside from simple opportunity, there's the racial-feud angle and—if anything Fielding said on this point is true—possibly a bit of overzealous payback for messing with her daughter. If Starrett actually harmed Shelly and Fielding didn't stop him, then they'd just compromised the sea witch's heir. There may have been nothing to it, but the appearance or accusation could have been enough since, for a lot of high-level paranormals, successful breeding is tricky and frequently fatal for someone. On top of that they're usually long-lived, which means slow to mature and slower to age. Even if she had more than one daughter or if Shelly wasn't harmed, the sea witch would not be happy to see her heir compromised or threatened. That's possibly dynasty-ending, and with paranormals that can mean the end of a species or at the least the total wipe of a local population. There are fewer of them than us, so they take that kind of threat very seriously. And she would be even less happy if she thought her clan's racial enemy—a royal dobhar-chú— had anything to do with it."

Solis nodded slowly, scowling. "It has all the twisted logic of a gang war. So . . . although he wasn't even aboard when the crime occurred, the sea witch would attack Reeve . . . to lure Fielding out of hiding."

"That's what I'm thinking, too. The sea witch would go after any of his remaining friends and family who might help him once he escaped from her—as he obviously did. And did we ever find Fielding's family?"

"No. There was no reply from his father's last known address and no forwarding address or phone number."

"Maybe we should find out if he's dead. . . ."

Quinton made a disgusted face at me. "How morbid."

"But if he is it would support the idea that the sea witch and her merfolk are wiping out all traces of the Fieldings and anyone who might have helped Gary. I suspect that if we could ask we'd find out that his mother is dead and has been for a while."

"Then if Shelly Knight was the sea witch's daughter, who is the sea witch?"

"Maybe *she* is, now. We don't know her status as virgin or nonvirgin or even if it's truly relevant. Shelly and Jacque could be the same creature with only a bottle of hair dye to separate them. What if . . ." I said, my speech slowing as I thought out loud. "What if losing the *Valencia*'s soul—the bell—also lost the sea witch her power, or limited it severely? She hasn't been very aggressive in attacking us and she must know by now that we're coming. And what if . . . it wasn't the mother that took the souls of *Seawitch*, but the daughter? Then she'd have quite a bit of power, while her mother had little or none. So *Seawitch* may have been just a pawn in a power grab."

"It is a very elaborate plan," Solis objected. "Not robust or simple enough to work."

I admit I'd been speculating rather wildly, feeling the press of time and the need for some kind of answers before we were face-to-face with the sea witch. "True. Simple is usually better. But what if it wasn't a plan but just opportunity seized? That might explain what Shelly was doing hanging around the marina for a few years: She was looking for chances to accrue her own power and topple her mother."

Solis wasn't quite convinced, if his scowl was any indication. "She comes to the marina to look for opportunities to wreck ships and steal souls, then accidentally meets the son of her family's enemy. So she watches him and gets close. Then things go wrong and she . . . what? Cries for help with the spell we discovered in her cabin?"

"Why not? No . . . wait. It was a complex spell—not something you'd cast in a hurry to get help—and the spell circle was broken. So whatever that spell was, it wasn't functioning when *Seawitch* was taken. I wish I knew what the spell was for. . . . But it might be enough to know who broke it. Because that's when the situation went to hell, according to Fielding—assuming he's not lying on that point, once again." I tried to talk the pieces of this puzzle into place. "If Shelly broke it herself, then that act brought down the merfolk. If someone is going to show up as soon as you break a spell . . . they'd have to be looking for you in the first place. So the spell has to have been some kind of . . . disguise or protection for the boat; she'd just use an amulet or a gris-gris if it were for herself alone. So . . . she breaks it deliberately to . . . get out of a bad situation with Starrett, wreak revenge on the dobhar-chú—or Fielding, as the case may be. But that doesn't make sense. You don't cast a complex spell just so you can break it later—that's a waste of resources."

"What if Starrett broke it when he . . . paid her a visit?" Solis suggested.

I felt myself smiling as I thought about it. "The result is still the same but the emphasis is different: The merfolk descend like hungry wolves, but now . . . all that bloodletting and crazy stuff Fielding described isn't Shelly attacking them . . . it's Shelly trying to repair her spell in a panic. A spell that was keeping *Seawitch* hidden from the merfolk or her mother. And it would take a complex spell to hide a moving object that weighed more than sixteen tons. Why she was hiding it, I don't know, but when things start to fall apart, first she panics, then she gets mad and curses Fielding, and, last, she tries to salvage what she can—and in the process she creates enough havoc that it's easy to snatch a few souls in the affray."

"Affray?" Quinton asked with a laugh. "You've been reading Agatha Christie again."

"Marsh. I wanted a break from the noir—my life's noir enough."

Solis sighed. "You who work with the darkest things do not find mystery novels . . . ridiculous and artificial?"

"Of course I do—that sort at least. Good triumphs over evil and the world is restored to order without a lot of angst and grotesquerie. That's why I like them: They are as far from my life as I can get without reading historical romances."

"Why do you not, then? Read romances."

"They depress me."

Solis looked puzzled. "My wife says the same thing."

"I like her more and more," I said, teasing a little but mostly serious.

Solis smiled—a real smile that actually moved his cheeks and creased the corners of his eyes. Then he glanced around as if looking for something mislaid. "Oh,

Zantree says that it's Quinton's turn at the wheel—his watch, rather."

"Already?" I asked.

"Yes. Two-hour shifts. He sees no reason for you or me to take the wheel with such a short distance left to go."

"But we've got a time limit and we don't know when it will expire. We may have to push on until we find Fielding's mystery cove."

"We should discuss the search with him, but either way, he expects to be in Roche Harbor before dark."

"So did Fielding. . . ."

June in western Washington is rife with vagaries of weather. It's warm one day, cold and wet the next, and a single twenty-four-hour period can turn back and forth between the extremes two, three, or four times before the day finally passes away. By eleven the sun had come out, the fog was long gone, and Quinton was almost half through his watch at the wheel. As I came up the ladder to bring him sunglasses and sit with him, the view from the flying bridge was clear and full of blue above and below with land visible but distant in nearly all directions. It was beautiful, if still a bit cold. Sun sparkled off the wind-ruffled surface of the water that was scattered with sailboats cutting back and forth and faster motorboats skidding along like water striders on a pond.

I handed Quinton the shades and he slipped them on, sighing. "Man, I had forgotten what this was like. It's gorgeous, isn't it?"

I agreed. "Did you spend a lot of time on boats when you were a kid?"

"Not a lot but it *was* quality. My mom's folks had a Hatteras—it was kind of like this boat but a little smaller overall and higher in front. My parents usually sent my sister and me up to stay with them for a week in the summer and we'd spend most of our time on the boat with Grandpa Quinn, just pottering around the Sakonnet river and in Narragansett Bay. It was great."

"Hang on," I said. "Narragansett . . . isn't that on Long Island?"

He rolled his eyes and laughed a little. "Rhode Island."

"You're from Rhode Island?"

"No, my mom is from Rhode Island."

"And you?"

"Not from Rhode Island. My sister moved in with my grandparents near the end of their lives. I . . . wasn't able to go. She really took to the place. Met her husband there."

"You miss it?"

"I miss them and I miss the way life felt easy when we were all together, tooling around in the boat. Rhode Island? Not specifically. What about you?"

"I've never been to Rhode Island."

"I mean . . . do you miss . . . people?"

I peered at him in confusion. "Which people do you have in mind? I miss the Danzigers."

"I wasn't thinking of them."

I cocked my head, curious. "Who, then? You'll have to be specific, because I'm just not following your train of thought."

He looked upset and I felt a spike of anxiety reaching between us. "I was wondering . . . about Novak, to be honest."

"Will? Why? He's been gone for almost two years now."

"Is he really? Dead doesn't always mean gone with you."

I tossed my head in exasperation. "Oh, for heaven's sake! When I say 'gone,' I *mean* gone. What was once William Novak is no more. I used to wonder if his personality lingered in . . . what he became, but I don't see any sign of that. Of course, I don't exactly spend a lot of time chatting the Beast up, so I'm not *entirely* sure, but if I had to bet, I'd say gone is *gone* in this case. You can't call the way it tosses me around affectionate."

"Maybe . . . he's angry with you."

"No. He isn't there," I explained, feeling my own frustration slowly drain away as I talked. "If anything remains, I would call that thing an echo of humanity—by which I mean the urge to be humane, not something endemically human. But I don't know that it comes from Will. I'm not even sure it's more than my imagination that the emotion exists in it at all; the Guardian Beast is not human. It's not even alive, really. It has substance and existence, but not . . . not a life, no soul of its own. And . . . Quinton, there is nothing—not a ghost or a monster or another human being—that can stand between you and me. And not just because of some silly magic thing. I love you so much and so deeply that if I could let it all flow out of me, it would fill up the whole Sound and spill out into the Pacific Ocean and fishermen in Taiwan would be finding big, sparkly pink shards of it in their nets a hundred years from now." I threw my arms around him. "I yearn only for you."

Quinton gave a self-conscious shrug and an embarrassed laugh. "I feel the same way about you and I'm sorry I'm . . . being an ass. Also, I suspect you just wanted to use 'yearn' in a sentence."

I gave my best Valley Girl imitation. "Well, like, duh."

This time he laughed for real and hugged me back. "You are half-crazy."

"More than half if you mean crazy about you," I replied, feeling silly even as I said it.

"All right: totally nuts. Like Chock Full o'Nuts nuts."

"Chock Full o'Nuts? You really *are* from the East Coast."

"And you really aren't. Chock Full o'Nuts contains no nuts—it's coffee. Which is appropriate, considering how much of it you drink."

I stuck my tongue out at him. Then I found myself pressing against him and neither of us had moved; the boat had moved under us.

While we'd been talking the boat had been motoring

along in increasingly busy water and now bucked a bit as it crossed the swell from a larger boat's wake.

Quinton frowned and looked down at the instruments. "Damn it," he muttered. "Pressure's falling."

"Oil pressure?" I asked.

"No, barometric pressure. It means there's a squall coming up, but . . . I don't see one. . . ."

Rising wind from the east and south puffed against *Mambo Moon*, pushing it a touch to the side and a touch more, then swung around and blew in our faces or on the stern—as if the rigid hull were a toy sail to be gusted across a pond—until we were out of alignment with our original path. Being a landlubber, I didn't think much of it. Having more experience with boats, Quinton figured we were a bit off but wasn't sure by how much or if it mattered with so much room to maneuver in the wide swath of the Strait of Juan de Fuca. He corrected the course and kept the boat moving ahead. After an hour I noticed that the distant shoreline seemed to be moving along more slowly. I pointed it out to Quinton.

"Well . . ." he started, clearly thinking aloud, "I suppose since the tide is still going out we might be encountering more resistance as we get closer to the mouth of Haro Strait, where the channel is much narrower, so the tidal current would be stronger and moving against us. . . . It should ease as we approach slack tide."

I had to shrug. "It's Greek to me. The currents of the Grey, I get; actual water . . . not so much. What's slack tide?"

"It's the point in the cycle where the currents have slowed as the tide is nearing the turn. In this case, just before the tide starts to come in, instead of going out like it is now. Areas of slow water like coves and harbors behind breakwaters become still and there's little to no current movement at the surface. It's very easy to maneuver in slack water because there's no current to oppose you."

"How long does it last, this still period?"

"Depends on the area but it's usually two to three hours."

"Then . . . we should be in slack water in an hour or two?"

Quinton paused a moment to consider the math. "Yeah. So the tide will be slacking about the time we have to turn for Mosquito Pass—the southern pass to Roche Harbor. We're still on the ebb tide now."

I scowled. "But if it's slowing down, why are we being pushed sideways more now than before?"

Something slapped the boat again, sending a shiver through the whole structure. I stumbled sideways and Quinton lurched the same direction with me, dragging the wheel around a few degrees before he let go of it. *Mambo Moon* wiggled in the water like a gaffed fish. I heard the doors below slide open and Zantree came zooming up the ladder to the flying bridge.

"What was that?" he shouted. "Did we hit something?"

Quinton started to answer but a sudden, violent gust of wind whipped across the flying bridge and stole the words from his mouth. Water splashed up over the railings and the boat rocked like a toy. Everyone looked out to see what we had struck or been struck by, but nothing was readily apparent.

Zantree took the wheel, saying, "All of you go down to the deck and look around in the water. If you can't spot what hit us, we may have gone over it. We don't want whatever it was to damage the propeller or the rudder—or the hull if it bounces back up. Logs sometimes float vertically and if they pogo, they'll knock the prop clean off her. And we *sure* don't want to be dead in the water here if this storm comes in. Those rocks off the port bow are mighty sharp."

We scrambled down the ladder and spread out around the boat, peering over the sides for any sign of what we'd struck. The boat moved sideways and leaned over as if it were being pushed by something in the water. I saw a bit of lambent color below the surface on the left side—the port side—but it moved away like a swimming snake and vanished. There was nothing else to see but water that seemed unusually agitated. Water splashed up onto the deck, spattering over the side rail where I stood, wetting my clothes from the hip down.

"What is that?" Solis shouted from the front. I gave up staring at the water and ran around toward him, heading for the bow. I could hear Quinton's footsteps going around on the other side but couldn't see him.

I cleared the front of the cabin bulge and started to the other—the starboard—side toward Solis, who was standing halfway up the open section of the bow deck and staring northeast out to sea on his right. He turned his head, saw me coming, and pointed over the rail toward the bulk of San Juan Island. "What is it?" he repeated.

I rushed to the rail beside him and grabbed on, astonished by the sight of what looked like a tower of water undulating across the waves toward us.

Quinton caught up to us and looked out, too. "Waterspout!" he shouted.

"Blast it!" Zantree yelled down from above. "There shouldn't be any of those around here!"

"What is a waterspout?" Solis demanded.

Quinton glanced at him and said, "It's like a tornado but on water, so it condenses moisture from the surface as mist. That's a fair-weather spout. They usually don't move much. . . ."

"Someone had best tell that to the waterspout," Solis suggested, watching the rising vortex of mist, water, and debris waver toward *Mambo Moon*. "How do we avoid it?"

"We stay the course we're on. The waterspout should continue on its line, east to west, and we're heading north. As long as we're moving at ninety degrees and faster than its intercept speed, we'll pass it safely. But it shouldn't be here—there's no cloud above it."

"I thought you said it was a fair-weather spout."

"That just means it's not part of a cyclonic storm. That one there's a micro cell, but . . . it should still have a cloud. . . ."

"You said they condense moisture from the surface?" I asked.

The boat shuddered again and swayed side to side.

"Yes."

"They don't suck water up?"

"No. Something that size doesn't pick up water or objects."

"Then that's not a waterspout," I said. "And I don't think we're going to have to search too hard to find the sea witch."

As I stared at it through the Grey, the waterspout was thick with creatures that writhed and twisted in the rising liquid. A handful of human forms spun, screaming, in the water, festooned in seaweed and trailing chain. In front of it, coils of blue energy reached and spun through the waves toward *Mambo Moon*. The sea witch—or her minions—had come to us.

Quinton and Solis both gaped at me. I felt sick and my cracked rib seemed to stab into my side, sending a cold chill of fear and pain through my chest. Or maybe it was Quinton who was feeling scared and sick, but I didn't think I was immune to common sense; the waterspout was not natural and it wasn't staying put or moving in a nice, straight line. It was coming to get us.

"I think the sea witch wants her bell back. . . ."

Solis turned to me. "You have it aboard?"

"Why wouldn't I? If we're going back to where it happened, we have to have all the parts of the mystery or we can't solve it."

"How would the sea witch know we had it?"

"The same way she knew Fielding was aboard: spies. I'll bet the dobhar-chú aren't the only paranormal intel-

ligence agency around. After all, they're the enemy, so
the sea witch wouldn't go to them. She'd post her own
observers. And it doesn't matter who; it only matters that
they found us."

That was when Zantree shouted down, "Hands on
deck! Prepare to fend off!"

TWENTY-ONE

"Fend off?"

"Well, you don't say 'repel boarders' when it's not human, do you?" Quinton shouted back. He snatched a pole from a pair of clamps beneath the rail and shoved it into my hand. "You go to the bow and smack down anything that tries to come over the rail—this is going to hurt and I'm sorry about that rib, but we have no choice. Solis, you stay on the side deck—your back will be protected by the cabin, but you'll have to move up and down the deck pretty quickly to keep off whatever's coming. I'll take the stern until Zantree tells us otherwise. We don't have time to tie off to safety lines since we didn't run any, so be careful, keep your flotation vests on, and grab or tie yourself to something whenever you can."

He ran back to the stern and returned in a moment with a wicked, narrow hook on a short handle. He thrust it into Solis's hand and then dashed back the way he came.

Solis blinked and paled, then turned to me. "What is coming and how will I know?"

"I think you'll see it just fine—these guys aren't being subtle. And if you can't tell, hit anything that isn't one of us or part of the boat."

"What about Zantree?"

"He's pretty busy on the bridge." I gave his shoulder

a steadying squeeze. "It's just like any other fight. Only wetter."

I didn't wait to hear him object but ran forward to take up my position on the bow, partially as the specially talented lookout, I realized, as much as a defender. I was puffing uncomfortably by the time I reached my spot and my side was already achy.

The waterspout was less worrisome than the roiling sea ahead of it. The gleams of Grey energy I'd spotted earlier were uncoiling now, reaching toward our boat and spreading like blind vines groping for us with seeking tendrils. And as they came, the strands formed outlines of shapes, monstrous and strange: creatures half-man and half-fish with wide mouths full of jagged teeth and extra appendages like the grasping tentacles of giant squid. The lines began to fill with sea foam whipped by wind and our own personal squall drew in fast, accompanied by harbingers of magical destruction and a high, keening song that caught across my ears and my throat, sharp as the metal taste of ozone. I risked a drop into the Grey to get a better look....

The ghost world roared with the voice of a storm and the cold blackness of the Sound flickered with lightning rising from the depths to burst through the surface in gouts of green, blue, and violet light. The colored energy from the depths reached into the smoky substance of the Grey, twisting it into vaporous shapes and running in quicksilver streams through the billowing eddies of ghost-stuff. Farther away, the Grey held a small cohort of more solid shapes that surged through the water. At this distance it was hard to be certain, but the things seemed to be the same shapes as the monsters projected in the magic and sea foam that was closing in nearby. One of the fast-running threads of energy snapped toward me with the sound of lightning and a stink of ozone; it clamped around my upper arm and yanked backward, trying to drag me off the boat. I snatched at it with my free hand and tried hooking one of my legs around the nearest upright on the rail and bracing my feet against whatever solid purchase I could feel to resist the strand's tugging me into the water, but the rail was insubstantial so deep in the Grey. I threw myself backward, pinching off the energy strand that had wound itself around my arm as I tumbled back into the normal.

And into a descending wave cresting over the rail.

"I'm getting . . . a little sick . . . of being wet all the time," I muttered, picking myself up, wincing and gasping.

A storm front pushed by the waterspout had closed in on the boat with unnatural speed while I'd been "out" and *Mambo Moon* was already pitching against thrashing water and gusting wind. Just keeping my footing on that moving deck was a painful task. Beyond the squall line the water was a little choppy but otherwise undisturbed and other boats seemed to have no trouble turning aside. But no matter how Zantree maneuvered, the waterspout closed on us, bringing bigger and bigger waves that soon broke over the rails. Trying to maintain my hold on the normal world and the boat, I didn't dare fall deeper into the Grey and had to content myself with glancing at the incoming storm from the corner of my eye, scanning for the horrors it concealed and breathing in uncomfortable gulps.

It wasn't so much a concealment as it was a literal front. The magic wasn't deep and it probably wouldn't hold up past a certain degree of damage, distance, or time, but how long or far we'd only know when it broke. The first real assault came over the side as blue-green figures of foam and water, reaching for us with tentacles and teeth. I heard Solis shout in alarm as the watery specters heaved aboard. I swung my boat hook at the nearest one, feeling the shaft connect with a slow thud to the mass of animate liquid. But the pole didn't stop; it merely bogged down against resistance and snapped out the other side too fast under the power of my muscles, causing me to stumble and twist forward as the hook came free into the air on the other side. The figure I'd swung through dissolved into a huge splash, as if I'd shattered an aquarium.

I swore as pain broke across my ribs and I jabbed the pole's butt backward into the next sea-foam monster. That, too, fell into a dousing explosion of water that knocked me down onto the deck, breathless and unable to refill my lungs as each heaving attempt was cut short by the sharp agony in my side. I needed to hold on to something or I'd pass out and the enchanted waves would wash me right off the other side. I rolled onto my back with care and started to shove my feet against the next one, but my foot passed through it and I felt a wet, electric shock as something gleaming wrapped around my leg and yanked me toward the rail.

"Oh no you don't," I gasped, getting a mouthful of seawater for my pains.

I braced my other foot against the rail as I was dragged to the edge and jabbed the boat hook into the gaping maw of the thing, shattering it. I dropped back onto the deck, free, but still down and hurting like I'd been beaten with a stick. I gagged on water and pain as I scrambled up, panting and not sure why the pole worked but my foot hadn't. My leg stung where the aqueous phantom had clutched me and my chest throbbed. I gulped mouthfuls of air to refill my lungs and stabbed at every shape that came toward me.

I cut my gaze to the side for a moment to check on Solis. He seemed to be holding out, though he was soaked and confused, moving in quick lunges side to side following the jerky turns of his head. I could see the whites of his too-wide eyes and he slashed and reposted again and again with a surprising economy. If I'd had time, I'd have admired his fighting form, but there was no such luxury.

"Just poke them. Don't waste energy; they're not real," I gasped, but my voice had no strength and he didn't hear me.

A few more of the sea-foam creatures boiled over the rails and I dispatched mine with simple jabs, conserving my strength so I could get up and fight the denser forms beginning to thrust through the vanguard of shaped liquid as the gleam of magical energy began to fade and the scraping, spiraling song with it. They were difficult to see through the water and spray, but I assumed the new assault was formed by the merfolk themselves—if the monstrous things I'd seen in the distance were they.

One of the merfolk—a creature only vaguely human above its muscular dolphinlike tail—broached the surging wave and snatched at Solis with arms like the leaf-shaped tentacles of a squid that shot forward and wrapped the sergeant tight before the monstrosity fell back toward the heaving surface. Solis gave a shout as he was lifted and dragged over the rail, flailing his hook against the thing's body, the point gouging into the monster's flesh. Red blood spattered onto the deck and the hook caught on a rail stanchion, arresting their fall for a moment.

"Rey!" I shouted into a gasping silence in the attack.

The illusions collapsed in a crashing wave and the horrifying monster forms of the real merfolk—a mere handful, though they'd seemed like a hundred—began to recede as the one grappling with Rey tried to yank him under the surface. It opened its mouth, showing the rows of shark teeth within, and I lunged forward, driving the prong of my boat hook into that dreadful maw.

The mer-thing made a gurgling cry and jerked backward, tearing Solis's hold free of the stanchion as it fell into the water. Solis fell after it, free of the tentacles for the moment as he vanished into the foam and spray of the merfolk's retreat. I tried to heave myself over the side after Solis, but I wasn't breathing well and my legs had gone limp under me while my ribs seemed to catch on fire. I squeezed my eyes shut against the pain.

"They're falling back. I'll get Solis," Quinton shouted in my ear, rushing onto the side deck to shove me back.

"You get to the bow and get ready to throw the life preserver to us."

"Life—" I started, forcing my watering eyes open.

"Big orange ring with a rope on it," he shouted back,
pointing.

Then he was over the side and gone into the water.

The noise of the boat and the storm dropped to a high
whistling and dull clanging and splashing, the merfolk—
stripped of their monstrous illusions, but still monsters—
sweeping back from whence they came. Zantree came
scrambling around to the side deck and got me on my
feet.

"You all right?"

I panted at him. "Just. Winded. You?" I hurt all over
and thought I was going to throw up from it, but I wasn't
going to say so.

"Had to cut the engine so we wouldn't run over the
boys and cut 'em up with the props. Why did those things
break off like that?"

"Out of power . . . I think."

"I hope they aren't just regrouping. . . . But I'd better
get back topside and keep an eye out for the boys. If you
miss with the ring, we'll have to circle around—if we can
and if this hole in the weather holds long enough. Can
you manage?"

I would have to: There was only the two of us left
aboard and I couldn't maneuver the boat like he could. I
nodded.

Zantree spun around and bolted back to the flying-
bridge ladder.

I held the rail near the life preserver and stared out
toward the water, looking for any sign of Quinton or Solis. I spotted something dark, splashing a distance out
from the side of the boat but well to the rear. I wasn't
sure how to throw the life preserver that far from the
bow, but I felt as much as heard the engines roar back up
to speed and the boat turned, coming around and moving toward a point above the splashing. The engines cut

back to a burble and the boat glided, turning a bit more so we weren't coming straight on it. In a moment the splashing resolved into the shape of two heads and a thrashing arm. I grabbed the life preserver and tossed it like a giant Frisbee, letting out a sharp squeal of agony as it flew free from my outstretched arms. I folded over the jabbing in my side, scraping my arms against the rails as I went, and forced my eyes open to see the ring splash down.

The orange ring skimmed out over the water and plopped onto the surface near Quinton's head with the grace of a belly-flopping eight-year-old. But it was close enough for him to stroke to and grab and I thanked every god I could think of that I wouldn't have to throw it a second time. The ring wasn't big enough to shove around any adult's head, but Quinton held on to it with one arm while he kept the other wrapped around Solis's chest. I ran the line around the anchor winch and started walking—crabbing painfully—backward to haul in the slack until the men bumped into the side of the boat.

It took a bit of mucking around with the rope to get Solis and Quinton to the swim platform at the back. Solis came up coughing and sputtering as Quinton lifted him, and the edge of the platform butted into his gut, forcing out air and water. He wasn't steady on his feet and Zantree had to push, pull, and haul him back up to the main deck and then into the main cabin, but he was alive and whole when he got there. By the time Solis was dried off and bundled up in new clothes and warm blankets, sitting in the galley with a cup of hot coffee, the wind had risen and the boat was being shoved by wild gusts and unexpected waves once again.

"I don't know why those monsters fell off—and thank God for it—but it's still going to be a fight all the way up," Zantree said, sticking his head in through the hatch to the enclosed bridge above the galley. He looked at me. "You think they're coming back anytime soon?"

I took my best guess and shook my head. "Can't maintain the storm *and* the illusions for long. There weren't very many merfolk and they retreated as soon as one was hurt. I suspect she can't afford to lose people. She'll put her energy into wearing us down with the storm and save the rest in case we make it to the cove."

"I'll take your word on that, 'cause the winds aren't dying down, but I sure don't see any more of those fish men. I'll keep the helm a while longer down here in the pilothouse station while you guys dry off and warm up. I may need a lookout on deck before that, but I can handle the wheel myself. You think you'll be ready to take over in an hour or two?"

"Yeah," Quinton replied from under a towel. "Are we still running for Roche Harbor?"

"That's my plan, though it sounds like we need to go on and find Gary's cove before we're out of time or battered to pieces. If this storm keeps up we may have no choice—we're way off course and fighting the shore current on the west boundary. The wind pushed us out a good bit and if it keeps on the same way, we'll be pushed back toward the rocks around the Chatham Islands. I'll have to work her out of the current and back into the main channel as soon as it starts to slack up. Then we'll have to scoot across to the west shore of San Juan and hope for a lift up the inside current once the tide's turning. We're going to be two or three hours later than we thought, if we can make it at all without overshooting Mosquito Pass."

"Doesn't sound good . . . That was a hell of a storm," Quinton said.

"I'd say hell's exactly where it came from. Never seen anything like that. It was like the squall picked us out. And now it's back, so I'd better hop to it." He vanished up the steps and we could hear him moving around overhead.

I looked at Solis, huddled in his blanket. He looked pale but it appeared he wasn't ready to give up just yet.

I was still a bit damp and battered myself but better off than he was.

"You still with us, Solis?" I asked.

He nodded with more vigor than I thought needed. "To the bitter end—if it comes to that."

"I hope not."

"This is becoming a most bizarre adventure."

"I'm not sure I'd call it an adventure," I started.

"What else can it be? It's no longer a case, per se. I cannot report most of what's occurred today without running the risk of being accused of . . . flights of fancy."

"You mean being crazy," I corrected.

He shrugged with a small bow of his head and half-raised shoulder. "That, too. I am finding it quite . . . eye-opening."

"If by 'eye-opening' you mean, 'staring in terror,' yeah, it is that," Quinton said. "If you'll excuse me, I'm going up with Zantree to take a look at the charts and nav and try to figure out where we're going and how to spot it before it's my turn at the wheel." He gave me a significant look—including a half-raised eyebrow—and turned to head up the steep steps to the bridge.

When he was out of earshot, I turned my attention back to Solis. "I'm sorry—" I started.

"For what?"

"For getting you into this mess and getting you half-drowned."

"You did not get me into any mess. This came with the case—which I requested—and while I find it uncomfortable, it is necessary. I would not be diligent if I didn't pursue this, however strange it becomes. I'm not of a delicate mind that cannot stand a challenge," he added, leveling a finger at me as if I'd implied any such thing.

"I never said so," I objected.

"But you think me inflexible."

"I find you . . . rather traditional."

He snorted. "Hidebound."

"No. Just somewhat . . . by the book."

"It depends on which book. . . ."

I laughed. "I suppose it does. Which book do you favor?"

"I no longer know. But . . . I am not what you think I am."

I raised an eyebrow but didn't say anything to stop whatever admission he held, trembling on the verge of words.

He took several slow breaths, glancing around as if he were gauging the room's ability to absorb what he was about to say without mutating into something even stranger than the creature that had snatched him from the deck. "I must be honest: I have looked into your background, Blaine. I . . . wanted to know if you were, perhaps . . ."

"Dangerous? Crazy?" I offered.

"Untrustworthy."

"Personally or professionally?" I asked. I wasn't offended; I would have checked up on him, too, if I'd had questions about the reliability of his information or person. And he'd had occasion to question mine once or twice, since I'm such a source of strange cases and freakish accidents. That was understandable and it didn't bother me . . . anymore.

"They're the same, in most cases. As you know."

I nodded. I'd done enough background investigation and legal discovery to know that people who aren't on the up-and-up in one aspect of their lives usually don't meet a higher standard in any of the others. Unless they're a particular variety of sociopath.

He spoke haltingly and without letting his eyes rest on mine for more than a second or two at a time. "But I found nothing of that sort, in spite of your . . . penchant for the unsettling. I have found you frustrating in the past—and still do—but I trust you."

I think I let a tiny smile sneak onto my face at that admission; it would have been inappropriate to grin. I just murmured, "Thank you."

"What we are heading into may require more than that. We may be stepping into the land of nightmares—my nightmares, at least. You seem to take such waking horrors in your stride, but I . . . When that creature pulled me over the railing, I fought because I did not want to die and I thought I might break free. But in the water where I was blind and couldn't draw breath, my old nightmare returned."

I sat still and breathed as quietly as my aching ribs would allow, letting him say what he needed to. He inhaled and exhaled slowly and went on, gazing directly at me for a moment as he asked, "You recall after we found the bell aboard *Seawitch* you asked what I had experienced? And I told you it was the bad dream of my youth: sharp circumstance closing in until I could only go helplessly forward. In the dark tunnel of the water with that song in my ears, I felt my death was inevitable, that I had no alternative but to go meet it."

"That was the song of the sea witch, not your dream."

"It was more than that. It was everything I fear. It is why I wanted this case, why I joined the police, why I found and married Ximena. . . . The dream is an allegory my mind torments me with: my inability to stop something horrible from happening, my inability to make it right—to retrieve the moment the evil became inevitable—because I have already lived through it and it will never be right. As a young man—a boy—I helped my mother hide from my father the bodies of three men she had killed in our kitchen. I had watched her kill them. I did not help her—I was too afraid—and I did not save her.

"My mother had been frightened, too, but it did not stop her. When they lay dead, she cried. She sat on the floor and wailed as if they had injured her, and she was so covered in blood I thought they had—you could not even see the pattern on her dress through the gore—so I came out from my hiding place and I tried to comfort her. At first she seemed not to know I was there. After a while she noticed and she got up. Now it seems almost humorous that she tried to straighten her dress and her hair, but that's the woman she was—very concerned for things to be proper. Perhaps even more so because the situation was so very improper. She put her arm around me and said we must clean up so my father wouldn't know what had happened. I did not question that. My father was a policeman. Such a thing—such a mess—in his house would not do. Now that so many years are past, I cannot recall how we did it, but we carried the men away and we buried them and then we returned and scrubbed and scrubbed and scrubbed. . . . My mother burned her dress and we never told a soul. I never felt I had a choice as we did it. It seemed my life had led inevitably to that unforgivable moment where one evil piled upon another and I could never take it back. When I left Colombia, I hoped for something better—for a cleaner justice—than what we had done. For the ability to make things right."

I was confused. "I can understand why you'd help your mother, but why did she kill them?"

Solis blinked and shook his head as if he had been sleepwalking and was now awakening. "They had come to rape her. The drug cartels were at war—Medellín and Cali—and she was the wife of a Cali policeman who would not take their payoffs to turn a blind eye. They thought they could destroy him by hurting her, by . . . making her worthless. You understand the culture of the place and time would have condemned her as much as the men who raped her. It would have reflected badly on my father to be married to a woman who was . . . soiled in that way. They told her what they wanted and she fought them. They tore her clothes and held her down, but they didn't know how fierce my mother was. She killed two of them with a kitchen knife and the last with a shotgun my father kept at the back door."

"And she didn't want your father to know."

He shook his head. "It would have embarrassed him. I told you she was a very proper woman."

"How old were you?"

He thought a moment before he answered, "Twelve."

"Your father never found out? Not even when the bodies were discovered?"

"They never were that I know of. Santiago de Cali lies in a fertile valley and there are places a body will simply melt into the ground. If picked bones were found some year after a cane burn, few people would ask where they came from."

My stomach lurched a little at the image that rose in my mind of blackened skeletons and remnant flesh gnawed by the rats and other things that might run through the tangled growth of sugarcane fields. I'm still a wuss about that sort of thing, no matter how many times I've seen death memories or dead bodies, or died myself, and I hope I never become inured to it. "It didn't bother you at the time?"

He blinked at me. "At the time I could not think at all—I only acted. But I have never forgotten the horror of it. Of looking down into the ruin of what was a man, of how my mother fought them and then cried over them, of the blood—how we scrubbed it and hid it and lied about the stains that wouldn't go. We told my father I'd killed a chicken—it's true, that saying about headless chickens—to explain the splashes on the walls that we couldn't remove in time. That was what decided me to come here and join the police—somewhere I thought the law and justice did not give each other a cold shoulder. I have learned that it is not always the way here either, and I despise that, but it's better than my home country was when I was a child and criminals thought they could harm my father by ruining my mother. There was no safe path once they came into the house. We let them dictate our shame, even if we did not let them win. My mother and I hid what had happened because dead criminals in her kitchen would have been almost as bad for my father as if she'd let them rape her. She killed them but they still owned a piece of her soul until the day she died, and they still own a piece of mine as well."

TWENTY-TWO

Solis's words echoed in my head. I swallowed a lump in my throat and couldn't think of what to say. "I . . ." I started in a weak voice.

Solis shook his head and looked aside. "An unpleasant tale. I offer it so you will know where *I* am broken and cannot be trusted. But if you do not want it . . ."

"Don't you dare."

Solis raised his eyebrows at me.

"Thank you."

"Why?"

"You can't take something like that back. It can't be unheard. And you are not broken or untrustworthy and I don't want to forget how much you've entrusted to me. No matter how ugly it is, it's still precious."

"But it is ugly," he agreed.

"So are my feet and I don't apologize for them. Of course, I also don't wear sandals. . . ."

He looked puzzled.

"You know I used to be a dancer."

He nodded. "It's in your record."

"Never seen a dancer's feet? I spent so much time in dance shoes as a kid, en pointe, or hoofing in road shows more weeks on than I was off that my feet look like they were run over by a truck. Dreadful, crippled-looking, knobby things. I earned them through pain and vanity. They remind me of what I left and why I left it. I don't show them to most people because they're . . . well, they're awful, but they are part of why I am what I am. And I don't regret that." I studied his face to see if he understood and it seemed he did. He nodded, scowling a little. I nodded back and gave a tiny laugh. "But they're still disgusting."

"More disgusting than those creatures in the waves?" he asked with a grimace.

"There's a lot that's more disgusting than those," I said. "Most of the things coming over the rail were illusions filled with water to give them weight. They wasted our energy and distracted us from the real ones coming up behind them. I tried to let you know, but I didn't have the breath to shout—I'm sorry about that."

He shrugged and I had an odd spark of hope for his nightmare's resolution. "I have survived. What manner of attack comes next?"

"I'm not sure. They may just try to batter us to death in this storm, since we've figured out their weakness."

"I haven't. What is this weakness?"

"The sea witch's power is limited and she has to choose where she'll spend it. The merfolk—or, more likely, the sea witch we keep talking about—casts illusions to create the impression of an army of her minions. But only a few are really flesh and blood. They aren't pushovers—though I'll admit the illusions are powerful, too—but once you know most of what you're seeing isn't real, it's easier to dodge the real ones and break the false. The merfolk aren't quite impervious to the motions of the water in the storm, so while the storm may continue to wear us down, I think they'll have to make their next sally against us in a less-unsettled circumstance. Anything else that comes at us will be magic, not meat."

"That may reassure *you*, but I do not feel better hearing it. What if she's holding the majority of her men and power in reserve against the eventuality of our arrival in her domain?"

I mulled it over. "That could be. But if you were her,

wouldn't you want to get rid of us as early as possible? Unless there's some reason she needs us in her lair before she tries to suck up our souls to power her spells, why let us get any closer than she has to? Consider that the *Valencia* was wrecked way out at the southwest point of Vancouver Island, west of here, but Fielding implied that her base is east of here, so her reach is—or can be—fairly wide. But the farther she wants to reach, the lower her power. So she has to play it close to her vest unless she's willing to come out of her place of safety."

"If, in fact, it has always been the same sea witch. But if Shelly usurped her mother and Jacque is doing the same now, each wreck would have a slightly different profile, since the perpetrators, though related, are not the same."

I hmphed and gave it a few moments' thought. "Possible. I guess we won't know until we are face-to-face with her."

"Is that wise?"

"I don't see any other way to fix the problems we have. We both need an explanation for the disappearance of *Seawitch*. You can understand better than anyone that I need to set some things right with those ghosts and Gary Fielding." I saw a question forming on his lips and cut it off. "I can't go into the reasons but I also have a duty to the world I live in—I didn't choose it but it's still mine. And that includes, at the moment, doing something to free the ghosts of *Valencia* and *Seawitch* and get Gary Fielding straightened out in some way."

Solis narrowed his eyes. "If he caused the deaths of the people on board *Seawitch*, it will require more than straightening out."

"That's another thing we'll have to deal with when it comes. We may not have any way to bring him to human justice. If that's even applicable. You may have to swallow dealing with this my way."

His face settled back into his customary stillness and he didn't say another word.

I wanted to tell him he couldn't do anything to change it, but I just shook my head and got up from the galley table, wincing as new bruises expanded the zone of discomfort in my back, side, and chest. "I need to dry off and warm up before my muscles freeze up completely."

"Your rib. My apologies; I'd forgotten."

"I wish *I* could. This is slowing me down more than I'd hoped. And it hurts!" I added with an attempt at humor that fell a little flat on our ears. "I'll tell you this, though: If we have any chance to catch one of those merfolk, we'd better take it. We could use some more leverage than just the bell."

I left him to put on an extra layer of clothes. While I was in the cabin Quinton and I had been sharing, I took another look at the bell. Fielding had mentioned it as he disappeared. Examining it now, at my leisure and without someone looking over my shoulder, I let my vision shift as I sank closer to the Grey.

The bell was no longer bronze but black, wrapped in green tangles that sent out long, thin streamers that vanished into the eastern distance of the Grey. The boiling agitation of the ghosts within pushed outward into a thick smoke of faces and forms twisted into one another. I put out one hand, wondering if I could just pluck the mess apart and let the ghosts go their own way, but a warning roar came from the ghosts and they flared red as if their agonized faces were washed in the light of a conflagration. I guessed that was a pretty strong hint that if I did anything to the spell that held them in the bell now—or here—the situation would only get worse. Though worse for them or worse for me, I didn't know.

I eased back a little, still immersed in the Grey, still concentrating on the bell. "Well," I whispered. "You wanted them and I've got them, but damned if I know what I'm supposed to do with them now."

I raised my voice a little and tried to call the Guardian Beast, concentrating on its form as if my thoughts could pull it to me. "I could use a little help here. . . ."

Nothing replied except the ghosts of *Valencia*, moaning like the wind. I tried reaching out into the Grey, gathering threads and pulling or shaking them, begging the Guardian to show its misty hide, but nothing seemed to have any effect. I couldn't even hear it in the distance as I sometimes did, going about its business. In desperation, I tried appealing to Will or whatever might remain of him, but to that the silence was even colder.

"Come on, you slippery bastard!" I shouted. "Get over here and tell me what I'm supposed to do! I've got the lost you wanted, but I'll lose 'em if you don't give me some clue what you want me to do with them!"

I turned again to the bell. "It said 'Find the lost' and I've found you. I think. But now it wants to play coy. Obviously just finding you guys isn't the end of this situation. It's not as if the Guardian actually cares about suffering, because it's never done a damned thing about it before, so what's the problem?"

"Power," the ghosts sighed. They stretched out from the mouth of the bell in wisps and eddies, curling around me, dizzying me with their ever-changing faces and forms.

"Yes, all right. Your souls represent a storage unit of power, but why does it care about that *now*?"

"Now the cycle renews itself. Now the floodgates open. We were not alone."

"Oh no . . . He—it—the Guardian Beast wants me to free *all* of the souls the sea witch controls? How do I do *that*? Without becoming one of you, too."

They made the incorporeal equivalent of a shrug, billowing around and moaning minor-key arpeggios that moved the mist of the Grey in swirls of smoke and blackness.

If she had other captive souls—and she certainly had at least four from *Seawitch* and possibly more—then she kept them where she'd kept the boat for so long. "Open floodgates . . ." So the door was open and where creatures like the merfolk who'd attacked us could get out, others, like us, could go in. But wherever it was, it would have to be a place with a twin in the Grey. It had swallowed up living things before, so . . . it was a sort of Grey Brigadoon—a magical place that appears for a while and then disappears again, going about its business, undisturbed in the ghost world, until the door is open again. The door had opened long enough for Gary Fielding to slip out with *Seawitch* and the ghosts of *Valencia*, but it was closing again.

"We have to find the cove. Where is it? Can't *you* tell me?"

The spirits sang on in their dreary, coiling tune of hopelessness and told me nothing. I pulled back toward normal, seeking warmth as much as respite from the company of ghosts, and sat on the edge of the bunk, staring at the bell.

It was heavy and plainly wrought with the little loop and a bead around the top and the flattened edge at the mouth upon which the name had been engraved. Not cast, so the ship hadn't been important enough to make a custom casting, but enough to cut the name into the bronze lip rather than let it go without; enough to tie it to one ship only. A ship so long lost that only a single lifeboat and a few pieces of timber had ever been recovered.

I flicked a fingernail against the bell's lip. It made a dull chime that rippled across the Grey and washed through me with a sensation of pressure and cold that made me cough and catch my breath. The green coils around the bell sparked bright for a moment, sending a pulse out into the distance along the threadlike tendrils that reached to the east. The ghosts moaned and flared into a bright curtain of terrified faces, frozen as if by an actinic flash. Then they faded away to no more than a distant whisper and the feel of ice water trickling down my back. The green light around the bell faded more slowly, lingering like a disturbed phosphorescence on the surface of nighttime waters.

I yanked a heavier sweater on over my still-damp head and found some thicker, drier socks to pull on before I resumed wearing my wet shoes. Then I tucked the gun I'd left on the bed earlier into a zippered interior pocket of my jacket and put that on, too, before I picked up the bell and carried it to the main cabin.

Solis, coming up from the galley, gave me a curious look. "The *Valencia*'s bell?"

"Yes," I said. "I've been wondering how we're going to get into the place *Seawitch* was held, since it remained hidden for twenty-seven years. So it's a place that exists more in the paranormal than the normal, though it has a normal twin. You don't just walk into that sort of location—or motor, as the case may be."

"Indeed?"

"Take my word for it. The easy way in is to die. I don't think any of us want to do that just to take a look around the merfolk's living room. We need a door opener. And after thinking about Fielding's last words, I think this is—literally—it."

"How?"

"Well . . . not only is it connected to two of the boats and crews who've been trapped in the mystery cove we're looking for, but it's a bell."

Solis looked puzzled and Quinton glancing down from the bridge hatch asked, "Why is that important?"

"What?" Zantree asked, out of sight.

"The bell," Quinton explained.

"What are bells for?" I asked.

"To ring signals," Zantree shouted down.

"And to ring for assistance. Or entry," I responded. "Magic is sometimes ridiculously literal. In this case, the bell is . . . also a doorbell. I think."

"What makes you think so?" asked Solis.

"I felt it. I flicked the edge of the bell with my fingernail and the ringing sent out a wave that I could feel passing in the paranormal fringes. Like a ripple on water. This bell is tied to the location it was hidden in, so ringing it causes a reaction there—in the paranormal 'there,' that is."

"Some kind of magical entanglement, like electrons?" Quinton asked.

"If you say so," I replied, carrying the bell up to the bridge station. Solis followed me. "Also I noticed that the merfolk made a noise as they retreated that sounded like something clanging in the distance. Or they were responding to the clanging—I'm not sure which. Either way, ringing or clanging, a bell is a bell and this one rings in the cove where *Seawitch* was kept for the past twenty-seven years. I'd bet my life on it."

"That doesn't mean it'll open the front door for us," Quinton said.

"No," I agreed, "but the sea witch will if she wants it back, which I'm quite sure she does. We just have to find the cove."

"That's not going to be easy."

"It can't be very far away, since the merfolk could hear the recall bell when they attacked us. And there is a practical limit to how far even the most powerful wizard can cast an illusion spell like the sea witch used on us."

"Sound travels easier and farther underwater since both air and water are liquids. Water is denser so the rate of energy loss is lower," Quinton offered.

"But even so, I'll bet it doesn't travel around corners," I said.

Quinton shook his head. "Only insofar as the sound waves fan out when they exit a restriction. The direction of travel from the source will be straight until the sound waves reflect off something, and the more they bounce around, the faster they decay."

I nodded. "Look at the chart and see where the sound waves could travel from to reach us without violating the laws of physics. The cove will be in that area."

"There're a dozen little coves and bays between us and anywhere that noise could have come from," Zantree objected, clutching the wheel and making a correction against the current and wind to take us farther into the safe center of the channel and away from the rocks at the edges.

"It would have to be farther from here than Lonesome Cove," I said, thinking aloud, "because Fielding said he missed that opportunity. Just where is Lonesome Cove, anyhow?"

"It's on the north side of San Juan on Spieden Channel," Zantree replied.

I set the bell down on the chart table beside the steering station. "Fielding said he had to pass up the northern entrance to Roche Harbor and was heading for Lonesome, but when I asked if that was where the *Seawitch* had ended up, he said no. He didn't get to say where the boat did finally come to rest, but it definitely wasn't Lonesome Cove. Unless there's another cove between Lonesome and Pearl Island . . ."

"Nothing you could hide a ninety-some-foot boat in," Zantree said.

"What about beyond Lonesome Cove?"

"I can't remember every blasted cove and bay in the islands! Quinton, take a look at that chart—page forty-six or so. Up and down Spieden Channel on the north end of San Juan Island, east of Vancouver Island."

Quinton flipped over pages of a massive chart book, laying one of them flat on the folded-back book and running his fingers across the rough-edged, inverted-pear shapes of the big islands and the shapeless blobs of smaller ones until he found Spieden Island and the channel south of it. He guided his fingers along the outline of San Juan's northern shore. "I see Davison Head . . . Lonesome Point . . . Lonesome Cove. . . . Maybe across the channel on Spieden, by Green Point? Or around the east side of San Juan into Rocky Bay?"

Zantree shook his head but kept his eyes on the view ahead. "With the wind he was describing, they couldn't cut straight across to the lee of Green Point. Rocky Bay would have been too rough—they don't call it Rocky for nothing. He said he'd tried for Davison Head, but he obviously didn't make it or he'd have been home and dry, as long as he avoided the submerged pilings—and there'd have been a famous stink if he'd taken her aground on them. Look straight on down the channel."

"There's nothing down the channel. It opens up at the end of San Juan Island and there's nothing else but Orcas unless you hook back over the top of Spieden Island."

"Jones! It's got to be Jones Island or I'm a gaffed marlin!"

"Why would it be Jones?" Solis asked.

"Because if what these two are saying about the sound traveling is right, Jones is the only landfall it could come from. It's straight down the throat of Spieden Channel! That big rock before you reach Orcas." He reached over and stabbed at the chart with his forefinger, mashing the page flat. "Right there."

We leaned closer as he straightened up to keep both hands on the twitching wheel. Where he'd pressed the map lay a modest lump of an island with a nibble taken from the north and south shores. Jones Island. An unobstructed line drawn through Spieden Channel to *Seawitch*'s last known location cut right through the island's northernmost point that guarded the nearly round little bite of North Cove.

TWENTY-THREE

It wasn't tiny but on the map Jones Island wasn't much more. There were smaller islands in the San Juans, but few as oddly alone as Jones. Smack in the middle of the confluence of several channels, the misshapen little island seemed isolated from its neighbors, though none of them was actually far away. The looming bulk of San Juan stood to its west and the long finger of Spieden pointed just over it to the massive curve of Orcas on the east. A few smaller islands stood below it like fallen crumbs and above it opened the passage to the northernmost islands, an empty stretch of churning water where the currents of the tidal race began their restless way through the riddles and gyres of the north Sound.

"North Cove's a pretty place," Zantree said, considering the chart, "but no one I know ever drops their hook there for long."

"I imagine that the merfolk make sure it stays that way," I said. Even if they aren't entirely corporeal all the time, the denizens of the Grey have ways of making their presence known and driving off the unwanted attentions of normal people without showing their true nature: cold breezes, unpleasant smells, disquieting glimpses from the corner of your eye that are gone when you turn around, and the sense that—for no reason you can name—you need to leave. With all that deep cold water to play in, they probably had a whole host of tricks I'd never seen

before, too, but I had no doubt I'd get familiar with them
soon enough.

Once *Mambo Moon* had fought clear of the rocks and
currents, the rest of the trip up Haro Strait was easy
enough. But even with the current now in our favor,
once we turned southeast above Henry Island the trip
down Spieden Channel was a bitter fight for every yard
in the teeth of a cold and adverse wind that sprang from
nowhere and rushed up the narrow passage like a fury.
Ragged white lines appeared where current-driven wave
tops were whipped into foam by the wind coming from
the opposite direction. The water in the channel became
a choppy ribbon of dark blue crossed with white that
sent the boat lurching up and then banging down like a
hobbyhorse with a squirrely front end.

We each took a turn at the bow—mine cut a bit short
by the swooning pain in my ribs—clipped safely in place
with lines from our flotation vests to the rails. We kept a
lookout for anything that might come under the boat as
it reared up, but nothing significant did and we all got
chilled in our damp, borrowed slickers as the sun started
its slow summer crawl to the horizon. With the bulk of
Vancouver Island far behind, the channel was cast into
shadow long before dusk.

As we bowed and reared, the *Valencia*'s bell gave out
occasional muffled chimes that sent a frisson through me
and plunged the world into a dark cloud of the Grey for a
few moments. The noise seemed to be folding reality, layer-
ing the normal and the Grey into a pleat where both appeared equally solid and real for the fleeting moments that
they remained aligned. Between the motion, my cranky
rib, and the fluttering of the worlds, I felt distinctly seasick
by the time *Mambo Moon* finally exited Spieden Channel.
Directly ahead lay Jones Island, shining gold in the wester-
ing sun between purple shadows lying on the water from
San Juan and Spieden islands, closing on the little nub of
land with their encroaching darkness like the pincers of a
giant black crab.

Within a minute of the boat's leaving the channel, the wind died down and the swells smoothed out as we hit the wider, more populated water. I was the last on lookout duty and I slogged my way along the deck sideways, bent and favoring my aching side. The bridge had its own doors that opened onto steps down to the side decks and I climbed them at a snail's pace to leave my moist coat on a hook just inside the starboard door. The three men were in the pilothouse when I entered, panting.

"You look done in, Harper," Zantree said from his post at the wheel.

I nodded. Quinton stepped close to draw me in tight against his chest so my back pressed to his heat while his arms circled my waist. Since I'm taller than he is, it was a little awkward, but I didn't care. Warmth is warmth and when it comes from an attractive man who loves you, you don't quibble about the way his chin hits your shoulder.

"How much longer?" I asked.

Zantree scrubbed at his damp hair with one hand as he answered. "Well, assuming we're in the right place and all, maybe forty minutes at this pace. But I don't get how we're going to see anything but the park service dock and a few tourists."

"I'll have to get our hosts to come out and open the gate to Neverland," I said.

I tried ringing the bell, but inside the confines of the pilothouse I couldn't generate a solid peal, only an anemic clank or ping that shuttered the world in darkness for a moment before it fell away again. The men all flinched as the overlapping world flickered in and out of view.

I looked at each of them. "What are you seeing or hearing that's making you cringe like that?" I knew what I was experiencing, but none of them were Greywalkers or even particularly sensitive to the Grey, though Solis seemed to take it in a bit more. Did the bell actually have some power to call up an entrance or was I imagining— hoping for—more than was possible?

"It's fast," Quinton said. "For just a second . . . it's like seeing the world in the light of an eclipse."

"Bleak," Solis said. "It is not just a darkness but . . . a loss."

"Storm light's what it looks like to me," Zantree said. "Like we're on the edge of a hurricane or a blow coming down."

"Do you feel something or is it just visual?" I asked.

"It's cold," Quinton said, and Zantree nodded.

But Solis frowned, shaking his head a little. "There is . . . expectation. Something waiting in the cold."

Maybe it's a cop thing—that intuition the good ones develop—that was giving Solis that extra bit of knowledge, but whether it was from his background, his family, his job, or being dragged in by me, he was picking up more than either of the other men. It was strange that Quinton wasn't getting more, considering how much time he spent with me, but perhaps the difference in perception was in kind rather than in degree. Either way, I guessed I needed a louder, longer tone before the phenomenon would hold steady.

"I guess I have to take it outside," I said.

"Why?" Quinton asked.

"The bell seems to resist ringing indoors. At a guess, I'd say the ghosts are deliberately muffling it and all I can think of is to try it outside. Don't know why they'd care but they do seem to."

"It doesn't have to be you who takes it," he said. "You're tired already and chances are good that a lot of whatever has to be done next will fall on your shoulders. So why don't you sit down and I'll do it?"

I didn't get to reply. Solis cut me off. "I will take it. You and Zantree know the boat. Blaine needs rest. I have been almost useless so far."

It looked as if Quinton would have argued but Zantree talked right over him.

"So long as you don't go overboard again," Zantree said. "If we're as close as Harper thinks, I doubt we'll be able to haul you back if those fish-tailed man snatchers drag you over this time. Get the harness on and clip in soon as you're out the door. Or I'll toss y'down below and lock you in till we're heading home. Not having any more rescue drills on this cruise, damn it."

Solis cocked one eyebrow but all he returned was a sardonic, "Aye, Captain."

Quinton helped Solis with the safety harness and the flotation gear, giving him a funny look. "Not wearing a red shirt under there, are you?"

"What?"

"*Star Trek*—the red shirt guys always get the ax."

"Ah. No."

"You only need to ring it once," I said. "I'll know if it works." I wanted to tell him to be careful but that seemed condescending. Instead I shut up and watched with a double flutter of anxiety—both mine and Quinton's—in my chest as Solis stepped outside with the bronze bell clutched in his hands and secured to his life vest by a line and clip through the loop on top. I hoped it wouldn't drag him down if he was again swept overboard.

Solis didn't go all the way out to the bow as I'd half expected, but stopped at the side deck, attaching his safety line to the nearest rail. He didn't need more room and it was foolish to go farther than he had to—a choice I mentally applauded. He didn't take any chances with grabby monsters this time but hooked his left arm around the hand rail on the stairs he'd just descended. Then he held the bell out and let it swing from its loop until the clapper struck hard against the body.

A loud, round peal rolled out from the bell like the report from a cannon, visible in the Grey as a rushing wave that rippled the material of the world and spun a hollow bubble of ghost-stuff around us, encapsulating *Mambo Moon* in a sphere that was both Grey and normal at the same time. The walls of the overlapping worlds shimmered and wavered like the skin of a soap bubble riding a paranormal breeze.

In the distance a chorus of unearthly voices roared in fury and an answering clang, and a shriek, less musical but more forceful, shivered the air, pushing on our bubble. The thin skin of mist and darkness around the boat held together, but quivered and melded to the arriving shock front, leaving us with only the thinnest barrier of Grey against Grey to hold back whatever had generated the opposing force.

I watched this odd phenomenon—like two soap bubbles kissing and then creating a flat section where they met, the surfaces shivering with reflections and the sliding play of storm light on the curved surfaces—and paid scant attention to my companions in the pilothouse until I heard Quinton whisper, "Is this . . . what it's like . . . ?"

I shook myself and turned my head to him, barely noticing the twitching of the chronometer on the navigation console.

"What it's like? I don't know. What do you see?" I asked, my voice low and uncomfortably rough in my throat.

Quinton stared out at the curved walls of our bubble and the sphere of the next pressing against it. "Beautiful and cold . . . like ice in the Arctic, colors buried in deep chill, running from the sky in ribbons like the aurora. . . ."

I felt the fleeting warmth and soaring sensation of his wonder but had to say, "Not to me. That's not what I see." And a colder feeling, born of memory and mist-touched terrors, dulled his reflected excitement and left me a little sad.

"I hate it," Zantree growled. "Give me the plain blue sea over this . . . pea-soup nightmare anytime."

So . . . like other aspects of the Grey, this one also reflected the viewer's own expectation and memory. Quinton saw cold beauty while Zantree experienced a mist filled with dangers.

I looked out at Solis and saw the interface of the two Grey spheres bow toward him. I threw myself out the door as the glassy surface between them shattered under a rush of water as white as a bridal dress and deadly cold.

Solis turned his shoulder to the falling wave, bending his body over the bell and crouching against the deck as the wave crashed into him. I shot down the steps with a sharp pang, oblivious to my lack of safety gear, and snatched at his lifeline.

"Solis!" I yelled as I yanked him toward the steps, only to feel my feet swept out from under me. I landed hard on my hip, dazed and breathless with pain.

Something hard and cold banged into my shoulder and I found myself scooped up and shoved back up the steps and into the pilothouse. Solis came through, dripping, behind me and slammed the door shut against the collapsing wall of water as both bubbles of Grey popped and dissolved.

Mambo Moon rocked violently and then bobbed back up, settling into the water again as the shadow of Vancouver and Spieden islands dropped away and let us back into the golden light of a summer's evening. The noise of the bells cut off as suddenly as the wave had receded and we bobbed again on a gently rolling sea of deep blue, Jones Island dead ahead and as large as Rushmore.

Solis coughed a little and pulled off his safety gear, untying the bell from his vest and laying it on the floor, mouth down. "Fifteen minutes," he said.

"What was fifteen minutes?" I gasped, trying to sit up without wincing.

"The elapsed time since I rang the bell. I thought it would be useful to know. . . ."

I blinked as I caught my breath and got myself upright. I hadn't thought of it and I supposed no one else had either, but it was helpful since the chronometer on the nav indicated a passage of only five minutes. The bell's Grey state lasted three times longer than the passage of normal time. Or was it the other way around?

"Whatever it was, we've drifted up close on Jones,"

Zantree observed. "I'll have to steer hard to port to make the turn around the point safely, so hold on."

The boat swayed as Zantree turned it away from the island, heading north, and then corrected back down in a few minutes to position us just outside the mouth of the cove. There he reversed the engines and brought *Mambo Moon* to a halt.

"Well," he asked, "do we go on as we are or do we ring the doorbell first?"

"I think we'll have to ring," I replied.

This time I made Solis stay inside and went out to strike the bell myself, the dark silver storm front of the Grey chime this time expanding outward and away from us to enclose most of the tiny bay instead of the boat. The bubble didn't grow evenly but seemed to cleave to some invisible edge, climbing the cliff on the west and leaving a crescent of untouched, normal water near the eastern shore while a fugue of mist and thrashing wavelets filled the space within the visible half of the sphere. Dead white things flashed below the churned surface and broached to reveal glimpses of glazed eyes and restless tentacles that trailed seaweed.

I swallowed hard, feeling my stomach flip over at the sight of the unsettled Grey waters. We waited but nothing gave any indication that we should advance or turn back.

Zantree looked at me. "What do we do now, commander?"

"I'm not sure. Can you make it to that clear stretch without entering the bubble?" I asked, pointing to the calm stretch of eastern water.

He studied the cove a moment, then nodded. "Yup. I can get her in there. But why do you want me to avoid the bubble, exactly? It didn't do us any harm the last time."

"We were alone inside last time. I don't really want to be inside with those things just yet," I said.

He nodded, brought the burbling engines back up just

a little, and then put the big boat in forward gear, easing it around the flickering mist edge of the Grey boundary, keeping us in the normal and the things inside undisturbed by our passage.

As we slipped between the two arms of land that enclosed the cove, he brought the boat around sharply to port once again, keeping as much safe distance between us and the bubble as possible. We slid without challenge into the tiny cove on the island's north shore.

The cove was nearly a perfect circle of water, embraced in the two reaching arms of the north and east points that enclosed the short spit of the park service dock at the south extreme of the bowl, directly across from the entrance. In spite of the early-summer weather, the calm little anchorage was abandoned; no other boat stood anywhere within the bay. The island beyond rose to a spine of rocky ground covered in still-green grass and tall, slim firs and cedars. The gentle slope at the dock's end rose into craggy, tumbled cliffs on the curving scarp of the encircling points that enfolded the cove. To the west lay the northernmost point of the island, tall, stark, and black in the shadow of the slowly creeping sunset. On the east the cliff fell into a scatter of massive stones that had rolled down from the treed, curving spine of the island. The sun struck the wet black rocks a burnished gold that writhed with creatures.

"Don't know that I've ever seen it this . . . empty," Zantree said, his voice hushed as if he feared something watching us with malevolent intent.

I pointed to the eastern cliffs and their strange movement. "What's that?"

Zantree peered at it, then pulled a pair of binoculars from a box fixed to the side of the steering station and looked through them.

"Otters. It's a colony of sea otters. Well, I'll be blowed. . . ."

TWENTY-FOUR

I found myself turning to watch the expressions of Quinton and Solis. Quinton stared toward the cliff, his mouth slightly open with excitement and awe. Solis looked haunted.

"Do you see . . . Fielding?" I asked Zantree.

He scanned the cliff with the binoculars. "Not sure. There's a dark shape in the water near the cliff base that *might* be him—it's a lot larger than the others. . . ."

"Can you get us near them without cutting into the bubble? We're probably safer near the otters than anywhere else," I said.

Zantree frowned. "I thought we needed to go into the . . . whatever you call that bubble thing."

"It's an overlap where both the near-paranormal and the normal are visible and operating simultaneously. I've seen something related before. This one is the merfolk's realm as it intersects ours. The temporary intersection acts as a gateway, or, as the ghosts put it, a gap in the worlds where both states exist in the same place and time until the gap closes when its operating schedule dictates. In this case I believe the cycle is twenty-seven years, because that's how long it was from the time *Valencia* went down until its lifeboat was found and the same amount of time from the disappearance of *Seawitch* to its reappearance. Since it's tied to water, I'm also guessing the cycle's tidal in nature—it ebbs and swells, so Fielding or his dobhar-chú relatives snuck *Sea-witch* out in the magical equivalent of slack water. And I'm pretty sure it's the only place to solve this mystery. I don't want you to take the boat in there if we can avoid it, and not until we're ready if we can't. If—when—the state that's keeping this gateway open collapses, *Mambo Moon* could be trapped in the merfolk's realm for the next twenty-seven years, just like *Seawitch* was. I don't think you'd enjoy *that* adventure."

Zantree shuddered. "Not my idea of fun, being drowned by merfolk."

"I'm not sure if that bubble will stay in place all of whatever remaining time we've got. . . ."

"It has been stable for more than the fifteen minutes our previous test lasted," Solis said.

"Really?" I replied.

He nodded.

"Then maybe it's going to hold steady. . . ."

"Hope for the best, but prepare for a storm," Zantree said, steering for the eastern rocks. "I'll keep the *Moon* out of the bubble for now. We can't get in too close to the cliff since we're coming on high tide, and as the tide runs out again the *Moon*'ll swing on her chain. We don't want to run aground out here—or slide into that freaky ghost wall when the boat tries to come around with the current. But we can drop the dink and set a stern anchor once we get the bow down. That'll keep her safe off the rocks and out of . . . that."

Quinton nodded and I mirrored him, though I had no idea what I'd just agreed with. Solis frowned at the lot of us as if he were rethinking the whole mad escapade and checked his watch again.

Zantree maneuvered the boat around about a hundred yards or so from the eastern cliffs until he found a location that satisfied him, then dropped the anchor off the bow with a rattling of chain running off the winch. Then he and Quinton took the dinghy out with a second anchor aboard and put it down a good distance out toward the mouth of the cove. They finished up by securing the second anchor rope to a cleat at the rear of the boat, which held *Mambo Moon* in position with her bow toward the distant dock and her stern toward the entry to the cove. "So we can cut and run if we have to," Zantree explained, though it didn't really help me visualize what he meant. I assumed our would-be pirate captain knew what he was doing since he'd got us this far intact, but I admit I was worried; our position was precarious and we were lying between the local version of Scylla and Charybdis. We'd have to wait a few minutes and see what the dobhar-chú and merfolk would do now that we were here. They had to be feeling the time pressure as much as I was, so I hoped they wouldn't dawdle.

The light in the cove seemed thicker and more golden on the normal side of the water, though the long summer day was nowhere near ending. Our "quick run" had taken nearly ten hours—double the time it should have, according to Zantree. I wondered how long we could count on the presence of the otters and their Grey kin to keep the merfolk at bay, or if the forces of the sea witch would hold off until the fleeting hours of night to make their move against us—and they surely would move. I didn't know if we could defend ourselves or even see them coming outside the bubble generated by the *Valencia*'s bell. I hoped it would hold, as I didn't think it was practical to strike the damned bell every fifteen minutes and I wasn't even sure that doing so would keep the layered zone of Grey and normal intact. I suspected we'd have only one short chance to confront the sea witch before the bubble collapsed and dragged us into her realm permanently—or close enough to make no difference. I might survive in her bit of the Grey, but my companions didn't have the same skills and their chances would be slim.

Once Zantree declared the boat secure and shut down the engines, I went out on the foredeck to study the Grey bubble.

The cove was about a mile across at most and we were only a dozen yards or so from the bulging edge of the fringe zone. Still no sign of the Guardian Beast, I noted, so nothing that shouldn't have been here was lurking nearby, but the things that *did* belong were frightening enough on their own. I felt more than heard someone walk up behind me and stop by the rail. I turned.

Solis was frowning out at the curving Grey wall as he held on to the rail. "It is a mirror," he said, without turning his head to me. "It reflects what you believe."

"That's an interesting thing to say." I don't know why I was surprised he'd come to that conclusion; as a detective, he must have been observing everyone's reactions and putting his own experience together with theirs to get a better idea of the situation as a whole. I supposed he'd finally thrown out his resistance to the idea of the paranormal.

"Do you not find it so?"

"Yes and no. I see a lot of things I never even knew existed, so they can't be just what I believe ... or the whole magical world would be a black blank to me."

"You believe in nothing?"

"I believe in people, both what's good and what's bad in them. And I think that's what I see, even when it isn't something I know. But I also see — or experience — more. Things that aren't just constructs of human belief, though I must in some way filter it through my own knowledge, memories, fears ... otherwise I couldn't recognize it enough to take it in through my own senses at all. It seems to be a state that's objective and subjective at the same time."

"When will it come for us?"

The boat swayed and lurched a little as someone moved around inside and the waves in the cove rolled gently under the keel. "It won't," I replied. "But the things inside it will—they want a resolution to this situation as much as we do—and they'll either bring the perception shift with them or drag us to it. They're ... I'd say 'real' but that's not quite the idea I want. . . . 'Corporeal' is the best I can do. These things aren't ghosts. Well, there *are* ghosts here and in the bell, but the things we have to deal with have physical bodies. They can do us physical harm."

"And can we harm them?"

I nodded, taking note of a slithering sound near the aft—maybe Quinton or Zantree was opening up the sliding doors. "Of course. You made some nice bloody holes in the one that grabbed you. I saw it bleeding."

He nodded. "Good."

"I approve also," said a rough, new voice from the side deck.

Solis and I turned around and looked back toward the aft. Quinton stepped out onto the stairs from the pilot-house and looked down at our visitor with a startled expression.

The man was only a few feet forward of the stern deck and he crouched, naked, in a pool of water. He glanced at each of us as he stood up slowly, unfazed by his nudity or our stares. He was about Solis's height, pale skinned and dark haired, and his eyes were a startling, clear blue—like those of some dogs. He appeared to be in his early fifties, judging by the lines on his face and the slight brush of silver hair at his temples, but he had the body of a sleek, young athlete—a swimmer or a gymnast, I'd have said, since he wasn't skinny enough to be a dancer or unbalanced like a runner. He also had the sort of strong, active aura I associate with magical creatures: This one was a bright halo of violet and green that whirled with tiny white globes of energy glowing like pearls.

He nodded to me, apparently having decided I was in charge. "Our cousin requires help beyond my ability," he said in his gravelly voice, exposing sharp teeth with pronounced upper and lower canines, a little more like a ferret's than a man's but not as mismatched as Fielding's had been. "You must come with me."

I gave him a doubtful glare and did my best to keep my gaze only on his face. "Must?"

He seemed puzzled at my reply. "Of course. That is why we sent him to you to begin with."

"This cousin would be . . . Gary Fielding?" I guessed.

He nodded with raised eyebrows, as if he thought me a bit dim, but wasn't going to insult me by mentioning it. "Please. We can go now? I find this form uncomfortable."

This form. . . . I made a not so wild guess. "You're Father Otter, then?"

He gave another, slightly impatient nod and pointed toward the eastern cliffs. "This is our holt. Within awaits our cousin, who will not live unless you come now." He turned and loped along a wet trail back to the stern, where the ladder came up from the swim platform. So that's how he'd come aboard. He scowled back at us once again. "We none of us have time to waste. Come."

I looked at Quinton and Solis. I didn't want to leave the boat, where I had allies and dry decks beneath my feet and any fishy adversaries were at a disadvantage. However, I was sure I'd need the help of the dobhar-chú to bring this business to a close and I knew I wouldn't get it unless I helped Gary Fielding. The thought of getting into the chilly waters of the Sound gave me a shiver as I remembered drowning as a child and all the times I'd been soaked since the beginning of this case, not to mention the dreadful things that lived in the water of this cove. . . .

Father Otter glared at me. "You will not help?"

I walked past Solis and Quinton to get closer to our visitor, but not close enough to be grabbed and hauled overboard. "I will if I can," I replied, "but . . . I don't do water very well."

"You cannot swim?"

"I can swim, but I get cold when wet. That will make it hard for me to help your cousin, especially since we have to act fast or we'll be stuck here."

Father Otter rolled his eyes and shook his head in disgust. "Bring yourself by boat to the crouch. It is dry within." He pointed to a particularly cluttered bit of the tumbled shoreline where there seemed to be an inordinate number of shadows that resisted the sunlight. "We will meet you there and take you within. Bring your assistant if you must. But soon. The merfolk gather their strength." That at least explained the cease-fire since we'd arrived and confirmed my thought that the sea witch had to husband her resources with care.

Then Father Otter turned his back, crouching and shrinking into the compact, dark-furred form of a massive otter. A cross of white fur marked his spine and shoulders. The huge otter turned its head to give us one last, annoyed glance before it dove under the rail and out, into the water, vanishing below the surface in a ripple that formed an arrow toward the cliffs before it dissipated into the rolling tide.

I turned back to Solis and Quinton and saw Zantree looking out of the pilothouse door also. "I guess I don't have a lot of choices . . ." I said.

Quinton and Solis both stepped toward me, saying, "I'll come with you." Then they stopped and glanced at each other.

"I'll go by myself," I said.

"You don't know that you'll be safe," Quinton objected, his aura spiking with alarm and sending little breathless jolts through our connection.

"I won't be any safer with an escort. There's bound to be more of them than us and I can't hope to fight my way out, so I'll have to presume their goodwill, because as much as I need their help, they need mine."

"What if something happens and you can't get back on your own?"

"I have my pistol in my pocket. If the dobhar-chú can't help me, I'm sure you'll hear it if I have to use it."

Quinton didn't like it but he knew I wasn't going to

budge on that point. Solis continued toward me with a determined expression.

"Now, wait a minute," I started.

"I am coming."

"No, you aren't. You heard what I just said."

"Yes. But I am not your boyfriend. I am your fellow investigator and Gary Fielding is material to my case as well."

Quinton scowled and I didn't have to experience his secondhand flare of confusion, jealousy, and discomfort to know how he was feeling.

I objected. "Solis—"

Solis shook his head as he came up to where I was standing. "There is no argument. He said to bring your assistant if you must. I am the only person who qualifies and I *will* come."

"Well, if it's that easy—" Quinton started.

I held out one palm to nip that in the bud. "It isn't. If I have to put up with you guys being high-handed, then Solis has the best argument. And here's one more: I don't think more than two humans will be welcome and even that number is obviously begrudged. Do not push it."

Quinton's mouth hardened and he looked belligerent, but after a second or two sorting out the battle between emotion and logic, he let out a hard breath and quirked one corner of his mouth into a resigned nonsmile. "All right. You are the boss and you know what you're doing. I'll stick here with Zantree and wait. For a while."

I gave him a grateful smile and went over to kiss his cheek. "Thank you."

"Just come back fast—those fish-butts aren't going to stay off our backs for long."

"I know. If they come, just keep them off the boat and away from the bell. We'll be back as soon as we can. And you know I love you and need you, right?"

"Yeah. And I love you . . . even when you're a bull-headed pain in my ass." He finally returned my kiss and then turned me around to face the aft rail before we got too maudlin. "Now get going."

Zantree had no interest in butting into the conversation or tagging along, but he helped us get the dinghy deployed again and heading for shore with me and Solis aboard. It was only when we were on the way that I realized the little vessel was in the hands of the half of the party who knew almost nothing about handling boats. Luckily the water on the eastern edge of the cove was nearly still and the boat was a simple outboard type without a lot of bells and whistles to deal with and no oars to pull. We drew near the tumbled rocks and cut the engine, letting it glide toward the shadow Father Otter had indicated.

Three wet, dark otter heads popped up, bristling whiskers and making chuffing snorts, sniffing at us as we neared. They eyed us thoroughly before the largest one turned back toward the rocks and the other two swam forward to guide us in by bumping the gliding dinghy into the proper path with their bodies. I had seen otters at the Seattle Aquarium and it wasn't until one of our escorts was cruising along the side of the boat only a few inches from my hand that I realized how big they are. This one was typical at about five feet long, including its rudderlike tail, and probably weighed between ninety and a hundred pounds. It rolled on its back in the water and yawned, showing off its mouthful of ivory-colored fangs. I've heard otters referred to as clowns and playful, but seeing one that close I knew "play" was relative—it would be no work at all for this giant seagoing ferret to snap off one of my fingers or break one of my arms if it got those teeth into me. And while they had a thick coat of fur, the body underneath was all muscle, and quick with it. I hoped I would have no reason to tussle with any of the creatures living under Father Otter's aegis, especially since dobhar-chú were even larger than the garden-variety sea otter swimming beside us.

In a few minutes the boat had come to a soft halt against the cliff base where a small, low cave had been carved into the rock by aeons of waves. Solis and I climbed out of the dinghy with care and jammed the little boat's rope between two rocks so it wouldn't drift away, though the otters looked at us with quivering-whisker expressions that implied they'd never seen a human do anything as silly as that before. At their vocal insistence, aided by nose prods and dirty looks, we scrambled for the cave and were met by one of the dobhar-chú—or I assumed it was since it was about twenty-five percent larger and had the telltale white cross on its back that I'd seen on both Fielding and Father Otter. Its bellow was something between a large cat's mew and a dog's bark. It looked us over and trotted off into the darkness at the back of the cave. Solis and I exchanged wary glances and followed it, stumbling on the slick, uneven rock of the upward-sloping cave floor. I winced with every jarring misstep and slip of the foot as we went.

In the dark all trips seem too long and perilous. Eddies and hollows of Grey washed around us, unnoticed by Solis, who kept his eyes on the dobhar-chú, while time rushed and lagged and broke into temporaclines that sparkled like shattered glass I dared not touch. The sound of muttering and mewling echoed ahead of us as we walked. In those weirdly dilated minutes, we passed through a ghost forest tilted at a disorienting angle and then through a flash of heat that dissipated into a bland, dim illumination the color of lichen. Before us opened a low-ceilinged cavern thick with half-lit things and the odor of fish and wet fur. Around the edges the cave seemed to writhe and it took a moment for me to realize the movement and the sound I'd been hearing all along was actually dozens of otters and dobhar-chú lounging, grooming, or moving in and out of the area through passages on each end that brought diluted air and light in from the outside. At our end a clearing had been made near the wall to accommodate a small group of dobhar-chú gathered around the misshapen bulk of Gary Fielding.

Fielding's situation had deteriorated badly since we'd seen him earlier in the day. The dobhar-chú had settled him in a depression in the rock and filled it with water, but either there wasn't enough water, or his brush with the merfolk had done him some new injury that brought trickles of blood from his eyes and nose running down his half-human face. The wet rocks around him gleamed with red streaks and he twisted in pain, rubbing more blood onto the rocks and his rough-furred body.

The largest of the dobhar-chú near Fielding started toward us, changing as it walked until Father Otter strode the last few paces across the cave to us in his human guise. He gave Solis an irritated glance and then seemed to dismiss him as he turned his gaze on me. He scowled. "You see what has happened? His forms must be untangled or he will die."

"How did this happen?" I asked. "He seemed stable when we saw him earlier."

"The world tide is changing. While it turns, the power of the merfolk rises and we lie so close to them that their evil magic is stronger."

"Then why don't you move a safe distance away?"

"This is our home. We will not leave."

"Isn't it their home, too?"

Father Otter bared his teeth at me. "But *we* do no evil. *We* do not sink ships and destroy men."

"At least not anymore," I said. "Your kind doesn't have the nicest reputation in the Old Country." That online research—thin as its yield had been—was paying off.

His face twisted with rage, his lips drawing back, and he hissed at me. He reminded me so much of Chaos when she was enraged that I almost laughed but I throttled the chuckle before it could escape. If he started jumping around and doing the weasel war dance, I really would lose it, and I thought that might be a very bad idea.

Instead I settled back on my heels and gave him a chilly look. "Let's not pretend either of us is a white knight here. You want my help; I want yours. Whatever the problem is, it's getting worse and I imagine there's not a lot of time to fix this. So how about we get to it?"

Father Otter rolled his shoulders and scowled but he nodded and led us toward Fielding. Solis shot me a glance that was a little too white around the edges, but he didn't say anything and he came along, if a bit hesitantly and keeping half a pace behind. This had to be horrible for him—being unable to stop or go back, powerless in the encroaching field of enemies—another fall into his nightmare. And yet he came of his own will.

At Fielding's side I crouched down to get a better look at him. He was rolling around from pain and making growling sounds in his throat. He didn't seem to register that I was there. I reached out and touched his wrist; it felt hot and the patchy fur on his arms was abrasive in my grip. I pulled back my hand and found my palm scratched and raw like a minor case of road rash. "Great," I muttered. "Gary? Gary? Fielding, it's Harper Blaine. Can you tell me what's changed? What do I need to do?"

His reply was an unintelligible whimper.

I turned to Father Otter. "I'll have to take a look myself. This is going to appear a little strange, so don't freak out." I didn't add "and attack us" but I thought it.

He scrunched up his face in what I took for an expression of confusion, though it was a little hard to tell since he didn't seem to have the same facial reactions as a human even with a human's face. He shook his head with a sudden snort that was more like a violent sneeze than anything else. Then he glanced at me and shrugged. "As you must," he muttered, turning his head away.

The rest of the dobhar-chú turned around also, giving me some kind of privacy, I assumed, or just not watching something as distasteful as dabbling with magic. I caught Solis's eye. "I'm . . . uhhh . . . going to get a little thin here. Keep an eye on our friends."

He nodded, his aura settling a bit at having an understandable job to do. His gaze shifted away immediately to scan the surroundings as I sank into the Grey.

The cave of the dobhar-chú looked like the remains of a wild party in the Grey. It was littered with knots of colored energy, tilted and tangled temporaclines, and mist alive with creeping strands of energy whose origin looked decidedly unwholesome. Fielding's aura was rendered into a seething boil of violet and blue pierced through by green and red spikes that seemed to dig deeper as I watched. Long threads of each color stretched away toward the cove as if the energy around him was literally spun from the water outside. Resting partially on top of him lay a shadow whose densities of darkness in shades of night, coal dust, and tarnished silver welled and ebbed like tar bubbling slowly from the ground. The shadow seemed to be knitted to Fielding by the strands of energy that defined and stabbed his aura. It was difficult to see exactly how the filaments of color stitched through the shadow form as it writhed and twisted. I concentrated on the dark shape, pulling myself by inches through deeper layers and sideways through variations of the Grey until I could see it better.

I seemed to have snuck into a pocket of the Grey that abhorred me: cold and shuddering like San Francisco during an earthquake, the air itself seemed to stab me with needles of ice and then slice with razors of fire. I did not wish to stay any longer than necessary and I wondered where the hell the Guardian Beast was—surely this wasn't a part of the Grey any living person should ever see. . . . But I steeled myself to the assault as best I could and stared hard at the strange form that was Fielding. As I'd feared, the shadow I'd seen on him was two shapes forced into the same space by the winding cables of colored energy. Each piercing thread of red or green caught a ripple of one or the other shadow form and pulled it toward the center of Fielding's energetic mass, constantly tugging and tearing the fabric of his dual forms into one another. I could barely make out the pale separation still remaining between them. I couldn't possibly pinch off every strand of magic that was knitting them so horribly together. I had neither the ability anymore nor the desire to try to reach into a living being and attempt to remove the burning twists and thorns of this unnatural torment. Especially not while I was being battered by an inhospitable corner of the Grey itself.

An icy shard of ghost-stuff ripped through my chest and I shivered so violently that I tumbled sideways out of the Grey.

I landed, wincing and trying to catch my breath as chilly tears welled over my lower lashes. Solis caught me and helped me back up to my feet. Work calluses on his palms and fingers felt like stones for a moment before the sensation faded.

Father Otter and his ilk had turned back around to watch me as I fell. Now they looked up at me—faces furry or human all curious and a bit repulsed by what they saw.

"He is no better," Father Otter accused.

"I can't do it here. I need to be in a more stable place in . . . the magic sphere," I said, groping for the right words to express the Grey to him. "Where it overlaps the normal world. I can't see what I'm doing under any other circumstances. You need to get Fielding and us out to the shore, where the two realms overlap." It was a place I did not want to go even though I'd known I'd have to. I'd hoped to put it off to the end, to draw the sea witch and her minions into my *own* sphere of control first. But that plainly wasn't going to happen and we had no time to argue.

"That shore is within the compass of the sea witch's power," Father Otter objected.

"I know that, and the gateway is closing, so we could all be trapped, but I can't do this here. We have to go where the overlap is already stable. It's too difficult for me to hold the two worlds steady and do what needs to be done at the same time."

"You will have to. We cannot fight her and defend you at once. We will attack—we will do whatever must be done, whatever you command us to do—to defeat her once our cousin is safe but we cannot do both in the same time and hope for any of us to survive. Including you and your . . . family."

I gasped out a laugh at the vision of the motley crew of the *Mambo Moon* as a family and regretted it as my rib sent a stab of complaint into my chest. A frisson of fear came with it: We had so little time and this was a desperate move.

"All right," I said. "I can try here, but it will have to be very quick. The only way to pull the two forms apart before they are knitted into each other too much to separate is to cut. There's no other way to get through the . . ." Again I stumbled for a word and settled for a gesture of shoving my spread fingers together in a woven steeple shape, while saying, "The joining magic fast enough. It has to go in one fast sweep and it has to be done very soon. I'll need some kind of knife. . . ." Part of my mind was gibbering in panic at the thought and the rest was doing its best to keep that element locked up where it wouldn't show. My hosts wouldn't have appreciated my freaking out and I didn't know where that would leave Solis.

The dobhar-chú barked and squeaked at the smaller otters and there was a frantic shuffling around as the assembled creatures searched for something for me to use. A collection of shells, rocks, and bits of rusted metal were shoved across the wet stone floor to me, but even the metal parts were too small or too dull to serve. I dug in my jeans pocket for my own little pocketknife. The narrow two-inch blade looked pathetically small for this job but at least it was sharp, and although the edge would serve more as an allegory than an actual cutting blade, this was a situation that called for a fine-honed symbol of incision, not a metaphorical butter knife. "It'll have to do," I muttered. "I wish it were something magic or at least something . . . bigger."

Solis tapped my shoulder and held something out to me. The dim light from the other side of the cave gleamed a moment on bright steel as he flipped the thing with care, hilt out. I blinked at him and took it gently. It was a karambit: an odd little Indonesian knife about eight inches long and curved the whole length. The handle and blade were all one continuous piece of steel. A ring at each end defined the handle as much as the grip scales did. The blade looked like the flattened silver claw of a raptor and it was wickedly sharp along the inside curve. It couldn't have weighed a quarter of a pound and it wasn't designed to stab, only to slice, but it would do that with elegant efficiency.

I looked a question at Solis, who shrugged his eyebrows and pulled a face as if to say "You know how it is." Except that I wasn't sure now that I did. Still, I nodded and thanked him and braced myself to go back to the inhospitable Grey.

Father Otter stopped me as I knelt back down beside the delirious Gary Fielding. "They will come as soon as they know our cousin is free or dead. Be prepared."

My heart was shivering and running rough, but I turned a cold look on him as if I weren't frightened to my very bones. "That will be your job, because my friend and I need some answers from your cousin before I go any further. And if I don't like them, you should fear me as much as the merfolk." Then I shook him off and turned back to Fielding.

Pure bluff and bullshit, of course, since there was no way I alone—or even with Solis's help—could hold off an army of shape-shifting otters as well as a cohort of pissed-off mermaids. But I still wanted to know what had actually happened on board *Seawitch* and if I was about to free a guilty man from punishment, or a falsely accused one.

One of the problems of the Grey is time; it proceeds strangely, sometimes too fast and sometimes too slow. It breaks and falters and remains like ice floes adrift in the cold, cold sea. This operation would have to go fast, but no matter how quickly I went, I had no way of knowing how much time would elapse in the normal world or how fast any adversary would arrive in the Grey. I hoped Solis would be safe; then I pushed my fear aside and got back to work.

Instead of sinking down into the Grey as I usually do, I tried pulling it over me like a blanket, keeping myself physically present in the normal world while surrounding myself in the world of magic. The Grey resisted initially, then flowed over me in a rush, almost knocking me down into its flood. I held myself to the rocky ground and felt the parallel worlds shimmy and slither together. The sensation of motion sickness swamped me for a moment but I fought it down to a level I could sustain for a little while without throwing up. I crept forward a few inches so I was pressing against the struggling shadows of Fielding's dual forms.

I reached for them and the world lurched. I slammed my hands down on the mist-flooded rock floor and heard the knife ring on the stone. The instability at my feet fled, leaving me anchored for the moment, but I was sure the ghost world would trickle back all too soon. I dug my toes under Fielding's physical body and he gave a banshee wail, arching up a little before he settled back down, pinning my sneaker-clad feet to the corporeal reality of stone.

I muttered to him, "Just hang in there a little longer, Fielding." Then I pushed my hands into the writhing mass of his shadows.

I pushed and tugged on the forms that burned my hands with alternating heat and cold. Representing the dual parts of his nature, they had polarized their representations in the Grey as well: the water form damp, icy, and fluid; the earth form spiky, hot, and resistant. While the water shadow moved aside easily under my push, it also flowed back fast and my first impulse to shove that aside and then sever the invasive magical strands exposed between the two masses was foiled by the material's ability to ooze around my hand.

But the shadow wasn't as fast-moving as water and it didn't pass through my hand but around it. I pulled the combined mass closer, ignoring Fielding's howl of agony by gritting my teeth until I heard them grind. Then I pushed my left hand into the thin cleft between the shadows, wedging it just wide enough to shove my shoulder into. I worked my way deeper into the combined forms, using my dense human body to hold the liquid shadow back long enough to expose a tangled net of energy. I blew out my breath to gain a precious inch and reached into the new-made gap to sweep the blade of the hooked knife through the nearest binding filaments of invasive magic.

The strands of red and olive sparked and burned away as I severed them and Fielding sighed and yelped at my feet, twisting with every virtual inch of separation gained. I worked deeper, toward the last dense area near the center of the entwined shadow forms. A roaring filled my ears and I forced myself to suck in a painful lungful of air and expand my chest as I leaned into the core of Shelly's curse.

Through the din in my head I heard Fielding whimpering and a cacophony of shouts, barks, and yelps underscored by a pounding that shook the cave and thundered on my eardrums. The oscillating pressure of the sound made me shudder with nausea. I didn't raise my eyes from the task at hand, even when I felt something cold and liquid spatter onto my legs and right shoulder. I shoved as hard as I could, paying Fielding's scream no heed as I reached through the moment's gap between his two forms and drew the knife down and back, the curved blade sweeping through the taut bundle of gleaming magic like a scythe through grass. The entangled, writing forms rushed apart and Fielding roared, bucking and shoving me away as I clutched frantically and snapped off the last clinging filaments of the curse as I fell.

I landed hard on my back and felt my abused rib pop. I didn't have the breath to cry out and barely kept hold of consciousness as the normal and ghost realms fell apart, leaving me beached on the wet rocks of the cave as the otters and the dobhar-chú leapt at the invading flood of waterborne merfolk.

At their back, held up by a wave that crested but didn't break, I glimpsed two humanoid forms with long, streaming hair: one pale green; the other vivid red. And then the two forces crashed together and the battle front was obscured by an explosion of salt water.

TWENTY-FIVE

Battered, wet, cold, and laced by pain with every movement, I rolled to my uninjured side and squirmed sideways until I could touch the wall Fielding had been leaning against. Bracing my hands on the wall and floor, I pushed and pulled myself up to my knees. I paused to look around. Nearby lay a colossal mustelid even larger than Father Otter. Solis stood in front of it, glaring down while the otters and the rest of the dobhar-chú clan pushed their enemies back out of the cave by sheer weight of numbers. They'd worked the watery tide of merfolk and sea-witch illusions into a bottleneck in the cave complex and were moving them backward and out by short rushes.

Solis noticed me and, as he looked away, the huge otter got to its feet and tried to run past him to the back exit. Solis dove past me and tackled it. They rolled together on the wet floor, the otter snapping and growling as it writhed and changed shape. The otter form collapsed suddenly into a slender, dark-skinned man with long, curling black hair hanging to his back and his naked skin slick with blood and brine. Fielding eeled out of Solis's grip and started for the back door again.

I threw the knife.

I'm not a great knife thrower and the curved form didn't fly well, anyhow. It flipped into a flat arc, the base of the grip smacking into the back of Fielding's right knee. He stumbled but he would have kept going if Solis hadn't launched himself from the ground like a sprinter coming out of the blocks and snatched Fielding around the waist and neck, half shoving, half dragging the dobhar-chú down to his knees. Solis released his grip on Fielding's waist and switched to his nearest wrist, twisting it up between the other's shoulder blades.

I heard Solis warn him, "Change now and your arm will leave the socket. You will not enjoy it."

Panting, Fielding hung his head. "All right. I give up. Just don't . . . don't tear off my arm."

Solis stood up, pulling Fielding up with him. "I won't. Unless you force me." Then he marched Fielding back to me.

Fielding kept his head down and I doubted it was strictly over his nudity. I was beginning to think I'd now seen enough naked men to fill my quota for the rest of my life. I started to sigh and caught myself cringing as my rib twinged. I kept my gaze up as the two men stopped in front of me.

The noise of the battle moved farther away but it was still there in the background as I started to speak.

"So . . . I take it you're not as innocent as you protested," I started.

"I don't know what you're talking about."

Solis glared at him and must have twisted Fielding's arm a little, making the former sea captain wince.

"Hey!"

"What did you do?" Solis demanded. "What did you really do to bring down this sea witch's wrath?"

"Nothing!" Fielding shouted back.

Solis's mouth was a hard, straight line and I could see tension gathering in the muscles of his shoulders and arms. I shook my head at him and staggered over to pick up the knife from the slick stone floor.

I walked back, turning the knife in my hand as I came. "This is a long way from anywhere. And there's a lot of water around, though I understand it only takes a few inches to drown."

"Are you threatening me?" Fielding demanded, incredulous.

"I'm reminding you of the situation," I said. "My friend's not in a good mood where you're concerned. See, he has a couple of daughters himself."

"I don't see how that's important."

I shook my head at him in disappointment. "Oh, Gary, is this the way you repay favors? You came to me to solve a problem. And I have. But now we have a new one and there's still a question my friend needs answered and so do I. Not to mention, what should we tell the insurance company? Should we take you back to Seattle and let Solis lock you up as a rapist and a murderer?"

"I didn't hurt anyone!"

Solis shook him. "You are alive and all the rest are dead. You say this came about because Castor Starrett attempted to sexually assault Shelly Knight and you didn't stop him. Or did you do it?"

"No!" Fielding shouted, looking indignant.

Solis bumped him again. "Did you rape Shelly Knight?"

"No," Fielding repeated but his tone was less adamant.

Solis continued to bully him, no longer twisting his arm but badgering Fielding with unremitting questions. "You worked together before. Why this time did she accuse you?"

"She was angry! She knew what I was!"

"She knew that before. Why now was she angry enough to curse you and call on her mother's help when she'd hidden you all from her?"

"I don't know!"

"Yes, you do."

"I made a mistake."

"What mistake did you make? Do not repeat that ridiculous story about going down below with Castor Starrett. What did you really do? Did you rape her?"

"No!"

"Did you find her with Starrett? Is that what happened? Castor Starrett had your woman before you could? You got angry, you hurt him, and then you had to get rid of witnesses—"

"No!" The single word came out in a long, agonized howl. "No! I didn't hurt him. I didn't hurt anyone. I just—" He cut himself off and curled on himself as if Solis had punched him in the gut. Then he sank to his knees on the slick rock floor of the cavern. "Les started freaking out. I still don't know what she said to him exactly, but Shelly must have told him his wife was dead while Cas and I were out after that damned halibut. She could do that sometimes—she knew things. She didn't like to say them, but Les probably badgered her into it. That's the sort of guy he was."

"Who broke the circle?" I asked.

"What?" Fielding barked, staring at me.

"Who broke the spell circle in Shelly's cabin? That was the real problem, wasn't it? Was it Leslie Carson or Starrett or was it you?"

Fielding stared at me. "What are you saying . . . ?"

"You lied to us about what happened on *Seawitch*'s last night. There was no spear mark and no blood on the deck or in Starrett's cabin, although there was plenty in Shelly's cabin. So Shelly Knight didn't shoot Starrett with the speargun as you said. There're a hell of a lot of marks on you, though. They're scars that shine even through your fur. In fact, they show more, which means it's your otter form that's got them. But you said you'd never known you were a dobhar-chú until that night—and I believe that—so you'd never changed form before and you've never changed properly since, so all those scars happened that night. How'd you get them, Fielding?"

He gaped at me, his mouth working like a fish's, but no sound came out. I just stared back as if I were only curious.

Solis poked him in the shoulder and peered at his face. "There is a scar here on his face. Like fingernails make, like a woman makes when she's angry or afraid and she claws at your eyes," he said, making a sharp gesture toward Fielding's face with his own crooked and raking hand.

Fielding flinched.

"Come on, Fielding. We don't have a lot of time. Maybe I can guess what happened and you can just tell me if I'm right."

"It's not what you think."

"I *think* you said that before. So what is it?"

"I was out with Cas after the halibut and . . . he found out. He found out about Shelly—about us—and he . . . he wanted to fuck the mermaid," he added in a mumble.

Solis fell silent and the sound of conflict still raged, but distantly and diminishing. Fielding's whimpering sobs of shame trickled into the noise like tears into a pool.

I leaned forward and returned the knife to Solis, pretty sure he wasn't going to use it on Fielding at this point but thinking I might. "So," I started, "you and Shelly were together."

Fielding nodded, still looking at the ground.

"Reeve disapproved, didn't he?"

"Yeah . . ."

"And that's why he didn't get to come along on this trip. You or Shelly made sure he was too sick to sail. Didn't you?"

Fielding nodded. "I put laxative in his beer at Charlie's the night before we went out. He was talking about seeing the water hound on the boat and he was half-drunk and already half-spooked, so it was pretty easy."

"You're a real sweetheart, aren't you, Fielding? How much did you know about Shelly then?"

"I knew she was special. She told me I was . . . something special, too. She couldn't quite convince me it was true, but I was starting to believe it. She said no one could know about us—and especially not about how we were different."

"But Reeve knew, or suspected, didn't he?"

"Suspected. But Shelly wasn't like that! She was . . . she was sweet."

"So she didn't come to the marina looking for victims for her mother. She came looking for something else."

"She wanted to see the human world. She said she didn't know any living humans. And when she found me she thought it was funny that I wasn't really human at all. I didn't understand. But I liked it. I liked her. I liked . . . being with someone forever, not just for the night."

"I can understand Reeve figuring it out—he was a salty old guy and pretty observant—but how did Starrett find out about Shelly?" I asked. Solis seemed to have decided this was my part of the interrogation—I was good cop to his bad cop, I supposed.

"He saw her at Port Townsend. I guess she was upset after what had happened with Les so she went swimming to relax."

"What did she tell Leslie Carson about his wife?"

"She knew Odile was dead—she just knew. He said she was teasing him since he complained constantly about how Odile threatened suicide all the time to keep him in line. Odile was messed up and unhappy and everyone but Les understood that. He thought Odile was just screwing with his head, because she'd told him she would do it this time and he'd come with us, anyway. So I guess when Shelly told him she was really dead this time and how and when . . . he was freaked, and more freaked when the cops called with the same details. Wouldn't you be?"

"Yes. And his accusations upset Shelly because he didn't take it seriously?

"Yeah. Well, knowing about it upset her, too. So she went swimming because that's what she did when she was stressed out. It's not very safe to swim in the Sound in the dark without dive lights—it's easy to get lost and then you tire out and drown. But Shelly was half-fish and it was only in the dark that it was safe for her to swim near people. But Cas wanted his damned stupid halibut and he stayed up all night to get it. We didn't have tank gear so he was using a mask and snorkel in the shallows where the halibut come up to spawn and he'd swum out pretty far from the dinghy. Shelly didn't realize he was nearby—she thought we were going the other way. He saw her under the water. When I got the fish out of the fridge in the morning for him to clean, he told me he had seen her. He told me what he meant to do—he thought it was . . . funny, like it was a joke and I wouldn't mind, 'cause we were buddies or something. He was that kind of jerk—he figured every woman was his to take. I was panicking—he was my boss's boss and I'd made Reeve sick to get the cruise, so the old man wasn't there to back me up and he wasn't going to take my side on anything when we got home, either. Hell, he was probably going to fire me once he figured it out. I didn't know what to do. I already had the engines fired up and was ready to take the boat out. Cas didn't seem in any hurry—it was like he was savoring the idea—and I didn't know how to stop him, except to act like it didn't bother me and try to get below ahead of him.

"It was my fault we were at sea when the call came in about Les's wife and I wouldn't go in to port because I was scared shitless about what was going to happen to me and what Cas would do to Shelly. I wanted to stay at sea so she could jump overboard and swim away, but . . . she didn't. She wouldn't. I got us out of Townsend and in the clear in the strait. I turned on the autopilot and I went down below, but she argued with me about leaving and we were still arguing when Cas came down. He laughed at us. And she . . . she told me I was an idiot. She told me to go away and take care of the boat and it wasn't anything girls like her hadn't been doing for centuries with guys like Cas. I didn't understand what she meant—I still don't. But I got angry and I shoved her and her foot slipped on the rug on the cabin sole. And then she was furious—it was like she'd flipped a switch and went from sweet girl to unholy bitch in a millisecond. I didn't know what the rug was covering up until she started screaming at us. She threw it away and pointed at this crazy charm she'd drawn and now it was all messed up and she was shouting at us, telling us we were doomed, that we'd done it to ourselves and she ... she was just crazy. She shoved Cas backward and he hit his head on the hatchway. She started pawing at the blood on his head and saying it wasn't right, it wasn't working, and I was trying to drag him away from her because ... I thought she was nuts. I didn't know she was trying to save us! I didn't understand. She grabbed my arm and she cut me—"

"She cut you, not Starrett?" I asked for clarification.

"Yeah. It's my blood in the cabin, but I figured no one has a DNA sample from either of us, so who'd know?"

"We didn't need a DNA sample. The lab said it was only partially human blood; the rest was otter."

"Crap!"

"Doesn't matter. What happened next?"

"Shelly was trying to redraw her spell or whatever and I was just getting in the way. I was freaking out. I was trying to pull Cas out of the cabin and he wasn't responding—he was barely conscious and he was bleeding and mumbling.... Shelly was angry at me and she was saying crazy things and crawling around on the floor.... And when I tried to grab her and make her help me with Cas, she screamed at me and started hitting me, hitting and hitting and calling me names. She clawed at my face and pushed me away and she cursed me and ran up on deck and threw something in the water. She was screaming the whole time. Then the rest of them came to carry her away. That's when they started killing people."

"You didn't write any of this in the log."

"I wasn't sure I'd make it, but if I did, I didn't want that kind of thing on the record. And if I didn't ... who was going to believe me if they ever found the log, any-way? I was going to steal the stupid thing when I brought the boat back but Father Otter convinced me to leave it—to bring you to us."

"*You* brought the boat back." As I'd suspected. "Good trick in the state you were in."

"The ghosts and Father Otter helped," Fielding ad-mitted. "Then he went to look after Reeve, while I came back here for a while. I knew the merfolk would try to find me—even though they missed me right under their noses for twenty-seven years, the morons—and Reeve would be the obvious place to start looking. Even if he was still mad at me, I owed the old man some protection. None of this was his fault."

"Wait. The merfolk didn't keep you and torment you for that whole time, as you implied before?"

He looked a little uncomfortable at being caught out. "Not the whole time, but I couldn't get any farther away than here until the gate in the worlds opened again. I found the bell by accident the first year and the ghosts said they'd help me hide if I helped them escape when the gate opened again. The sea witch was trapped in the cove until that time, too, so she wasn't using the ghosts and wasn't paying attention to any of the objects they were stuffed in. I had to keep on dodging her for the next . . . twenty years or so. When the gate started to form, the dobhar staged a raid and she was too busy to notice when I moved *Valencia*'s bell into *Seawitch*'s bilge. I'd been making my plans to get to you for a year or more after the raid, and when I left, Father Otter warned me the sea witch would know I was out in the world again. He was pissed off about the business with Reeve so I didn't tell him I was planning to go find him at the hospital and tell him what had happened to me and the boat—I figured that was another thing I owed the old man. I thought the merfolk would leave him alone once Father Otter foiled them once. But I guess not." He didn't seem as broken up about it as I'd have expected. He was unhappy about what had happened to Reeve, but it was almost a self-pitying kind of misery.

I shook my head in disgust. "Your Romeo and Juliet romance turned into a grudge and you didn't try to clear up the misunderstanding; you just made it worse and spread the tale around. Why didn't you just tell us the truth?"

"Because the truth is that it's all my fault. I would have let him hurt her. When the ghosts saved me and the boat, I was still so angry and confused . . . I didn't understand what had happened for years. I didn't see what I'd done until it was way too late to fix it and Shelly and her mother . . . they've been looking for me ever since. Mermaids don't forgive much. Sea witches forgive nothing."

"This love story was never going to end well. Her mother wasn't going to want a dobhar-chú for a son-in-law."

"I hadn't thought that far ahead."

"Sounds like a regular problem of yours. So now it's not just Shelly who wants your hide, it's her mom, too?"

He nodded. "She's one hard bitch."

"She wouldn't happen to be a redhead?" I asked.

"Yeah . . . why?"

"I think we've met."

Fielding finally looked up at me. "Oh . . . God, no."

I shook off his fear. "I'm not working for her. In fact I'm not working for you, either. All I want is the ghosts."

"But . . . you have them."

"No, Fielding. I want *all* of them. You found one. I'll bet you know where the rest are, too."

The cave had fallen nearly silent and then a new sound started at a distance but came closer: a shuffling, snuffling, and squealing. The otters were returning.

"I can't—" Fielding objected.

"I think you can. I think with you as go-between to your ex-girlfriend, we can offer the sea witch her bell back."

"But . . . I thought you wanted to keep the ghosts."

"I intend to. This is just the bait to move her where I can see her. Then you're going to grab the rest of the receptacles. You know what they look like and where they are, don't you?"

"Yeah, but . . . it's suicide. She'll kill us. Well, she'll kill you and then she'll kill me. And then everyone else."

"I don't think so. There are more of your cousins than there are of the merfolk, and once we have the ghosts, the sea witch has no power but what she gets from the merfolk. She's a blood mage and she hasn't got little merfolk batteries, so if she intends to use them, she'll have to cast her magic the instant one of them dies. She's not going to squander any more of her people for that. That's counterproductive. She won't diminish her population further. She may be a pissed-off hard-ass and half-insane as you and I see it, but she's not stupid."

"You are totally wild-ass crazy," Fielding said. "I won't do it."

"Yeah, you will. Or you'll go back to Seattle and stand trial for piracy and the murder of everyone on board *Seawitch*—since it is, as you said, your fault. You broke the protection circle, you would have let Starrett do what he wanted to Shelly, you made the bad decisions that put the boat in harm's way. As the captain that makes it your responsibility legally and morally."

He scoffed, though there was a certain amount of false bravado to the sound. "How are you going to make it stick? They're not going to try an *otter* for murder. Your policeman friend isn't going to keep my arm in a lock forever and you can't stop me from changing form."

"Don't count on that, Gary. I cut you loose. I can tie you back up, too." Blatant lie, but I wanted to see if Fielding was willing to risk it. I had other ways to get to the ghosts if I had to do without Fielding's help, but I didn't want to use them. Father Otter might not like it, but we had an agreement and he owed me. Magic creatures take that kind of thing seriously. Which reminded me . . . "You owe me for that, not to mention the lying and the underhanded way you got me into this pile of otter poop." I wasn't going to mention the Guardian Beast, since that wouldn't get me anywhere and I'd already tried asking *it* for help and gotten nothing.

The noise of returning otters and dobhar-chú had drawn close so I wasn't surprised to hear a short scrabbling sound followed by the rough clearing of a throat. I could feel Father Otter's presence at my shoulder even without seeing Fielding cringe. Solis flicked his gaze a degree or two aside but his attention didn't move away from Fielding.

"Does our cousin offend?"

"He's not being cooperative," I replied, keeping my eyes on Fielding. "I've rendered all the services I was asked to perform and I still have nothing to show for it. While it's of no interest to you, there is a small matter of human law and the death of the people on board *Seawitch* to be resolved. And beyond that is the sneaky way your cousin used me and you and still let people die because he didn't have the spine to do what he ought. He didn't help his girlfriend and he endangered the crew and got Reeve killed by leading the merfolk to him at the hospital. While I'm willing to let the human matters go if I must, I'm not ready to leave the situation here as it is and simply excuse a debt of honor because Gary doesn't want to get his paws dirty."

I could tell by the way Fielding pulled back that Father Otter's attention had turned on him and it wasn't pleasant. "Have you not had enough of exile from your proper form? Will you prefer to be outcast and outlaw, too, now that you have regained it? We shall make it so—"

A light came on in my mind at his use of "we" and "our"—they were not the common plural, but the royal usage—as Fielding lurched forward and down, putting his face to the rock floor of the cavern.

"No! No, Uncle," he gurgled even as his form flowed

and shifted from human to otter in front of us. Even though he was the largest of them, he wiggled forward like a pup, keeping his head on the ground and rolling onto his side in front of Father Otter, exposing his throat and belly.

Father Otter shrank down to his own otter form beside me and lunged forward, biting down on a mouthful of Fielding's nearest ear and scruff. Then he shook the larger dobhar-chú hard until Fielding squalled and flailed with all of his paws as he was flung about. A stench thickened the air and Father Otter held his miscreant relative down until Fielding made a docile yipping that sounded like "Pax, pax, pax . . ."

Father Otter spat out the fold of Fielding's hide and glared at him with disdain. He made a barking noise at Fielding and turned his back on the younger creature before stalking away to join the rest of the returning otters and dobhar-chú redistributing themselves around the cave. The others watched but none interfered or gave any sign that they were upset at what had just happened. A few furry faces even looked a bit pleased.

Solis and I stood still and watched Fielding resume his human form, shivering and sweating as if the scene between him and Father Otter had been a sickening ordeal. Perhaps it had been in a way we mere humans couldn't understand. Fielding didn't get to his feet this time but curled up to sit on the floor with his knees drawn up against his chest. "I'm to do as you tell me." He sounded like a chastened child.

"Or?" I asked.

"Or I'll have no home among otters *or* men. They'll hound me to death. Father Otter is really pissed at me." He was in his fifties no matter how he looked, yet he sounded like a teenager.

I kept my growing dislike in check. "I see. What about the merfolk?" I asked.

"They've withdrawn for now. Father Otter and the others will attack when you say so. But I think it'll have to be soon—before the fish faces can regroup and come after us or Paul's boat."

I was ashamed to admit that I'd almost forgotten about *Mambo Moon*. It lay outside the overlap but that didn't make it safe and I had no idea what may have happened to it while Solis and I were in the dobhar-chú's cave. I looked at my watch and picked a course of action, no matter how wild and stupid it was—even the faultiest plan put in action swiftly is better than working out a perfect plan and squandering the time to execute it.

"I assume they'll move at or just before sunset when we'll have the sun in our eyes. There's not much time. So we'll have to be ready to go before they move. How long until sundown?" I asked Fielding.

"It's pretty dusky now so . . . maybe two hours to darkness, ninety minutes to red sun—that's what the dobhar call sunset."

"All right. In one hour the dobhar-chú and the otters need to be in place as far into the overlap perimeter as they can get without being spotted. Father Otter will know the strategic points for placement. You need to scout and find where the other ghosts are and get into a hiding place where you can get to them quickly once the sun is nearly down. I'll deal with the sea witch and her daughter."

"I thought you wanted me to be the go-between."

"I need those ghosts more than I need you dangling like bait. Besides, I don't think Jacque will let you get close enough to issue the invitation I need."

"Jacque . . . ?"

"You said the sea witch is a redhead. The woman who was on *Pleiades* until Father Otter came to talk to me at the marina is a redhead. The name she gave was Jacque Knight, and if she's not the sea witch, I'll be the proverbial monkey's uncle."

Solis interrupted. "Could it not be Shelly who is the sea witch, as we discussed?"

"I don't think so," I replied. "The revised story doesn't

fit that scenario, and if you were a powerful magic user looking to unseat your parent, would you keep her around afterward?"

Solis shook his head. "No. Then this business about virginity and power was the truth? But how does one have a child if that is true?"

"I don't know that it's true or not—I can't even guess at this point. Shelly was a mermaid. She's still a mermaid. She just never became the sea witch, but there's no way to know why and my speculation may not be correct in any case. The sea witch used to roam the Sound and destroy ships but she couldn't keep the door open this time and then she lost a significant percentage of her ghosts. She's got to be pretty angry at Fielding here."

"Didn't I say she carried a grudge?" Fielding asked. "She never lets go of anything."

"You did. And I intend to use that to my advantage. But we have to get back to *Mambo Moon* first. Fielding, you find the other ghost receptacles and get ready to grab them when the sun goes down and bring them to me. Recruit other dobhar-chú or the otters if you need to; we have to get those things away from here or there will never be any peace."

"What about Jacque and Shelly?"

"What about them?"

"Aren't you going to . . . destroy them?"

"I said I would deal with them; I didn't say I'd kill them. That's not what I came here for. I won't stop your clan from doing what it needs to and if my goals force me to do it, I will kill them both, but I won't put my job aside to do yours."

"But—"

"I already helped you and your clan. Now you return the favor. That's the deal. That's as far as it goes."

Fielding looked flabbergasted, but it was the truth: I hadn't come here to play avenging angel for the wrongs done to the dobhar-chú or the merfolk. "Someone once called me the Paladin of the Dead and that's what I am.

My job is to get justice for the dead, not to settle scores for the living, no matter how magical."

"But I hired you—"

"When? I was already on this case when you showed up. And you never offered me anything but false answers. You've never offered me any payment. I am not working for you. I'm working for something bigger and meaner than Father Otter or any clan of sea witches or even the insurance company. You'll get what you want if it works with the rest of my own plans, not because I owe you anything or feel you're the injured party. If you don't like that, maybe next time you should offer something better than lies."

I turned my back on him and started for the dark passage that led back to the bay. Solis fell in behind me in a few steps, saying nothing as we were joined by an escort of otters and a single dobhar-chú the size of a rottweiler.

Nothing stopped us all the way to *Mambo Moon*.

TWENTY-SIX

When Solis and I stepped back on board, the decks of *Mambo Moon* were a mess. The skirmish between the merfolk and the dobhar-chú had sent a lot of sea life tumbling over the sides of the boat, and Quinton and Zantree were still clearing it away when we returned. Finishing the job killed about twenty minutes of the hour or so that we had before I'd have to be in place to bargain with and distract the sea witch from the snooping presence of Fielding and his relatives. Explaining what I needed to do took another ten minutes and resulted in an argument I didn't win.

I'd just finished summarizing the events and discussion in the otter cave and said, "So, Quinton and I will take the bell to the dock while Paul and Solis move the boat out as close to the bay's mouth as possible. I'll use the bell to get the sea witch's attention—"

Solis said, "No."

I stared at him. "What?"

"I will not allow you to put yourself into the first line of fire."

"Not your decision, Solis."

"I believe it is. I am a policeman; you are not."

"This is no longer a police matter. You have the answers you came here for. Your case is closed one way or the other. You can attempt to take Fielding in or not as you see fit, and I have the background info I need to put the insurance case to bed, too. All that's left is the concerns of the dead and the magical. That's my field."

He shook his head. "Nonetheless, I will not be sidelined while you put yourself in danger. I can't allow it."

"I can't take you both: *Mambo Moon* requires two crew, since Paul will need a lookout while he pilots."

"Quinton is the more experienced boat hand. And it makes more sense for me to come with you than to stay here."

I sighed and shook my head in exasperation. "Things are going to get very weird out there—"

"And the earlier parts of this day were not?"

"Not like it's going to get. A few ghosts in the engine room and some talking otters is not even in the ballpark. Quinton's been through this sort of thing with me before."

"And you trust him more?"

Way to put me on the spot. "That is not the issue."

"Then what is?"

"Well, if you want the truth, I don't think your family would forgive me if I got you killed."

He laughed a single hard bark of irony. "Eventually Ximena would understand. But Mama Gomez . . . she's the one you should fear."

"I do."

"Most of the neighborhood is afraid of her."

"Which surprises me not at all."

"And does not change the situation. I will go with you."

Quinton cleared his throat. "Far be it from me to get in the middle of this . . . interesting argument, but I really am the better boat hand and if this is going to turn into another sea battle, we frankly need the best hands aboard. Not that I'm dissing you, Rey, but—"

"The right man in the right position is more important than hurt pride," Solis said.

"Yeah. But while we're on the subject of who won't

forgive whom . . . I've already lost Harper once." Quinton gave Solis a meaningful look.

Solis returned a somber nod. "I understand."

Zantree cackled. "I feel like I should break out the rum and cutlasses!"

"You might need to yet. Those merfolk aren't numerous, but they seem to leave quite a mess. If they come after the boat again instead of focusing on me and"—I hesitated for a moment while I adjusted my mind to the change in my plan— "me and Solis, you may need a few sharp blades around."

Zantree looked excited. "Really? 'Cause I have an old navy cutlass I've been dying to swing."

Dying . . . I hoped not. "Much as I hate to say it, now would be the time. They may be magical and they have an illusory cohort, but these merfolk are corporeal enough to stab," I replied.

Zantree looked ready to dance a jig and I wasn't sure I'd just said the wisest thing. "Arrr! They'll never take us alive. Eh, Mr. Quinton?"

Quinton laughed and saluted. "Aye, aye, Cap'n Zantree! All hands to stations and prepare to repel boarders!"

I felt a strange tickle of adrenaline from Quinton and I stared at them, incredulous. "Hey, this isn't a game, you two. These creatures kill people."

Quinton sighed. "Then all the better reason to get our humor on now. A little levity helps ease the sheer terror I'd otherwise be feeling at the thought of being gaffed by fish men." I wanted to laugh, also, but I was too aware of how much responsibility I had for these three men and how terrible I'd feel if any of them were injured or worse. This responsible-friend thing? It bites.

We had a few more words about the details and I felt more and more desperate and afraid for them, but I didn't speak up—what would have been the point?— even when Solis and I were ready to head out for the dock that stuck out from the shore, while Quinton and Zantree prepared to move *Mambo Moon* out as close to the cove mouth as possible to offer the surest escape. If Solis and I couldn't rejoin them, we'd decided to ditch the dinghy, walk across the thin neck of forest to the other cove on the south side of the island, and wait there for the boat or a message. It was only a little more than a mile to hike, but we were sure the merfolk would not follow us across the ridge of dry land.

And although I had denied it to Fielding, I was prepared to destroy the sea witch if it was the only way to keep the men with me safe. I wondered if my mixed feelings of fear, frustration, and resolve were as strange to Quinton as the flood of excitement and trepidation he was sending to me.

Before we left, Quinton and Zantree did some flitting about with the dinghy to free the anchors. Once they were done, Solis and I, carrying one handheld radio between us, bundled up in waterproof jackets against the rage of the sea witch and her clan. Then we took the little boat and, with the bell from the *Valencia* tucked into a compartment in the bow, headed for the dock. As soon as we were clear, Zantree eased the big boat's engines up enough to make way and turned her gently toward the exit. Solis and I continued on alone, running across the gold and orange reflections of sunset on the water. I hoped Fielding and the dobhar-chú were doing their part....

This time there was no storm to weather and summer clouds picked up the reflected colors of the sunset and striped the sky in red and pink as Solis and I sped across the water to the dock. We had to cut into the edge of the paranormal bubble as we neared our goal, disturbing the calm like a pounding on the door, and the world turned dark and silver with washes of thin color, as if we'd plunged into an impressionist film version of the cove.

The water around us began to roil as if heated, though only a preternatural chill rose from it. By the time we'd tied off the dinghy at the short pier whose seaward half stuck into the overlay of Grey and normal, the water seemed to be alive.

I snatched the bell from the boat as it heaved on the unnatural swell. The green energy ribbons imprisoning the ghosts of *Valencia* within its bell burned vivid emerald spiked with ruby red and the spirits billowed around us in a howling chorus. I checked my watch; then I swung the bell hard and felt the clapper strike, the peal rolling outward like a shock wave of white light on a note that shook the sturdy little dock under our feet. If Solis was right in his observation, we'd have fifteen minutes until this bubble collapsed—and most likely took the gateway with it.

An answering shock of sound and light rolled back to us in a moment, and the water at the end of the dock belled upward like soft plastic deformed from below and lit by moving fireflies leaving sickly yellow-green trails below the bulging surface. The water rose higher until it was head height and then the surface peeled away, letting something come through.

Water shed off the writhing shape as it came up, as if it made the liquid and spat it forth until the air had dried it out too much to bear and the surface had to crack and peel away. The bulge differentiated slowly into three shapes riding a hillock of water: two slender women of nearly equal height and one wriggling, miserable man. The three were borne down to the dock as if by a giant watery hand.

The first woman stepped forward. Her long red hair fanned and billowed around her as if she were still immersed in the water and she gave a cruel little smile that showed serrated teeth. She seemed to be dressed in the shimmer of moonlight on the sea that obscured the details of her body without hiding the sensual shape of it. The face that was still that of Jacque Knight but, stripped of the illusion of boring humanity, she was more beautiful and terrifying. Behind her came her paler version:

Shelly, whose white skin and silver hair both held a pearly greenish tinge that gave her the look of something fragile and ephemeral. In this overlapped world I could see the faint impression of scales under Shelly's skin and a long scar ruining the symmetry of her coltish legs and awkward feet.

From a swift, hard glance deeper into the Grey I could see that Jacque's form was more true, if somewhat glamorized, while Shelly looked more truly a woman who was half-fish, walking uncomfortably on her split tail.

Shelly held on to Gary Fielding's right arm but it was Jacque who reached back to yank him forward. She held him out toward us and shook him. Shelly stumbled a little as she was dragged along.

"Did you send this creature into our realm to steal from us? Or is he as presumptuous as ever all on his own?" the sea witch's voice ripped the air.

Fielding crumpled to his knees as Jacque let him go. I wanted to yell at him and demand to know what fool thing he'd been doing to get himself captured but I restrained myself.

"Where ever did you find him? I thought he'd taken off when Father Otter was busy with your fishy friends."

"Does that fur-bearing fool think he can spy on me with the likes of this shabby thing? Or wreck my plans a second time by stealing my heir away?"

I held on tighter to the bell. "Has Mr. Fielding ever been one to do as he was told?" I asked, carefully skirting the question.

"And do you come to me now to ransom him back?"

"It's not quite what we had in mind," I replied.

As Jacque kept her attention on me, Fielding huddled into a ball. Shelly crept forward and dragged him backward a little, out from between the two of us. She kept her eyes turned away from mine, and her mother never turned her own gaze from me.

Jacque gave me an imperious raise of her eyebrows. "Then what brings you?"

"There is a small matter of the boat you took twenty-seven years ago—the *Seawitch*. . . ."

"What of it? I have it no longer, thanks to this one," Jacque added, aiming a kick where Fielding's head had recently been.

"It's not the boat I want so much as the souls you took from it."

Jacque crowed with laughter. "Paltry things!"

"Then you won't mind trading them to me for these," I said, holding up *Valencia*'s bell but making sure to keep it close to my own body so she couldn't snatch it from me.

Jacque tried to dart forward, but she wasn't built to do so out of the water and I fell back, luring her closer to the landward end of the dock. Solis was now nearly next to the sea witch and he made a face and stepped aside as if to avoid touching her, but his move put him slightly behind her, as we'd planned.

Then Fielding sat up and turned to look at Shelly. "I'm so sorry," he babbled. "I didn't mean what I did—I was so stupid and I let horrible things happen to you. And," he went on, repeating himself compulsively, "Shelly, Shelly, I love you and I'm so, so sorry. . . ."

Jacque sneered and turned to look back at Fielding. I wanted to scream at him to shut the hell up.

But any sound I would have made was instantly drowned in a roar of churning water and the shriek of creatures throwing themselves into battle.

The water within the bubble of overlapping worlds burst upward as the shapes of otters and merfolk charged at one another and clashed violently all along the encircling edge. Too soon and bringing far too many, the skirmish couldn't have been more ill-timed with Fielding's babbling stupidity.

The sea witch whirled back to me, her face a rictus of fury. "A trap! I'll tear you into chum!" she shrieked, and lunged at me.

I backpedaled as fast as I could and heard Shelly

scream for her mother to stop. Fielding continued to cry
out to Shelly and tried to grab her. She shook him off and
chased after Jacque. He spun and came back toward me.

I ducked the sea witch and ran toward the free-
floating end of the dock, hugging the bell to my chest
until I could reach Fielding. "You giant furry idiot!" I
yelled. "Stop mooning after your lost love and get the
damned ghost receptacles. *Now!*"

He ignored me and threw himself at Shelly again,
moaning her name. She skipped to the side but missed
her footing and fell into the bay with a yelp of surprise.
Then she flipped in the water and swam away.

"No! Shelly!" Fielding cried.

Jacque rushed up after me and snatched at him, tangling her hands in the shadow of his otter form. "I'll
show you once and for all, you meddling cur!"

Fielding screamed. I reached out with one hand to
steady his form, snapping off the tendrils of Jacque's
magic as quickly as I could—which would never be fast
enough, but I'd be damned if all the work I'd done would
go to hell this way, and I didn't want her and her magic
reinforcing the merfolk against the dobhar-chú until I
had what I needed.

"Goddamn you," I muttered between gritted teeth,
focusing my thoughts on the Guardian Beast, wherever
it was. "Why aren't you lending a hand if you want these
damned souls so much?" But it replied not at all, nor
showed any sign it was nearby. It's nice to know manage-
ment thinks you can handle the messes on your own but
I really could have used more help.

Solis tried to grab on to the corporeal Fielding. The
other man was squirming around and his shape was
heaving and fluctuating too much to give the cop a grip,
but the sergeant continued to try to hold his subject.

The sea witch abandoned the men with a howl of rage
and turned her ire on me. "Give it to me!"

Mute from lack of breath and the jabbing agony in my
side, I shook my head. Behind her I could see the bubble

of the overlapping worlds shivering as if some wind had touched it and I thought we were about out of time. If I couldn't break her power before the gateway collapsed, I wasn't sure that we'd ever leave.

The sea witch bared her jagged teeth at me and I could see the wisps of ghosts drawn to her through the ether of the Grey, streaming like mist filled with faces that screamed in panic and pain before flowing into her. She threw her arms upward; the sea rushed up, too, and then rained back down in torrents of red as the sky seemed to catch fire. Fish and firelit water pelted back down and I cringed, still holding the bell to my chest. Beyond the end of the dock full-on war raged in the heaving waters of the cove.

Holding on to the bell with one hand and trying to steady the writhing Fielding with the other, I had no way to defend myself. I rolled on top of the bell, my broken rib stabbing at my side and sending dizzying pain through my chest. Jacque gestured and the air seemed to fill with small, voracious sea creatures that swam through the falling bloody rain to attack me, needle teeth biting into my face, hands, and the back of my neck. I could have swatted them aside with the barest effort, but that would have taken my hands off the bell or Fielding and I couldn't risk either. Time seemed to jerk and start, coming and going in washes of blackness as I fought to stay conscious, and tingles of Quinton's reflected adrenaline jolted across my nerves.

"I have him!" Solis shouted. I assumed he meant Fielding but I didn't turn to look.

I shook off the biting things long enough to plunge my hands into the bell. The green energy net sizzled and burned against my skin, pulling a strangled whimper from my throat. This time they did not resist—I'd brought them to the right place and the right moment. I yanked at the magical restraints without plan or thought, ripping them aside so the ghosts spilled out, and the searing feel of the magic gusted away on a puff of bitter wind.

The ghosts of *Valencia* whirled around Jacque in a maelstrom of tormented faces that screamed and cried and spun her away from me. She fought them—or for them—grabbing at them and trying to clutch them to her chest or stuff them into her mouth, but they continually slipped away and soared, spinning upward to spread out in the dome of the bubble like a white cloud.

The ghosts screamed and sighed and wailed as they lashed past her, seeming to tear the strength from her in wisps that rose with them until they rushed upward, free. Their howls of horror and agony slid into shouts of joy at their escape as they touched the edge of the overlapping worlds and burst through the silver wall of ghostlight, sparking in the last rays of the sun.

As the last of them slipped out of her grasp, Jacque let out a scream that rose and shook until the edges of the worlds shook with it. The silvery bubble of the Grey collapsed with the sound of a gong reverberating across the water and the last impressions of the ghosts vanished into the darkness of the natural sky thickly spread with stars and smeared here and there with the smudges of summer clouds still holding the ruddy tinge of the sun that had already slipped below the horizon. It hadn't felt like fifteen minutes had elapsed. . . .

But, against my hope, the sea witch was still here, or, more to the point, not *there*. The gateway had collapsed but she was here in the world—the normal world—and I didn't have the ghost receptacles, which meant she still had power. I didn't know why she was still here and not locked away again in her bubble of Otherplace, but I'd have to worry about it later as my mind threw out a stream of curses I didn't have the breath to vent.

The sea witch threw herself at me, no words this time, no declarations of hate, only action meant to bring me down. As long as the other ghosts remained unclaimed she still had power, but she seemed too angry to use it and turned to her fists and teeth instead.

I dropped the bell and fought back, but I was slow

and dizzy from the pain in my chest that seemed to be shutting down my ability to breathe, to focus, to see. . . . I struck back more by instinct than anything else, blind and desperate and flailing.

I managed to duck her next blow, diving to the deck and rolling forward, but the cost in black agony was high and I staggered, trying to rise again. I turned around as she flung herself at me with taloned hands outstretched, jaws opening improbably wide to bite at my face. I hopped sideways, falling as much as anything, and turning to get behind her, but she still managed to gouge a bit of waterproof nylon and flesh from my left arm as she whirled around.

I stifled a cry as the yellow slicker shed tears of my blood. She turned back and grinned as I lost my footing and landed hard with one knee against the wet dock boards. Then she darted forward again, swooping lower this time, knowing I could only go down to avoid her.

I knew Solis was somewhere behind me but I wasn't sure how far away or if his hands were full. I couldn't spare the attention to find out. I'd have to fend for myself. My vision was unfocused through tears that welled with the agony in my side and arm but I could still see her coming. I shoved my right hand into my pocket and hoped I wouldn't pass out. . . .

She raked her hands toward my throat, scoring lines in my skin.

I fell flat backward, clutching the gun in my pocket and tilting it upward. I squeezed the grips and trigger, feeling the jolt and burn as the bullet ripped through the fabric, scattering burning residue and jetting hot gas against my hand in the confined hollow of my coat pocket.

She made a guttural sound as she passed over me, kicking, then turning with a jerk, unharmed. She was laughing. She stomped at my head and I rolled aside but she still connected. I screamed as her foot dug into my unbroken ribs, jarring the rest of my body and heaving me a short distance forward, where I folded into a half-fallen heap, unable to breathe or move out of her path, barely staying as upright and conscious as I was. I squeezed my eyes against the pain and tried to rise past my knees—I did *not* want to die again. Not now and especially not crushed down like a broken toy.

I could hear her moving closer, speaking, her voice rising with a wind that came to her call. Electricity hummed and crackled in the air, raising the hair on my neck and arms and prickling across my skin. I didn't know any counters to this but to shut her mouth, and though I struggled to point the gun at her again, I couldn't see her well enough between my pain and tears to be sure I would hit her.

There was a scrabbling sound behind her and the sea witch gasped, lunged down against me, then squealed and went limp, her weight shoving me all the way to the deck. I pushed her weakly aside and crawled away, turning my head to see why she had collapsed.

Panting and wiping red fluid from his face, Solis backed away from the crumpled, still body of the sea witch. The karambit, clutched in his fist, dripped blood from its claw-shaped blade.

Fielding yelped behind him and rolled onto his side, his shape shifting toward otter. Solis spun, the knife low and ready to take on whatever came next. Then he dropped it to the decking and dove after the mutating dobhar-chú. It eeled out of his grasp and bounded for the seaward end of the dock. Solis scrambled to catch the creature but the odds seemed to be in Fielding's favor.

I managed to pull my pistol out of my inner jacket pocket and from my prone position it wasn't so hard to fire into the wooden planking just ahead of the fleeing otter. Pure dumb luck, I assure you, because I was shaking too hard for it to be anything else. Fielding skidded to a stop and looked around for another escape.

I gulped in a breath. "Don't try," I warned him. "I will shoot you. Next time. And damn to Father Otter." I felt like I'd been steamrollered, but I must have been terrifying: still dangerous even flattened to the deck.

Fielding stayed, cringing, where he was and slowly shifted back to his human form. "I'm sorry. Please don't shoot me. I won't run."

I glanced up at Solis and watched him turn to collect Fielding and bundle him into the boat.

I put my head down for a moment and lay on the wet dock until Solis returned to help me up. "That wasn't fifteen minutes," I whispered. "We failed."

He shook his head and kept me moving forward. "Not yet."

I staggered with him to the boat as he dragged the bell along. I tried not to look weak as a newborn until it was too late for Fielding to change his mind, but maybe no one cared, since I was sure I looked as helpless as I felt. I needed to stop making a habit of this sort of bravado, especially when my head was reeling and I was barely keeping my feet under me. I figured my luck was nearly over.

I oozed into the dinghy and literally sat on Fielding to keep him from shifting form all the way back to *Mambo Moon*.

TWENTY-SEVEN

The waters of the cove fell still and silent as Solis guided the little boat back to the larger one. The surface no longer churned and there was no sign of the battling creatures of fur and fin, though I was sure they were somewhere. As we maneuvered to come next to *Mambo Moon*'s steps, I thought I heard a woman's voice from the deck just out of view. Quinton, seeming prescient but probably just hearing the engine, leaned over the side and caught the line Solis tossed to him to help us tie up and come aboard. I needed a lot more help than I had when we left, and keeping Fielding in line had to be put in the hands of another.

The other being Father Otter, who jumped down into the dinghy as we left it and hauled Fielding out, fairly chasing him up on deck with sharp pinches and snaps of his teeth, reminiscent of the way he'd bitten and shaken the other dobhar-chú earlier when they were both in otter form. I was so startled to see Father Otter that I stared in bold silence as Quinton and Solis helped me on board and along the deck. But there was more yet to shock me: As we rounded the side and came onto the aft deck and into the glow of electric light shining from the cabin, I saw Shelly Knight standing beside the fish hold and talking to Paul Zantree—who was holding a slender, curved sword that was certainly not a pirate-show prop.

Shelly's pale green hair swirled around her as if she

were floating in water rather than standing on the deck in plain air. She was the same woman I'd seen in the photos and a few minutes before on the dock and yet she had changed dramatically—she glowed now and had a regal air, seeming taller and moving with ineffable grace. It appeared Zantree had lent her a bathrobe and that seemed a faintly ridiculous cover for such arresting beauty. Her skin reflected the light from the cabin like the surface of a pearl—a sheen of rose, green, and blue hovering over her exposed limbs and face. Her voice was very low but it cut through the creaking of the boat and the lapping of waves with the clear, quiet sound of water trickling over rocks, softly, gently wearing them away.

Zantree turned toward the commotion raised by Father Otter chivvying Fielding along and Fielding himself drew up short, taking a nasty smack across the head from Father Otter for doing so.

"Shelly," Fielding breathed.

She gave him a cool glance, then looked past him to me as Quinton eased me into a chair. She pointed at a pile of barnacle-crusted objects at her feet with a finger tipped by a hooked white nail. "I believe these are what Gary was after. I'm sorry to have left you to confront my mother on your own but I knew the gateway would collapse soon and I had to take the chance that presented itself."

Father Otter started forward, scowling, as if he meant to confront Shelly in some fashion.

Quinton put out his hand to restrain him. "Let's not do that again," he suggested.

Apparently things had been much livelier than I'd imagined here on *Mambo Moon* while Solis and I were in transit. I glanced at Quinton, who gave a tiny shake of his head. I wasn't going to argue with his brush-off; all I really wanted was to fall into bed and sleep until I stopped aching.

Father Otter issued a guttural hiss, but took a half step back and made another ill-tempered snap at Fielding's ear. Fielding flinched.

Shelly looked disgusted. "I won't say I'm happy about the death of my mother," she started, sending a quick glare at Solis, "but it is better for all of us that she's gone. And I don't need these, nor do I want them. Since I found Gary snooping around them and you had the *Valencia*'s bell on the dock, I assume it's you who wants them. Though I suppose it could have been the dobharchú who sent him, trying to steal them and break my mother's power."

She gave Father Otter a dirty look. He curled his lip and gave a low growl in return.

I leaned back in my chair like a boneless thing, not caring how weak or impolite it might look—I hurt too much to play that game. "Why?" I asked, panting a little against the painful constriction of breath in my chest. "Don't you need them?"

"No. When I realized how my mother's power worked I went looking for something else. I knew how to make sure we weren't closed in the cove again but I wasn't going to do it for her sake—not after what she'd done to me. And now that she's dead I can claim my own power; I don't need this filthy stuff."

"So the whole virgin thing . . ." I started, making a rolling gesture with my hand to encourage her explanation.

She rolled her eyes. "Oh . . . Mother . . ." She shook her head. "She couldn't very well tell me I didn't need her, could she? As long as I was a sheltered little fry, hidden away in her cove, she could control me and my magic. When I went outside, bad things happened and she used that to convince me to stay under her thumb. But I'm not stupid. I realized she had lied to me about power and about . . . your kind. I couldn't and won't do what she could do, but I can do my own tricks. I don't need these," she added, pointing again to the relics on the deck. She looked at Fielding. "And I don't need you or anyone else to show me what I really am and what I can do for myself and my folk."

Fielding looked stricken and moaned her name.

She sighed. "Oh, Gary. You're such a selfish jerk. A pretty one, but still a jerk. My people have been devastated but we can survive—as long as we don't have to fight our neighbors all the time. I could take you as a hostage, I guess, like some kind of royal insurance policy, but, frankly, I just don't want you. If that makes Father Otter angry, we'll have to find some other way to bring peace here. But you . . . ? I think we'd all be better off if you left."

I cut in, trying to keep the conversation on track. "So, you can't even use these?"

Shelly made a face and shook her head. "I could do that kind of magic but I won't and I don't want them here. They stir up bad feelings. Take them and do as you like."

Father Otter inched forward and started to reach for one of the objects in the pile. Shelly sucked in a breath and made fists of her hands at her sides, as if she were restraining herself from slapping him away. I did it for her, though the movement sent a flare of nauseating pain through my chest and sides. Father Otter flinched and glared at me.

"Don't. It won't help you or your people and now is not the time to get greedy." I turned back to Shelly. "You don't plan on . . . using your siren wiles on other boats, do you?"

"No. Well . . . not that way. I might like an occasional frolic, but I have seen too much death and pain and I don't have any taste for killing if I don't have to."

"Then I'll thank you for giving these to me." I wasn't quite sure what I was supposed to do with the things, writhing and foaming as they did with shadows and shades.

Solis glanced up from his watch. "Fifteen minutes," he said.

I frowned. Fifteen minutes from what?

The surfaces of the objects on deck—bells and bottles,

bowls and boxes—shimmered and sparked a moment; then the gleams of color that bound them fell away, unraveling like rope decayed to dust.

"Just touch them," Solis added. "I think I've guessed it right."

I bent forward like an arthritic old woman and brushed my fingertips over the nearest of the crusted trove—another bell, this one much smaller than *Valencia*'s and not as heavy, gleaming a bit of brass through its veil of seaweed and barnacles. A flood of silver mist and white light burst out of the bell, flashing for a moment into four images: two young women and two men. They let out a sob and a cry, then leapt for the night sky above us, spiraling away into the scattered starlight of the Milky Way's spangled band.

I turned an amazed glance on Solis. "Everything balances out—we lost fifteen minutes the first time we rang the bell, so this time we had to regain it."

"What about the bubble around the cove?"

"Why would ringing the doorbell count on that timer?"

It was loopy, but it made as much sense as anything else in the Grey and more than some things. "How did I miss that?"

He shrugged. "Busy."

I suppose they would have responded as well to anyone, now that the spell was broken, but everyone seemed to have agreed it was my job to let the ghosts out of their shells. As uncomfortable as it was, I managed to creep to each of the receptacles and brush away the last remaining strands that held the souls of the drowned at bay. Each time they poured out and upward in swells of lambent mist and shimmering light, sighing and weeping, then crying out in joy and vaulting for the deepening night sky that stretched above us, pierced like black velvet with the brightness of stars. The river of the Milky Way, tipped for a while into our planet's tilted, whirling view, seemed to grow brighter and thicker as the ghosts rushed away from their captivity into freedom. An uncanny wind blew them away in coils of silvery mist that turned a massive head in our direction just long enough for me to recognize the passing shape of the Guardian Beast shepherding the spirits of the dead onward. It didn't pause to say thank you and the velocity of its passage rocked and shook the boat as easily as an autumn leaf. I got no sense that it cared the deed was done or done by me. The balance of power in the area had been leveled and that was all that concerned it. There was, indeed, nothing human or humane remaining in the Beast and I finally put that niggling thought away, relieved.

When the last spirit was no more than a memory of sound and light in our senses, I eased back into my chair once again, satisfied but struggling with my exhaustion and discomfort. I glanced at Shelly, who was still standing, looking up at the sky, smiling a bittersweet kind of smile.

It seemed wrong to break the moment but I had to. "I think . . . we're done here," I said.

She lowered her eyes to mine, her expression growing more grave and a touch sad. "I still need peace with the otter people."

I glanced at Father Otter and she took that as I meant it; it wasn't up to me.

"Will you stay a moment as my witnesses?" she asked, looking from me to Zantree and back. . . .

As we nodded to her, Father Otter cast rapid glances at each of us, lingering longest on Shelly and Fielding. He stared hard at Fielding, who shrank from his gaze, for a moment, then turned back to Shelly, asking, "You don't want this one?"

"What would I want *him* for?"

"Revenge. He harmed you, he broke your power, he ruined your value, and he allowed your mother to imprison you."

"Why should I care after all this time about what was or could have been? None of that is important anymore.

Do *you* want to keep on living in the past? Living in a state of war because of some stupid dispute hundreds of years old? We could do a lot for each other, my people and yours. We don't have to keep on killing each other. You and me . . . we don't have to be friends but we could at least call a truce and let our people heal."

Father Otter scowled but it wasn't the angry expression he'd had before. "Your people, our people . . . That may be enough for the Puget folk, but none of the others will abide by such a truce."

"Not at first but we can do our best for ourselves and let the rest come around in their own time."

"What about the Columbia people? They will kill and die and they will not respect our truce if we cross the bar."

"Then maybe we should send an emissary. Someone who's *from* the Columbia." Shelly turned her gaze and looked hard at Fielding. "We can net two fish with one cast: Send Gary away from here *and* let him be useful elsewhere. And never come back," she added under her breath.

"What does it net us to send him away?"

Shelly laughed and the sound set my teeth on edge. "You don't actually *want* him to stay? Disruptive, whining, self-centered idiot that he is."

Fielding sat down hard on the deck. "I'm not *that* bad!"

"In a shark's eye," Shelly shot back. She looked at Father Otter. "Am I right?"

Father Otter was clearly calculating something. "We can send him back to his mother's people . . . Though we hate to give such a prize away. . . ."

"Gary's no prize," Shelly said.

Father Otter turned his head and cocked it to one side. "To the Columbia people he is. His mother was the last royal dobhar-chú on the river."

Fielding made an ugly face at Father Otter. "You lied to me! You said you didn't know anything about my mother!"

"Her *where*abouts. Who she was—certainly we knew that, whelp!"

"You didn't say so."

"Why should we give such information to you when you brought us nothing but trouble? And you didn't ask the right questions." Father Otter turned his attention back to Shelly, as if Fielding had disappeared. "We will consider sending a message. . . ."

"Don't pretend you don't want him gone as much as I do."

"What do you offer us to make it worth our effort to conduct him safely back to the Columbia? Our folk outnumber yours and we could order them to attack again."

"That battle will not be as easy as you think, Fa Dobhar-chú. My mother's power no longer restrains mine and you don't know what I can do. . . ." She gave him a cunning look and stared him down for a moment. Having made her threat, she paused and then her face brightened and she added, "Besides . . . I have treasures: pearls and the salvage of hundreds of lost ships. . . . Such knowledge as your folk could do much with. And I will share with you if you become my allies rather than my enemies."

Father Otter smiled a little; it wasn't a greedy smile but an appreciative one.

"What if I don't want to go back to Oregon?" Fielding objected. "You can't compel me, either of you. Not if I choose to live in this form."

Solis cleared his throat. "In this form you will return to Seattle with me and stand trial for what happened aboard the *Seawitch*."

Fielding looked smug but the expression was wobbly. "By what evidence and under what charge?"

"Piracy, perhaps, or criminal negligence as the captain who allowed his ship to be taken and his charges killed. And as you are the only surviving member of the crew, the questions will be pointed. If your answers don't please the court, you would be remanded for psychological examination at Western State Hospital, which could take quite some time in that landlocked and miserable place."

Quinton cleared his throat, looking a bit uncomfortable. "Actually . . . if his answers or actions—like turning into an otter in the holding cell—set off the wrong alarm bells, he'll be made to disappear."

We all turned to regard Quinton with a range of emotions from curiosity to terror.

I raised my eyebrows at him. "This wouldn't have anything to do with your dad's little project, would it?"

He was pale and upset. "Yes." He looked at the others and continued. "I can't tell you much but certain groups within the U.S. government know that there are . . . people like Fielding and Shelly and Harper. One of these groups is headed by my father, who is even less agreeable than Father Otter here. If Dad gets wind of someone like Fielding, his agents will hunt him down and snatch him. He won't even make it to court." He shifted his focus to Fielding. "Once that happens, you get to be the biggest rat in their lab and these guys . . . they redefine the term 'living hell.' You really, really don't want them to find you. Or even hear of you."

"You'd narc on me?" Fielding asked, appalled.

Quinton gave an adamant shake of the head. "Not in a million years. Not to anyone and especially not to these guys. No one here would." He cast a desperate glance around and all the humans nodded. "But if you are booked on charges, information about you will get out. That's just the way the booking databases are connected to other parts of the electronic world and there are specialized programs cruising that information pool like sharks looking for the right kind of food—food like you. Once they figure you out, they'll descend like ninjas and you'll disappear in a small puff of paperwork that will claim you've been transferred to a special facility that doesn't exist. No one will see you leave or where you go, and if guys like my dad have their way, you'll never come out."

Fielding's eyes widened, his mouth gaped, and his chest began to jerk as his breathing went panicky and shallow. He was ready to bolt but there was nowhere to go.

I caught his eye. "I recommend that you go to back to the Columbia. As their royal dobhar-chú, you'll be a lot safer than you are as Gary Fielding."

"Only if you behave," Father Otter put in. "Kin they may be but the Columbia folk are not easy. They will make you earn your place—as we should have done."

Fielding nodded like a broken doll. "All right. OK, I'll go back to the Columbia."

Father Otter bared his teeth. "We will know if you do not."

Fielding flattened himself on the deck, a cowed and horrified expression on his face. "Pax, pax," he muttered.

Shelly gazed at Father Otter. "Can he be trusted to swim the whole way?"

"I'll take him," Zantree offered. He stood with his arms crossed over his chest, the gleaming cutlass in his fist making him look every inch the pirate captain, although the starstruck smile he turned on Shelly did somewhat ruin the effect.

Shelly seemed bemused by it all. "Will you? Why?"

"Well . . . I've got this big ol' boat to myself these days and I rarely take her out, but now I'll have a top-notch bar pilot along. I always did have a yen to cross the bar on my own. I'm sure Gary can teach me a few things— being half otter he must have a feel for the water I don't. I think that would be a fine adventure. And . . . well . . . it would be my pleasure to do something for you."

"You would take this risk for *me*? How can you trust him after what he has done? His presence nearly got your boat destroyed," Shelly objected.

"Oh, I imagine your folk and his folk will want to check in on us once in a while . . . won't you?" He turned his attention to Fielding with a gimlet eye. "And you won't dare give me trouble. Will you?"

Fielding looked horrified but he nodded docilely enough.

Zantree looked back to Shelly. "First we'll have to drop these folks off, though. If it's all right with you."

"Yes," she replied. "It's a wonderful plan. If Father Otter agrees . . ."

The dobhar-chú gave a stiff nod.

Zantree turned to me and asked, "You have any objection to being dropped off at Victoria? You can take the hydroplane in the morning and be home before lunch. I think Gary and I'd be best served to head straight on down the coast as soon as possible. Don't you?"

I agreed. "That sounds like a plan. Can we pause long enough to drop this off?" I added, pointing to the *Valencia*'s bell lying on the deck.

"Where do you want to take it?" Zantree asked.

"Back to its proper home. Out where the *Valencia* went down."

"Well . . . it's a bit of a ways . . ."

Shelly smirked. "Not with my help."

Zantree smiled like a kid with a present. "Would you?" I had the feeling Paul Zantree was utterly enchanted with the new sea witch—though not in the usual way.

Shelly's smile warmed to something genuine. "Of course." Then she turned to Fielding. "Be a better man this time, Gary. The nature of a second chance is that you only get one."

EPILOGUE

As wonderful as it had felt releasing the spirits that had so long lain imprisoned by the previous sea witch, I was exhausted, sore, and miserable, and I wasn't convinced I was the only one—just the worst off. The human vote was to head out in the morning, after we'd all had a chance to rest. Fielding went off with Father Otter, unhappily but not actively resisting, to be watched over by his furry kin for the night—just in case. With the assistance of Shelly and her merfolk, the cruise back up Spieden Channel in the morning was as smooth and swift as an ice cube sliding down a satin tablecloth and we passed the turn for Victoria Harbour about ten in the morning, making Pachena Point less than two hours later. There we broke a bottle of red wine over the bell at Zantree's insistence, and, asking for the help of Poseidon—I was a bit leery of this, but Zantree claimed we had to—we ceremoniously heaved the *Valencia*'s bell overboard and let it sink to rejoin the last remains of the ship from which it had been taken long ago.

We entrusted the emptied shells, bells, bottles, urns, bowls, and boxes that had contained the spirits of the drowned and shipwrecked to the merfolk for disposal in the most appropriate places. All but the first brass bell, which we carried away to return to *Seawitch*.

Shelly's merfolk, though not much seen, were in evi-

dence throughout the trip in the persistent strangeness of
waves and wind that ran fair on our stern even when every other boat in sight was caught up the other way. We
couldn't do much about the tide, but with Zantree's
knowledge of the currents, we didn't have to. We slipped
back to Victoria ahead of the turn of the tide and Quinton, Solis, and I disembarked on the pier at Victoria Harbour at last, carrying our baggage and feeling altogether
grubby, sore, and disconnected from the normal world.
Since it was Sunday, the Victoria Clipper's morning hydroplane was full and we had to wait for the next boat. We
did have some complications because we had appeared
pretty much out of nowhere, but both Solis and I had our
passports with us all the time and I am still not quite sure
what Quinton said to earn a startled look and a quick
escort to a private office before he was released again under a barrage of nervous smiles from the Victoria Harbour master.

On the high-speed ferry trip back to Seattle, Solis and
I discussed the reports we would file. For the first time in
my experience of him, he had no interest in telling the
unvarnished truth about a case. As far as I could tell, he
was as ready to bury this one in obscure paperwork and
oblique wording as I was. It was weird to feel so much in
tune with him and I wondered if I was going to feel this
new oddness forever. I found myself calling him Rey
more often than I'd meant to. It was a strange way to
build a friendship but it looked as if that's what we had.
Solis even invited us to come home with him for dinner
but we declined. I didn't want to know what he would
say or not say about our trip—not yet at least.

It was a long bus ride from the Clipper terminal
downtown to my place in West Seattle, since the sporadic
foot ferry to Alki was not running. Quinton and I leaned
our heads together and didn't talk. I loved the quietness
we fell into after our hectic weekend of monster seeking
and ghost saving. We barely spoke for the next two days,
thinking about what had passed and simply enjoying the

quiet of being together at home again, while I gave my
ribs and my arm the rest they needed.

Quinton's anxiety about his father died away once
we'd been able to talk for a few minutes in bed one night.
I still felt sore and delicate in body, but my emotions
were calm. I did not need to fret about my friends, my
lovers, or the vicissitudes of guardians and ghosts.

The first day at home I checked my computer for anything that really needed my attention before I stuck myself in the shower. In the backlog of weekend e-mail, I
found a note from Mara and Ben Danziger. It was long
and rambling, as Mara often was, and I found myself
tearing up a bit over the familiar tone.

On the subject of the dobhar-chú, I can't say as I'm
the best source. Although they're of Irish origin I've
never seen one and most folks say they're long
gone—by which I mean the beastly ones, not the
common otter, as the term is now used. All tales
agree that they are vicious and entirely animal in nature, having only the instinct and cunning of a beast
and none of the reason of higher creatures. I do hope
you haven't had to tangle with them. Perhaps Ben
and Brian will wish to go in search of them. . . .

But it's truly a pleasure to hear from you! We've
been out in the English countryside with a circle of
mad druids preparing for the summer solstice and
entirely out of touch with the computer for weeks.
It's a pleasure all of its own, yet I'm missing my friends
in Seattle terribly. I had not thought I would feel so
much a foreigner, yet I often do—and I am no longer
the cleverest witch in the room—which quite puts
me back on my heels. But the news is that Ben has
been offered another teaching position here in England now that the primary work on the book is
done, so we are likely to remain a while longer on
loan, so to speak. I shall certainly miss you and Quinton and now that the research is over, I suppose I

shall pine for the excitement of investigating things. I know we had a rough patch before our parting, but that has not put an end to our friendship. I hope that in distance we may rediscover the value of compassionate friends. . . .

If Mara meant me, I was afraid I didn't really measure up, though I was trying. I was struck by the phrase "compassionate friends." This was what the Guardian Beast was not and what I had been lucky enough to find in the people I was able to call friends: the Danzigers, Quinton, Solis—I found it strange to think of him as a friend, but that was surely what he was now—and Phoebe Mason, with whom I needed to do some fence mending. Friendship wasn't always easy and I thought of Linda Starrett and her lost friend Odile and wished there was something I could have done to comfort that lonely woman. But there was nothing in my power. No amount of compassion in me would mend the hole in her life.

It occurred to me that human compassion, as much as my ability in the Grey, was what had forced me into the role I had. I wasn't very good at compassion—I tended more toward the hard-ass side of the line—but I had considerably more of it than the Guardian Beast. And I had friends who reminded me of the need for it. That was perhaps the real reason I was the one tasked with being the Hands of the Guardian. I'd met one other Greywalker in my life and he was not like me—a colder, harder man whose better impulses rarely broke past the shell of his bitterness. He felt little need for friends or to seek justice.

Solis sought justice in the law, but in the end it was not the law to which we had turned in the matter of the *Seawitch*. We had agreed, with a pang of guilty conscience, to lay the legal blame on Gary Fielding—a negligent captain who'd been busy with his private relations with another of the crew and allowed his boat into dangerous waters on autopilot, where it had been taken up in the tidal race in the straits and swept out to sea with all aboard lost. We claimed the boat had drifted in and been returned to her berth by an odd stroke of luck and a sailor who was in the country illegally and had been deported the same day he'd dropped off the boat. Having laid the blame, we then let Fielding disappear in the fiction of an anonymous death rather than become a lab rat in a nightmare experiment—or be hounded to death by his own people. We were both a little surprised that the police and the insurance company bought the story, but in the end they did. I even got a bonus from the company for wrapping it up so quickly—which made me laugh all the way to the bank. Perhaps we would regret having tempered justice with compassion someday, but not today.

AUTHOR'S NOTE

First off, a note about the name of the marina: It really is called Shilshole Bay Marina and yes, I know how it gets mispronounced. Everyone who makes that joke thinks they're the first to notice how easy it is to mistake that first L for a T. But in fact, it's not a silly slip of the tongue; it's a name the Duwamish people gave the area that means "threading a needle" and probably referred to getting your fishing canoe through the once-narrow opening between the bluffs and mudflats on the way to Salmon Bay, just east of the present-day Hiram M. Chittenden Locks. So, you can stop sniggering now and get on to the next bit.

As always, I borrowed from real events and places as much as possible and faked it where I had to. I did my best on the Spanish for Solis's family, but had to rely heavily on help from Spanish-speaking friends and my copy editor, who stepped in at the final stage and fixed my errors. Anything incorrect, stupid, bass-ackward, or outright wrong is all my fault. Now, on to the research!

There are persistent tales that a ghost ship haunts the Strait of San Juan de Fuca, near the southwestern tip of Vancouver Island, and, of course, I couldn't resist looking into them for this book. But I hadn't really expected to find a real-life story behind them as chilling as the tale of the S.S. *Valencia*. Accounts of the sinking of the steamship vary in some details and can be a little contradictory and confusing but all agree it was a tragic and harrowing event. I actually played down some of the facts and historic descriptions, since the reality was so terrible as to seem surreal, with accounts of women and children freezing in the rigging and so on. The captain's and navigator's errors may account for some of what went wrong, but a lot was plain bad luck, fear, and bad timing—like the first landing party turning the wrong way and the crew making only one attempt to shoot a line onto the cliffs without recalibrating the gun sight and trying again. It's true, however, that the only surviving lifeboat was lost for twenty-seven years and the big ship's wreck remains at the foot of Pachena Point (sometimes referred to as Cape Beale or Beale's Point in the historic records) to this day. The section of hiking trail that passes the ill-fated ship is sometimes referred to as Valencia Bluffs in honor of the wreck below. Memorials to the passengers and crew have been erected near the wreck site on Vancouver Island's West Coast Trail and in Seattle's Mount Pleasant Cemetery on Queen Anne Hill. You can learn more about the sinking of the *Valencia* online (HistoryLink.org being one of my favorite sites, though the article at Wikipedia is surprisingly good) and at the Maritime Museum of British Columbia in Victoria, B.C., where the nameplate from lifeboat number five is on display. But I'll warn you: If you thought my descriptions went a bit too far, you may find some of the historic record stomach turning; those old-time reporters and sailors had some creepy turns of phrase.

I didn't make up the Graveyard of the Pacific, either. North America's upper West Coast does, indeed, have a sinister history and there are plenty of rusting wrecks you can still visit up close or spot from a cliffside vantage point along the coasts of northern California, Oregon, Washington, and British Columbia. Most have less-horrifying tales attached than the *Valencia*, but a few are the stuff of nightmares. It's also true that the mouth of the Columbia River is a place of danger where boats are damaged or capsized with frightening regularity. The United States Coast Guard maintains a lighthouse and rescue station on the Washington side of the river mouth at Cape Disappointment—aptly named—specifically to keep watch over the treacherous Columbia Bar. And, yes, you can see the silt plume from orbit. There's a nice scientific explanation for why the area is so dangerous at Oregon State University's Ocean and Air Magazine Web site (http://oceanandair.coas.oregonstate.edu/index .cfm?fuseaction=content.display&pageID=85) if you want to know more.

All the locations mentioned in the book are real (even the obscure and tiny Neil Bay), including the islands, coves, harbors, and waterways Harper and her friends visit while aboard the *Mambo Moon*. The northern Puget Sound around the San Juan Islands is so well-known for its bizarre tidal currents that a special "current almanac" exists for the area that shows the directions and strength of the prevailing currents for any day or time you need. On boating trips around the islands, I've witnessed and been aboard light sailboats with full sail on and engine engaged standing still and even going backward in the grip of the adverse currents, which can move at greater than eight knots there. It's a tricky place to travel by boat, but since there's ferry service to only three of the islands, there's no other choice if your destination lies on an island other than Vancouver, Orcas, or San Juan. Despite the perverse currents and twisting passages, the San Juans are a wonderful place to visit. Most of the area is protected as U.S. or Canadian parkland, and it's breathtaking. The water is a deep clear blue, and small towns and villages among the islands offer delightful tourist opportunities, while the uninhabited islands are home to natural beauty and a haunting sense of isolation difficult to find so close to civilization. And there are other stories to be found in the San Juans, such as the true tale of the Pig War, how the area was discovered by a Greek sea captain but given a Spanish name, and a host of native myths and legends as well as tons of U.S. and Canadian history.

The dobhar-chú are an Irish legend, although the word is now used, as Mara explains, to mean any ordinary river otter. I changed the beastie a bit to suit my purposes, with many apologies to the Irish. Although I've never seen it, I've been told that the tombstone attesting to the deadly attack of a dobhar-chú does exist in Conwal, in County Latrim. Anyone who can send me a verifiable photo of such a marker will have my undying thanks.

I admit to playing fast and loose with the investigation of possible crimes in inland and international waters. The jurisdiction of such crimes is rather convoluted and arcane, so I simplified it and I hope the Coast Guard, FBI, International Maritime Organization, and everyone else involved will understand the necessity. As to the rest, I warped, snitched, borrowed, cribbed, and made things up where I couldn't find what I wanted. And I always thought merfolk needed tentacles, so I gave them some.

All the other characters, events, boats, crimes, and relationships included here are solely my invention and any resemblance to real stuff is unintentional.

Read on for an exciting excerpt
from the next Greywalker novel,

POSSESSION

by Kat Richardson
Available in hardcover in
August 2013 from Roc.

I don't usually acquire clients in secondhand stores; books, jackets, furniture, knickknacks — yes — clients ... not so much. I was lurking in the nook at Old Possum's Books and Beans where the books about music, theater, and philosophy were currently kept — more a comment on the owner Phoebe Mason's sense of humor than any practical filing system — when a woman approached me. Even before I saw her, I felt the touch of her desperation and fear like a cloud of bad perfume.

Her footsteps stuttered as she walked across the scarred old wooden floor and I looked around and down to find the source of the uncertain noise. Thus, the first thing I actually saw was her shoes: good-quality leather loafers with low heels that had become unevenly worn so each step wobbled just a bit, the dark brown leather scuffed along the sides and toes as if they'd been scraped repeatedly through rough stones. Her designer jeans were baggy at the knee, cinched in with a belt that didn't match the shoes, and fit like they'd been meant for a curvier body, while her blouse was so rumpled it looked as if she'd misbuttoned it.

I looked up to study her face and saw a once lovely middle-aged woman with shoulder-length black hair, the gray roots leaving an undyed band about an inch wide along her part. Her cheekbones stood in high relief, hinting at some mix of Asian ancestors with taller Europeans, under skin that was dry, fine-lined, and too tight, as if she'd given up eating and was subsisting on nerves and dry toast. She stopped, her eyes widening as she bit her lip, and stared at me for a second. Then she drew a deep breath and asked, "Are you the detective? A friend of Phoebe's?"

Her question seemed to hang on the air and I took a beat before I replied, frowning a little at the weight it seemed to add to room. "I am both of those things. Whether I'm the specific one you want, I'm not sure." The fading ghost of a former customer wafted obliviously down the aisle and through the pair of us as we stood there.

The woman didn't see it, but she twitched at its cold passage and gave me a deer-in-the-headlights stare. "There's someone else?" The drained olive-and-charcoal shimmer around her told me she was terrified of the answer.

I put up one hand to stop her turn away. "No. I'm sorry. That's not what I meant. Phoebe has a lot of friends. Why do you think it's me you're looking for?"

"I need—um, I have a sister—" She stopped and shook her head as if she could shake her words into the right order. "I need help. I came here because I'm desperate to find out what's happening. I was told I should talk to you—" She wrung her hands as she babbled, her posture bending, stooping forward as if her chest ached.

I touched her hand and felt a chill of distress twine up my fingers like the tendrils of a climbing vine. I didn't jerk away, though that was my first impulse. "It's all right," I started, patting her hand very lightly and then closing mine over hers to stop her churning motion. "Let's sit down and you can tell me about it then."

She returned a jerky nod, her hands stilling as she let her gaze slide away from mine. I led her down the aisle and around the corner to the coffee nook, where there were a few cushy armchairs set between a fake fireplace and the espresso counter. A three-quarter-scale replica of a triceratops skull looked down on us from the wall above the espresso machine, just a few feet from a round traffic mirror that showed the alcove to whoever was manning the front desk. We were alone, but not unobserved, and that was fine.

One of the chairs was occupied by a massive golden feline that laid claim to being a house cat only because we'd never been able to prove it was a mountain lion. "Hump it, Simba," I suggested, with a dismissive jerk of my head.

With impressive languor and a yawn that showed off white fangs and a long tongue of barbed pink velvet, the cat flowed out of the chair and prowled off to intimidate one of the lesser cats out of its sleeping spot. I waved to the two now-empty chairs nearest us and watched the woman stumble and nearly fall into the one just vacated by Simba.

I got a cup of water for the woman rather than coffee, since I figured that although she looked exhausted, she didn't need to be any further wound up than she was. She clutched the cup in both hands, her shoulders hunched. Her skin had a sallow cast over its natural lightly bronzed color and blue shadows of worry smeared her eye sockets. She peered at me like a frightened cat from under a bed.

I sat down and started the conversation, since it seemed like she wasn't ready to. I did my best to give the impression I was earnest, honest, and safe to talk to. "I'm Harper Blaine and I am a friend of Phoebe's. I'm also a private investigator and I help people with problems. What's your name and what can I help you with?"

"I— My name is Lillian Goss" she started. "Lily. Phoebe says . . ." Her gaze darted around, looking up at me, then down, then side to side in nervous jumps. "She says you see ghosts."

I was a little surprised: Phoebe hadn't seemed entirely convinced when we'd had "the talk" about my weird abilities that had caused her some grief in the past. Of course, she might have still been mad at me and it's hard to tell precisely what Phoebe's thinking when she's displeased. "Do *you* believe in ghosts?" I asked.

"I don't. Or I didn't. Or— I don't know. But I believe in God and I believe in the Devil and I believe that whatever has my sister isn't either one of those."

I blinked, but I didn't balk. "Is your sister missing?"

"No. Or yes. She's . . . not home anymore. But someone else is."

"Someone else is in your sister's house?"

"Not her house—her body."

She watched me absorb that statement and took my well-schooled poker face as rejection. She looked at the floor, her hands squeezing the cup so hard that the plastic sides deformed with a popping sound that made her start and gasp. "You don't believe me!"

"Yes, I do. But why have you come to the conclusion that someone or something other than her own self is . . . occupying her body? That is quite a leap for most people."

She bit her lip, clamping down on sobbing breaths. She wheezed and snorted a moment before she regained some control and was able to speak. "My sister is in what they call a persistent vegetative state. She's not really awake, even when she has her eyes open and seems to be looking around. She breathes on her own and sometimes she laughs or cries, but the doctors and nurses tell me it's not real laughter or sadness, just an involuntary function of whatever's still working in her brain. She can't do anything but lie in bed or sit in an armchair. The doctors say if her state doesn't change soon, it never will; she'll just deteriorate slowly until she dies.

"But a while ago she sat up on her own and she started drawing or painting something on her bedspread. I thought she was getting better, but that's not it. She just paints. She doesn't improve. The machines indicate that she's not doing anything—that her brain isn't sending these signals that move her body—but she's sitting up and painting. I started bringing her supplies so she wouldn't use food or blood on the bed. . . . Now she just sits up at random times and paints. And then she lies down and whatever spark she had in her goes away again. The machines say she never did anything. Her blood pressure and breathing go up, but that's all. But these paintings—they're real paintings—not crazy finger paint smeary things."

"Is it the paintings themselves that distress you?"

"No. She paints landscapes but they're . . . they're odd. Someplace you almost know but can't name. She paints them—it's not a hoax or a prank. But my sister doesn't know how to paint or draw or anything like that. She never learned. But it's not her . . . it's not her doing it." Goss gulped a sob and tried to drink from the crushed cup, getting water down her front for her pains.

I took the cup from her hand and fetched her a new one, along with some paper towels to mop up the mess. Flustered, she patted at herself, looking embarrassed and finally hiding behind her cup of water for a few sips. Once she'd settled down again, I resumed the conversation.

"You've seen her do this?" I asked. "The painting."

"Yes. She lives with me now—if you can call what she's doing 'living.' I sit with her all the time. Night and day. Everything is falling apart, but I don't know what else to do. Nurses come twice a day to help me, but she doesn't move or do anything unless she's painting. There're so many machines . . . but they all just beep quietly away as if she's only lying there like always. And now it's getting worse."

"In what way?"

"She paints all the time, so many hours, and not all the same kind of paintings anymore. Now it's like there's more than one person painting. Even when she should be sleeping, she sits up and paints. If I take the brush away from her, she just grabs something else and goes back to painting. And just in the past few days, she's started babbling—it's nonsense, not words, but she . . . talks. Some of the nurses don't want to come anymore—it freaks them out to be with her. The doctor said I was imagining things until she started doing it in the exam room. Now even he's spooked. And all the time she's doing it, it's as if her mouth or arm is moving without the rest of her doing anything. She'll move her head around, open and close her eyes, laugh, cry . . . wet herself . . . and keep on painting. It's like *she* isn't the one talking or painting at all. It's just her body being moved around by someone else. Like a puppet."

"Does she finish the paintings?"

"Not always. But she paints faster now, like she's racing—or whoever is inside her is racing to finish before they have to leave again. If she doesn't finish one the same day she started, she'll never finish it at all. She just goes on to the next painting. Sometimes she'll do three in a day."

"I think I need to meet your sister."

Lily Goss's face seemed to flower with hope. "Then you'll help me? You'll find out who or what is possessing my sister?"

I had to shake my head. "I can't guarantee that. I don't know what's happening to your sister or if it's really in my purview. There are some things I can't do anything about. If this is really is some kind of demonic possession, then you need to talk to your priest."

She gaped and looked on the verge of crying, her aura turning a bleak, muddy green that seemed to drip downward like rain. "No . . . I already talked to Father Nybeck! He can't help me! He said he can't help me . . . won't. Don't—don't say you won't either. Please."

She crushed the second plastic cup, sending a gout of water into her lap. She jumped up with a sob and I think she would have bolted if I hadn't caught her shoulders and steadied her. She felt like a bundle of dry twigs barely held together by her rumpled clothes and I was too conscious that I loomed over her, but there was little

I could do to make myself smaller. I braced her and held her still, saying "Miss Goss, I didn't say I wouldn't help. I said I might not be able to."

She looked back up at me, her lip trembling and her jaw twitching as if she wanted to say something but couldn't remember the words.

"It's all right. I'm not saying no. I'm saying let's go see."

Kat Richardson

The Greywalker Novels

A detective series with a supernatural twist,
featuring Seattle P.I. Harper Blaine.

ALSO AVAILABLE IN THE SERIES

GREYWALKER
POLTERGEIST
UNDERGROUND
VANISHED
LABYRINTH
DOWNPOUR
POSSESSION
(coming August 2013)

"The Grey is a creepy and original addition
to the urban fantasy landscape."
—Tanya Huff

katrichardson.com

Available wherever books are sold or at
penguin.com

R0113